ANIMAL INSTINCT

To Larry,
In the animals
Dot Hayes

September 2006
Hayes@AnimalInstinctHotel.com

ANIMAL INSTINCT

Dorothy H. Hayes

iUniverse, Inc.
New York Lincoln Shanghai

Animal Instinct

iUniverse books may be ordered through booksellers or by contacting:

iUniverse
2021 Pine Lake Road, Suite 100
Lincoln, NE 68512
www.iuniverse.com
1-800-Authors (1-800-288-4677)

All major characters in this novel are fictional and are not to be confused with those who play similar roles in the animal rights movement. The campaigns depicted herein deal with some of the current issues and programs of the animal rights movement.

ISBN-13: 978-0-595-36489-3 (pbk)
ISBN-13: 978-0-595-80922-6 (ebk)
ISBN-10: 0-595-36489-6 (pbk)
ISBN-10: 0-595-80922-7 (ebk)

Printed in the United States of America

Dedicated to Tyke and Lisa
A thank you to my husband and family for their unfaltering support.

Five percent of the proceeds will be donated to animal advocacy.

CHAPTER 1

▼

THE MIRACLE

Eleanor would forever consider what occurred in the newsroom that mid-December afternoon a miracle.

It had been the usual grueling week, but for unknown reasons, instead of rushing back out into the cold for home, she remained anchored to her desk chair in her typical Thursday stupor, her legs stretched out in front of her like two dead weights. One suburban editor labored in the dusty shadows of the warm sprawling room, as Eleanor gazed straight ahead focusing on absolutely nothing. She faced the two messy, pea-green walls that banked her corner desk and were covered with clippings of her favorite stories and a poster.

It occurred to her that during her five-year journalism career she'd written virtually every type of story, ranging from the opposition to the Gulf War to a bio on a Tibetan Buddhist monk. She'd hustled herself out of the sleepy burbs of Derbe, where she still resided, to cover the teeming city of Norfolk. She'd exposed corrupt town officials, cornered politicians, conned drug pushers, and charmed the toughest, all to get the story. And just two weeks ago, she learned that she'd won a prestigious journalism award for her series on Vietnam veterans.

It might be the award, she thought, that kept her seated and gazing back over her career and personal history. Although she flourished as a reporter working in the dingy but hospitable *Norfolk Daily News* newsroom, hers was not a tidy little life: the painful discovery of her husband with his belly-dancing lover, followed by divorce; returning to school for her undergraduate degree; her late-starting career in journalism pitted against alpha twenty-somethings; and then the depression that demanded she address the childhood scars caused by her alcoholic father.

It was far from grim. Once she resurfaced from life's tumult, she had rediscovered herself.

With each contemplative moment, it was becoming clear that she had accomplished everything at the *Norfolk Daily News* that was humanly possible. An inchoate idea began to bubble: maybe it was time to move on? Time to specialize? That's what reporters did, come to think of it, she told herself. But the thought was brand new. Her tired body squirmed in her seat with the sad realization that she had neglected to develop a specialty. She had been too busy. She began to examine the two walls in front of her. Perhaps they held clues to what could loosely be considered "a specialty."

That's when the miracle occurred.

As she stared at the walls, eyes stared back at her! She bolted up astonished: a calf, a deer, and a black Labrador retriever stared at her with imploring dark eyes that stirred every inch of her. The life-sized, colored poster of the calf tied to a crate marked "veal" was directly in front of her. His backside was facing her, and he strained his neck to turn his head and stare directly at her, begging the question, "What are you doing to get me out of here?"

To the calf's left was the black-and-white newspaper clipping about the three-legged doe in Derbe maimed by a hunter; she appeared to be calling attention to her missing right hind leg. Underneath the doe was the clipping of a doomed black Lab as he sat alone in a South Norfolk shelter, reminding her of the 5.7 million dogs and cats in public shelters across the country that were euthanized each year.

Other clippings were tacked on the wall, but they turned into a blurred background for the three faces. She opened her top drawer to view the countless clippings of stories of missing and shelter dogs stored there and her most recent exposé on deer hunting in the suburbs.

The epiphany resonated as if the three on the wall knew her better than she knew herself, as if they were kind envoys sent from her patiently waiting soul. They looked so benevolent, as if they had faith in her and knew it was only a matter of time until she discovered them. After closing her drawer, with both hands placed on the peeling lip of her green metal desk, she pushed back her chair, needing a little distance. The creaking wheels of her chair, however, sounded like a ringing alarm clock in the newsroom silence. She rose to her feet and, with a look of amusement, took a few sobering steps away from her desk, her back to the three animals. When she pivoted around, the magnetic qualities of the three had only been enhanced.

She then had to admit that of all the hapless victims in her countless stories over the last five years, the animals were the only victims of a legalized system of perfidy in her country, their lives sacrificed within the law, and as a matter of course. She learned of their suffering through indisputable facts and photographs: pigs squeezed in pens, their ears and tails chewed off; chickens hanging like widgets on assembly lines; cows skinned while alive and kicking; the authentic stories were endless. With each revelation, it became clear that the meat and dairy industries were a tragic and horrible mistake of modern times, a gross crime against the innocent, against nature, with the masses as unwitting accomplices, herself included. Until her conversion, that is.

Her heart pounded as she returned her gaze to the three. They, no doubt, were the face of her mission. She remembered Joseph Campbell, who said that when one finds one's mission there is a sense of "knowing." "Knowing"—that was the overriding sensation, she concluded. In her next breath, the practical side of her ventured to ask, "Where will I find a job?"

That's when Honor Vine sprang to mind. She was the president and chief executive officer of People Against Animal Cruelty, PAAC, virtually the only national animal protection organization headquartered in the Northeast. During the last two years, Eleanor had depended on Honor for spicy quotes. The outspoken president never hedged her criticism of state officials, fellow movement leaders, or anyone else, as a matter of fact.

She hesitated. Wouldn't Honor think she was crazy? Calling her out of the blue for such a rare and precious job just because she happened to have an epiphany one very tired, cold Thursday afternoon? Her doubts echoed with a hollow, gutless clunk as she gazed into the patiently waiting eyes of the animals, who seemed to be reminding her that they too were created by a superior being. They, indeed, were a part of her.

Eleanor took a deep breath, crammed her chair under her battered desk, stretched to her full five foot seven inch height, and vowed to the three that she'd call the president of PAAC after deadline the next day no matter how ridiculous she might appear. To her amazement, the next morning, Honor welcomed her as if she'd been expecting her call. She had read Eleanor's hunting story and might be hiring a staff writer/public relations director. Did she want to come in Monday for an interview? Eleanor sat back in her chair stunned by providence for the second time in just hours. It seemed as though she had just been officially

…into the small army of disciples who understood. No longer was she someone eking out a living at a discipline she loved; she was part of a bigger plan. After hanging up, she sat frozen in place, her hand still gripping the receiver of the phone. A jarring thought crossed her mind: an angel of mercy had moved Honor Vine to dangle a job before her that touched her heart and stirred her soul like no other, but was Honor calling other candidates?

"No," she muttered aloud, her hand tightening around the receiver. "Nobody's going to steal this golden opportunity from me! This job is mine!"

On Monday morning, December 15, 1997, Eleanor Aquitaine Green pulled up to the ice-dappled parking lot of the headquarters of People Against Animal Cruelty in Westport on Compo Beach Road. The contemporary driftwood-gray professional building was across the road from the shore of Long Island Sound. Eleanor stepped from the warmth of her car into the frigid sea air as if it were a balmy summer day. She gazed dreamily beyond the quiet snow-lined beach road and the snowy beach to the miles of wide-open sea and sky. The vast mysterious seascape cast its magic, and she sighed with welcome relief at the sight.

Off in the distance, Long Island was a little strip of land set before the offing of the Atlantic. At the shoreline, several ring-billed gulls walked on the beach unimpressed by the snow and oblivious to all human endeavors. One sailed above the frigid waters, her long, white wings floating as if she were free of all mortal cares. Eleanor closed her eyes and inhaled the entrancing sea odors teeming in the brackish waters from the nearby salt marshes. She imagined her toes sinking into the warm sand on summer days, and saw herself swimming in the calm, sea-green waters at lunchtime.

"Is this all too good to be true, or what?" She peered up at the heavens.

Upscale beachfront homes with wide porches lined the street, their roofs and lawns laden with several layers of snow. PAAC's headquarters was one of only two commercial buildings on the precious strip of land. The other was a convenience store next to it. Hancock Insurance occupied the first floor of the building. Eleanor climbed the short flight of open stairs to a narrow hallway with two doors, one on the right marked "Rest Room," and the other "People Against Animal Cruelty."

She opened PAAC's door and walked into a warm, dimly lit lobby that seemed a kind shelter for one troubled by the plight of animals. Across the small room sat a smiling receptionist behind a glass partition, a young, pretty girl with dark hair and eyes, dressed in a black wool-ribbed turtleneck and black woolen slacks. Eleanor smiled down at her and gave her name. She felt like a soldier reporting for duty.

"Eleanor Green is here for her eleven o'clock appointment," the receptionist said into her phone. Her voice possessed a hint of street toughness. After removing her beige parka and black knitted cotton gloves, Eleanor eased into one of two chairs to the right of the receptionist as if it had been waiting for her. She placed the black nylon briefcase that held her precious clippings on her lap. Across from her was a colored photograph of chimpanzees in the wild that immediately held her attention. She heaved a sigh of relief, grateful to be reminded that not all chimpanzees were prisoners in laboratories. As the seconds ticked by, her euphoria deepened in the kindly atmosphere of the animal protection organization. This is the place, every fiber in her body seemed to be saying. It was a caring place, an egalitarian place—one that respected the rights of those less powerful. Yes, she thought, life had been a tough teacher, but at age thirty-four she seemed to be on the shore of the promised land.

In a few minutes, rapid footsteps approached the closed door to the left of the receptionist. An abdominous, nervous young woman swung open the door and nearly tripped over her own feet in her haste as she stepped into the lobby. Her flushed cheeks matched the large pink flowers on her oversized, black wool sweater. "She'll see you now," she said smiling.

They passed through a boxy, windowless room with wall-to-wall desks, computers, typewriters, and filing cabinets. There were five female employees seated behind desks and intent on their work, taking no notice of them. As the two filed past the women's desks, different and distinct fragrances perfumed the air: sophisticated, sweet, flowery, and the fragrance of fresh air. The only sound to be heard was the tapping of two keypunch operators. The silence struck Eleanor as eerie even for a Monday morning. As they approached an office, one of several that lined the outer wall, she felt eyes on her back. She turned to find the women staring at her. Like children caught in the act, they were quick to return to their work. She thought it weird. One employee, however, a young African-American woman, smiled with an impish grin. Eleanor flashed her a responsive smile.

They entered a doorway that led into a kind of inner sanctum with abundant plants and a view of the Sound. The room's atmosphere was at once uplifting. A young blonde woman, who seemed like an executive assistant, glanced up from her desk, offered a brief smile, and continued filing cards in the Rolodex set before her. Leaning against the end of a desk adjacent to the president's door stood a matronly woman who looked like a guard. She had a floppy bulldog face with jowls that hung pretentiously. Without uttering a word, she held up her beefy left hand like a traffic cop, signaling the woman escort to stop while she waved Eleanor on. With a perfunctory smile of approval, the woman rapped on Honor Vine's door.

The office atmosphere resembled that of IBM, Eleanor had observed with some concern. But as the woman opened the president's door, all doubts faded with the sound of Honor's mellifluous contralto voice, the most cordial voice she had ever heard, which rang out a full-bodied, "Hello!"

Honor Vine, the animal rights icon, stood behind her desk across the wide room, tall, graceful, with ramrod-straight aristocratic posture. And under the artificial recessed light, she appeared to be every bit the charismatic celebrity in the spotlight. Her ecru skin was radiant, the brass buttons on her navy wool blazer glittered like gold, and her dark brown hair shone with white streaks reflecting the overhead light as if it were silk.

At once Eleanor was taken aback by Honor Vine's resemblance to the actress Sigourney Weaver. Her tiny nose was almost lost in the sharpness of her powerful, square jaw and the high chiseled cheeks. Each strand of her hair was combed back and turned under obediently at the collar, except for a small wave that fell on the left side of her creamy forehead, as if it were called upon to soften her professional persona. Honor, sixty-one, appeared to be in her early forties and endowed with the effervescence of a young woman; no doubt a benefit of her vegan diet.

"We meet at last!" Honor said, smiling with delight and gliding around her desk with her hand extended as if she were welcoming a long-lost friend. Much of Eleanor's initial apprehension melted in the warmth of that first handshake. And she was enchanted anew by Honor's slight English accent.

The contemporary office was decorated in minimalist style, with glossy stucco walls and sleek Scandinavian furniture. A spectacular view through a floor-to-ceiling window of the Long Island Sound dominated the room and faced Honor's desk. Six black-and-white photographs of a variety of dogs and cats, framed in stainless steel, hung on the wall behind her desk. A credenza was against the far wall, to the right of the desk, with a pair of spotless, black nylon ankle boots obediently lined up underneath.

They exchanged compliments like mutual fans. Honor thanked her for all the coverage, while Eleanor in return voiced appreciation for her spicy quotes. Eleanor proceeded to sit in the closer of two teakwood chairs that faced Honor's desk and to which Honor graciously pointed. She then turned around to peer at the floor-to-ceiling window behind her, offering an obligatory comment on the spectacular view.

Honor responded as she returned to her executive chair. "This time of the year, you can sometimes see harbor seals on the rocky islands." Her dark eyes searched the distance. "I spent many summer hours watching them when I was a little girl," she said. She swallowed several times and slurred her words. She explained that she'd had a wisdom tooth extracted that morning at eight o'clock. She gently placed her right hand on her puffy right cheek. "I haven't been indulging. If only that were the case! There's a little swelling, nothing more."

But she clipped her words in what seemed an attempt to avoid pain. Then she began to act like a clown, blowing up her cheeks to exaggerate the swelling. "Ouch!" she yelled, obviously unhinged by the unexpected pang. "There's a couple of stitches." She was grimacing and her words were garbled. "The pain comes and goes! It only hurts when I laugh!" Then she held her cheek, closed her eyes, and slumped over the right arm of her chair in a mock faint.

"Honor, how can you be so charming and funny when you're in such pain?" Eleanor rose to her feet laughing. "Please, I'd be happy to come back tomorrow."

Honor braced her jaw and raised herself upright. "Charming, that's me, but no, no, absolutely not. Please sit, sit!" She waved her left hand, palm down, in a motion for Eleanor to sit, while keeping her right hand on her tender cheek. "I'm not digging ditches here, am I?" she said. Although she minimized her condition, her ashen pallor revealed the truth of her pain. "Not even my triple bypass could keep me out of touch for more more than three days," she noted. But silence followed for a few seconds as the pain overwhelmed her. "Oh yes, I know how to turn on the charm all right."

Honor stared past her to the view of the Sound, and the gray December day with a reminiscent gaze. As she began to speak, she fondled the single strand of cultured pearls with her left hand, the subtle pearl color of her nail polish matching perfectly. The necklace sat comfortably on the jewel neckline of her white silk blouse.

"Charm was considered one of the arts in Elizabeth Kendell's School for Girls, where my parents packed me off at the tender age of eight," Honor said. Her tight lips revealed that her childhood pain still remained. "Why would anybody send an eight-year-old to boarding school?" she asked, as if the hurtful experience had occurred yesterday.

"That's brutal!" Eleanor said, while she considered her next move. She didn't dare place the clippings that she had withdrawn from her briefcase on the slippery man-made fabric of her teal suit; they were sure to slide off, and that would be disastrous. She eyed the tempting desk in front of her while Honor spoke of her boarding school experience. Without asking, Eleanor placed her clips on the desk just inches beyond her panty-hosed knees.

Honor swallowed several times, looking like she was attempting to control the building saliva in her injured mouth. "You seem prepared to conduct the interview entirely on your own. As fate would have it, you might have to." With that she sat back in her chair.

Eleanor tucked her thick shoulder-length hair behind her ears as she gazed at the clippings in front of her. "I left out the 'Hunting in Suburbia' story because you mentioned it on the phone. Imagine people hiring sharpshooters to kill neighborhood deer. The same deer some people move to Derbe to see."

"Deer will eat the low growth on anything when they're starving! There's been a foot of snow on the ground for weeks, and it's only mid-December."

"I know," Eleanor said.

"The animals are fighting starvation," Honor added. It was clear that her outrage was building. "The damned bushes grow back in the spring!"

"I know!"

"Why don't they move to New York City then?"

"Exactly!"

She stared at Honor. Their eyes locked in silence for several seconds. It was definitely a moment of bonding, and Eleanor offered a silent prayer of gratitude for writing the story and for her editor publishing it.

Then Honor's mellifluous voice turned into a seething hiss. "What a hellish act of betrayal!" she said. "What asses these slobs are!" Her face had turned to granite. "A deer hunt may occur any day now at Denmark Cliff State Park in Soundview! The deer share the park with hikers, joggers, families on picnics, and some well-meaning idiots who even feed them! They're not wild deer by any stretch of the imagination! They won't know what the hell hit them! And any respectable hunter wouldn't dare participate in this imitation of a hunt! It's a hellish act of betrayal!" she repeated. "It's no hunt, it's a bloody massacre! A step up from bait and kill!"

Eleanor attempted to hide her mystification as, within seconds, the amiable and even clownish Honor transformed into a bitter, ranting woman unable to control her hatred for those involved in the state park hunt.

"It's politics!" Her eyes flared in her outrage. "The governor is facing reelection next year, and the NRA is among his ardent backers! He can't wait to open the state park to hunters and wear that badge of honor in his reelection lapel! The bloody carnage is as much as guaranteed. Fifty thousand animal advocates are also residents of this state! But our concerns are the butt of jokes for this administration and most legislators!" She gazed down again at her clenched hands that rested before her on her desk. "This is the worst winter in two decades. No doubt some of the deer will perish: the sick ones, those who are genetically weak, the old, and some of the very young! But not the 200-plus healthy deer that the slobs will kill, quote, 'to save them from starvation!' The huge trophy animals, the hardy magnificent stags, that's who these bastards will take from the herd to decorate their tacky family room walls! They'll donate the bodies of the deer to the homeless shelters as a grand display of charity. As if these bloody cowards, wife beaters, and sex perverts give a damn about the poor! The state plans to leave only twenty-five deer out of a full herd of an estimated 200 plus!"

She winced and paused for a moment to swallow several times. "The state lies," she said. "Then the press prints the lies and the lies become truth as we know it."

The words oozed out of her like the pus of a deep, festering wound that she had carried in her soul for the last forty years. She jerked her chair back and rose to her feet, and in her fit of frustration walked past Eleanor to the huge window as if drawn to it to seek some solace in the peaceful order of nature. The sunless winter light accentuated the hard edges of her drawn face.

Eleanor wasn't offended by Honor's indictment of journalists. She even understood her outrage, no matter how misplaced it might be.

"I found out early on about how the state lies," Eleanor said. "I called the Department of Conservation for roadkill numbers when I wrote my first anti-hunting piece." She spoke to Honor's slender back. "They sent me their yearly report that bragged about 'harvest' numbers. I was shocked! They referred to the slain deer as if they were crops, like corn or potatoes. Then I realized they were in the business of stocking the woods with wildlife for hunters. As a reporter you learn to follow the money. The hunting and fishing license fees and the taxes on firearms and ammunition set their yearly budget. Up to that point, I thought state environmental protection bureaus were established to actually protect wildlife, not to fill the woods for hunters. Silly me!"

Honor walked back to stand next to Eleanor, who continued to peer out the scenic window. The hem of Honor's light beige, wool skirt brushed against Eleanor's knee.

Eleanor stiffened at the touch of the skirt. She didn't dare move her leg. She was so flattered to have her stand so close to her. I'd follow this woman anywhere, she thought. She's like a Malcolm X, seeing through and telling off the high and mighty politicians unapologetically for forty years! The woman's tough and authentic! She predates Tom Regan's writings and Peter Singer's *Animal Libera-*

tion bible by twenty years. What a courageous woman! What moral stamina! Eleanor leaned a little toward her, and her eyes gazed up at Honor's in adulation. She screened out her silk and wool clothing.

Then Honor glanced down at her for a second before she returned to her seat looking like she carried the weight of the deer on her back. She examined her pad, which had a list written on it, and then glanced again at Eleanor.

"My operations manager has yet to determine if our budget will allow for a writer, so I'm not free to offer anyone the position today." She rolled her eyes as if she were annoyed. Then she swallowed hard three times and leaned back, obviously bothered by the pain. A few seconds later, she began again. "I asked you in, anticipating the job opening." Again she gazed down at the list on her notepad. She seemed to be mumbling to herself as she stared at it. "I can't see how I can do without a writer."

At that moment, a fit of coughing took hold of her, the saliva again building up and gagging her. From a tissue box on top of the computer at her left, she pulled out one tissue after the other and coughed into it. The coughing accelerated into a hacking fit. For several seconds she choked, coughed, and spat into tissues, using one after the other in rapid succession, and tossing them into a wastepaper basket hidden under her desk. As the coughing subsided, she gestured to Eleanor to commence.

But Eleanor cringed at the thought of the inflamed and irritated stitches, and had to force herself to forget about them so she could launch into her pitch. Fifteen minutes later, Honor's huge desk was a collage of clippings.

"In Derbe, I pleaded with my editor to print the photographs I'd taken of the dogs in the shelter, including this one," she said. She presented the picture of the black Lab that was on her wall. "After a visit to the shelter, it honestly seemed a matter of life and death to both me and the dogs that I find them a home while I worked at the weekly. And I did! For every single one of them, including this one." She sighed with relief. "I even convinced the cavalier dog warden to allow me to walk them in my spare time to keep them from going crazy in their little cells so they'd be more adoptable.

"I wrote a hunting piece inspired by a three-legged deer, which I believed was a Derbe myth until I received this photograph from a loyal reader." She placed the photograph of the deer that she had removed from her wall before Honor. "The deer inspired a major compare-and-contrast piece on hunting, which challenged my journalistic ethics. I squirmed in my seat writing the evenhanded piece while detesting the actions of those legions of hunters who each year, equipped with power scopes, bionic ears, and high-tech rifles and in the name of male bonding, invade the woods, where life is hardly a piece of cake to begin with."

Her finale consisted of her full-length features on battered wives, teenage drug pushers, and finally, her prizewinning, in-depth series on Vietnam War veterans. Honor gazed at her with parental pride. "What a prodigious amount of excellent work!"

"Honor, the journalism award encouraged me to take stock of my career and myself. I looked around my desk, and animal faces stared back at me. Of all the stories I've written, all the issues they addressed," she allowed her eyes to sweep Honor's busy desk, "this was the issue that searched me out. I didn't seek it. That's when a career in animal rights first occurred to me. The epiphany struck on Thursday. I called you Friday, and you seemed to be waiting for my call!"

Honor's smile indicated that she was pleased and intrigued by this touch of karma.

"Ten years ago I became a vegetarian because of the health craze," Eleanor continued. "First I gave up red meat, then chicken, and then I became sensitive to the plight of animals. Then I couldn't eat fish or dairy products. I call it galloping vegetarianism." She chuckled at her own joke. "I have a RUFFFF poster of a calf tied to a veal crate on my wall so my veal-eating colleagues will learn. But the pathetic calf's eyes keep staring at me and asking, 'What are you doing to get me out of here?' My answer obviously was, 'Not enough!'"

When Honor squirmed in her seat at the mention of Rights Unlimited For Fur, Feather, and Fin, Eleanor wondered why. No doubt she was committing the mortal sin of interviews: talking too much. She began to collect her clips to form one neat pile for Honor. As she stretched across the large desk, the plastic buttons on her teal suit jacket softly scraped the desk. She gazed at her eager fingers. Why did her soft cranberry nail polish seem so coarse?

"Can I keep those?" Honor asked, nodding at the pile of clips.

"Of course, I was just straightening up." Eleanor decided to throw her final pitch. "I'm usually the hardest-working person on the job, and for you I'll work even harder. Hey, who wouldn't want to work for Honor? Excuse the pun, I couldn't help myself."

Honor chuckled, and her expression revealed that she enjoyed the flattery. "Laughter is a must in this business," she said. "The salary for the position is $30,000, with two weeks vacation."

Had Honor just given her the job?

With her right hand bracing her sore cheek, Honor dashed around her desk, her long legs stretching with the agility of a twenty-year-old. She opened the door.

Eleanor rose to her feet, traversed the office, and crossed the threshold like a woman walking in a dream.

"I should know by the end of the week," Honor said. "You can expect a call Friday afternoon. Please follow me, I'll show you your office."

Honor dashed past her blonde assistant as if she didn't exist. She turned left and scudded past the busy employees in the large room and paused at the third door in the row of offices that lined the outer wall. The small, modest office had a large window on the far wall with a partially opened mini blind. In front of the window sat a beige metal desk, a computer to its right on a corner extension. A matching two-drawer file cabinet was against the south wall with a printer on top of it. In the north corner was a black folding chair.

To Eleanor the small office was just as good as a corner suite in the Chrysler Building. A glimpse of the Sound was possible, she was sure of it, if she pressed her nose against the windowpane. "It's perfect," she thought. "Each letter I write, each key I strike will help the animals, the seagulls and geese outside my own window! The fish, the mammals! Could I be this lucky? Eleanor, you don't have the job, yet! God, you wouldn't find me a mission and then not provide a job!"

As Honor escorted her to the lobby door, the employees' heads were still bowed over their desks like worker ants. Eleanor smiled at the office at large, shook Honor's hand, and remembered to say good-bye to the friendly receptionist.

That evening she attempted to push the job possibility out of her mind as she covered "Father's Night" at the Martin Luther King Youth Center in South Norfolk. She returned home wired and unable to focus. She'd pound out the copy tomorrow morning. Since the incredible happenings of the day made sleep impossible, she settled into her cranberry winged-back couch at 10 PM. In a comfortable daze, she sipped hot chamomile tea to abate a chill. She listened to the howling north wind rolling down Route 7 in front of the house and whistling through the towering trees and bushes in the nine-mile set-aside that bordered the back of the property.

As she worried about the animals surviving the severe winter, she thought, wouldn't it be wonderful to work for a woman who shared such sentiments? As the fierce wind blew, she eyed the redbrick fireplace before her—but she was too tired.

Rusty, her orange tabby, purred in her lap while the aged Friday, a gray tabby, warmed her feet. If PAAC hired her, she would be more financially stable, with a salary increase of $4,000. Her modest Derbe residence was pricey when she rented it, but it was within walking distance of her parent's former home. The owner, a California resident, saved the upstairs apartment for his rare visits, so she virtually lived alone in the small colonial. It seemed like her own.

The brass bed, double maple dresser, and mirror of her childhood occupied most of the space in her small bedroom, which was just off the galley kitchen. On her bed lay a patchwork quilt, a symphony of delicate floral patches of unobtrusive yellows, blues, and pinks. It was pretty, but mainly it was a gift from her mother. In hard times, and in her exhaustion, she wrapped the softness around her and was braced by her mother's unconditional love. At this moment she missed her. But her mother was far better off, she noted, since she retired from teaching two years ago and moved from Fairfield County to more affordable Jupiter, Florida, with its healthier climate and landscapes of paradise. There she also had the companionship of her two retired sisters. It had been painful for her mother, Eleanor recalled, to leave her only child behind to pursue her journalism career. It would be best to wait until Friday to call, she decided.

But as she sipped her tea, it became clear that she would have to talk to somebody. She reached for the phone on the lamp table to her right without disturbing Rusty and dialed Lydia Grant. With all her connections, her backyard cat sanctuary, and her local group, Animal Independence, Lydia could give her the skinny on Honor. Lydia was the one to talk to. She was a wise, plainspoken person with common sense; she often sounded like a primary school principal.

Eleanor revealed the happenings of the last few days. "The job's mine, if the budget allows for a staff writer position, that is. I'll know for sure Friday!"

"I'll pray for a deficit," Lydia said. "I doubt that you'll last more than three months. You're too ethical."

Honor began her career working at the South Norfolk Humane Society. Lydia credited her for coming a long way from her humane roots, but like many of her ilk, she was more rightly labeled an animal protectionist. Honor was not 100 percent vegan, Lydia explained, and she wore silk and wool. She was also a known tyrant and was characterized by past employees as "impossible" to work for. Lydia warned Eleanor that Honor's famed paranoia led to the hiring of relatives and friends, those she believed she could trust. Although she tyrannized them too, she endowed them with special privileges. "That's a double standard and purely unprofessional," Lydia said. "I'll be honest, I cross the street when I see her coming. I think it best not to tangle with a tyrant."

Tyrant?

Eleanor sat Rusty on the couch as the heat of anger surged within her in indignation for her hero. She rose to her feet to pace the pine floorboards of her living room. Lydia's intolerance seemed so unlike her!

"I've called her for over two years, and I know she's a true animal rights advocate," she began. "I wouldn't work for her otherwise! And Lydia, she's so comical! And she treated me like a long-lost friend!"

"You're a reporter, and she needs the ink. Honor knows where to butter her bread, pardon the expression. To be fair to her, I wouldn't work for her or for Leona Nesbitt, Alison Barrington, Rutherford Gee, or any of them. They're all tyrants in my book."

At that point, Eleanor was convinced that her friend's wisdom was clouded by jealousy. No doubt, Lydia would love a full-time job in the movement.

"Even if she's not 100 percent vegan," Eleanor said, "nothing could diminish her contribution to the movement. She's a pioneer. When she began there were fur commercials like, 'What do you want to be when you grow up? I want to be a fur coat at Canadians.' Try that today!"

They said their good-byes. It was premature, but given Lydia's response, she decided to telephone her mother.

"Eleanor," Lillian Green said, "this woman, Honor Vine, don't trust her, darling! Zealots lead revolutions. And they often cause as much harm to their followers as their adversaries. You're entering a dangerous game. She'll use you. Eleanor, you'll always be expendable for the cause. Promise me you'll protect yourself?"

She almost expected this reaction from her mother. Yet it was strange, because she'd encouraged her to be an independent woman. She'd even named her after the twelfth-century queen of England and France after a prenatal dream that revealed she was carrying a girl. When Eleanor was eight, her mother explained that she respected Eleanor of Aquitaine because she was one of the original liberated women. Eleanor, however, always sensed that her mother held back some aspect of the dream.

"I'm happy for you. But darling, be careful! Think of Dr. Martin Luther King Jr., and Gandhi. For all of the great men and women who suffered death for their convictions, thousands of nameless crusaders were also killed."

"Mom, this is a peaceful revolution! It's a revolution of the heart waged by caring people! Eight billion farm animals, for the most part raised in factory farms, live horribly and die horribly every year. And their numbers are expected to reach ten billion by 2004! Mom, just the sheer numbers represent the worst suffering in the modern age. It's legalized treachery!"

In the silence that followed, she could hear her mother worrying. "Don't worry," she said. "I promise you, I will take care of myself."

Eleanor was tempted to laugh at her mother's reference to such historic heroes, but she knew better. Her mother was no fool. On that Friday, she received the confirmation of her employment, and what seemed to be the answer to her prayers.

CHAPTER 2

▼

"KEEP YOUR CONTACTS!"

On Monday, January 7, Delores Best introduced Eleanor to the five women in the center office and the mail clerk, Patroklos Evers. It was Delores who had delivered her to Honor's office on the day of her job interview. They then went out to the lobby for a formal introduction to the receptionist, Ellen Milani.

Finally Eleanor entered her own office. Smiling with contentment, she hung her beige parka on the wooden hanger behind her door. The hanger's hook clicked as it hit the door's hook. She walked behind her desk and bent down to open the bottom drawer, which uttered a squeak. She placed her black shoulder bag inside and patted it as if she were putting a baby to bed, and closed the drawer. Then she lowered herself into her desk chair and took possession of her office.

For the first few minutes, she gazed at the open door directly in front of her. The precocious Coretta Washington, who had offered the impish grin on the day of her interview, sat only a few feet away keypunching, but Eleanor didn't notice. Her eyes were glazed over. She was not only getting paid to write, but paid to write about the animals she loved. It didn't get much better than this. A sigh of relief revealed that she didn't think herself undeserving.

She rolled back her chair. There was just enough clearance between her desk and the wall with the huge window behind her. She stood up and pressed her cheek to the cold glass for a glimpse. A thick blanket of clouds hovered over the choppy frigid waters whose whitecaps reached the offing, and at the shoreline, small waves slapped the snow-covered beach. She straightened up and turned her attention to the cozier Grandma Moses winter scene directly below. The expanded summer homes, of all styles, were squeezed on small parcels of treasured land, and capped with snow. Straight ahead, the tree-lined Compo Beach Road rose up a steep hill and faded into the western sky. The thick branches of the stately elms, oaks, and maples hovered over the road their bare branches coated with a layer of white.

She sighed with tranquility and turned around to retake her seat and utter a prayer of gratitude. No more dated pea-green walls and ugly, treeless South Main Street. There were letters in her double-tiered in-box at the far left corner of her desk, no doubt deposited by Honor. She uttered another prayer of gratitude for her new boss. With an unhurried move, so unlike meeting a daily deadline, she reached for her first piece of correspondence. This action seemed the first in a career that would last a lifetime.

It appeared that the manatees were vanishing in Florida, and a class of junior high school students was asking for guidance to help them. "How much farther away from teenage drug pushers can I get?" Eleanor asked herself.

The job kept getting better. She placed the letter in front of her, on the new beige desk blotter with its imitation leather brown corners, and rose to her feet to venture to the outer office. She felt uncommonly centered, as though life was at last falling into place like a Mozart symphony.

Standing in her doorway, she eyed the claustrophobic room. The large gray filing cabinets directly across the room were her destination, not the eight-foot-high filing cabinets used to store computer data sheets that lined the south wall to her left. The silence again struck her as strange, as she observed the five women before her all dutifully engaged. Again, they seemed oblivious to her movements. She squatted before the first bottom drawer, which was labeled "Aquatic Mammals." She had to yank on the drawer to pull it out. It hung heavy from its cavern while she thumbed through it to find the slender manatee file. At a glance, she saw at least two Miami groups to recommend. She withdrew the file, eager to learn whatever she could about the mammals.

Wearing her new smile of tranquility, she hugged the file and its precious information. How wonderful it was to "specialize," she thought. No more frenzied trips to the library because you were asked to report on a subject you knew nothing about with a turnaround time of hours.

"Are you going to the library to research?" asked a low, deep, contralto voice with a Jamaican accent. It was Betty Miller, another keypunch operator. She sat closest to the file cabinets, with her back to Eleanor. The question startled her. It was as if Betty read, or misread, her mind. Betty wore a creamy wool pants suit, and her hair was cut to mold her head. "That's what all the other writers did. They had to go to the library to do their research."

Before Eleanor answered, she closed the heavy drawer, stood up, and returned to stand before her doorway. Mary O'Donnell, the young bookkeeper at Betty's left, waited for her answer. So did Carla Jones, an attractive middle-aged clerk who sat in front of Betty. Even Lisa Raves, Honor's administrative assistant, sitting in the front of the room, stopped her typing to listen. Only Coretta continued working.

"OK, I'll bite. How many other writers were there?" Eleanor asked.

"I've been here for seven years," Betty said, "and I tell you, there's been a parade of them, whew! They last about a year."

"A parade?" Eleanor swallowed hard. "Were they animal activists?"

"No, no! None of us are! We like our meat!" She gazed at Eleanor daring her to object. Meat was part of her family tradition, she explained, and besides, she was certain that some meat was required to nourish her teenage son and daughter.

"Oh. Well, but I am a vegan, and an activist," Eleanor said. "So I'll have staying power."

"Good luck!" said Betty. "Whew! Honor! Is she hard to work for!" Her voice sang in her Jamaican rhythm, and she turned her head from side to side for emphasis. To the room at large she asked, "Remember the fights? Remember how she yelled at Russ?" A chorus of "Ah hums" responded. "Russ, he was the last one! He left running out of here one Friday at 5 PM as if his pants was on fire!" Everyone laughed. "He didn't even wait to find a new job! He started temping just to put bread on the table. He was a reporter too, like you, from the same paper, the *Norfolk Daily News!*" She stopped keypunching to stare at Eleanor. "There's been at least two or three of those!" She shook her head from side to side. "Lots of yellin' goes on in your office! Whew!"

Coretta, who had blithely continued to enter the amounts of donations from a stack of receipts set in front of her, glanced at Eleanor's feet. With exaggerated lip action and a stage whisper she warned, "Your job's high turnover. Keep your contacts. Honest, I give you a year." With her right hand she brushed back her imaginary long hair and again returned to her work.

Eleanor joined in the laughter. Coretta had the timing of a comedian. She had a cute, animated face, like a female Mike Myers, with large expressive eyes and a small nose. Her prominent lips, painted a tulip red, complimented her skin's yellow tint.

Patroklos was drawn to the laughter from the mailroom, which was next to the rear file cabinets. He folded his arms over his wide chest and leaned on the left side of Coretta's desk, as if it were his reserved spot.

"Eleanor, in case you didn't figure it out yet, the princess and her ladies-in-waiting have left the building. Oh, we don't know where they went! Or when they'll come back! And what's new? Claudia, her assistant, called in this morning that she was 'unable to come to work today.'"

Coretta's fans chuckled.

"That's OK, because she's Honor's cousin, so she only has to work when it's convenient," Coretta said. "No problem! But we can't be five minutes late! But no kidding, Eleanor, you look like a really nice person, and Honor, she's something else, and you work hand and glove with her. We're here for years because we worked for our former office manager, Geraldine. But now she's gone. But we stay out of Honor's way. She don't care about us. But you, she's always working with you. Your job, man, it's a revolving door. Honest, keep your contacts."

Her audience chuckled again.

"Thanks for the tip," Eleanor said. She was now leaning in her doorway. "But if the other writers weren't activists, they probably weren't aware of all she's done."

Honor and she were comrades, she explained. They shared a sense of outrage over society's treatment of animals. Critics had been ridiculing Honor for forty years behind her back and in print. "But she continues the good fight. That's what makes her tough. I know these things; maybe the other writers didn't. She's taken a lot of crap!"

"'Crap's' a key word around here," Coretta responded.

"Well, I've worked with macho editors," Eleanor said. "I can take a little crap. I've had an alcoholic abusive father, went to Al-Anon, did reparenting, survived a cheating husband who I discovered in our own bedroom with my neighbor, and worked during the day and went to college at night for my undergraduate degree. Then getting a late start in my career, I hustled. I hustled to scoop reporters working nights and weekends to get ahead. I'm talking long hours seven days a week. For the good of the cause, I think I can handle a little 'crap.'"

"Well, Eleanor," Coretta said, "all that stuff that happened to you, I'm so sorry you went through all that, but that's definitely only a warm-up for this place. Would I kid you? Honest, keep your contacts." She stood up and smoothed her royal blue sweater over her black skirt, taking no notice of her chuckling audience.

"Coretta, how about the comedy channel?" Eleanor asked.

"Nothing's funnier than this place!" she said.

Betty explained that the former office manager who had hired them, Geraldine Preston, was forced to quit a month ago after a series of insulting encounters with Honor. Betty also revealed that Freda Barty, the operations manager, who seemed like Honor's security guard, was hired just six months ago. "She's an old friend of Honor. Honor, she don't fire you, she just whips you out of your job! T'ings change," she said. "People change, times change. Maybe in a few months we'll all be gone!"

Betty's prophetic words summoned a murmur of agreement from around the room. At that moment the front door slammed, jolting the walls, and angry voices followed, resonating from the small lobby. The workers' eyes darted back to their work. In seconds, Patroklos disappeared and the eerie silence reclaimed the room.

"I don't give a fuck what you say, I'm the bloody president!" Honor Vine screeched out of control, her English accent in full tilt. The lobby door flew open and in she charged like a raging queen ready to punish her erring subjects. Her thin body leaned forward in agitation as she stomped across the office floor into the conference room. A trail of fretful figures followed like a humbled retinue: Freda Barty, Carol Conrad, the New York director of one year, and Delores Best, the jittery new office manager.

The conference door slammed shut, but Honor's fury penetrated it and continued to send shivers up the spines of her cowed employees. The women bent over their desks, seemingly absorbed in their work as they grasped pens and frantically wrote, avidly keypunched, or fiercely typed. They didn't dare look at each other, as if Honor could detect betrayal from behind closed doors.

Eleanor, however, with her reporter's curiosity, was rooted in her doorway. Honor's screeches continued to escalate, hovering now on the edge of violence. It was similar to overhearing a violent domestic dispute in the next apartment, one that would tempt Eleanor to summon the police. Some softer rumblings no doubt belonged to Carol Conrad as she attempted to defend herself, but her words only seemed to fuel Honor's fire. At that point, Eleanor's frightful memories of her father's drunken tirades were stirring, setting off a stream of adrenaline. Her heart began to pound. She wanted to take flight into her safe office. But before she could escape, Coretta leaned forward and curled her index finger, beckoning Eleanor to her desk.

"Better get used to it," she said. "Honor, she loses it when the pressure is on. We knew this was coming! Although the Princess told everyone she wanted everything calmed down before you started."

"She did?" Eleanor asked.

"Yes, honestly. And Delores, she warned us too. They have a conference every Monday, but we never go to any meetings. We're nobody around here." She rolled her large eyes. "You'll see. Geraldine used to tell us things, now Delores does, but she uses us too. You see, she's Freda's friend, that's why Geraldine got fired. We know everything we tell Delores gets back to Freda, who tells Honor. Delores, she told us that today Carol was going to tell Honor that she wouldn't stay if Honor didn't treat her better. Carol, she organized a big fund-raiser at the Hilton in New York. They made a profit of $25,000! Anyway, Honor, girl, she was so nervous about the fund-raiser! For weeks, every day she called her, yelling at her. I felt so sorry for Carol! The fund-raiser was December 17; it was like a Christmas party fund-raiser. We used to be invited, no more. Freda thinks it's a waste of company money to invite us. But last week, Carol told Delores, she took too much from Honor already and she would probably quit today. Poor Carol! She's divorced and has a girl in high school." Coretta shook her head in sympathy. "She needs her job!"

Honor's hysterical voice continued, with the four-letter word used liberally, but Eleanor persevered, sticking close to Coretta's desk. "She has one cousin and one friend working for her?"

"No, she has two cousins. Claudia, and PAAC's lawyer is her cousin too. Leonard, he don't do nothin'! He never here and he don't get no mail, and no phone calls," she said, using homegirl speak for emphasis. "You know what I'm sayin'?" She lifted both hands up in the air with the palms out to indicate her disapproval. "He wears alligator boots, and eats ham sandwiches in his office! We can't do that!"

With that, Eleanor escaped. She empathized with the women as Honor's shouts of outrage permeated the environment. They needed a fallout shelter, she thought, but they were stuck in that fishbowl. She put the manatee file on her desk as she took her seat, and turned her attention to the students' letter. Her hands trembled. It was impossible to concentrate.

She wanted to rush down to Honor's office to save Carol. She considered herself a witness to the poor woman's abuse. "Eleanor," she mumbled to herself, "if you were witnessing a defenseless dog being whipped by an abusive owner, you'd rush to the rescue!" Then she put her hand on her forehead and chastised herself for the ridiculous notion. "Given your status, you'd have the shortest employment in PAAC's forty-year history, including the parade of previous reporters!"

The conference room door opened and the voices were suddenly amplified. Eleanor raced to her door, her back flush against the wall, and peeked out like a spy.

Carol, who seemed the type of person who would be perky and cheerful in normal times, stood in the doorway, the vision of disillusionment. She was a short, attractive woman, with dark hair and eyes, most likely Italian. Eleanor could see into the conference room. Honor sat at the head of an oak table with Delores and Freda on either side.

"Honor, three weeks before the fund-raiser," Carol said, "you refused to speak to me! I had decisions to make. Me and your handpicked steering committee. I informed you of our decisions in memos, which you approved."

"What the fuck is this! I didn't want boring classical music! And the menu was a damn bore, wasn't it? Your décor was over the top! And I dare say, tactless. Worse yet, you commandeered this project! I'm through with this little bloody power struggle!" She hesitated, her eyes examining Carol. "You're demoralized, aren't you?"

Carol bolted up as if Honor had struck her. "I'm exhausted!" she said. "If I am demoralized, you demoralized me!"

Eleanor could hear Freda telling Carol to wait in her office. Carol closed the conference door. Her faux beaver fur coat hung over her right arm like a dead body as she walked to Freda's office.

"Bollocks!" Honor could be heard screeching behind the door. "Either she apologizes before the end of the day or she's out of here! The cow is demoralized! That's not my fault! Tell her to grow up! And I don't need a depressed woman working for me!"

Eleanor watched as Freda raced to her office and the waiting Carol. Just a few minutes later, Delores's jittery voice called Freda back to the conference room. Once outside her door, Freda pointed her demanding index finger at Carol, silently instructing her to remain seated until she returned.

"Is she quitting? I don't have all day!" Honor yelled.

Freda told her that Carol had given two weeks' notice. "But you don't want her going back to the New York office alone! You have to search every file she removes from her office. I'll confiscate her keys now! You don't want her leaving with stationery!"

"Good! Freda, you handle this," Honor said.

"We'll just shut down the New York office!" Freda said. "We should shut them all down! DC, Boston, and Los Angeles! Run the whole show from here!"

"An animal protection organization cannot be run from one central office," Honor said. Her voice showed signs of disgust. Eleanor heard Delores asking if Carol would receive two weeks' severance pay.

"No!" Freda said. "What for? She won't be working. She's entitled to one week's vacation money, and we owe her for the days she's worked since her last paycheck. That'll add up to two weeks. That's her severance!"

"Great!" Honor said. "See, she gets two weeks severance! She's out of the office tomorrow! Good bloody riddance! Piss off, please!"

Delores's softer tones were inaudible through the closed door, but it was clear that she was explaining that the labor board expected businesses to provide two weeks' severance pay or at least two weeks' notice. Honor grew impatient with her. Severance pay was discretionary, she insisted.

"And I choose nothing!" she shouted.

Eleanor watched as Carol, who no doubt had heard enough, walked to the lobby door with her dignity intact, but with her coat wrapped about her body as if to hold together her jagged wounds. She understood. Carol was quitting her dream job.

Back at her desk, Eleanor sat at the edge of her seat, her right hand clasped over her gaping mouth while she eyed the cowed workers outside her door, their words of warning reverberating.

Even Honor had warned her that things got "intense," but she had no idea! Obviously, no checks and balances curbed Honor's abusive treatment! If anything, it seemed that Freda, Honor's right-hand toady, fed into the worst of Honor. "This would never happen at IBM!" Eleanor thought to herself. "Cursing out employees in front of the office staff! How reprehensible! But this is a tough business! Feelings run high! Honor is obviously frayed at the edges from 40 years of combat! But nobody should be treated with such disrespect, no matter how low they are in the hierarchy! Carol wasn't exactly at the bottom of the heap, either. But what is a hierarchy doing in a national animal protection organization, anyway? It isn't supposed to be survival of the fittest! Egalitarianism, isn't that the way?"

She picked up the letter from the Miami students. Her hand trembled. It was impossible to focus. "And I thought journalism was a high-wire act!" She recalled the dilapidated—but somehow lovable—newsroom.

It was only ten o'clock. She decided to do more research on the manatees in an attempt to calm herself. She ventured outside her office to the small library off the conference room for a book. No one dared to glance at her in her travels. Freda and Honor were in Honor's office speaking in conspiratorial whispers. At five past twelve, she decided lunch was an innocent enough move, but on second thought, the last thing she wanted to do was run into Honor on the way out. She decided to wait until Honor had left the building. She removed her purse from the creaking drawer and picked up the black cotton gloves that would protect her hands from the icy steering wheel.

She heard Honor, Freda, and Betty leave for lunch. She waited for five minutes, putting on her beige parka and her black knitted gloves while standing in the middle of her office. The pretty young Lisa poked her head in the door. She looked professional in her gray business suit.

"It's not always like this! We do a lot of good things that make it all worthwhile. It's managing people that seems to get the best of Honor," she said. Her green eyes were intense, but smiling.

"Glad to hear it!" Eleanor said. "Thanks for the encouragement!" Lisa left and she followed seconds later, walking to the lobby door while absorbing the fear still adrift in the half-empty office. No one dared to even glance at her.

Outside in the parking lot, her gray Nissan seemed to represent a normal world. And the bitter January wind that whipped off the beach was refreshing. Eleanor heaved a sigh of relief when the lock on the car door proved to be unfrozen. She sidled into the cold seat and suddenly smiled. She was strangely comforted by the thought of Rusty and Friday curled up on her grandmother's cherry wood table watching the Route 7 traffic and the local birds.

As the motor warmed, she gazed across the road at the tall grass in the tidal flats flailing in the wind. What an effort it seemed to be for the roots of the scrub bushes and small trees to cling to the sandy earth. In the high marshland the wind was even fiercer, with the bare bayberry bushes, the wispy marsh elders, the faded sea lavender, and the lithe black grass being whipped about mercilessly. Covering the bases of the plants were clusters of sparkling icy snow that appeared to help anchor their roots to the earth. The tall grass also grew in the low marshland, the home of fiddler crabs and blue herons, all hidden from sight at the moment. The struggling cord grass was whipped about, the wind spreading the grassy clumps in half, flinging the tall stems this way and that. The tenacious reeds also grew out in the distant tidal flats, where the ribbed mussels, mud snails, and black-bellied plovers lived. Through the horizontal waves of thrashing brownish grass Eleanor could glimpse the choppy waters of the Sound. At the shore, the usually serene beach was being beaten to a pulp by the oceanic surf.

She was mesmerized by the coastal turbulence as she drove north on Compo Beach Road to downtown Westport and entered the congested Post Road. She sat forward in her seat, anxious about the snarled lunchtime traffic. It took ten long minutes to reach the Harvest Moon, a popular health food store. Her stomach was in a colossal knot as she maneuvered around the small mountains of snow stacked in the parking lot from eight snowstorms thus far, with predictions for about twenty more. She parked facing the Post Road for a fast exit, and hopped out of the car and raced to the supermarket's front door.

During her high-speed dash through the market, the organically grown fresh produce tempted her. There was no time. She sped past the vitamins and herbs, and the cruelty-free toiletries and makeup. She needed soy milk, breakfast sausages, and had a desire for pepperoni. That was too bad. And cat food too. Yes, she needed cat food. And she was low on tofu and tempeh. They'd all have to wait.

"Our food is made with love, minus animal products, pesticides, hormones, or antibiotics," read the sign over the deli counter. "Cancer: Meat invites it, Veggies fight it!" was written in smaller letters underneath. The counter was three rows deep in waiting customers. She took heart. Two juicers roared while manned by two female attendants, and another man and woman reached into the glass display case for fresh salads, sandwiches, and other prepared dishes with the swiftness of major league baseball players. The aroma of lasagna tantalized the patient crowd. Within five minutes, she gave her order to a thin, dark-haired young man who, she decided, had a Kevin Bacon type of face.

"A large juice, please," she ordered. "Carrots, celery, beets, parsley. Make it strong. I need all the nutrition I can get! In fact, make it a double!" The young man smiled and was obviously attracted to her. Eleanor cast her eyes down to the food in front of her in the deli counter to avoid his stare as she ordered an unturkey sandwich.

Then she experienced the uncomfortable sensation of being watched. She peered behind her. Two young men were admiring her. She pulled a pamphlet from the countertop and hid behind a wall of books and magazines.

"Harvest Moon recommends that you read John Robbins's best seller, *Diet for a New American and Diet for a New World*," the pamphlet read. Her pride swelled. "I'm in such good company."

The pamphlet described, in Robbins's words, the connection between heart disease and diet. Robbins's books were replete with independent studies to prove his point. One study proved that vegetarian men lived about six years longer than meat-eating males. "Six years!" she said.

Some 30 to 40 percent of cancer deaths were related to diet in men, and as many as 60 percent were related to diet in women. Breast, uterus, lungs, mouth, pharynx, larynx, esophagus, stomach, colon, liver, pancreas, and prostate were listed. Vegetarians suffered a lower death rate in all types of cancer than did meat-eaters.

Cancer had never entered her mind, given her diet. Glancing defensively at the two gentlemen, she grabbed her juice and managed a smile to the Kevin Bacon look-alike. Robbins was a devoted husband and a man of great integrity, she thought, as she sidled into her car which was still warm. He refused to benefit from his father's Baskin Robbins ice cream fortune, professing that he couldn't reap the profits gained from a harmful product. "Maybe there's hope for me yet," thought Eleanor.

She headed back to Compo Beach Road, driving past PAAC's office to the beachfront parking lot a few blocks away, and pulled into a space that faced the shoreline. The ring-billed gulls foraged on the wide beach. Gray and white, with skinny, yellowish legs, the gulls poked about in the shell beds along the shoreline. Their folded wings created a black-and-white polka-dotted tail that tilted up as they dug for sand crabs, mud snails, clams, ribbed mussels, oysters, and other sea life. With prey in their beaks they'd flutter straight up in the icy wind and then drop it, the impact calculated to split open the shell. Several flights were often required.

How she loved the gulls! She leaned forward to gaze up at the misty globe of the sun behind the clouds. "I love my food," she said to her creator. "It keeps me healthy and it doesn't hurt anyone! It doesn't hurt me or them! 'Behold, I have given you every plant yielding seed…and every tree with seed in its fruit; you shall have them for food.' Who needs more?"

Back at the office, an hour later, Honor paid her a surprise visit. "Eleanor, get me the deer population figures some twenty-one years ago when the state yahoos established a hunting season, and the present figures. I expect a call from a reporter at 2:30 PM. Grill the bloody nimrods on the numbers. They manipulate numbers to justify their liberal hunting regs."

And with that Honor ripped back out of Eleanor's office.

She had all of fifteen minutes. While she fingered through her Rolodex for the state wildlife department number, she prayed the line wouldn't be busy. Her fingers snapped the small Rolodex cards back in her haste. A sigh of relief escaped her with the card's discovery. With a rate of speed new to her, she punched in the numbers. A special pride filled her as she realized that for the first time she was assisting Honor, her hero. But her heart was pumping away, and she thanked God when she heard the number ring.

"Calm down!" she told herself. "All this anxiety over one damn telephone call?" She thought of the many exposés she had written with far less stress. "You're OK. Just keep your mind on the text."

It took a brief conversation with the state's clerk to obtain the information. In just minutes she was jogging down to Honor's office with a legal-sized yellow pad in hand. There was plenty of time, she told herself, another four minutes, according to her watch. Honor, however, was already engaged in conversation with the reporter.

"The department stocks the woods with 'natural resources' for their hunting customers," Honor was saying. "Hunters purchase the hunting licenses and also pay taxes on firearms, which sets the department's budget each year. In the twenty-one years of established hunting seasons, the deer population grew from 20,000 deer to 60,000 deer, thereby tripling the deer population."

Honor's numbers were wrong, Eleanor realized, as she stood before her desk. Her credibility was at stake! Animal rights organizations are perceived as prone to exaggerations and emotions, she thought. She prayed Honor would be able to read her expression and put the reporter on hold.

Instead, Honor's gaze turned brittle. Eleanor hesitated a second, like one does when one is about to risk one's own neck. But motivated by loyalty, she raised her two index fingers to form the letter T, for time out. Honor asked the reporter to hold.

"The numbers are incorrect, Honor," she said. "It was twenty-two years ago that hunting seasons were established on state grounds, not twenty-one, and the deer numbers grew from 25,000 to 55,000—they doubled plus 5,000. They didn't triple."

"Wasn't I clear enough?" Honor asked. "They fudge the numbers. I just got these bloody figures from my hunting friend. Who should know better?"

"You're quoting the wrong figures, Honor," she repeated.

Honor looked at her as if she were seeing her new employee for the first time. "Just what part of this don't you get?"

The sting from the humiliating question produced a flush of heat. "Honor, you have the wrong numbers."

"You mean to tell me you're taking the word of a department clerk instead of my inside source?"

"Didn't you say your source was a hunter? Maybe he's not telling you the truth. The clerk had no reason to lie to me. I never revealed my name to her. She told me." Eleanor gazed down at her yellow pad and read her quotes aloud.

"Twenty-two years ago there were an estimated 25,000 deer in Connecticut, and this year, 1998, there are an estimated 55,000 deer."

She glanced at her boss for a brief second and then departed with Honor's glare on her back. "If she doesn't want to correct the figure that's her damn choice!" Eleanor thought to herself. She had fulfilled her obligation, that's all that counted. Yet her heart pounded as she raced past the employees knowing they had heard every word. Never in her career had she engaged in an emotional argument with her boss. Honor had impugned her intelligence. She plopped into her chair, slapped her pad and pen on her desk, and stared at Coretta, Betty, and Carla, who never looked up. "Well, that was a first," she told herself. Her heart still pounded. "It's the first day of my dream job, and I'm having an argument with my new boss? An animal rights icon? Me the novice! Great!"

A half hour later, on her way to the hall lavatory, she and Honor crossed paths. She cast her eyes toward the floor to avoid contact. But Honor approached her. "I called my friend. You were right," she said. "I misunderstood him."

"You're a hard person to correct, aren't you?" Eleanor asked. The candid comment curdled the unsmiling Honor. She watched as Honor continued toward her office without responding. "I've annoyed her once again! What can I do? I'm used to the newsroom! We don't have prima donnas!"

Back in her office, she answered the Miami student's letter. Speedboats and infringements on manatee habitat were endangering the mammals, she advised them. Two local animal advocacy groups were promoting statewide regulations that would widen the areas that were off-limits to speedboats and enforce reduced speed limits. The friendly manatees would be preserved by such restrictions, she revealed, and she thanked the students for their worthy efforts. From her reading, she learned that manatees are cousins to elephants and like their cousins loved swimming and romping in water. Elephants swim? This was a revelation, since for decades she had only viewed elephants in dry landlocked terrains such as circus tents and bone-dry zoos in the middle of cities. Next she constructed her first punchy letter to the editor regarding the blood sport of hunting. The two letters reduced the afternoon to what seemed like minutes.

At 4:30 PM her phone rang. "Hi, I'm Tina Tripper. I'm the director of the DC office. I'm sorry, but I have to whisper. Please don't think I'm too strange, but I have to whisper because there's a spy in the office! Pamela Roberts, she's Freda's best friend. Need I say more?"

Eleanor threw back her head and howled with laughter. A strange woman's voice whispering of spies was a fitting finale for her first day of working in the movement.

"I do sound funny, don't I? But Pamela's our receptionist, and she just stepped out so I'm calling you now, while I have the chance. But I'm going to keep whispering just in case she sneaks back in. I just had to welcome you. Nuts there today, right? I heard that Carol quit. Is that true?"

"I'm not sure, but I think so," Eleanor said. She sat back in her chair, the tension of the day dropping from her. "I'm glad to meet you. Tell me what happens on Tuesdays?"

"Get accustomed to people coming and going. Carol was a true activist. I hate seeing her leave. She worked her heart out for a fund-raiser! It was great! Shamefully, Honor never even thanked her! But tell me, was there a big blowup?"

"Yes!" Eleanor described the incident in detail with her eyes on her opened door.

"Honor runs PAAC like her own fiefdom, yet she's always the victim," Tina said.

Eleanor decided to whisper her reply. "I thought they'd come to blows at one point."

"Don't worry, you haven't been here long enough to be barbecued," Tina offered.

"I've got a news flash for you!"

"No! I'm sorry!"

"Yes. But I'm not too scarred. And I don't want to talk about it. Freda just passed my door." She cupped the phone and her mouth to smother her voice.

"Right!" Tina said. "Because of this thing with Carol, Freda will be skulking around eavesdropping to see who you talk to. Oh, I hear our front door. The spy's back. Talk to you soon. Watch your Ps and Qs, kiddo, and welcome aboard. Sorry you got the treatment already."

Eleanor heaved a sigh of relief. She realized that she had felt emotionally safe talking to Tina for the first time that day. Was it always like this at PAAC? Why did Honor spy on her own staff? Something horrible must have happened to her to produce such paranoia. It took more than her parents' neglectful treatment, Eleanor thought, thinking of the stories she heard at meetings. She'd pump Tina next time.

Her phone rang again. It was Ellen Milani. "Eleanor, there's a woman on the phone. She's having a fit. Can you please take this call, please! I don't want to ask Honor! She's in too much of a bitchy mood. You know what I mean? And Eleanor, can I ask you? Was Carol fired?"

"No. I think she quit, but I'm not sure."

"You mean she had to quit!" She transferred the call.

"I'm a teacher in Norfolk," the woman said. "I got out of school late and there were five small dogs, about three months old, under my car! Some creep dumped them! They're half starved! They're skin and bone! And freezing! And they're afraid of me. I could only get one in my car. They look like a beagle mix. I called the Norfolk Shelter. Everyone's gone. I can't leave them. Will you pick them up?"

"No, we don't do that," Eleanor said. "But thank God you can't leave them! Look, I'll give you some numbers."

From her personal address book, she offered a vet's number who was known to place abandoned dogs. As a backup, she gave her the telephone numbers of two local activists.

"Get some water and food and put it in the car," Eleanor said. "If you have a rope, attempt to pull and push them in. I've rescued a few myself. You can do it. You might have to keep them overnight, but they'll get them in the morning. I'll give you the number of a small group that won't destroy them." She referred to her small address book for the PAWS number and recited it to her. After she hung up, in seconds, she regretted not taking the woman's number for a follow-up call.

The phone rang again. It was Ellen. "Eleanor, I'm sorry, but there's a woman on the phone, she's frantic, her dog fell off her balcony. His jaw is broken! But the vet refuses to treat him because she has no money. He's one of the vets that we recommend!"

"Sure! I'll take it." She pondered, "The vet won't treat a dog with a broken jaw?"

"Hello," the woman said. She was on the verge of tears. "I don't have a charge card, so the vet won't allow me to pay it off in installments. Can you help? My dog! He's in such pain! I can't take him home like this!"

"We don't pay vet bills. But let me speak to the person in charge." Her temper was rising. The female assistant vet came to the phone, but Eleanor failed to change her mind. "It's policy," the assistant said.

The woman caller was back on the phone. Eleanor explained, "There is a group in New York, but you're in Pennsylvania, so this is not going to work. I don't know what to do for you."

The woman began to sob. "I can't take him home like this!"

"Look," Eleanor said, "I'll give them my credit card number if you promise to pay them in installments." She was surprised at her own generosity. But it was impossible. How could she let the dog leave the vet's office with a broken jaw, with nowhere else to turn?

"OK," the woman said. She heaved a tearful sigh of gratitude. "That's so kind of you." She began to weep again.

Eleanor pulled out the bottom drawer for her black purse to fish out her Visa credit card from her wallet, doubting she'd ever see the money. The assistant vet informed her that the medical treatment would cost approximately $200.

The phone rang again, "Eleanor...."

She jumped in at the sound of Ellen's voice and said in unison with her, "There's a woman on the phone."

Ellen chuckled. "She's a very poor, old, old lady from South Norfolk, and she's so upset! Somebody gave her a puppy for Christmas. But she can't afford shots!"

"Sure. But do all the crazy calls come in from 4:30 to 5 PM?"

"Most of the time!"

"I love him," the octogenarian said. "But I don't have the money for the shots. Do you give free shots?" Her elderly, thin, and squeaky voice shook with emotion.

"No, we don't do that. I'm sorry."

"I thought you did." The woman sounded forlorn.

"I'll give you numbers to call. You'll get some help. Don't worry. First call your health department and the local shelter. They sometimes offer free shots. Also, some local animal protection groups will help. They'll direct you to vets who sometimes offer a free clinic and shots for a day." She found two numbers in her personal directory and read them to the woman. "If that doesn't work, look up humane groups in your yellow pages."

It was 5:03 PM. Eleanor rose and peeked out of her door. She laughed aloud to find the office empty. "Only furniture!" she thought. "Barren as the Sahara! I can't imagine why!"

With a satisfied smile, she returned to her seat. "I'm so satisfied, so grateful that PAAC is here to direct people," she thought. She spoke to herself and God. "So what if it's a little crazy! It's a business in a movement. What did I expect?"

She thumbed through several issues of *HOWL*, PAAC's quarterly magazine. The magazine addressed issues from animal experimentation to the cruel production of fur coats. And without apologies, it expressed admiration for the "magnificent" animals and drew parallels between humans and nonhumans. Its voice spoke for those who understood the worth and the plight of animals. It was unafraid of being accused of anthropomorphizing, and in doing so, it offered Eleanor a sense of peacefulness.

The magazine was Honor's baby and it was well-done, with detailed descriptions of the issues, including supporting facts and figures. PAAC definitely served the purpose of speaking for the voiceless, Eleanor concluded. She placed the magazines in her nylon briefcase for some night reading.

"If PAAC and organizations like it didn't speak for them, who would?" she thought. "Who could question Honor's integrity toward the animals? How could PAAC's motives ever be questioned?" she wondered. Lydia's harsh comments came to mind. "Yes, world, we confess! PAAC is guilty of wanting to end animal suffering! So jail us!"

After donning her parka and gloves and retrieving her purse from the bottom drawer, she headed toward the lobby door. The lights were still burning in Honor's and Freda's offices. It was close to 6 PM.

"Good-bye!" she shouted.

"Good-bye!" Honor's mellifluous voice answered. With a brilliant smile, Honor came to the door in an obvious show of approval for Eleanor working late. Freda, wearing a skeptical smile, joined them while remaining in her doorway, which was to Honor's left.

"You survived your first day!" Honor said.

"A new reporter at the *Norfolk Daily News* went to lunch on his first day and he never came back!"

Honor threw back her head and filled the office with laughter. She walked up to Eleanor and stood only inches away.

"We're having a minor employee crisis," she said. "Managing employees is the most difficult part of my job. It should calm down in a day or two. But then there'll be something else!" She rolled her eyes and threw her arms up in the air, and then turned around to head back into her office. Without speaking, Freda disappeared into hers.

Eleanor was so inspired by Honor's confiding in her that she decided to return early the next morning with a plant and the photographs of her three departed dogs.

"Have a good night," she sang.

"Night!" Honor said. It was the full flowering of her musical voice.

"That's the fun-loving Honor who hired me," she thought.

With a smile of satisfaction, she stepped outside into the forbidding weather.

CHAPTER 3

▼

STEEL-JAW LEGHOLD TRAPS

On Friday, Eleanor was in the coffee lounge with the staff getting a cup of tea when Honor paid a rare visit. She casually announced that Carol Conrad had applied to the state labor board, testifying that she suffered the symptoms common in Battered Wife Syndrome. Carol said her condition was caused by Honor's treatment of her and the nature of the work.

As Honor spoke, Eleanor noticed a predatory gleam in her eyes as she stared at her employees, and concluded that her visit was calculated to head off possible corroborating witnesses. Yet she rushed to Carol's defense. "Maybe she did feel abused. It does get a little intense in this business."

Her words cleared the lounge as fast as they fell from her lips. She wondered what had motivated her to come to the defense of a total stranger. Then visions of the wounded Carol popped into her head.

For the next three months, however, Eleanor worked in her peaceful office, having little to do with Honor. They merely exchanged friendly smiles. But with each passing day she met members of her humane family, all of whom seemed like lost cousins. They called from near and far for literature to distribute at local campaigns, for advice to help abused neighborhood animals, to announce demonstrations and protests, to request information and fliers, or to seek financial and membership support for legislative and other worthy campaigns. Just as Eleanor had suspected, she was a member of a quiet lifetime army of professional and volunteer foot soldiers.

She was the beneficiary of a certain cachet as PAAC's representative. An elderly woman from Iowa called because she couldn't persuade the local police to budge on behalf of a neighborhood dog chained outside and freezing. A few words from Eleanor and the police rushed to the site to speak to the family. She got the impression that the police feared that PAAC's members were massing at the state line. A weeping Pennsylvania woman revealed that her condo's new rule limited each unit to only one animal, forcing her to choose between two beloved canines. Eleanor suggested to the chairman of the condominium association that the new ruling apply only to new owners.

It worked. It seemed that whatever the issue, a solution jumped to her mind as if all her past experiences had been in preparation for this job. When PAAC failed to pack a punch, she employed the not-so-subtle art of threatening an exposé. If nothing else, she was a shoulder to cry on.

As the days slipped contentedly by, her dream job became her life; she had found her Holy Grail. The blissful smile never left her face even with the grating hair dryer blaring in her ears each morning for twenty minutes. She traveled from Derbe to Westport without a cloud in the sky. Each evening she returned to Rusty and Friday, walking in the door and greeting their inquiring faces with caresses. She felt soulfully at peace with her day, as if she were living in an "earthly paradise." Her leisure time was filled with her journalism colleagues and Lydia. On weekends, skiing allowed for communing with the opposite sex at a safe distance, and then there was church.

As the daylight hours lengthened, she jogged a couple of miles after work or in the mornings on the back road that paralleled Route 7. It cut through the woods and ran along the Norfolk River. She felt akin to all of the woods' bird and animal inhabitants, thanks to her newly chosen profession. At the house, the resident chipmunk sunned himself on the stone wall outside the kitchen window. A family of raccoons, a woodchuck, and a skunk also emerged from the surrounding woods. Families of whitetail deer, usually a doe and her two fawns, also gathered near the kitchen casement window to feed on the ivy that grew on both sides and the berry bushes underneath. With the reappearance of each animal, she heaved a sigh of contentment.

On Friday morning, March 28, Honor and Freda departed for a noon flight from LaGuardia to Denver. They were scheduled to return on Tuesday, April

Fools' Day. Honor was to meet with movement leaders who had formed a coalition to launch a Colorado state initiative to ban steel-jaw leghold traps.

Eleanor was shocked to discover that the traps were outlawed by approximately ninety countries and were almost universally detested by Americans as well. Except for American hunters and trappers. PAAC's files revealed that the traps were placed by commercial and hobby trappers who sold the pelts of fur-bearing animals such as raccoons, minks, lynxes, ermines, beavers, foxes, coyotes, and wolves to those in the fur trade.

Nontargeted animals were designated as "trash" animals, she learned. The traps so mangled their small bodies that when the unintended victims were finally released, they were killed and "trashed"; hence the name. Skunks, woodchucks, squirrels, badgers, hawks, falcons, and a variety of other birds and animals, including unwary family cats and dogs, were the "trash" animals.

PAAC's employees were periodically freed from their own leghold trap. Eleanor noticed that the eerie silence disappeared in Honor and Freda's absence. On Friday, at 3:30 PM, Carla, usually a frightened mute, chatted freely about a young man charged in the murder of Bill Cosby's son Ennis. As the women moaned and groaned with sympathy for the Cosbys, Coretta informed everyone that she still thought OJ was guilty. And to the delight of her fellow employees, she also called the White House comment line, asking President Clinton to offer cut rates for the poor so she too could sleep in Lincoln's bedroom.

The fun came to an abrupt end Tuesday morning when Honor and Freda returned.

"That lame trapping initiative has a loophole in it large enough to run a bloody eighteen-wheeler through it!" Honor's shouts emanated from Freda's office. She had wasted her money traveling to Denver, she said.

It became clear that all unity between the animal advocates had come to an end when Allen Dey, the CEO of the North American Humane Society, had caved in under federal pressure. And the coalition members went along. So Honor had stormed out calling them "spineless."

The employees worked with their heads lowered. Ellen was so afraid to speak to Honor that she begged Eleanor to take a call. It was from a Colorado woman who shared Honor's opinion of the "lame" bill. As Eleanor was on the phone with her, Honor charged into her office.

"Those jokers at the Connecticut Humane Society should offer free spay/neuters for dogs and cats statewide!" she yelled. "They've got more money than God!"

Eleanor put the Colorado woman on hold.

"I want you to take this call," Honor said, pointing to the blinking red light on Eleanor's phone pad. "Approximately 30,000 cats and dogs are euthanized each year. Nationwide some 5.7 million family dogs and cats were killed in state shelters across the country. We should be digesting these numbers with our oat bran muffins in the morning!

"They have the money to advertise this carnage! They have an unseemly nine million dollars in investments. Connecticut residents don't donate their money to the humane society so they can sit on a sweet little nine-million-dollar nest egg, do they? While animals die every day? That goes beyond anyone's idea of a rainy-day slush fund!"

Eleanor laughed at her spitfire of a boss and grabbed the legal-size manila pad sitting on the right side of her desk and jotted notes. Since her first day on the job, she had yearned for this level of excitement, working with the movement icon, even though their initial collaboration had ended in a set-to.

She finally blurted out the news about the outraged woman on hold. "Her name is Mary Browning, and she's head of Colorado Citizens for Animal Rights, CCAR," she said. She pronounced the word "CAR." "And she hates the initiative so much that she's mobilizing her group in an attempt to kill it!"

Honor took the phone and asked Mary to hold on while she returned to her desk. "Thanks for the call!" she shouted back to her in full gallop. "I can't wait to hear what this Mary Browning has to say!"

Eleanor continued to gaze at her door, wishing she were more involved with the Colorado initiative as she listened to Honor's feet pounding their way to her office. She realized that she felt like a little kid who'd been patted on the head by her parent.

Ten minutes later, she scurried down to Honor's office full of pride for PAAC's firebrand who had stood boldly in a Denver room full of parroting activists and cut through the hypocrisy. These leadership qualities seemed to Eleanor to justify her devotion to the mercurial Honor and her propensity toward insouciance for heartbroken employees such as Carol Conrad. With her pad and pen in hand, Eleanor tentatively approached Honor's open door. She hadn't been in her office since her first day.

Honor pointed to the first of two chairs in front of her desk, taking a few minutes to wrap up the call. Honor and Mary Browning agreed to collaborate on a series of negative advertisements in key Colorado newspapers in an effort to kill the coalition's initiative.

Honor revealed to Eleanor that the initiative began with a local Denver group that had decided to promote a simple referendum to prohibit the use of leghold traps, padded or unpadded, by hobby, commercial, and government trappers. When the group appealed to Allen Dey for contributions, he created a coalition. Dey believed it would take a united effort to succeed. But when the federal government intervened, he then said that to succeed, the initiative must exclude the ADC allowing it to continue to use the traps.

Eleanor recalled that the ADC was Animal Damage Control, which had a thousand employees and a yearly budget of forty million dollars. Honor wanted to put them out of business.

"Dey said we couldn't fight the NRA and the ADC. He swore that they'd wage a fear campaign with images of rabid animals in people's backyards! We'd be misguiding the voters who placed their trust in us! They'd think their wildlife and dogs were safe from at least one trap! And taxpayers haven't a bloody clue that their hard-earned money is paying for this ranching subsidy.

"What horseshit! But the stupid cows in the coalition are charmed by Dey. He's convinced them that without him, and the cooperation of the ADC, the initiative would be struck down! It's the same old tune I've heard for the last forty years from the same tired welfare voices!"

Honor picked up a National American Humane Society leaflet on leghold traps from her desk and held it up. "When you read this, the NAHS appears to be totally against leghold traps. But of course, we know it's actually willing to allow the ADC to continue business as usual. In NAHS brochures you're led to believe it espouses veganism and opposes all animal experimentation and hunting!" She placed the leaflet back on her desk. "But actually, when an organization is labeled 'humane' or 'welfare,' it is fair to assume it approves of some hunting and supports some animal experimentation, and it approves of eating meat if the animals are humanely slaughtered. Never use the terms 'humane' or 'welfare' to describe us!"

"Why is the coalition buying this initiative, then?" Eleanor asked. "Oh, I know," she said, "they think the bill will stop the commercial trappers, at least."

"Bullshit!" Honor said. She bolted up in her seat, her large feet hitting the floor. "Government officials hire local trappers to set the traps. The trappers get to keep the pelts. It's the good ol' boys network. If this initiative passes, Dey takes the credit. His salary is a hefty $200,000. Need I say more? The trappers continue as usual, they're happy. And his donors hear about this phony initiative, and they're happy. And the ADC is happy! But the pathetic animals—for whom he works—they remain trapped in Dey's rusty jaws of complacency! And Dey thinks he justifies his hearty salary by pulling off such political stunts! Some criticize my salary! It's a pittance next to bloody Dey's!"

Honor's briefing helped to answer a few of the nagging questions about the movement's disunity. Eleanor's admiration for her was rising.

Honor rose and walked around the desk to stand next to her. "Then Dey gave this standard speech that saving some of the animals from the traps each year is better than saving none of them. I've heard it all before."

At that moment Honor seemed to collapse into grief. Eleanor sprang to her feet. "Honor, what is it?" she asked. She stroked her thin slumped back and shoulders. "I'm sorry."

"I'm OK," she whispered.

Eleanor withdrew her hand, feeling Honor's resilience return. She remained standing.

"I've heard this sorry excuse for cowardice before," Honor said. "Save half if you can't save them all. That's what they always say, and you wind up losing them all." She returned to sit behind her desk.

Mary Browning, she revealed, had refused to appeal to other local groups for additional cosigners for the advertising campaign, saying that the locals wouldn't want to be used as pawns in a battle between national organizations. Mary also said that the local groups didn't trust the national organization in the best situations.

"Fuck them!" Honor said. "There are too many bloody small groups anyway! I know of 8,000 of them nationwide. It just divides us even more, doesn't it?"

"Honor, about the Connecticut Humane Society article," Eleanor said. She gazed at her notes. "The reporter finds it hard to believe they have nine million dollars in investments, and she's going to look into it. I doubt she'll criticize them. If our information sees print, it'll be because she quoted us!"

"They should have stores in malls like pet stores; instead they're hidden away! Almost as bad as our shelters on the outskirts of town near the dump!"

"But the papers print half-page photographs of animals being rescued by the inane humane society as if they're heroes. Even though the animal has to be near death before they act!" Her eyes were bulging. "They never push the envelope. They're too bloody busy playing footsie with government officials. They steer far away from controversy, just like our buddy Dey! They're more concerned with their insider status than with significant change.

"The San Francisco Humane Society urges businesses to adopt a cat colony," she said. "They're actually making strides in eliminating euthanasia. What's the damned humane society doing here? Sitting on their nine-million-dollar nest egg!" She abruptly stopped her harangue.

"Cats made life tolerable for me in my early boarding school days. I've loved each and every one of them since. They lived off the garbage pails placed in a building behind the school. How weary and lonely they were!" she said, sitting up and folding her hands before her on the desk. "They'd creep on my lap for a cuddle. I'd pet their tattered bumpy coats. I'd smuggle food from a plate hidden under my jacket or skirt, and give them all I could swipe from fellow students or whatever I could bully or shame out of them." She started to laugh. "I actually got into the big commercial kitchen refrigerators a couple of times in the middle of the night!" She gave a belly laugh and looked at the ceiling, and continued to howl. "Then they feasted royally! At first I was so homesick, yet I hated my parents. I told myself over and over again that it didn't matter that they didn't like me or love me. How pitiful I was."

Freda rushed into the room, obviously in a panic. Her loose-fitting dress waved from the trembling of her plump body underneath. She stopped at the corner of Honor's desk. "We have to talk."

With a nod of the head, Honor insisted she speak in front of Eleanor.

Paul Rossi, age thirty-seven, the new Seattle director who operated out of his small apartment, had been missing for two days. He called and told Freda that when he took the job five months ago, he understood that it was not nine to five. He was annoyed at having to account for every minute of his time.

"I know he's accustomed to sitting up in trees for days, but that's not what we're paying him for," Honor said. "Why didn't he bloody mention that he'd be unreachable for two days?"

Freda flushed a bright pink. "I quote: 'I told Honor I'd be out of touch for two or three days,'" she said. She read her notes in machine-gun fashion. "'I told her on Friday. I arrived in Quebec on Thursday night. I traveled all day Friday to reach the north shore.'" Freda stopped and glanced at Honor. "He has the rest on an attached e-mail," she said, waving the single-page e-mail in her right hand.

"Read it," Honor said.

"'Dead seals are washing ashore by the thousands,'" she began. "'Sunday I saw around 400 animals: blue backs, beaters, raggedy jackets, white coats. Their bodies are mutilated, their penises amputated. Some bear the wounds of cuts that circle their whole body. The Department of Fisheries and Oceans had the audacity to claim the wounds could have been caused by jagged ice. Dr. Donald Bavlock from the Canadian Marine Mammal Association, who saw photographs, said he's certain the cuts were done with knives. He's witnessed carcasses of seals with similar wounds floating in the North Atlantic. The DFO continues to refuse to accept the scientific information and blames anything other than the seal hunt that took place three miles off the North Shore of Prince Edward Island. I'm on top of this, and I've got photos and statements. Also, I'd like to take off Wednesday. I should be back in Seattle by then.'"

"He can't take off Wednesday!" Honor screamed. "This is a moral nightmare, but a PR wet kiss! I want him banging out press releases today! And doing interviews tomorrow, which is Wednesday! Every bloody spring, young seals die horrible deaths!"

Honor told Eleanor that the fishing industry supplied seal penises and other organs to China and Japan where some believed them to be aphrodisiacs and to possess medicinal powers. It was obvious that this barbarism was going on with the tacit permission of the Canadian government and the sealing industry. "Men and their damned obsession with their penises," Honor cried.

Freda explained that Paul said he didn't have time to do mail. And when he was hired, he understood that he would not have a nine-to-five job.

"He's done a good job," Honor said. "But you tell Mr. Environment that if I have to answer the bloody mail, so can he. If he has to work weekends, too bloody bad. Our hours are Monday through Friday, nine to five. He talked to Claudia, not me. I never approved this two-day disappearance! Tell him he talks to you or to me. I have employees in India and in China working with organizations that rescue strays. They travel on dirt roads. Yet I always know where they are! But we've lost Paul three times in five bloody months. Bollocks!"

Freda read her last note. "He said, 'I'm used to working as close to the site of the abuse as possible. I'm not your typical PAAC armchair activist.'"

Honor smiled at Paul Rossi's spunk, to Eleanor's surprise. Then she rose to her feet and waved her hand, dismissing Eleanor and Freda. Eleanor headed to Lisa's desk. Paul had risked his life to spare several baby seals for just a few precious moments, she revealed. That's why Honor hired him. He was tall and husky. His muscular body could withstand the rigors of animal rescue. Among other feats, he had sat atop floating dolphin traps so he could chase them away, saving them from a life at Las Vegas hotel swimming pools.

Paul's acts of bravery on behalf of the seals occurred a year ago, when he had joined other environmentalists at the Gulf of St. Lawrence. They risked their lives for a few symbolic minutes when they prevented the sealers from clubbing and spiking the heads of countless three-week-old baby seals. Then they acted as witnesses to the deaths of the crying babies as they were bludgeoned and skinned alive.

Lisa revealed that Honor, in 1967, had viewed one such massacre from the shore through a pair of binoculars. Her life was threatened in telephone calls she received at her hotel. But she returned home to purchase her first nationwide mailing list. Fur coats were being made from the skins of baby seals, she told potential members. The sealing industry was endangering the species. She instructed them to write the Canadian government to demand an end to the massacre. After two mailings, PAAC's donor base leaped from 6,000 Connecticut members to 30,000 people nationwide.

In her office, Eleanor learned that the baby seal hunts had been accidentally discovered in 1964, according to PAAC's files. It seems that a Canadian film crew, assigned to film the seals in their natural habitat, had stumbled upon the massacre and filmed the clubbing of 100,000 baby seals to produce fur coats. The exposé united environmentalist, animal protectionists, and celebrities including Brigitte Bardot.

Canada placed restrictions on the sealing industries as a result. "Protecting just enough of the seal babies to allow the species to continue does not end the brutal murder of newborns, most of whom will be skinned alive," Honor wrote her membership. "Many biologists will attest that sea mammals are the most advanced form of nonhuman life."

Eleanor sat at her desk overwhelmed by her glimpse into Honor's world. Her own work seemed clerical in comparison. She gazed at her trusty in-box filled with letters and pink telephone message slips. She was relieved to be interrupted by her phone. It was Tina talking about Laboratory Animal Day.

In Norfolk, Alison Barrington, of People For Animals, PFA, would be holding her yearly demonstration outside of Surgical Pride, Tina said. Surgical Pride was a suture company that used live, stray dogs to demonstrate its surgical staples. After mock operations with real surgeons, the dogs were killed.

Alison tipped off Helen Graves, the director of PAAC's Boston office. Helen was planning to rescue some of the dogs. It seemed that Surgical went on the road with its staples and dogs show. And the dogs would be stored in vans waiting in the parking lot of a hotel while the operations took place inside.

"Dogs are being used as live models in operations to demonstrate surgical staples to surgeons?" Eleanor asked.

"It's been going on for years!" Tina said.

Tina was to lead a group of protesters outside the National Institutes of Health, the NIH, which issued millions of dollars of taxpayers' money yearly to finance animal experimentation in Washington and in universities and commercial laboratories across the nation.

A half hour later, Honor invited Eleanor to lunch. At noon Eleanor practically skipped down to her office, sure that she'd be part of the Colorado initiative one way or another.

Frankie's Italian Restaurant was an overcrowded, noisy seaside eatery on Compo Beach Road a mile north of the office. The bright daylight filtered through the restaurant from its generous windows, one of which faced the Sound. The square room resembled a large patio sitting under an atrium. The business crowd's steady chatter echoed uproariously off the pink brick floor, while in the background Dean Martin sang, "When the sky hits your eye like a big pizza pie, it's amore." The music was the finishing touch to what seemed more like a cocktail party than business luncheons.

A young waiter weaved the four women through the crowded floor to a circular patio table in the center of the room. A large wooden bowl of complimentary salad sat in the center of the glass tabletop, and a busboy dashed over with a basket of steaming Italian rolls. They squeezed into their chairs to avoid pushing against patrons sitting inches away. Lining the right wall was a row of occupied wooden booths, and straight ahead there was a view of Long Island Sound seen through sliding doors. Honor took the seat that faced the view. Freda sat across from her, and Eleanor sat to Honor's left, facing Delores. After they ordered drinks and a large eggplant pizza, without cheese, Honor helped herself to one of the rolls, her fingers breaking through the thin crust and allowing a puff of steam to escape. She bit into the bread with gusto. The rest of the women followed her example.

After a few bites, Honor shouted to be heard above the din. "Dumb cow that I am, I thought I was free of problem employees with Carol gone. She was way over her head as the director of the New York office," she said gazing at Eleanor. "Now we have the activist supreme performing his famous disappearing acts!"

"He's ridiculous," Freda said. She gazed at the diet Cokes and straws being served by the young waiter, and Eleanor's glass of water. "I'll straighten him out!" she said. She lowered her head, glowering as she removed the white straw wrapping and rolled it into a tight ball.

Eleanor noticed how Freda glanced at her as if she were uneasy discussing managerial matters in her presence. Then Freda reached for the two clear plastic serving utensils set in the large wooden salad bowl, serving a helping of salad to Honor and then returning them to the bowl. Delores helped herself and offered the serving utensils to Eleanor while the conversation continued.

"They're all children," Honor shouted. She chewed on a mouthful of salad. "Pat and Betty are always five minutes late! And nobody in that entire room has any social graces! Not one of them offers a simple 'Good morning!'"

Eleanor swallowed hard. The salad stuck in her throat. It was Honor's place to offer the "Good morning," she thought. She longed to defend the staff. But she didn't dare. Throughout lunch, disrespectful comments were directed at PAAC's managers. At the mention of Tina, Freda revealed bitterness. By the time the pizza was served, it was difficult for Eleanor to swallow. Her throat was too clogged with unspoken words. The best part of lunch was its conclusion.

Honor and Freda spent the remainder of the day sequestered in Honor's office with her cousin Leonard Workman, PAAC's lawyer, who made a rare appearance. From the voices she overheard, Eleanor knew that they spent the entire afternoon discussing present and potential employee lawsuits, including Carol Conrad's claims.

CHAPTER 4

▼

COLORADO WILDLIFE

The following morning, Wednesday, April 2, a few minutes after nine o'clock, Honor rushed into Eleanor's office, pulled the corner chair to her desk, and sat inches away from her like a teenager at a school lunch table. Eleanor gazed at Honor, content to have her shoulder leaning against hers. Honor's CEO robes were gone. Once again, she was her comrade.

"I want you to do the groundwork in this campaign against the initiative," she said. "This thing can't reach the polls. I need you to engage the local groups. Mary will start you off. She's faxing names and numbers of contacts."

Mary and Honor's collusion to take down the Colorado coalition kept Eleanor tossing all night. She found PAAC's files on the subject rich with possibilities for a positive campaign. The solution, however, failed to materialize until 3 AM. For the remainder of the night, she rehearsed her pitch.

Eleanor tucked her thick hair behind her ears and began. "Honor, let's really stick it to Dey! Why not create our own initiative? Let's expand the simple leghold trap initiative and go beyond leghold traps to padded leghold traps, the body-gripping conibears, snares, and all poisons! Including sodium fluoroacetate or compound 1080, sodium cyanide, which the government uses liberally, and the local groups have tried to outlaw for years! This will force trappers to use one trap only, the have-a-heart trap! And what's more, Honor, the ADC will not be able to trap animals for ranchers and farmers. Trapping will be restricted to public health issues. Even at that, the ADC will be required to use have-a-heart traps.

"The local groups will love it. We conduct demonstrations to collect signatures on petitions across the whole state of Colorado, with their help of course. Oh, we're not going for the hundreds of thousands of signatures required for an initiative to be placed on a ballot, but just enough to show Dey that we've got a chase.

"We tell the grassroots groups that the coalition is creating a less powerful initiative, but we're certain that with their help we can encourage the coalition to broaden it. I'm new to this game, but even I know that Dey's initiative won't fly without the support of the grassroots!"

She raised her hands to indicate that the simple truth was unassailable, and more: it was the basis for a victorious campaign.

"Here's the sexy part, Honor: since taxpayers don't have a clue that their tax dollars pay for the removal of so-called nuisance animals, the subject is ripe for editorial pages and should raise debates across the state. At the same time, we should run ads listing the ADC's telephone numbers and e-mail addresses."

Honor rubbed her smooth hands together as her elbows rested on the desk, and then she gazed up at the ceiling. "This ought to tweak that son of a bitch," she said. Gazing at Eleanor, she nodded her approval.

Satisfied with her reaction, Eleanor sat back in her chair, relieved that she had spouted everything in a coherent manner despite her lack of sleep.

"How many groups do you think you can get?" Honor asked.

"How many do you need?"

They both laughed at Eleanor's confidence.

"Honor, honestly, it's an offer they can't refuse! I won't have to sell this! There lies the beauty in this plan. Don't you think the local Colorado groups know the power of the ADC even better than we do? They'll welcome a positive campaign run by a national organization if it's presented in the right way. We'll provide the organization, literature, petitions, and PR. At the same time, I'll let them know we know, that this initiative won't fly worth a damn without their foot-soldiering!"

Eleanor gazed down at a legal yellow pad that was filled with her mad nighttime scribble. "We'll call it the Colorado Have-A-Heart Campaign. Honor, we know that thousands more animals a year are trapped in Colorado using poisons. There are two to twelve others for each target animal that's killed. I got that right from our files."

Honor stared spellbound at her. "He's a greater fool than I think if he bucks the grassroots! What demanding interlopers they are! So arrogant! Give volunteers an inch and they take the bloody campaign!"

Eleanor chose to remain silent.

After staring down at the desk blotter for a few seconds, Honor gently tapped the fingertips of both hands against it several times while she nodded her regal head in agreement, as if sealing Eleanor's Colorado Have-A-Heart Campaign. She reached for the calendar on the desk and began thumbing through the small loose-leaf pages. "We have no time to lose," she muttered. "Our initiative has to hit the ground first before Dey's. There's the filing date with the Colorado secretary of state to consider."

April 28 was Laboratory Animal Day, so that weekend was out, she noted, and flipped the page. Her eyes finally rested on Saturday, May 17. It was just short of seven weeks away. Honor suggested the date, her eyes darting to Eleanor's to measure her reactions.

Eleanor knew people who gave more advance notice for a birthday party! The deadline sent a minor chill through her. Hundreds of groups and people to be enlisted, maybe thousands, and the literature to research, write, proof, publish, and mail! And no doubt a million other details of which she had no idea. The campaign for the initiative was a two-year project. But her eyes stared firmly into the icon next to her as she said, "Honor, you're the veteran here. If you think we can pull this mother off in six and a half weeks, let's go for it."

"Of course, we'll just 'do it'! We don't have a choice! We have to be the bloody early bird!"

Honor stood up and returned the chair to the corner and walked to the doorway where she hesitated and gazed at Eleanor, shaking her head from side to side as if overwhelmed with Eleanor's ingenuity. She then scudded to her office.

Worried that if Dey pulled out, leaving the leghold trap initiative up to PAAC, Eleanor's first call was to the office of Denver's secretary of state. A mere 67,829 signatures were required for a referendum ballot, not hundreds of thousands! "My God," she pondered, "that's a piece of cake! If we get forty demonstrations, and the activists collect 500 signatures each, we'll be one third of the way there!"

At that moment, Lisa dashed in obviously annoyed. She was delivering Mary Browning's fax, a single piece of paper with the Colorado numbers, which she handed to her. Then she leaned across Eleanor's desk, her lush brown hair falling forward. She was twenty-four, with alabaster skin accenting her large green eyes that at the moment bulged with indignation.

"I'm only allowed one pen," she said. Her voice was deep and controlled. She held a blue ballpoint pen in her right hand. "If there's more than one pen on my desk or in my drawers, after I leave at night, Freda confiscates them. Or Delores. I don't know which. They put them back in the supply cabinet. It's not just the pens, Eleanor, which is ridiculous all on its own, but this means that they're searching our desks every night! I feel like I'm a teenager and my parents are snooping through my room!"

She also revealed that she had seen Freda and Delores sifting through everyone's wastepaper baskets the night before. "Ask Coretta about the desk searches."

Eleanor tore herself away from Mary's fax and approached Coretta. She wiggled her index finger, beckoning Eleanor to her side, and opened her desk's top drawer to reveal a stash of prophylactics, feminine pads, and loose tampons rolling around. "Shouldn't they find something interesting when they search my desk? I'm thinking of putting some used ones in here."

Eleanor rolled her eyes and shook her head laughing at Coretta's antics. Then she raced back to her campaign. The animals are the priority, she instructed herself, attempting to put PAAC's dysfunctional office in the proper perspective as she dialed her first call. Without the plight of the animals, nobody would have a job. On that score, she'd like the whole office to be unemployed.

At 11:30 AM Honor appeared in Eleanor's doorway, personally inviting her to lunch and implying that such lunch meetings would be a regular occurrence from now on. In the glow of Honor's approval, and Frankie's minestrone soup, salad, and hot Italian rolls, the indignities suffered by the office staff soon faded from Eleanor's mind. Honor and she laughed like old cohorts with Honor imitating Allen Dey, while puffy-faced Freda scrutinized them looking like a bride left at the altar.

An hour after they returned from lunch, Eleanor could hear Honor's feet as she pounded her way to her office for an update on the enrollment of the local groups. Eleanor knew it was just the first of many such visits for the next six plus weeks. She looked up as soon as Honor arrived at her door. "I feel like an IBM saleswoman," Eleanor told her. "When they say 'No,' that's when I begin to sell!"

Honor's hopeful face soured.

"I'm only kidding, Honor! There's no selling to be done. They're jumping on board, wanting to put an end to the poisoning along with all the other traps!"

Mary Browning had underestimated the grassroots groups. Activists were offering to be contacts and were furnishing her with new names. At 5:30 PM that day, Eleanor tramped through the empty main room toward Honor's office. "This is good!" she thought. "This is very good, to be this important to PAAC, and to Honor." Charging straight across the room to Honor, who was seated behind her desk reading the *Times*, Eleanor presented her glowing report. "We'll have the state covered like a blanket, pardon the corn."

Honor smiled with respect, and placed the newspaper on her desk spread open. "I don't have that vigor to start from ground zero. Oh, I can still charm the high rollers. But mobilize troops of activists? No bloody way. You'll easily have a following here in the state and across the country."

Honor's words multiplied Eleanor's devotion to her, and crowned her faith in her mission. That evening with Friday and Rusty purring at her side, she thanked God for women such as Honor who had dedicated their lives to the children of the Earth for the last forty years. Again she was overwhelmed with gratitude for being among the lucky few who discovered their mission and even managed to get paid fulfilling it.

But the next day offered a more sobering insight into PAAC. It was Thursday, April 3, and over linguini primavera, Freda proudly announced a newly installed employee surveillance routine. Periodically all employees' desks would be searched, as well as their computers. Copy machine numbers would also be recorded nightly and checked each morning.

This plot has a J. Edgar Hoover ring to it, Eleanor thought. She watched as Freda's pale and powdered jowls wiggled from the brutal force of her words as she rattled them off in staccato fashion.

"When you want to get rid of somebody," she said, "I'll retrieve any information we need in minutes. No more surprise attacks, like Carol Conrad! Humph! I'm also going through every long distance number on our telephone bills. We'll have a thick file to draw on for the labor board! I'm making note of their character in their personnel file. Whether we can trust them or not will be a matter of record." She laughed. "Screw 'em!"

Honor chuckled, obviously proud of the covert operation. "Well, that's perfectly legitimate. You're responsible for job evaluations."

Eleanor suffered instant indigestion. She gazed down at the cluttered glass table as she attempted to swallow the indignation she felt on behalf of herself and her fellow employees. She noticed Freda scrutinizing her, trying to read her thoughts, so she quickly shut them down and commented on the delicious primavera. Following lunch, her office was a welcome sight and her ringing phone a diversion from her thoughts of the fascistic Freda. In between calls on the initiative, she researched trapping numbers in Colorado and general leghold trap information, and jotted down thoughts for the drafting of the literature and donor letters. Thursday proved to be too long, with telephone calls flooding most of her day; and it was the prototype of days and nights to come right up to the demonstrations, with telephone calls following her home and reading and researching stretching into the night.

The next morning, Friday, April 4, began with Mary O'Donnell's tears of indignation. Mary, PAAC's bookkeeper for five years, stood behind her desk and wept into a tissue. The whole staff including Patroklos surrounded her. Her pocket change, retrieved from her top drawer, sat on her desk. Attached to it was a yellow note from Freda written in red pen: "Is this PAAC's money?"

"I've handled hundreds of thousands of dollars over the years. How could she question me?" Mary asked.

Eleanor had seen few people more innocent-looking than Mary. She was in her late twenties, efficient, dependable, and the mother of a two-year-old. She smelled of baby powder but seemed virginal and no more than seventeen. Several freckles were sprinkled on her pure Irish milkmaid skin. If Freda was willing to cast aspersions on Mary to please Honor, she'd accuse Mother Teresa of serial murders.

Noticing how the staff soon rushed back to their desks, wanting to place a safe distance between themselves and the accused, Eleanor remained to comfort Mary. She also imagined what Freda might have noted in Mary's personnel file, recorded without Mary's acknowledgment or response.

"When Freda and Honor took the trip together to Denver," Mary whispered, "they became so close that Freda acts like she's running the company. She handles all the finances! She even orders our accountant around. Honor needs her. She's in charge of all the books. If Honor needs funds for an unexpected campaign, Freda can fix it for her."

Mary revealed that Honor was always on friendly terms with the person in Freda's position. "But this is different. Nobody ever questioned me! And every day Honor becomes more exclusive, talking only to Delores or Freda!" She dabbed her runny nose with a white tissue. "Freda encourages it. She's jealous. You can see it. She's so insecure. Sometimes I even feel sorry for her because Honor uses her. But Honor used to come out here and work at a desk and talk to us."

While Mary spoke, she stared in the direction of Freda's office. "Eleanor, Freda insults one of us almost every day. I think she wants us all to quit so she can hire her own people and have spies all over the organization."

Mary's thoughts seemed right on the money. To keep Mary's spirits up, Eleanor offered encouraging smiles through the day. She was grateful to have the excuse of the Colorado campaign to avoid another lunch at Frankie's peppered with managerial plots. At five, Mary peeked her head into her office offering her gratitude.

Eleanor couldn't wait to escape for the weekend. At her kitchen table sitting behind her typewriter, or busy on the phone, her crusader's heart was never more content. One Colorado activist faxed her state trapping statistics to the office. She rushed to Westport Saturday afternoon to retrieve it. Back home, she began her draft of the demonstration flier.

Knowing that indiscriminate traps caught two to twelve nontargeted animals and birds for every targeted animal they caught helped her do the math. She learned that 30,000 animals had been trapped in Colorado the previous year. So some 200,000-plus innocent animals each year could be saved if their initiative were adopted.

She'd had no idea the stakes were that high.

Even though she slept with Rusty and Friday at her side and she nestled under her mother's comforter, her dreams were trundled by ideas that woke her. During the spring weekend she forgot about jogging in the sun-dappled back road; she was knee-deep in the Colorado Rockies, talking to activists from all points of the state: Durango, Alamosa, Pueblo, Colorado Springs, Castle Rock, Greeley, Loveland, Boulder, and on and on.

When she arrived at the office on early Monday morning, April 8, she discovered a fax from Pamela to Freda that said one word: "Gotcha!" It was obviously a code. She called Helen, who promised to investigate. Ten minutes later Helen revealed that Pamela had discovered a number of long-distance telephone calls that Tina had placed. She had informed Freda with the "Gotcha" signal.

"Honor uses rivalry as a key employee motivator," Helen added. "Whether the calls were justified or not is immaterial. It gives Freda another opportunity to prove her loyalty. You know that Honor is paranoid? Trust is a constant issue. Besides, Freda wants to continue to gather evidence of insubordination on Tina's part, believing in the 'three strikes and you're out' philosophy."

"Helen, I can't work like this," Eleanor said. "Freda accused Mary of stealing; Delores and Freda search our desks and read our garbage every night; and Freda's installed a surveillance routine that rivals Communist China! We have no civil rights here!"

In a motherly voice, Helen explained that Honor was suspicious of almost everyone, which was not unusual in the movement. Spies came in several varieties: there were various industry spies, political and governmental spies, biomedical spies, hunting and trapping spies, and intra-movement spies, to name just a few.

"At our conferences, for instance, we know there may be spies from the different segments of the population that we're targeting. Alison Barrington's office was bugged by a pharmaceutical company she was protesting. And at our demonstrations, our target will often have their own photographers posing as part of the media, and even interviewing Honor. The in-house spying has escalated to new heights since Freda was hired, I must admit. Freda was an office manager for a marketing company, and perhaps that's the cause. But Honor thinks we're disloyal if we participate in other campaigns, especially RUFFFF's."

"That's hard to believe," Eleanor said. Her eyes were glued on the open door.

According to Helen, Leona Nesbitt, the head of RUFFFF, called meetings for the sole purpose of humiliating her employees; it was her managerial style. Helen and Tina had worked for Nesbitt in the heyday of the animal rights movement, in the early 1980s. "We're the only former employees who lasted. Activists quit RUFFFF and join PAAC, and then quit in a few months. Honor welcomes them with open arms because she wants to hear the dirt on Leona, whom she considers her nemesis. Although Leona hardly knows Honor's alive. At RUFFFF they say, 'The movement doesn't end at 5:00 PM.' Lunches are a half hour and you're on call twenty-four hours a day, including weekends. And Leona works the longest hours of all. Here my hours are regular and Honor trusts me. I have autonomy. But I'd never survive working in the same building with her. For that I sincerely feel for you. But I don't like to talk on the phone. I'm sure someone is listening."

With that she hung up.

Stunned by Helen's words, and her hasty good-bye, Eleanor sat at her desk numb for a few seconds. Then her telephone rang, jarring her nerves. It was Tina.

"Freda is Honor's worst enemy!" Tina said. "If anybody says anything to me, I'll quit!"

While Eleanor was overwhelmed at the prospect of working for PAAC without her, Tina revealed the reason for the long-distance calls. She had called PAAC's New York members to alert them about RUFFFF's MacDonald's protests. "Honor's dragging her ass on the agribusiness issue. Eight billion animals a year killed, the numbers rising every year, mass slaughtered, cows skinned alive, and packed in saran wrap on your grocer's shelves! And we don't have a plan! Yeah! I made a few damned calls about these hamburger joints! So fire me!"

A few minutes later, Eleanor entered Claudia's office for files on the ADC. Honor's open door revealed Freda standing before Honor's desk looking irate. She held a copy of the incriminating telephone bill in her right hand.

"I expect a little of this," Honor said. Her voice was cool. "I expect employees to occasionally use office equipment for personal use," she said. With that she dismissed Freda and her incriminating information.

"You should at least question her!" Freda sputtered. "It cost us money! What was she doing, anyway? Who was she calling?" Both her arms were flailing as she spoke, and the telephone bill rippled with a swishing sound as it swirled in the air. "Was she working for another group?" Her fury heightened with each question she posed. "Why don't you question her? You should give her an official warning. Put her on probation! Why don't you do that? Why don't you do that?"

"Because I don't bloody want to," Honor said. She then turned her attention to her work.

Freda stood for several seconds before the huge desk fidgeting, as if she were waiting for a token sign or word that would soothe her battered pride. She walked past Eleanor as she left. Eleanor was quick to lower her eyes. Eleanor then rushed back to her office to inform Tina. To her surprise, ten minutes later, Freda charged into her office as if seeking validation. She silently paced from the door to the window in her agitation. Following three fierce laps, she stood in the center of the small office and broke out:

"She always complains to me about Tina! She even told me she wants to fire her! I supply her with incriminating evidence, and she refuses to confront her! To hell with her!" She swung her thick right arm in the air, as if she were throwing a baseball. "I'm not doing this shit anymore!"

"Freda, she loves Tina," Eleanor said. "That's obvious. Besides, nobody's perfect. Tina's a great campaigner. That's an art in itself."

"Then why the hell is Honor wasting my time complaining about her? I found evidence that will allow her to fire her. That's what I thought she wanted from me!" She stood perfectly still for a second, and to Eleanor she seemed a victim of her own deeds. "I guess she just doesn't want to fire her. That's it—she really doesn't want to fire her!"

With that realization she left.

Eleanor felt a tinge of guilt for her harsh judgment of Freda. She didn't have a significant other, her job was important. But, on the other hand, she thought, Freda obviously had enough friends to fill PAAC positions in different parts of the country at the drop of a hat. As she returned to her work, Honor rushed into her office full of anxiety. The coalition's signature gathering would commence on Saturday, June 9, and the members were contacting social clubs throughout Colorado. "They're campaigning for one million dollars for advertisements!"

She peered at Eleanor as if it were a state of emergency. "Social groups are jumping on the bloody bandwagon. It's a warm, fuzzy, noncontroversial issue that makes them feel good about themselves! We've got to get moving! I want the demonstrations to take place on Saturday, May 17, at 10 AM." In her haughty manner, she strode to Eleanor's desk.

"I don't want the demonstrations spread throughout the whole weekend. I want them all on the same day at the same time: 10 AM. I want them to distribute a flier that you create and I want press releases in every local weekly and daily in each vicinity!"

Eleanor tucked her thick hair behind her ears and reached for the yellow note pad on a stack of folders to her right. She was nervous as she searched her notes. She had to calm Honor down and convince her that she was on it.

"I worked over the weekend, Honor. I know we have the support of the general public. People think the leghold trap is already illegal. They're shocked when they find out it's still being used! They won't buy the ADC's argument that they need the traps to protect the public. A young woman told me, and I quote, 'Let the ADC use have-a-heart traps to catch rabid or dangerous animals.' I got that quote from several homeowners, and local groups verify the sentiment. And people are ready to call the ADC and complain. And, like I thought, taxpayers don't want to subsidize farmers and ranchers by paying the bill to catch predators for them. As one voter said, 'Let the ranchers bring their sheep into a barn at the end of the day!'"

The initiative had been posted on PAAC's Web site, and twenty local animal activist groups representing various sections of Colorado had signed on. Eleanor had spoken to representatives of the Tiger's Club, volunteer firemen, church groups, and political clubs who were considering signing on and circulating the petitions. Lisa was e-mailing the petition to hundreds of social groups throughout the state.

"The League of Women Voters is on board with us; that's straight from the president's mouth! They just have to formalize their support. They have 5,000 members. That's 5,000 signatures. Several activists have even contacted Dey."

Honor grabbed the corner chair and pulled it to her desk.

"The activists reported that Dey was encouraging," Eleanor said. "He's assured them that he's working on softening the government and he's considering expanding the initiative."

Honor's expression soured. "He'll work this. We'll get the signatures, work our bleeding butts off, and then he'll jump in at the end and take credit for it all. That would be bloody pissass Dey."

"Do we care? We will have met our objective! We're talking a lot of animals, Honor. Some 200,000-plus 'trash' animals whose lives will be saved each year. After all, I think Dey wants to save these animals too!"

"We better damned well care!" Honor pulled herself back to broaden the distance between them. "It's our campaign, and we had better hang on to it! Our donors need to know we're out there, not Dey! This is a business!"

"We will hold onto our own campaign," Eleanor said. "PAAC's label will be on this campaign through the media, in particular in editorials with our objections to the ADC; that'll keep it ours. Dey's allergic to such controversy, right?" She didn't wait for a reply; she flipped the page of her legal-sized yellow pad. "The ADC records showed—I got these straight from our files—that the ADC trapped 15,000 Colorado animals the previous year, which equaled the numbers trapped by commercial trappers, 15,000, making a grand total of 30,000 animals."

"Really?" Honor said. Her voice softened along with her expression.

"If we can believe the numbers, we know there are so many more unreported." Eleanor retrieved a manila file from the stack on the right side of her desk and withdrew the two sheets of paper with the trapping information faxed to her by the Colorado activist. "Honor, in one county, 42 target coyotes were caught and 91 nontargeted species were also reported trapped. Mathematically that turns out to be about two nontarget animals to one targeted animal. In another county, 7 targeted coyotes were reported caught along with 85 nontargeted animals. That's what, about twelve to one?" She stared at Honor with a look of horror on her face. "Twelve to one!"

"Disgusting!" Again, Honor hissed her words.

"And Honor, no state or federal government regulations obligate a trapper to report the number of untargeted animals trapped. So you can bet there's a hell of a lot more that we know nothing about." She again referred to her pad. "If you take an average of the two numbers, 2 and 12 animals, we'll be saving more than 210,000 birds and animals a year who stumble into the traps and are mangled and trashed. If you want to take the lowest number, 2, we'll be saving 60,000 of them a year. Honor, the ADC listed a million birds killed each year by various means, including the steel-jaw leghold trap: starlings, magpies, gulls, blackbirds, pigeons, ravens and crows, grackles, and can you believe great blue herons, finches, egrets, owls, red-tailed hawks, snow geese, meadowlarks, pheasants, woodpeckers, wild turkeys, robins, and house finches—the list goes on. Many of them, including hawks and falcons, are listed among the squirrels, badgers, woodchucks, and others, not to mention dogs and cats, who are 'trashed.' We'll select photos of them, whoever you want to be in the flier, with the stats."

Eleanor pulled a photograph from another file set directly in front of her on the desk. It was an old photo she'd found in PAAC's trapping files of a golden retriever. He was spread-eagled on the ground under an oak tree in the forest, his snout fatally caught in a leghold trap. She selected his image to be the icon for the Colorado campaign. "He died so painfully right there on state-owned land that bordered his home," she said. She handed Honor the photograph.

"That's perfect. They'll get that."

Honor sighed and rose to her feet, placing the chair back into the corner. Her anxiety quelled, she returned to her office.

Later that day, Eleanor landed an interview for Honor in the *Denver Sun*. Over the ensuing days and nights, her endless hours of work were rewarded with responses from thousands of PAAC's Colorado members, along with those of women's clubs and political and social clubs. The phones rang nonstop from early morning until late at night. Eleanor could easily have used an extra pair of hands. Adding to the burden, PAAC had no message line that recorded after hours, so it became routine for her to arrive early and stay late, given the three-hour time difference, and she often left her home phone number.

Ellen Milani complained of an overload and requested assistance. Before the Colorado initiative petitions even hit the streets, the whole state would be involved. As a result of the flood of editorials, several legislators had promised to "look into" the subsidy for farmers and ranchers.

In the midst of this all-consuming campaign, Eleanor's other daily obligations continued. The *Stamford Advocate*'s tepid story about the Connecticut Humane Society appeared. It merely noted the investments of nine million dollars. She rushed to Honor with the disappointing article. But Eleanor received only applause for the growing Colorado campaign. "The *Advocate* hates controversy!" Honor said.

Hurrying back to her busy office, Eleanor thought, "I can't seem to do anything wrong these days."

At this special time, it appeared to everyone that the two women grew closer with each passing day. The office staff watched with faint amusement and some envy. Lisa noted, "She's living in your office!"

Eleanor understood. It seemed that instead of the staff hearing raucous laughter emanating from Freda's office, it came from hers. When Honor requested her advice regarding minor employee problems, it seemed like she needed Eleanor's advice to run the office. Honor's time with Freda was reduced to their lunch meetings.

Throughout the day, Eleanor and Honor worked in full tandem. Before Honor left the office for any reason, she would poke her head in and shout a cordial, "Eleanor, I'll be back in an hour." When she returned, she'd peek in her door with a friendly, "I'm back!" During one of their conversations, Eleanor confided in her sister-in-spirit, "This is not work, Honor; this is a dream come true." Each night exhaustion never prevented her from thanking God for the worthy marathon effort to save the animals from the variety of traps. And nightly she thanked her creator for Honor.

On that Friday, April 11, after working until 7 PM, Honor invited her to go out to dinner. The Jade was on the Post Road, a short distance away. After the dinner of grilled black mushrooms, string beans, and sesame noodles, Honor seemed lost in thought while she gracefully sipped her second Dewars on the rocks.

"If I could ever trust a damned man!" she blurted.

Eleanor roared with laughter, pressing her head back against the high booth, almost dizzy. The one glass of wine in her exhausted body made her lose all reserve.

"Let me begin again," Honor said. She raised her glass. "If ever, ever I could, and this is most unlikely, you understand, ever trust a man enough to marry him, I'd marry Grumpol!"

Grumpol, Eleanor had learned, was Honor's lifetime lover. She overheard a couple of telephone conversations and Lisa filled in the rest. Grumpol was a celebrity, having tried high-profile sexual harassment suits. Recently, however, he had taken on several animal abuse cases.

But Honor was presently focused on her first love, a college freshman. Effrom Roosevelt had been her fiancé when she lost her virginity to him under the seclusion of a willow tree set back from the St. Charles River in the late fall.

"How much did I love him? For the first time, I was grateful that I had a lonely childhood because I could tell Effrom. I was confident that such confessions brought us closer and sealed our love forever. We planned to marry right after graduation. That was the plan until I found him with my best friend in my dorm room after returning early from the Thanksgiving Day holiday."

At the sight of them, Honor had spun around and left school and refused to return, to her parents' dismay, she told Eleanor. Only a few days later, she landed a job as a receptionist at the South Norfolk Dog Pound, which was one of the many thousands of shelters opening around the country at the time.

"At first, it was therapy. I was totally absorbed by the owners as they tugged the dogs up to me." Her voice began to change. Even her look transformed; her expression was that of an impressionable young girl. "I was at the front counter and they handed them over to me as if they were old and useless luggage. The dogs looked around the strange surroundings and at me scared to death, and forlorn. They knew. And I knew they knew.

"I looked the owners in their eyes, but I could hardly believe they could be so cruel. They explained why their family pet had to be euthanized. They were too old, too expensive, had grown too large for the apartment or the owner to handle; they caused asthma or allergies; the nursing home didn't allow dogs; they were Christmas gifts the owner couldn't return; they had personality disorders; they refused to behave; they wet the carpet; or they ran away. Certainly all the complaints were correctible, nothing to bloody die for! They use the same excuses today. I'll never forget the dogs' stricken expressions as they watched their owners walk out the door without them."

In the dogs' erect, nervous stance, their wide, frantic eyes, their quick head movements while being held tightly on their leashes, Honor revealed that she had recognized the pain of betrayal. They searched the door out of which their owners had disappeared, and then switched back to the young woman behind the desk. "They turned to me with pleading eyes; I was their last hope. But the compression chambers would be the last stop for all but a rare few. By the end of my third week of employment, I was so depressed.

"That Friday evening, I broke down and sobbed," she continued. "Once tears began to flow, my buried disillusionment with Effrom, Barbara, and even my parents washed out of me."

In the ensuing weeks, she cried each night for those dragged up to her each day, she told Eleanor. But the crying failed to wash away the wrong. After a month of weeping, she became determined to act.

"I sat on the edge of my bed, in my comfy not so little bedroom, and I made a vow that would guide me for the rest of my life. I sat on the edge of my bed, my hands turned to fists. My eyes squeezed shut so I could conjure up each tormented individual, each pleading canine face that had turned to me for help since my first day on the job. I remembered every bloody one of them, and I made a lifelong vow to dedicate my life to their memory. I promised them I'd make sure that their lives were worthy and their deaths remembered."

She hesitated for a moment, the dreadful memory overtaking her. Eleanor's eyes filled with tears. She reached over and caressed the tight fists resting on the table.

"The vow," Honor continued, "quieted my conscience. I slept for the first time in weeks." That Friday night crusader's vow was Honor's initiation into adulthood, she said. The following Monday she launched her career in animal protection. "At that time, 20 million dogs were euthanized each year. The numbers are still horrible: 5.7 million, and that's cats and dogs. But no one can deny the tremendous gain.

"Two years later, at the age of twenty-one, in 1957, I opened PAAC's storefront office on the Post Road in Fairfield. Lenny's father, Eliot Workman, my uncle, a loud-spoken, cigar-smoking lawyer, processed our nonprofit corporation papers. We were just a little local group. He's much like Lenny minus the cigars. Of course, my parents mellowed and took a great interest. They aided with connections to deep-pocket donors, and they took some pride, at last, in their only child. Instead of marrying Effrom Roosevelt, I married a business. PAAC is my partner for life. Control, I learned, offered the only lasting serenity."

"When you slammed the door on Effrom, you slammed the door on your youthful dreams," Eleanor said. She sipped some burgundy. "I know the kind of hole that leaves in your heart."

The night she discovered her husband with his lover, Eleanor told Honor, she too had returned early from school, night school. It was a winter night and the roads grew icy and she decided to return home. She entered her apartment and the bedroom door was closed. But she could hear music playing. When she opened the door, her husband was watching her neighbor do a belly dance in full costume. He lay on the bed wearing nothing but an unbridled smile. It looked like a routine thing.

The scene was so painful that she had only described it to her mother.

"Since then it's seemed foolish to believe that a man could be devoted to one woman all his life. Or that you can really know a man. I came to the conclusion that I had no idea who my husband really was. I didn't know I had a stranger in my bed. My mother never trusted him. He drank like my father. Let's face it, I married my father!" She waved her two hands in the air in hopelessness. "Nothing new here!

"But Honor, since then a closed door has symbolized betrayal. I fear depending on anyone, male or female, anyone who can ruin my peace of mind, and in particular a male, anyone who can close the proverbial door in my face."

In that moment Eleanor felt that she and Honor had bonded as easily as they did on the day of her job interview. For her, the moment sealed their friendship forever. And in the retelling of her story, the painful betrayal seemed to have occurred to someone else: the woman she was before therapy, the woman she had been before responding to the eyes on the newsroom wall. Now that she had rediscovered herself, her writing, and her mission, she'd never gravitate to a hurtful man. As she sat there smiling at Honor, it seemed so clear that her wounds had healed.

That evening, as Eleanor curled up in bed with Friday and Rusty, she realized she felt secure in her job, as if she had found a solid place in life and a solid foundation for her life's work. Her friendship with Honor bordered on the sacred, she mused, while enjoying Friday's soft fur under her caressing fingers. Now it was time to trust again, she told herself while smiling into his hairy, whiskered sweet face. As she prayed that night, she thanked God for her wonderful boss who was a hero to all the animals. Through the weekend, she thrived as never before as she shouldered the awesome responsibility of the Colorado campaign. Her belief in her sacred mission had been fortified by her conversation with Honor.

Monday morning, totally engrossed in her notes, Eleanor rushed out of her office to update Honor. Coretta, sitting at her desk, called to her sarcastically, "How's your new friend?"

These days, Eleanor realized that she raced past those in the outer office in the same way that Honor did, as if they were invisible. She smiled back at Coretta, but didn't respond. She and Honor bonded several times daily in their work, something she couldn't share with the meat-eating staff. And she had only recently realized to what extent management played an adversarial role in employee-employer relationships. She willingly accepted the distancing from the staff when it meant gaining Honor's confidence. Honor, after all, was her animal rights leader, the one whom she was destined to assist.

Nearing the third week of the Colorado campaign, forty small Colorado organizations were signed on, and the sites were nailed down, from Grand Junction in the east to Burlington in the far west, from Trinidad in the remote south to Fort Collins in the north. That Friday evening, April 18, Honor dashed into Eleanor's office and announced that she was leaving for a week's vacation in London. Eleanor gazed at her like a wife whose husband had failed to mention a planned trip. Her bleary eyes managed to turn wide with fake enthusiasm as she looked up from her busy desk and managed to wish Honor a pleasant trip. While Honor remained standing haughtily in the doorway, Eleanor requested that the demonstrations be allowed to take place over the weekend, from May 16 to the 18th, a Sunday, in order to accommodate the activists. Honor reluctantly agreed.

One day in the middle of the subsequent week, Coretta stood in Eleanor's doorway. "Every year, she goes to London at this time. She has to brush up on her English accent. Oh, you'll see. Her voice, it'll be deeper and she'll end everything she says with a question. Like, 'It's a nice day, isn't it?' That's very English."

Eleanor chuckled and was grateful that she wasn't excommunicated from the office staff altogether. The campaign continued with gusto. At each planned demonstration, she appointed a volunteer to act as PAAC's spokesperson. The flier was finished, and she had mapped out the newspaper dailies that reached the highest demographic areas, and listed the weeklies to carry their ads. All that was left to do was to pack and mail the fliers and petitions.

Her phone was like a constant bell ringing, and it would continue ringing until the day before the demonstrations. While she talked to one person, Ellen was taking messages from others. She accepted the reality of infinite calls, realizing that the moral support she offered kept women and men who were thousands of miles away and would never set eyes on her, feeling as familiar with her as if they were with their local librarians. The phone calls were a small price to pay for their full weekend of foot-soldiering, and to maintain their trust. Like Honor they wanted updates about the coalition and the progress of the initiative. They discussed site problems, the numbers of activists expected, and the number of fliers required. If anything changed in their arena, they called her. If they had any doubts, they called her. She invited the constant calls; they kept her connected to those on whom the success of the whole campaign hinged. Moreover, to the novice Eleanor, their loyalty and trust proved her worth to PAAC, and therefore to the movement, and therefore to the animals. Again, she surprised herself with her ability to solve problems; it seemed to be a natural talent, like playing the piano, she joked to herself on one of her many late evenings in the empty office.

The nonstop work hours were similar to those required to write the Vietnam veterans' stories. The payback there had been the vets finding their missing souls; this time, it was saving tens of thousands of wildlife beings annually.

Eleanor's mission and the campaign were on point. Then Honor returned from her vacation.

CHAPTER 5

▼

THE OMEGA

Honor returned on Monday, April 28, three weeks before the demonstrations. Eleanor trembled with excitement to see her, wanting to share every detail with her partner. Several of her memos were waiting for Honor, including the latest list of demonstration sites and participants. Belying her state of exhaustion, Eleanor dressed to look fresh and crisp. She trotted down to Honor's office first thing that morning. She offered Claudia a smile and tapped on Honor's open door as a polite gesture.

Honor was seated behind her desk signing letters. She continued as if she hadn't heard her knock. Eleanor rapped on the oak door again, increasing the impact. Again Honor failed to respond. After a few minutes, Eleanor turned away more puzzled than embarrassed. She shrugged her shoulders at Claudia, and walked back to her office. "Honor must be out of sorts," she thought. "It is her first day back—the week's backlog must have overwhelmed her. I shouldn't have approached her so early in the morning."

At 11:30 AM, anxious to update Honor and obtain her approval on pending decisions, Eleanor again approached her office and tapped on her door, but this time she also took the initiative to cross the room and stand before her desk. She gazed down at Honor's gleaming dark hair, anticipating her attention. Honor continued to sign letters.

Eleanor stood there waiting, and each passing second offered new humiliation. The objective reporter in her deemed the scene unreal, and she thought that in her entire work experience she had never come across such gross disrespect. Rob DeOrio, her editor, had produced a daily newspaper without demeaning a single employee, yet here she was gazing down at Honor as she continued to sign her name. Eleanor could count each strand of hair on her shiny head, and yet she was invisible. It made little sense to speak. It would only invite more of the same.

So she exited. Returning to her office, she began to ponder. How could this be? Really, what the heck is going on? What is the matter with Honor? In her growing concern, the thing uppermost in her mind was the development of the campaign, so she wrote Honor another memo asking for permission to proceed. For the third time that morning, she ventured into Honor's office, this time walking in and depositing the memo. Ten minutes later Honor tore into her office in a fit of anger, slapped the memo into her box, and stomped out. Again Eleanor felt like a wife, but this time like one watching her angry husband give her the silent treatment.

At least Honor's permission was scribbled across the bottom of the memo.

At lunchtime Eleanor heard Delores, Freda, and Honor leaving for lunch, their voices raised above the conversational level and accompanied by boisterous laughter that she knew was meant to hurt her. Like a homing pigeon, the laughter seemed to find her and deliver its bitter message. She was ostracized and as good as pilloried on PAAC's village green while the three chums departed for Frankie's, leaving her behind. She felt the heat of the humiliation. Not one person in the office spoke to her or dared to look at her as she walked to the lobby door. What a fool she must seem, to have worked twenty days and nights only to be the object of such indignities, she thought.

Going to her car, Eleanor drove by the serene sea on automatic pilot and headed for the busy Post Road and the Harvest Moon to purchase an organic juice. The exhaustion, held in abeyance during the last twenty days, fell on her like a metal yoke, and she became a beast of burden. Back at her desk, sipping her juice, she reminded herself that hers was a labor of love. And her boss was God. She had sufficient work to keep from dwelling on Honor's punitive and inexplicable behavior.

"I hated those lunches anyway," she told herself. The most troubling part of all of it, she thought, was Honor's refusal to talk to her. Why couldn't she just discuss what was bothering her?

As Eleanor endeavored to work that afternoon, nagging questions persisted: "What's wrong with her? What did I do? As far as I know, I'm guilty of only one glaring fault—working to carry out her orders! But obviously she's unhappy. There must be something!"

The next day, Tuesday, April 29, Eleanor woke with a knot in her gut. Early that morning, when she and Honor crossed paths in the front of the large office, Honor recoiled at the sight of her. She actually shielded her eyes with her right hand, and her upper body twisted and ducked from the waist awkwardly in the opposite direction. Honor's bodily contortions stunned Eleanor anew. She objectively studied the action, wondering if she were reading it wrong. She was far from a stranger to rejection. Her father had seen to that, but even he didn't cringe at the sight of her. Her beauty and personality typically generated the opposite response. The eyes of the staff again were politely diverted from the incident, but they saw everything.

That day and the following days of the week, the three women left for lunch with much banter while Eleanor sat in her office, trapped in self-doubt and nameless guilt. She was bewildered, hurt, demoralized, and wondering what unwitting sin she had committed against her boss, and her abandonment issues rose to the surface. And each memo she delivered to Honor's office was another act of humiliation. Yet she waited like a pining lover for Honor to barge into her office and resume their relationship. Eleanor was quite alone. At this time she realized to what extent she had alienated her office family. No one spoke to her as she traveled to and from her office, except for Lisa and Mary's occasional remarks. And although the staff was angry at her, and fearful of guilt by association, they did manage to venture "I told you so" smirks.

She didn't dare confide in her colleagues, Tina, Helen, or Larry Knowles, the Los Angeles director, they might be Honor's present partners. Her mother would worry, and Lydia was outside the office family. It was best to withdraw, not trust anyone but herself, and mimic the others outside her door.

The respect from the Colorado activists allowed her to reenter PAAC's office each day with her head held high. Her exhaustion grew, however, as the week and the indignities plowed on. A good night's sleep became a thing of the past. She was demoralized and being beaten up by her boss, yet the weight of the campaign lay heavily on her shoulders, not Honor's.

Thursday night she considered going to the movies to see *Jerry Maguire* or *The English Patient* just to relieve her tortured mind, but she dismissed the frivolous notion; instead she played Chopin CDs and worked.

That night she again tossed and turned with the dread of being fired. She must have done something wrong, she told herself. She had a tendency to be overconfident, too assertive. She was a reporter and was not used to taking orders; perhaps she had been unwittingly disrespectful. She was not used to kowtowing to a boss. Rob had met them on equal terms, but then again, he hadn't started a company from scratch either. Perhaps she treated Honor too much like a friend and not like a boss, and that had offended her. Thank goodness Friday morning dawned, and with it came some relief from her nagging questions. In her quiet office, the work restored her sanity. The endless inquiries from the Colorado activists served as tranquilizers that allowed her to forget her doubts and all the indignities.

On mid-morning that Friday, May 3, Eleanor rose from her crowded desk to gaze out her window. The cumulus clouds seemed too beautiful to believe. Why hadn't she looked at them earlier? The horizon's indigo, that shimmering and indistinct blending of sea and sky off in the distance, seemed a place that hovered between earth and heaven. Earth was not her home, the indigo reminded her, and beyond the vast blue sky was God and reality. Eleanor took several deep breaths in which she exhaled her self-doubts and inhaled serenity. Her eyes closed and a natural meditation took hold.

She sat down, for at once crystallizing thoughts overwhelmed her. Like a harbinger of things to come, she recalled Carol Conrad in tears and her claims of wife battering, and how Honor had cut Carol off during the planning of the Christmas benefit she organized; how Honor had insulted her to the point of refusing to accept her telephone calls, how Carol was forced to reach key decisions without the benefit of Honor's input; how Honor had accused her of a power play; how the loyal, hardworking but demoralized Carol had opted to quit her dream job rather than apologize for a job well done. Then there were Tina's warnings about the stormy times when Honor would turn on her.

Now it was Eleanor's stormy time, and Honor had turned on her. She must hold on "for them." She remembered the eyes on the newsroom wall.

She judged herself innocent of all crimes against Honor. She was certain of it. She had done nothing to offend her. It was just Honor being Honor! The revelation offered instant relief. The tightness in her gut eased just a bit. Eleanor knew that she need not admonish herself for committing foolish mistakes.

Prayer never failed to help her. She sighed, rolled her chair back, and returned to the window. "I may forget you in the midst of turmoil, but you never forget me."

At 2 PM that afternoon, Honor finally broke her silence. She telephoned Eleanor requesting an updated distribution list; the May demonstrations were just two weeks away. Eleanor dashed down to Honor's office, her list in hand and the enthusiasm of old. But to her surprise, Claudia was seated in the far chair facing Honor's desk. Eleanor decided to remain standing and at the side of Honor's desk. Claudia gazed up at her with the timidity of a captured bird.

"This list has the numbers of fliers and petitions to be sent and distributed at each demonstration," Honor said. She was referring to Eleanor's distribution list, which both she and Claudia held. "Do you think 1,000 will be enough for the Loveland demonstration?" Honor smiled brightly at Claudia, waiting for her response.

Clueless, Claudia searched Eleanor's eyes. She nodded her head in the affirmative.

"Yes, 1,000 fliers," Claudia said. "That looks like enough."

Eleanor remained standing at the side of Honor's desk, ignored and puzzled. Why would Honor ask that question of Claudia? Claudia was a stranger to the campaign and possessed no knowledge of the sites or the demographics. An updated distribution list dangled from her right hand.

"Make sure that Pat has enough copies of the fliers," Honor commanded. "And Claudia, I want you to write a letter to the activists to insert into the packages. Helen will list your name on the newspapers ads and on the press release along with Helen's and mine as contacts."

"I'm the director of public relations!" Eleanor said. "Why wouldn't I be a major contact on the press release? Isn't that my job, not Claudia's?"

She leaned across Honor's desk. Honor rolled back her chair as if she were afraid. "Didn't you read my memo?" Eleanor asked. She straightened up. "I wrote the press release. I identified the newspapers with the desired demographics! How would Claudia know how many leaflets are required?"

"Fuck it!" Honor shouted.

The four-letter word delivered a solid blow to her pride.

"I see you have Colorado names and numbers as contacts!" Honor said. "This is our bloody campaign! Who OK'd that? The good fairy?"

It was now clear. She had been charged and found guilty of favoring the Colorado activists at the expense of PAAC and now she must pay. She responded with patience; perhaps an explanation would clear up the whole matter. But her knees quivered from her injuries as she began.

"Honor, I wrote you a memo and you approved it. A local contact is necessary for us to get the weeklies to cover our demonstration in their area. That way we'll reach more people. You want signatures. Right? Weeklies will not cover our demonstrations if they don't have a local contact. Honor, it'll be a missed PR opportunity.

"Honor, I spent a good deal of time rooting out forty reliable spokespeople, getting their proper names and correct spelling, addresses and telephone numbers, and coaching them, all of whom have declared themselves our volunteers. So they will be speaking for PAAC, not for their respective groups. I sent them a prepared speech, for which I requested your approval and you signed off on."

Honor sneered with renewed contempt as if Eleanor were a stupid fool. "So they'll bloody have to call us!"

"Honor, we, in Westport, Connecticut, will not receive a call from a reporter from the *Durango Weekly*, I can guarantee you that! Or the *Canyon City Gazette*."

"Well they can bugger off then!"

It was Eleanor's initial encounter with stupid authority. Her knees buckled as she realized the worst of all possibilities: Honor had the power to ruin the campaign, and the animals would pay. Now she understood why her job was a "revolving door."

"We're finishing this thing today," Honor said. She peered down at the list. "Your list was incomplete. Poor Claudia's been calling people for hours finding the missing addresses." She offered Claudia a smile of gratitude. "She has spent enough time on this!"

In her exhausted state, Eleanor winced again. Her voice was reduced to a whisper as she attempted to control her building rage. "Claudia doesn't have to do any of it, Honor. I can do it. Honor, you haven't been in touch. The distribution list you and Claudia have is incomplete. You should have asked for my updated list earlier today and you could have spared Claudia's valuable time! I expected to finish this list this afternoon and send the material out Monday!"

"I don't need an incomplete list. I need all of the names and all the addresses! And the material must go out today."

Honor's words stunned her. Was Honor totally delusional? How could they run off the petitions and letters, and pack and address forty parcels in two and a half hours? And on a Friday afternoon?

"We can't wait until the last minute," Honor said. "You're disorganized! No matter, the list is done. Claudia did the work! Humph! Claudia, let's run down the list."

Eleanor continued to stand at the side of Honor's desk determined to oversee the transaction between Claudia, who knew nothing, and Honor, who could ruin everything.

"Denver, 5,000 handouts and petitions. Do you think that's enough?" Honor asked Claudia.

Claudia gazed at Eleanor, who nodded her head in the affirmative. Claudia answered, "Yes."

"Boulder, 4,000?" Honor asked. She smiled down at Eleanor's list and up again at Claudia waiting for an answer.

Claudia's eyes again flashed at Eleanor, who nodded her head in the affirmative. "Yes," Claudia answered.

Eleanor was numb, but reviving. This part of the campaign, at least, was safe from Honor's interference. It should all be this easy! For each of the forty sites, and for a long forty minutes, she and Claudia played the charade. Once they concluded their business, Eleanor turned, eager to put distance between herself and her abuser. As she approached the door, she heard pounding footsteps behind her. She turned to come face to face with Honor, and a door slammed in her face.

That was the final blow. She stomped back to her office past the observant staff. On her desk were several urgent messages from Helen. Eleanor remained at the front of her desk staring at her open door. She reached for her phone with a trembling hand and dialed Helen. Her neck was pulsating furiously. As soon as Helen heard the rage in Eleanor's voice, she appealed to her.

"Eleanor, I'll write whatever you want. I need direction. I haven't a clue. But please, don't quit! I don't know why she pulled you off this. You did a great job organizing this campaign. She does this every time we approach a major event. She gets nervous! She doesn't want to be wrong!"

"Helen, don't worry, nobody can force me to quit this job," replied Eleanor. "I owe all the activists, and the animals. But Helen, you can't let her screw up this campaign! For all our efforts we might gain nothing! She doesn't have a clue, and she's asking Claudia's advice!"

"Oh."

"I promised the local activists acknowledgment so they'd join us. Don't make a liar out of me, or us! They'll pull out on us, and there goes Colorado!"

Helen assured her again of her cooperation. Again, she described Honor as isolated from other leaders in the movement, feeling alone and afraid. "To be honest, she's in over her head. She works from a base of fear, fear of being wrong, and fear of employees taking over, fear of losing the company."

"Helen, she acts like you're her best friend. Then she slams the door in your face, literally. She gives you authority and then takes it away after you've worked to satisfy all her demands. This is a gross misuse of power. She's a bully. A tyrant."

Eleanor had dared to trust again and she had been betrayed again. "I feel demoralized not by our meat-eating society, but sabotaged from within by my own leader! What kind of leadership is this? This hurts! I thought she was my sister. Does she have any idea how she hurts?"

"She aims to hurt. She once told me 'If employees don't fear you, then what?' It's all about control, Eleanor. She doesn't care if people think badly of her, or say she fights dirty. The lower the blow, the stronger she perceives herself. Don't forget, she's the victim. In her mind, she's fighting fire with fire. I've seen the best activists leave PAAC. Whatever you do, please don't quit!"

"A friend of mine said the movement was dead! Maybe the national leaders are killing it."

"There's a place in the movement for national organizations," Helen said. "But the small local groups are the engine of the animal rights movement. Look at the Colorado demonstrations. We organized it and we're supplying literature, and PR, but who's going to be out on the street? Don't forget, Eleanor, you are the national leader they are following, not Honor."

"Has anyone heard that 'if a house is divided against itself that house cannot stand'?" Eleanor asked. After the conversation, she was numb.

Her telephone rang. "Hi, Eleanor, it's Ginger. Well, we're supposed to be outside a supermarket for the demonstration, but I've learned that there's a special meeting in our high school that night. I think we'll get many more signatures there. So I wanted to alert you so you can change the address on the press release. Sorry for the bother. Oh, I got a fax this afternoon that I'm supposed to call a Helen at a Boston number from now on regarding the protest. Is that right?"

A new wave of humiliation assaulted her body, making her knees tremble and her heart race. "Yes, I know," she lied.

"I can't do that, Eleanor. I don't know this Helen. I know you. I'm involved in this because I trusted you. So if you don't mind, I'll just keep calling you. Is that OK? To tell you the truth, Eleanor, I'll be surprised if any of the activists call anybody but you. You're our contact."

She hung up stunned by the activists' trust. A half hour later, Mary rushed up to her desk.

"Freda is going to Denver with Honor for the Saturday demonstration. They leave Friday. I'm sorry. It should be you. But I wanted to tell you so you didn't hear it from Honor or worse, Freda. It would be another slap in the face! I just booked their flight reservations."

"Thank you, friend," she said. Tears stung her eyes from Mary's show of kindness in the middle of the volley of bruising attacks. It made good sense for Honor to be on hand for the national coverage.

She dialed Tina's number, and then with her narrowed eyes fixed on the open door, she walked around her desk to lean on the other side of it.

"Did you hear, kiddo?" Tina asked. "Helen rescued five of the ten dogs slated for the staples demonstrations: two beagles; a large, black Lab mix; a yellow Lab; and a German shepherd. Helen and six others broke into a van sitting in the parking lot. The dogs were all in kennels; it took two people to handle the Labs' kennels. But the alarms went off and the security guards charged after them, yelling. They barely escaped. But I feel so bad for the others."

"Helen never mentioned it. She was too busy listening to my complaints." Eleanor described the stripping away of her authority and the charade in Honor's office.

"I'm sorry," Tina said. "I'm sorry. It's the pressure of the job. Don't let it get to you, kiddo, please promise me. Each time it gets close to a major event, and this is major, she attacks the person in charge. You're the whipping girl! Hitting you relieves the pressure. Wait, you'll see it happen to me too! We take turns being PAAC's outcast."

"PAAC's outcast?" Eleanor smiled.

"Sure! Look, kiddo, don't you know that every wolf pack has one outcast? That's the omega wolf. If things are OK, well, then the outcast is OK, but when things get tight, watch out. That's how it works here at PAAC. We all get our chance to be PAAC's omega."

Eleanor laughed. "I guess that makes Honor the alpha wolf!"

"Oh, well, yeah. But she's 'the alpha, and the omega, the first, and the last, the beginning and the end.'"

"In other words, she's God!"

She was laughing harder now, it felt so good! She noticed that the pain in her gut was subsiding. She regretted not confiding in Tina and Helen sooner.

"Last year," Tina continued, "in the middle of our largest demonstration, FFAD, an anti-fur campaign in DC, she did it to me. I led the campaign. For weeks, she insulted me every day. Every single day she flung debasing garbage at me. Three days before the event, surprise, surprise, I came down with the flu. I ran a high temperature and stayed home that day. Make no mistake about it; this place makes you sick! The afternoon I was out, she demoted me from the director of the DC office to the entry-level position of outreach coordinator. She kindly called me at home to inform me. In the same afternoon, she promoted Larry to director. I had such pains in my chest that I thought I was having a heart attack."

"Oh my God! I'm sorry, Tina! But I have two more weeks to go. You mean she's going to continue this harassment? Every day?"

"Kiddo, you can count on it. Because each day you get closer to the event, she gets more uptight. Don't let her get to you. Don't quit! Hold on for them. It's like riding a tidal wave, but you can handle it!"

As if talking to herself, Eleanor uttered, "How much more of this can I take before I crack? Tina, Honor seems incapable of pity or remorse when it comes to her employees. What turned her to stone?"

"I don't know."

"What horrible thing turned her to stone?" Honor's grief-stricken face of some four weeks back flashed to her mind. Then she remembered the forty packages that would never get mailed today. "Tina, get ready, I think our venerable leader may be losing it."

CHAPTER 6

▼

THE TYRANT

An April rain began to fall that evening filling Derbe's air with a woodland dampness. On nights like this, the house took on the atmosphere of a cabin in the woods. Fading from view behind the curtain of moisture, the two-lane highway seemed even more of a country road. Derbe was an eighteenth-century town settled in a forested valley and surrounded by hills. The valley was the recipient of the moisture that flowed down from the hills to the wetlands to rest in the aquifer beneath the town. In summer its greenery glistened with morning dew, in spring the rain flooded its wetlands, and when winter came Derbe often turned into a snowy wonderland while neighboring towns had but a dusting.

The premature darkness triggered the streetlights on Route 7 early that evening, yet Eleanor hardly noticed. She paced the floorboards of her living room enraged to near madness by Honor's insults. Periodically she reminded herself that it was just two weeks until the Colorado demonstrations, and Honor's insulting behavior that afternoon was of no consequence. What mattered was saving the lives of tens of thousands of Colorado wildlife each year. Most of all, Honor's slamming a door in her face shouldn't feel like a death sentence.

But it did. How could she have been so wrong? The twisted and flawed leader who abused her bore no resemblance to the Honor who had been her willing animal rights contact for two years, and her sister in spirit. Desperate to ventilate, Eleanor halted her pacing at the lamp table and opened its shallow drawer.

"Good old Tina! She's definitely the one to hash over this whole thing with," she thought. But before she finished dialing she recalled that Tina was out of town for the weekend. She found Helen's number. No response! Helen was too political; she'd never return her call. Her mother would worry, and Lydia, well, she didn't want to talk about Honor to outsiders.

She resumed pacing. Her path ran from the red brick fireplace on the east side of the room to the double colonial windows that overlooked the porch and Route 7 on the opposite side. The multi-paned windows dripped with rain, and the white gingerbread colonial porch was soaked with small puddles lying in its warped slats. And beyond, the rain-soaked highway gleamed under lamplights and the headlights of the Friday night traffic.

She didn't notice. She wore her favorite faded jeans, a white T-shirt, and sneakers, which she had put on as soon as she arrived home, attempting to regain some normalcy. But her pacing began soon after. Rusty, stretched out on the floor in front of the fireplace, measured her every move, and Friday slept curled up in a corner of the couch. Her needs were beyond their companionship. The descending chilly night activated the heater in the forty-year-old house, making the pipes creak and groan like the hull of an old sailing vessel. The sound usually captivated her. But tonight it evoked a ship engulfed in fog and destined to float aimlessly at sea.

The tension continued to grow until a crescendo of words erupted from her; a volcanic explosion of words were hurled at an imaginary Honor standing to the left of the fireplace.

"How could you accuse me of handing the campaign over to Colorado activists?" Her words filled the room; her cats gazed in her direction. "Haven't I worked day and night for four weeks to be your loyal soldier?" she asked.

Eleanor stood at the lamp table, her right palm pressed against it, and she twisted to stare back at the beguiling Honor. "Here's the worst cut of all, I trusted you! For the first time in years, I trusted someone other than my own mother with this painful secret. I loved you for all you've done for the animals. I felt I owed you my loyalty before I even knew you! But I misjudged your character! Oh, I thought you were my friend. But you flung my personal life and my trust at me like shit when you slammed that door in my face! You used my heartache to punish me, and for what? For some fictitious, nameless crime against you! A crime I haven't even been charged with! Why are you so hard? What or who has scarred you?"

"Why did I trust her?" she asked herself. She rolled her eyes at her own naiveté. "Didn't I learn anything in all the years, in all the meetings? In all the therapy?"

The words stopped for a second. But her rage flared each time she recalled the insult. She continued to rant and pace with even more vitriol, spilling her guts over and over again, rerunning the same hateful words, adding a new charge here and there. It was so satisfying! She reveled in the imaginary justice that was available to her in this impossible situation, and she took full advantage of it. Telling Honor off felt so good.

It felt too good. At 10 PM she gazed through the rain-spotted front window at Route 7 and realized there was virtually no traffic. The suburban town had closed down for the night. The hours had flown by like minutes. Friday night was spent. She had paced for virtually five and half hours, and the healthy ventilation, a psychotherapeutic technique, had soured into an obsession. Meanwhile, Honor, no doubt, was enjoying her Friday night with friends.

"It's always like that with tyrants," she said aloud. "You spend your night in anguish while they go to a party!"

She turned off the lamp, and headed to the narrow hallway past the kitchen and down to her bedroom door, her two cats following. Perhaps unconsciousness would stop the words. She'd concentrate on rising early for a good jog before the Colorado calls began. Even wrapped in the softness of her mother's comforter, sleep evaded her. She soon found herself again hurling hateful words at Honor. After an hour, she surrendered, and bolted up in bed. "She's more omnipresent than God!"

With her pillow in hand and her two friends trailing after her, she headed for the couch and her VCR, knowing relief was readily available in her favorite movies: *Howard's End* and Henry Fonda in *War and Peace*. For comic relief there were Mel Brooks's *Young Frankenstein* with Gene Wilder and *High Anxiety* with Madeline Kahn. Vegan pizzas, popcorn, Panda licorice, handfuls of Brazil nuts and dark chocolate, and Tofutti ice cream also armed her against the rampaging words. When sleepiness finally arrived, she stumbled to bed.

The next morning her anger propelled her for a seven mile jog before she could ebb the flow of bellicose words. Not even the magnificent woods bursting with new life could compete with the satisfaction of telling off Honor just one more time.

"You've got the tools, use them! Meditate!" She moved to the side of the road and placed her hands on her hips, closed her eyes, and adopted a smile of tranquility. She inhaled the energy surrounding her and exhaled all negative thoughts. At once she could feel the bumpy, hard macadam beneath her gray Saucony shoes and the cool spring air on her cheeks and bare legs. After several breaths, she opened her eyes to gaze at the sun rays streaking through the forest, the baby blue sky with its white cumulus clouds overhead. In seconds her problems were reduced to the size of an acorn.

The Norfolk River, nothing more than a stream at this point, was filled to the brim from the rainy night. She closed her eyes to enjoy the sound of the gurgling water rushing over the glistening rocks lining its banks. When she opened them she heaved a sigh of contentment at the sight of a determined mallard couple hugging the river's fringes. The water's foam swirled around them as they endeavored to evade the current. They mated for life, she recalled with a smile of satisfaction. Her mind rested even more as she gazed at the endless new leaves on the bushes and trees, the fresh lime green a miracle in itself.

Then like a dam that broke, the flow of angry words gushed forth again. She succeeded in gaining a few more seconds of serenity by taking another deep breath. To expect more than a few seconds of freedom at a time was apparently unreasonable. It wasn't a day at a time, it was a moment at a time, she decided. She resumed running. Every few seconds, she reminded herself to listen to the sounds of her running footsteps and the gurgling river to her right. She'd target one brand-new lime-green leaf off in the distance, staring at it until she finally reached. She fixed her attention on its symmetrical lines, its individuality, the way the sunlight illuminated it and added yellow to its hue, and how it promised long, lazy summer days. "A second at a time, a second at a time," she muttered to herself to the beat of her jogging feet, "a second at a time!" She continued this process for a half hour before returning home where again she employed "the tools." In between calls she meditated to rest her worn psyche, which had had so little reprieve during the night.

The telephone calls kept her mind in the present for the rest of the day, while her stockpile of library videos did the trick that night. On Sunday morning, she awoke to the comforting sound of rain tapping on the wide oak leaves in front of the house, just outside her double colonial windows. The worst of the weekend was behind her. And she had managed to even enjoy some of it. But at St. John's Episcopal Church, while kneeling at the communion rail, her hands cupped to receive the holy Eucharist, she thought of nothing but Honor, for which she apologized to her creator and prayed that the Almighty would crack her fixation. At coffee hour in the large dining room, the kind and cheerful faces of her church family surrounded her, but they were distant figures, living in another land.

That weekend, the more she tried to forget about Honor the more she thought of her. At the same time, her countless conversations with the Colorado activists encouraged her dream of a movement united for the sake of the eight billion animals slaughtered each year for food. It seemed only a matter of time.

As she tossed and turned Sunday night, Carol Conrad's sworn testimony regarding her battered wife syndrome grew ominous. That Monday morning Eleanor's fastidious grooming was motivated to boost her self-esteem. With each step she proved that she was worthy of the respect and dignity she believed due her. On another level, her efforts were an ardent wish for their friendship to resume. During the ride to work she managed to bury her fury, but the effort tapped the last of her energy.

When she entered the large office, Honor was coursing full tilt in the direction of the mailroom. As Eleanor stopped to allow Honor to pass, her feet were flat-footed and lifeless, as if anchored in cement. Honor gazed at her for a second and made a slight effort to muffle a chuckle of satisfaction.

One hour later, Lisa barged into her office. Honor had cut Eleanor's name from the circulation list, and a memo about the Colorado campaign was being distributed. Eleanor called Tina and concocted a covert system of communication so that she could do her job. Tina would telephone to alert her of an incoming fax, giving her sufficient time to rush to the back of the room next to the file cabinets to retrieve it before Honor or Freda discovered it.

During the first three days of that week, whenever Honor filed information in the file cabinets at the back of the room, Eleanor left her desk to skulk behind her door to detect what file drawer Honor was using. When Honor scurried away, she'd dash to the file cabinet and put her powers of deduction to use. To eavesdrop on Honor's telephone calls and conversations, she pretended to be filing in the cabinets stationed in Claudia's office. The humbling days clunked by. On Thursday, after only a few days of the skullduggery, she grew weary of the subterfuge and wrote a memo of appeal to Honor, asking her to return her name to the routing list for pertinent information. She waited for Honor to leave for lunch before she deposited the memo in her in-box. During the humbling trip to and fro to deliver the memo, Eleanor wondered how she had arrived at so debasing a moment in her career in the cause for which she was willing to give her heart and soul. As she walked to Honor's office and back her steps seemed unsure and her body lacked its usual vitality. There was no pride or purpose in her actions, it seemed to her. She was in store for only more fear, trauma, and humiliation. Minutes after Honor returned, she charged in and out of Eleanor's office, slapping a memo in her in-box without a glance at her. Eleanor lifted the memo out of the box; it was merely her own memo returned with Honor's comments sprawled at the bottom of it. "There have been no new press releases or interoffice memos. Go to the files for the rest." Honor lied in perfect penmanship.

Coretta peeked in the doorway. "So where's your good friend now?"

The staff had showed no pity for her during these trying times. But after Coretta's comment, the chill thawed. Eleanor was again included in the roll of the eyes over the antics of the "princess," and in the office scuttlebutt. Even better, Coretta resumed her position as her loyal sentry.

The Colorado initiative continued to receive overwhelming support. It was clear that if the movement managed to raise enough funds and signatures to deliver the anti-trapping initiative to the ballot box, the voters would do the rest. That afternoon, Eleanor received a call from Grace Rayburn of Denver's Have-a-Heart Trapping Coalition that jolted her to her feet. The legendary country and western singer Tommy Joe Adams would write and perform a song on behalf of Colorado's wildlife at their demonstration. Tommy was a converted trapper, and he'd perform in front of the state capitol building.

"We're ready, honey, we even have our permits!" Grace said. "You can expect thousands of Tommy's fans to attend this show. I've got them to announce the event on radio, and we're posting it at the college student centers."

In her excitement, Eleanor paced as she listened. No doubt the major networks and CNN would cover it. This called for a memo. She alerted Honor about the new prospects of coverage by the networks, CNN, and the print media including the *New York Times* and *USA Today*, and delivered it to Honor's office. As she charged across the presidential office in obvious elation, Honor continued to read the federal document she had before her. Eleanor hesitated, staring at the top of Honor's shiny, dark head and hoping she'd drop the charade and gaze up out of sheer curiosity.

No chance. The hours clunked by. The next day, Friday, late in the afternoon, with no word from Honor, Eleanor paced her office in a fit of outrage. Just a couple of weeks ago, she and Honor would have had their heads together promoting the great Tommy Joe's song! No doubt Honor was on the phone with Grace, and maybe Tina or Helen, working out the details of the superstar's appearance!

Just as she had visions of her campaigns, she now had visions of quitting. A few minutes before 5 PM, and with still no response from Honor, Tina's warning words about an insult every day echoed in her mind.

There were ten whole days left, and most likely ten more insults! While she collected her belongings to participate in the 5 PM stampede, she decided to join the Derbe YMCA. Working out every morning would kick off her endorphins and prepare her for her daily fight; her "thriller in Manila," her "rumble in the jungle." It might even save her job!

As the staff raced to the door, she revealed her plan. "And I'm going to hide a five-pound weight under my desk, and every time Honor insults me, I'll pump iron."

"You'll have the muscles of a man," Betty said.

That night Eleanor dined with her former colleagues from the *Norfolk Daily News*. They munched on chips and salsa while seated around a rough-hewn circular table in the South Norfolk Mexican restaurant. "You'll never know how 'normal' it is working at the paper!" she said. She joined in the laughter. "And Rob, he's a saint!"

She had forgotten the feel of mutual respect and esteem. How good it was to be out of Honor's reach and away from her insolent superiority. How normal the outside world was! Athletics and the respectful Colorado activists guarded her sanity that weekend. On Sunday after church, she touched base with her mother, saying nothing of her problems. But Lillian softly offered, "I love you."

Monday morning she plunged into the YMCA's pool, the blue water enveloping and chilling her body. Sixty minutes later she hoisted herself out, her legs wobbling; but she was fortified. In her office, with satisfaction, she rolled her metal five-pound weight under her desk.

It was 1 PM when Claudia rushed into her office, hysterical. Honor had appointed her to contact the media. "I'm going to college at night to become a graphic designer! I'm not the PR director!"

"She's reduced me to a clerk," Eleanor thought. "Will my private office be next?" She fought for self-control with every bit of toned muscle in her body. Honor was willing to risk the public relations of the campaign to punish her? Did her vengeance have no limits?

She fought her urge to confront Honor. "I must do what is best for the animals," she told herself. She reached for the list of media contacts at the corner of her desk and stood up and walked around to face Claudia while actually wearing a supportive smile. PAAC had an opportunity to influence millions of people nationwide on the issue of trapping wildlife through the demonstrations in Colorado, she explained. "Thanks to Honor, you are now a key player!"

Eleanor surrendered her media contact sheet. Then she reached for one of the campaign fliers she had written and stacked on another corner of her busy desk. "Remember this?"

"How could I forget! But I never read it!"

"Claudia, we could be saving at least 30,000 animals from torture, and maybe as many as another 200,000 from death each year by banning several kinds of traps! That's the message for reporters."

The Colorado activists were expecting PAAC to deliver national coverage, Eleanor explained. "The deal is that the local groups pound the pavement while PAAC delivers TV and print coverage. Do all your calling from in here. Honor knows you'll come to me, she's no dummy!"

Claudia offered a smile of relief and turned to leave. Then Eleanor rushed after her, remembering the Denver demonstration. She questioned Claudia only to discover that she was clueless regarding Tommy Joe Adams. Eleanor instructed her to call Rather, Brokaw, and Jennings.

Ten minutes later, Claudia returned and stretched across her desk to whisper that Honor told her "the big boys" weren't interested in Colorado state trapping laws. When Eleanor insisted that she call anyway, Claudia began to cry. With that Eleanor decided to take back her contact list.

"I'll use your name. Don't worry, Claudia, Honor will love you for it!"

A half hour later, after talking to the networks' assignment desk editors, Eleanor relayed the good news to Claudia.

"Damned bloody good!" Honor shouted. She strode out of her office toward Freda's, calling Delores and Lenny and ordering both of them to follow her. "Wait till you hear about our Claudia's coup! Brokaw, Jennings, and Rather, CNN, and the *New York Times*!"

In the following crucial days of the campaign, it seemed that Claudia yo-yoed back and forth from Eleanor's office to her own in an escalating state of panic. Eleanor bit her tongue when she heard Claudia stumbling through interviews. As stories were published on the upcoming demonstrations in newspapers across Colorado, Honor like a vengeful teenager faxed copies to all her managers and excluded Eleanor. But Tina called, and Eleanor would rush to the fax machine for the contraband.

PAAC had grown so weird and unprofessional that Eleanor began to question why she remained on the job. Why had she allowed herself to become the victim of abuse? Once again?

On Thursday, Freda and Honor left for Denver with much fanfare, with Honor's vicious laughter filling the office with the obvious purpose of taunting Eleanor. She sat zombie-like at her desk. The taunting laughter flowed down to her office and hit its mark. Patroklos, who was to drive them to the airport, rolled their suitcases on a dolly trailing behind the two women as they headed out of the office. In the lobby Honor said to Freda, "Took the jelly out of her donut, didn't we?"

When he returned, Patroklos stood in Eleanor's doorway and addressing everyone in the office, he imitated Honor. "'Took the jelly out of her donut, didn't we?'"

Everyone burst into laughter, but Eleanor rushed over and hugged him.

With the two gone, the office heaved a grateful collective sigh of relief. Betty opened the office windows soon after the women left. "Let the fresh sea air sweep the office clean! Even the smell of rotting crabs is better than some perfumes."

Using Claudia's name, Eleanor continued to do the job for which she was hired. By Monday they'd know if the campaign worked. Even if Dey stuck to the coalition's initiative, the animal rights movement would still be credited for cutting the numbers of animals killed in traps by half each year, and it would have educated the public about the gruesome contraptions. "Yes," Eleanor thought, "the winds of change are abounding."

That Saturday, May 10, 1998, the burly Tommy Joe Adams sang his poignant tune, "Cries in the Lonely Night." He stood before the steps of the capitol building performing for a couple of thousand fans and activists in the cordoned-off street. In the Denver sunshine, the transcendent music moved many in the swaying audience to tears of sympathy for the trapped wildlife, while the cameras focused on fifty dogs that wagged tails, sniffed each other, and stretched out in the sun filtering through the thick crowd.

In their separate homes Eleanor, Lisa, and Lydia taped the TV and cable coverage. There was an aura of history in the making when Dan Rather, Peter Jennings, and Tom Brokaw introduced the demonstrations in Denver and Boulder at the top of their shows, with Brokaw asking, "Could this be the beginning of the end of trapping?"

Lydia called after the event. "It was the highest-profile campaign in PAAC's history. Congratulations! You did it!"

Sunday, in the noon sunshine, she and Lydia read the *Times*'s story together. They sat on the back porch of Lydia's home in Norfolk that overlooked her small cat shelter. In the national section, on the first page, above the paper's fold, on the right-hand side was the article.

"Ban Leghold Traps: Adams Croons for Colorado Wildlife." It was a full quarter-page story, with a photo of the dogs, Tommy Joe Adams, and several smiling young women activists holding handmade signs. At a glance they could see that Honor was quoted at length, spouting trapping statistics.

"Great!" Eleanor said. "Now it's up to Dey."

Lydia put together a celebratory Italian dinner. For Eleanor it was fitting to spend such a landmark day with a true sister-in-spirit and her many rescued cats. And she smiled with some satisfaction upon realizing that she had survived a rite of passage at PAAC. She had managed to successfully lead Honor's Colorado campaign even in the face of great odds: Honor's self-destructive nature.

The next morning, the stilled atmosphere in the office reflected that of a courthouse waiting for a jury to render a verdict. Honor was sequestered in her office. Nobody was talking. It was lunchtime when Eleanor got the call.

"Eleanor," Tina said, "pat yourself on the back, kiddo, Dey caved, just this morning. Before I forget, congratulations on the *Times* story and the out-of-sight TV coverage! The coalition's expanding the initiative to go beyond the steel-jaw leghold traps to padded leghold traps, the body-gripping Conibears, snares, and all poisons."

A grateful sigh escaped as Eleanor listened and tears of gratitude and exhaustion filled her eyes.

"Those who campaigned for years against compound 1080 are exhaling," Tina said. "But the government can still use Conibears, snares, and padded leghold traps for animals that, and I quote, 'threaten the safety or health of humans.' Kiddo, there are no exceptions. The ADC will no longer trap 'nuisance animals' for ranchers and farmers. Dey assured us that government officials will not contest it; this is as good as law! Nothing but have-a-hearts in Colorado!

"Remember the positive approach was your idea? Kiddo! Honor and Mary would have gotten diddly from the activists with their negative garbage. Denver would never have happened! Not only Denver! For you, kiddo, they covered all four corners of Colorado. Congrats!"

"Thanks…but it was for the animals, Tina," Eleanor said. "I didn't have to sell this. Remember, the activists began the whole thing. Without the local groups and their hard work to get people and activists out, and Adams, there'd be no TV coverage or anything else. And I'm grateful that Dey found the courage."

She was talking to herself as well as Tina, mulling over her first encounter with the intricate anatomy of a full-blown campaign, and one taking place thousands of miles away. "It was a team effort," she concluded.

"Kiddo, you promised the grassroots and you delivered!"

The rest of the week, Eleanor hovered somewhere just above the late May clouds over the Atlantic estuary with her beloved seagulls, getting a bird's eye view of PAAC. She was more objective now, being out of Honor's inner circle, and no longer under her influence. What was wrong with being the outcast, she'd ask herself. At least she wasn't subjected to Honor's whims.

She'd never felt so privileged. All the abuse was worth it. And if it weren't for Honor, she wouldn't have the job. The success of the campaign continued to fill her with contentment and professional satisfaction, although Honor still ostracized her. Each morning, as she dressed for her swim at the YMCA, she gazed into her bathroom mirror and issued herself a pep talk:

"You work for God, the animals, the activists, the little old ladies from the backwoods of Iowa who send their two dollars in. That's what it's about. Write your letters to the sweet members, write your punchy letters to the editor; you're valuable to the movement." She pointed into the mirror and said, "The movement needs you!"

On Friday, June 13, Honor returned from lunch in a veritable fit, pounding her feet as she rushed to Freda's office, slamming the door and sending chills up the spines of her staff. Eleanor was surprised to find that she cringed, and when her phone rang, she jumped as if an ambulance siren had grated full strength in her ears. What an immense relief it was each time to hear Ellen Milani's voice at the other end.

This time Ellen was in a panic. "Eleanor, please, I beg you, please, please take this call. It's a Jean Ellington from Citizens for Animal Rights in New Jersey. It's spelled C-A-R-N-J and pronounced 'carnage.' She's calling about a puppy mill bill. I know," she wailed again, "it should go to Honor, but please don't make me do it. Not in this mood! You know what I'm saying? I've got a kid and a mother to support. I leave here and work at UPS! I need the two jobs! Honor's pissed because Carol Conrad, she's still getting unemployment, and Paul Rossi's missing again! So Honor's going to fire him! But I heard he'll sue the organization for $200,000 in damages."

"Oh, my God," Eleanor said. Her outburst was a sincere prayer for immediate intercession. "Of course, I'll take the call." She bowed her head while speaking to the caller in the hope of avoiding Honor's rage.

"Hi, Eleanor, you must be new." Jean Ellington had a kind, homespun voice and a persona that soothed Eleanor's nerves. So much so that Eleanor was determined to keep her talking.

Jean wanted PAAC's donor list to aid in a proposed New Jersey bill to ban the sale of puppies and kittens in pet stores. The previous night a truckload of sixty puppies had died from heat prostration when a ventilation unit failed, she revealed. The New Jersey state police discovered the dead puppies after the truck was in an accident on the turnpike. The truck belonged to a Missouri puppy mill that regularly delivered puppies to pet stores in New Jersey and New York. "Only God knows how many times this kind of thing happens!"

The air seemed to leave Eleanor's lungs as she envisioned the horror of the stilled small bodies trapped in their cages.

Jean explained that puppy and kitten mills were factory farms that produced so-called purebred puppies and kittens, misguiding people into believing that they were bred with care. The puppies and kittens were stock for pet stores. "They come with American Kennel Club papers too. People think that's some kind of insurance. But the AKC will tell you that it only means that they're purebred; it doesn't guarantee humane standards! It's so misleading!"

Tens of thousands of mothers suffered in the filthy farms where they were forced to breed until they died. They were boarded in crowded and bug-infested pens coated with feces. The farms were generally in the Sun Belt, so the mothers and their pups also suffered from heat exposure.

"The cages are made with wire mesh flooring that injures their paws. It deforms and cuts them," Jean informed her. "But the mesh allows the feces to fall to the ground below, since the pens are usually raised about two feet or so off the ground on stilts. Of course, the feces fester and create an odor so foul you'll remember it for the rest of your life. The sickening smell also comes from the decaying corpses left in the cages for days. It's the smell of death."

Eleanor's eyes remained on the doorway beyond which Coretta, Betty, and Carla continued to work under duress. She played with a pen nervously, taking sporadic notes on her yellow legal-sized pad as Jean described the conditions of the canine "concentration camps." The mothers suffered from general neglect, eyes filled with pus, festering cuts, matted coats with infected sores, and general poor health from overbreeding. They often produced sick puppies that the unwitting pet store customer paid for in doctor bills and heartache.

"I've seen NAHS's film of puppies being born right next to their mother's feces," Jean said. "You know this isn't natural. The mothers are known to prepare a safe birthing place for their young.

"When you walk by them they cry for you to take them home," she said. "They're hyper, you know, from being penned up, and they constantly bark. The puppy mills are one of the reasons why more than five million animals are killed in our public shelters each year. Are you getting the whole ugly picture?"

Eleanor got it all right. Honor and her tirades faded from her consciousness while she contemplated yet another aspect of the animal rights movement. She wondered if there would be any end to this "specialty."

"Some die right after birth from diseases because of the filth and from being born to sick and worn-out mothers. The frightened little things, taken prematurely from their mothers, are packed in crowded cages that are stacked one on top of another in the back of a small dumpy truck.

"We had one last year—puppies being shipped to the Northeast for pet stores for the Christmas rush. The truck's propane heater tipped over and set fire to the inside of the truck. Only ten out of the ninety puppies packed in the truck survived after being hospitalized for weeks. A cop stopped the truck, seeing the flames licking out of the rear! Sometimes the stressful trip alone kills them. There's poor ventilation, or poor air-conditioning or heaters, and little food or water.

"If they outgrow their shelf life, some storeowners kill them, or worse, sell them to a research lab. Good people buy the little 'puppy in the window.' They're sorry for them. That's what pet stores thrive on. That's where the bill comes in."

PAAC donor labels were confidential, but Eleanor promised Jean that she'd write to PAAC's New Jersey members about the bill. She asked her to fax a press release on the proposed bill. In minutes the fax arrived; a half hour later the letter was done. Eleanor located the zip codes in New Jersey in the zip code book on Betty's desk and generated a computer printout of 2,000 labels.

At that moment Honor raced into her office, to her great relief. She looked as though she were about to break the long eight-weeks' silence. Then Honor's eyes focused on the letter displayed on Eleanor's computer screen. She glanced at the large sheets of labels sitting on top of Eleanor's filing cabinet. Her eyes opened wide in accusation at Eleanor. Eleanor's heart stood still, and the color drained from her face. Honor, full of fury, spun around with her large flat feet pounding the floor as she rampaged out of her office and stomped over to Freda's office, where she shook the building with the slam of the door.

Eleanor's heart roared in her ears. She fell against the back of her seat. "What have I done now?" She examined her computer screen. She continued writing the letter as she waited for Honor's other shoe to drop. A half hour later, she asked Lisa to deliver the letter to Honor's in-box for her approval.

Suspense hung in the air like a Hitchcock film until 3:45 PM, when Freda arrived at her doorway. She remained just outside the doorway holding up the letter.

"You have no business printing computer sheets and sending letters like this out without permission from me or Honor!" Her voice carried throughout the office. She observed the donor labels on the file cabinet and charged into the office and ripped the large data sheets off the cabinets. She returned to her stand outside the door.

"What?" Eleanor asked. "I've done this as a matter of course in the past! Delores instructed me to automatically go ahead with such requests! It makes sense. The local groups receive our help, and we let New Jersey members know that their donated dollars are working in their state. It's a win-win situation!"

"We have a tight budget. We can't afford these gifts right now! Call this person back. You tell her our budget won't allow this mailing. By the time we're through it'll cost us hundreds of dollars. We're not a funding agency. Understand?"

"Why didn't Honor tell me this herself?" Eleanor asked as she walked closer to the door.

"She's too busy to be bothered with you! OK? This issue isn't big enough even for me to bother with. Any more questions?"

In the rush of humiliation, Eleanor stared back at Freda speechless. After Freda left, she telephoned Helen, her eyes glaring at the door.

"Can you tell me why both Honor and Freda went to Denver, and I hear they'll both soon be traveling to China, if we can't afford a few hundred dollars to support a worthy New Jersey puppy mill bill? Certainly, Dr. Tsoi will be holding her hand. She doesn't need Freda too!"

"I don't know," Helen said. "She seems to be spending so much more money on traveling and luxury hotels since Freda was hired. I think it's burnout, Eleanor. Honor used to stay at the homes of donors to cut costs; she did cake sales, car washes, and potluck dinners to raise funds."

After hanging up, Eleanor pulled up the blinds and searched for sanity in the new green leaves now grown to their full June thickness on the trees surrounding the seaside homes below. Battered wife syndrome and Carol Conrad leapt to her mind. When she called Jean, Jean kindly reminded her that Honor had helped them in other situations. As she hung up, she remembered that PAAC had spent a good deal of money for the wildlife in Colorado.

Eleanor walked to the end of the window to peek out at the beach. For the last few weeks it had been alive with sunbathers. But the water remained cold, and besides, if she swam at lunch Honor would think she had lost interest in her job. According to Tina's description of PAAC's omega, the outcast position should have terminated with the completion of the Colorado campaign. She had morphed into Honor's in-house whipping girl. She was definitely wounded, as wounded as if she had an arrow stuck in her heart.

In her dilemma, she leaned forward in her chair in a Rodinesque pose. Without moving, she lifted her eyes to her three canine pals on the wall over her desk. "I feel chained to this desk! I guess this is what it's like being at the mercy of a tyrant! What a cold place!"

She stood up and removed the three photographs and stacked them on her desk. "I'm taking you home."

But she had to return! The repugnant prospect so overwhelmed her that all her instincts ordered her to quit. But how could she?

The epiphany six months before came to mind; the pure and trusting eyes of the calf, the lab, and the deer on the newsroom wall. Then the Colorado wildlife: badgers, prairie dogs and jackrabbits, red foxes, beavers, muskrats, minks, weasels, porcupines, squirrels, rabbits, wolves, coyotes, moose, deer and elk, and on and on. And the scores of species of birds: willets, sandpipers, yellowlegs, snipes, dowitchers, herons, grebes, hawks, golden eagles, and so many others—and the domestic cats and dogs that she had helped to snatch from the steel jaws of the leghold trap.

"Does one walk away when the going gets tough? Look at Tina, Helen, and Larry!"

Still, she shuddered at the thought of Monday morning. How could she gaze into the insolent eyes of Freda after what had just taken place? Or Honor? "No!" she mumbled in full rejection. It was too humbling to comprehend! Too much to ask! It was impossible! She could not do it! She would not do it!

She gazed at the heavens and began to pray in a cry of desperation, her voice a painful whisper. "'I'm letting go, and letting God,'" she declared, peering at the fading sun. "I'm turning this thing over to you, God. My life at PAAC is out of control. It's over. I can't do this anymore."

She closed her eyes and drew a long, deep breath. In that mystical instant, the heavy weight of the animal rights world was lifted from her shoulders. The inner storm was replaced by stillness. She turned from her window knowing that no longer would she endeavor to carve a path to Honor's heart, and no more would Honor's degradation force her to question her employment. She was delivered beyond Honor's reach.

Tranquil beyond all reason, she picked up the three wood-framed photographs of her beloved friends and cradled them. She glided through the office indifferent to her surroundings. For the first time in three months, she was headed home free of Honor.

CHAPTER 7

▼

FREEING EVE

A silver mist had settled on Derbe during the night. It rolled and billowed over the wide, sprawling lawns, the wetlands, and the gullies that bordered Route 7. The long-stemmed wildflowers along the roadside seemed like brides with misty veils flowing from their purple and white blooms. On the bushes surrounding the colonial homes, the mist draped from one bush to the other, forming ethereal scalloped borders.

That Monday morning, two weeks and two days since her deliverance, Eleanor in her daily commute was blissfully admiring the mist's amazing transformations. But as she drove past Derbe High School, she did a double take. Peering through the fog, she saw what appeared to be a life size statue of an elephant standing on the high school lawn! Accelerating, she drove across the highway's busy outside lane, swerved onto its gravel shoulder, and edged on to Oak Tree Lane, the street that bordered the south side of the school. As she got closer she saw an elephant chained all alone on the edge of the high school's southeast field. She was chained to a red-and-white trailer truck owned by the Anderson Bros. Circus. The truck was parked along the curb behind the elephant.

Eleanor pulled up behind the truck and hopped out of her idling car. Immobilized by her chains, the elephant stood under a yellow-and-red striped awning in the center of a small, cordoned-off, grassy area. Her back left ankle was shackled to the chain connected to the truck; her front right ankle was chained to a metal stake in the ground. With chains pulling from both ends, it was impossible for her to take one step backward or forward.

Eleanor, stupefied at the sight of the harsh confinement, treaded softly on the dewy lawn, the inch-sized pieces of cut grass clinging to her black shoes, which were getting damp. The elephant seemed small, and her eyes were sunken, with dark, unhealthy circles. She looked depressed. Curling her trunk in slow motion, she set her bidding eyes on Eleanor. Then she picked up her front shackled leg as if showing it to Eleanor and begging her to remove the chains!

In that moment, the elephant in her cruel chains moved into Eleanor's heart and soul right up there with the animals on the newsroom wall. Her eyes darted to a sign posted on the truck which revealed that the Asian elephant's name was Eve and her first show began at 6 PM, with elephant rides commencing at 5 PM. "Could it be," she pondered, "that she will be chained until 5 PM? After being chained all night? Immobilized for nineteen and a half hours straight? Or maybe even more? The good people of Derbe would never leave their family dogs on a short leash, never mind with two paws shackled," she thought. "Why an elephant?"

She watched horrified as Eve began to sway back and forth to alleviate the strain of her confinement. Eleanor gazed at the steady Route 7 traffic slowed by the mist. "Am I the only curious person in Derbe? This is an upscale town, a bedroom community, populated by privileged, educated, intelligent, and caring people. Derbe isn't the sticks. Here we should know better!" She gazed at the traffic as if to admonish everyone on Route 7 who cavalierly drove by.

Than she saw a man emerge from the first of the three campers parked in the back field and cross the paved road that ran around the rear of the school. She ambled over to greet him. "Good morning, you've got a wonderful elephant," she said.

The man looked old, crooked, and grouchy. He gazed at her with suspicion and issued a "Humph." He was of average height, in his late sixties, with hunched shoulders and a complexion as wrinkled as old parchment. He resembled the iconic Uncle Sam with his gray mustache, goatee, and his circus outfit, which was a red-and-white striped shirt with red suspenders and dark blue baggy jeans. The only thing missing were the stars, thought Eleanor.

Like a chained dog, Eve begged him to free her by lifting up her shackled front foot and staring at him. He ignored her, although he stood facing her and just a couple of feet away from the cordoned-off area. Eleanor began to ask the ordinary questions. He gazed first at the wet grass and then up at her. She stood to his right and a foot away. Eve was twenty-one, he revealed, born in Thailand, and was two years old when the circus had purchased her nineteen years ago.

"Don't know what I'd do without her," he said, sounding folksy. He smiled with unctuous fondness and pride at Eve. "She's my partner," he said. He stepped closer to her and stretched out to pat her thick right shoulder, still dismissing her pleading eyes.

"How long will she work for the circus?" Eleanor asked. She walked around him to stand to his right and gaze into Eve's miserable eyes.

"Until she's fifty or sixty. She's my partner," he said again. "I wouldn't want to be without her." He then turned to stare at Eleanor, tight-lipped.

There were pink bull hook scars above Eve's eyes, right ear, and behind her thick knees. "Are those scars over her right eye?" Eleanor asked.

"Oh no, that's sunburn," he said. He gazed at Eve with a parental frown, as his eyes inspected the "sunburn."

"Yes, their skin is so sensitive to sun," she said. "That's why rolling in the mud after a nice swim is great protection." She had just written a circus protest flier. "You say she'll be with you for fifty, sixty years? Isn't that a long time to be chained up like that? Don't they get arthritis and other foot problems and suffer from isolation and severe psychological problems from extreme boredom? I read somewhere that they rock from the isolation. It's like solitary confinement. It can drive them crazy. They lose their sense of knowing where they are. Is that true? Or am I misinformed?"

"She's out of the chains for shows and rides. We're preserving the species, you know! They kill them in the wild! We treat her good. She has a tire to play with—that's her exercise. She don't have to forage for no food, we give her the best! She's worth $35,000!" He peered at Eleanor as if she were a sentimental fool. "You think we'd damage her, do you? That would be bad business!"

At that moment, a tall, muscular man with a bald head and a strong resemblance to Arnold Schwarzenegger's Terminator emerged from another camper in the back field. He stomped over the school road and headed toward them, crushing the blades of grass under his black-booted feet. His chest was barely covered by his sleeveless white undershirt, and his biceps were tattooed. He held a bull hook in his right hand. He walked up to the side of the baggy-pants trainer and folded his arms over his chest. The sharp point of the bull hook jutted out from under his left arm. He stared at Eleanor in defiance. Her eyes darted to the metal hook peering out from under his folded arms as if it were a weapon.

"This is Eve's keeper," the trainer said. "We're invited here, you know," he said.

Again, Eleanor noticed that Eve searched her out. Her eyes were pleading, asking her to free her. It was as though she recognized a friend in her, and again she raised her shackled front foot.

Eleanor stared into the elephant's eyes and recognized the being within. A compulsion to leave and do something, anything, took hold of her. She thanked the two men and scurried to her car. She stepped on the gas, backed up from the circus truck, and made a U-turn heading for the highway. Not knowing exactly what she would do, she circled back home, driving ten miles above the 35-mile-an-hour speed limit. She had barely parked in her driveway when she ripped open the car door to exit and slammed it shut in mid-run. She scudded up the porch's three stairs, her heels clacking against the painted white planks, and fumbled with her keys. She couldn't get the front door open fast enough. She bolted into the living room. Rusty and Friday watched her as she dashed by them, whipped out a large sheet of white poster paper stored under the cranberry couch, and rushed into the kitchen and slapped it on the small cherry card table. Her heart pounded as she bent over and wrote with large broad strokes:

"Circuses Enslave Animals! Boycott the Anderson Bros. Circus!" She squeezed the plastic marker with such determination that her fingers ached. "Oh, how good does this feel," she said. "This, God, is activism…this is really the 'movement' you wanted me to join. Not all the garbage infighting at PAAC! The movement is not about the little games that Honor plays to torment her employees! It's not all armchair activism!"

It was then that she recalled turning her life over to her creator on that Friday. She scrambled in her kitchen cabinet junk drawer for masking tape and a scissors. She cut four square pieces of tape, rolled them up to attach the poster's corners, and slapped the sign on her front door on the way out. It was back to the school with her fully loaded, faithful Canon Snappy LX camera while she wrote the cut-lines in her head: "No Garden of Eden," or perhaps "Paradise Lost?" or "Chained for life for a few minutes of entertainment."

She prayed that the trainer and the keeper would be preoccupied with circus business when she pulled on to Oak Tree Lane minutes later. This time she parked nearer the highway. At that moment a police cruiser rode up Oak Tree Lane, and Brian Lipser waved at her. Having been a town reporter for two years, she had made some friends. As Eleanor focused her camera, Eve lifted her shackled front leg for the third time begging to be freed. Eleanor swallowed hard and vowed a lifetime of dedication as she gazed into the sunken, depressed eyes. "Don't give up!" she begged. "Don't give up!"

She dashed back to her car, wanting to escape the heartless men without another encounter. She realized her dogs and cats had taught her about the nature of animals, wild or domestic, and Eve's agony was too much to bear without a plan. It was when she reentered Route 7 that the idea struck her. "Why don't I chain myself," she thought. "If an elephant is chained in Derbe, damn it, I'm chained in Derbe. I'll be damned if I'll snuggle up in my comfortable bed while she's suffering in chains unable to take one damned step, and just down the street from me! In my own town! A wild creature!" The inspiring idea melted the twenty-minute drive to Westport to mere seconds.

When Eleanor arrived at the office at 8:45 AM, Freda as usual was ensconced in her office, fifteen minutes before Honor's expected arrival. Eleanor charged into her office, deposited her shoulder bag in the squeaky bottom drawer, and without bothering to sit down dialed her former editor, Don Martlett, at the *Derbe Weekly*. Within seconds he had agreed to cover the chaining event and to photograph her door. In conservative Derbe, protest signs on the front door were news. He also warned her not to bully the Tigers Club members. "They renew their circus contract every January; you may be more successful working that angle."

Jack O'Brien, her contact at the Tigers Club, promised to call back at lunchtime. As she dialed the *Norfolk Daily News* she heard Honor arrive; her heels slapped the carpeted floor in her usual rush to her office. Meanwhile Briana Kelly, a suburban reporter, took her call, telling her that they'd cover the chaining. "Can't you hear Rob saying, 'Don't you think people want to know why a young woman is chained along Route 7?'"

As expected, the three local TV channels and Cablevision also jumped at the photo op. Her next call was to Lydia, who insisted on spending the night with her. "You're threatening their livelihoods. And the portable toilet is in the back field!"

Lydia also suggested approaching them about next year's contract before harassing them. Eleanor's next call was to Tina, who offered the name of a movement contact dedicated to captive elephants: Lenore Davis, the president of Taskforce United to Save Kindred Spirits, or TUSKS. Headquartered in California, Lenore tracked every captive elephant in circuses and zoos throughout the country and kept a chronological record of deaths and injuries caused to captive elephants dating back fifteen years.

Small traveling circuses like the Anderson Bros. were every bit as brutal as Ringling Bros. and Barnum and Bailey, Lenore revealed. She agreed to fax Eleanor the information immediately, and to overnight a video of elephant rampages.

"Your Eve is pitiful. Forcing an elephant to live without another member of her species is the worst punishment. They bond with their mothers for life, and are a highly socially evolved species. Tell your Derbe Tigers Club they'll need extra insurance! That'll shake them up!" Lenore started to chuckle. "But to tell you the truth, I gained more ground by joining them. I became a member of my local Tigers Club several years ago. It took awhile, but now circuses' fund-raisers are history." She chuckled with fondness for her fellow Tigers.

Lenore's video included Tyke's rampage and death in August 1994. The twenty-one-year-old African elephant had been rented from an Illinois-based organization to the circus for a show in Honolulu. At the Saturday matinee, in the center ring, she stomped her trainer to death before thousands, traumatizing the audience, most of whom were children. A groom was also injured in the ring, and a dozen bystanders suffered injuries and trauma. Tyke's trainer was reputed to be heavy-handed, Lenore revealed.

The August 22 Associated Press story recounted a witness hearing someone in the ring yelling just before the attack. "He was yelling in an angry voice, very mean." The attack followed.

"Tough trainers take pride in dominating elephants because of their size," Lenore continued. "All you have to be is caring and affectionate, and elephants respond. Tyke ran when she got the chance. The chains are off during shows. She just wanted to escape the abuse."

To learn demeaning tricks and wear costumes, their wills must be broken, Lenore explained. She had photographs of trainers using heavy machinery to smash their massive skulls and backs. In the wild, elephants protect one another, act as midwives, and mourn their dead. Mothers and daughters bond for life. They submerge in water as often as they can to keep cool, swim, and frolic. They are fun-loving and always touching each other. They roam for twenty hours a day, foraging on migratory paths that range from 25 to 125 miles, and they sleep a mere four hours a day in nests of soft ground cover. "In captivity they're chained for twenty hours a day, the opposite of all that is natural for them," she revealed.

"If they're spooked by movement or a weird sound, they'll revert to their natural instincts, they'll stampede. I think that's what happened to Tyke. She was spooked and saw an opportunity to escape. There are serious accidents every year. I tell people that it's crazy to put a kid on an elephant—it might be the last straw!"

Lenore had just returned from Harrisburg, Pennsylvania, where a trainer stabbed a baby Asian elephant numerous times with a bull hook during a performance because the baby refused to behave. The shocked audience booed him and reported him to the police. "I flew to Harrisburg to rescue the baby. But it was useless!"

The USDA laws imposed a small fine on the circus, but the baby, considered by law as the property of the circus, was returned to the circus owners. Lenore followed the baby back to the circus to observe his living conditions. He rocked feverishly, driven by natural youthful vigor, pulling at the chains hysterically. "He was chained to a wall, his eyes wild as he rocked. He looked around him, to the side and in back of him, desperate to get free to play. They were torturing him. I can't get the image out of my head. And his mother was chained on the other side of another adult elephant, trying to reach him with her trunk! Just to comfort him! I'm considering suing the USDA for not upholding its own regulations."

Tyke was the same age as Eve! That thought struck as she hung up. Tyke was gunned down in the industrial section of Honolulu, towering over a fleet of police cars filled with men aiming assault rifles up at her, after a chase of several blocks. Her bloodshot eyes were frantic as she searched for a way out, a way back to the jungle.

Eleanor thought of Tyke's eyes, and recalled Eve's. There was no time to lose. She could follow the circus through Connecticut and even Massachusetts, bull-dogging them. Of course, as PAAC's employee she was obliged to inform Honor of her protest plans, even if they would occur during her off-hours.

It had been two tranquil weeks with absolutely no communications with Honor, and she had no intention of being rejected again. So she decided to lobby Honor as she would legislators in Hartford. While pounding her keyboard to create a circus flier, she listened for Honor's step. With her anemic in-box and her name rescinded from the interoffice routing list, Honor endowed her with time. It was only a half hour later that she heard Honor's feet pounding in the direction of the back filing cabinets. Eleanor darted around her desk to stand a few feet from her doorway. When Honor slammed the file door shut and prepared to walk back to her office, Eleanor called to her casually.

"Honor, the Anderson Bros. Circus is in Derbe and I'm going to chain myself to a stake along Route 7, tonight, right after work!" Eleanor smiled with humor as she blurted the basic facts across the room. The cautious women in the office continued working with their heads down. But Honor stopped in her tracks and turned to walk to Eleanor's office and stand in the doorway. Eleanor remained in the center of her small office, facing her. She related her discovery of Eve in the fog that morning, and her plan to chain herself that night and the following night with the assistance of Lydia. She detailed her strong reception from the two local papers and local TV stations and promised positive coverage for PAAC.

"Circuses are great photo ops," she told Honor. "The big top, the elephant and other animals, I expect a great reception," she said. "Besides, the weekends are slow news days, generally speaking. Especially in the burbs!"

Derbe's residents, she explained, were for the most part conservative whether they were Democrats or Republicans. "They want to sweep the dirt under the carpet. They won't cotton to negative publicity, I guarantee you that. But they're good people. I'm sure I can convince them that circuses are inherently abusive. I also have contacts in the Tigers Club. I did several profiles of the club. They actually offered me an honorary membership which, of course, I turned down because it would be a conflict of interest."

"Campaigns begin in just that way," Honor said. She stood flat-footed in Eleanor's doorway with a thick file in her arms. "You might even succeed in taking Eve away from them." She perused the office as she spoke. "If the Tigers Club drops them, cancellations might just snowball. The word gets around. The elephant's gone or they lose the circus. It could be as easy as that."

Honor stepped into the office and leaned casually against the wall next to the door. Eleanor moved back to rest against her desk, keeping a safe distance.

"It was funny, Honor," she said, "when I spoke to the two trainers this morning, I was fearless, even though this Terminator type, a body builder with huge tattooed muscles, held his bull hook like he wanted to bury it in me. But strangely, I felt nothing. My eyes gravitated to Eve. Just the sight of Eve gave me strength. Like a mother protecting a child. The mother doesn't think about herself. My baby was already suffering."

She recognized a look of reminiscence as Honor stared at her. For a couple of seconds, she and Honor gazed in silent understanding, the bond between them revitalizing. Honor again lost the robes of the reining monarch and became her sister-in-spirit. But to Eleanor's surprise, her wounds still smarted from the Colorado campaign. Her initial feelings of trust seemed to be sealed behind the door Honor had slammed in her face. She found it impossible to rekindle the feeling of sisterhood generated on the day of her job interview.

Without anything said, Eleanor knew that she would represent PAAC in the chaining protest that weekend. But barring incarceration or injury, she was expected at her desk by nine o'clock on Monday morning. As Honor left her office the phone began to ring. Tina's voice boomed with excitement at the other end. An anti-fur protest was scheduled in New York City in July for Fur Design Week, and she was doing the organizing. "We'll finally meet!" she cried. "But let me warn you, Honor will be jumpy! Leona Nesbitt is expected to protest. She'll share the same small, designated protest area. The protest maven and the pencil pusher! To tell the truth, those are the times when I feel sorry for Honor."

Eleanor asked Tina why the two groups couldn't work together.

"It's complicated."

She told Tina about the planned chaining. "Why don't we protest circuses traveling through our own state?"

"We protested three Ringling Bros. and Barnum and Bailey Circus performances, in Pennsylvania, DC, and California. Honor never took up that challenge. I don't know how you've got her to agree to this chaining thing. But good for you, kiddo! Go for it!"

At exactly 12 PM she was surprised to see Honor back at her office. Eleanor remained in her seat, staring at her. Honor leaned against the wall inside her office, next to the door again, as if she were silently mulling something over.

"What is it, Honor?" she asked.

"Eleanor, what about doing a protest on Sunday in Derbe?"

It was a question, and it appeared that whether to do the protest or not was Eleanor's choice. "I'm not sure how many people we'll get on such short notice, but I think that's exactly what we should do. Honor, since my first day on the job, I've been collecting names of volunteers stored in that metal index box on my desk for just such an occasion. I have about 150 people I can call. I think it's a great idea!"

"Bloody good!" Honor smiled with satisfaction as she dashed out of her office, appearing to be once again infinitely grateful for her new employee.

Eleanor could barely wait to dial Lydia, who was quick to tell her that her group routinely protested the small traveling circuses along with several others. She gave Eleanor a list of names and telephone numbers. "Christians For Animal Rights, CFAR, pronounced 'See Far.' Be sure to call them; that's Steve Roberts's number."

A few minutes later, Lisa rushed in holding sheets of the USDA regulations faxed from Lenore and looking disgruntled. She rushed up to her desk, handed Eleanor the fax sheets, and whispered that the circus protest wasn't Honor's idea. A board member, Kwame Cummings, had called Honor early that morning asking what PAAC was planning for the Anderson Bros. Circus in Derbe that weekend. "Honor told him, and I quote, 'We're doing a Sunday protest!' And then she came in here pretending it was your idea."

Eleanor merely chuckled at her conniving boss. The possibility of freeing Eve now consumed her, while Honor and all her frailties were of no consequence.

"Eleanor, all of us are fed up with Honor's ten-week campaign to break you. Now after all that, she expects you to plan a protest with one day of preparation? She could never do this protest without you! She's using and abusing you!"

"It's impossible for her to 'use' me. I want to do the protest. I appreciate you all worrying about me. But I thank God a board member can push her buttons! Lisa, the more I can antagonize this circus the better."

She and Honor were again working shoulder to shoulder. Honor was faxing the press release while she worked on the circus handout. Lenore's charges against the USDA were on her mind, and the curled-up sheets of fax paper that sat at the corner of her desk tantalized her. She finally grabbed them for a quick read. A magnifying glass would have come in handy, but at least she was familiar with the language from reading litigation reports, state statutes, and proposed bills as a city hall reporter in Derbe and Norfolk. Within minutes, it became clear that Lenore's claims against the USDA were valid.

The regulations stated that each and every captive animal should be in a state of "well being." The elephants rocked back and forth in their chains and lost a sense of their surroundings; this was a kind of madness brought on by a life in chains, she pondered. Was this considered a state of "well-being"? She thought of the poor baby in Pennsylvania. It was too unbearable to comprehend.

The USDA inspector for the region that she managed to contact from a number in her Rolodex boiled it down to a few essentials. "As long as the animals are fed, clean, and have shelter, they are considered within USDA regs," he said apologetically.

Her next call was to Steve Roberts of CFAR, who promised to send somebody. But his group was busy with another traveling circus. "Oh, don't worry about a sign, we bring our own."

Signs? Why hadn't she thought of signs? What else had she overlooked? She called Lydia, who agreed to create ten extra placards in calligraphy. "Look in PAAC's closets," Lydia advised. Eleanor hung up and dashed to the mailroom, and Pat led her to a storage closet where they unearthed sixteen dusty, warped generic circus protest signs used for Ringling Bros.

As a result of the press release, Eleanor received a call from an irate Derby politician. Marissa Appleton was a Democrat on the Board of Selectmen. Eleanor could hardly believe it was her. She had always been so calm and collected.

"I personally checked out this circus! I thought they were humane to their animals."

Eleanor launched into her concerns, and described Eve's scars. Quite unexpectedly, Appleton grew even more indignant and irritated as the conversation ensued.

"Historically, Connecticut towns, volunteer firemen, boards of education, polit- ical groups, and church groups have all used circuses for fund-raisers," she yelled. "Derbe and the Tigers Club shouldn't be singled out!" With that she hung up.

Appleton was more worried about her reputation as a fund-raiser than she was about Eve's abuse; that seemed clear. Eleanor's reputation as a reporter also seemed to be at the root of her concerns. Eleanor charged down to Honor's office. "We got the Tigers Club by the tail," she said.

Honor invited her to lunch, but she had no time. As soon as she returned to her office, a raspy Irish voice was on the phone instructing her. It was Jack O'Brien, her Tigers Club contact. He had arranged for the club's president and vice president to meet her at the Derbe Diner on Saturday morning at 8:30. "Don't try to strong-arm them. You catch more ornery old bears with honey. They can be stubborn."

Eleanor jotted down the men's names and numbers and gazed up to see Honor standing in her doorway, having returned from lunch. She related the good news about the breakfast meeting. "I know these people, Honor, they're good people. They'll come around!"

"I wouldn't bet on it."

Derbe High School was surrounded by virgin woods and protected wetlands. The school's property spread from Pine Road to Oak Tree Lane and was ten acres deep. When Eleanor arrived, the sylvan setting had been transformed by the big top in the center of the field, facing the highway. The red-white-and-blue ticket booth was halfway up Oak Tree Lane. A few feet in back of the booth was a makeshift petting zoo comprised of a portable pen spread out under the hot June sun. Irritated sheep and goats of all sizes scuffled with each other in the close con- fines. A few feet away were six ponies tethered to a huge mechanical wheel that went round in circles, also set in the glaring western sun. The horses were blinded by a strap that connected their harnesses to the slow turning wheel. The strap slipped over their squinting and irritated eyes while they walked around in circles with children on their backs. In the back field, a befuddled llama was tethered on a short leash to a truck, while tethered dogs sat under campers to escape the sun.

Eleanor parked in the lot at the end of Oak Tree Lane, opposite the circus, and carted her tent over to the field. She was relieved to see two TV trucks pull- ing up. On the field were circus personnel dressed in the patriotic colors, with organ music blasting and barkers hawking, while the smells of popcorn, hot dogs, pretzels, and cotton candy blended with the scent of hay and manure. Costumed acrobats, clowns, and jugglers jumped, spun, and juggled on the sides of the field, warming up, while families arrived. Children clung to their parents' hands as they walked from the familiar school parking lot and ventured into the unfamiliar world of the circus. But when the children set their sights on Eve, excitement mingled with affection filled their faces. Eve laboriously trucked around in circles like one in a trance, with her "exercise" tire dangling on the tip of her trunk.

Eleanor walked across the front lawn in the direction of Route 7, she stopped at the edge of the lawn's slope, which led down to the highway below. It was important to get as close to the state road as possible, since what was considered public domain allowed her the constitutional right to a peaceful demonstration. She did, however, inform the police.

Lydia stood near the center, close to the eight-foot slope. As they set up their army-issue tent, the arriving media recorded and photographed every move. Two police cruisers parked near the ticket booth and two patrolmen ambled over, giving Eleanor a nod as they approached. She had informed them of the protest. Lydia placed the stainless steel chain around Eleanor's ankle, which was protected by a white tennis sock, and she sank the stake into the soft soil inside the tent in order to hide the chain from the eyes of late night yahoos riding on Route 7.

As Lydia sank the stake into the ground, Eleanor groaned to herself at the sense of entrapment because it was but a taste of Eve's life. She tugged at the chain and stared into the TV camera, her face bold and defiant. She wore khaki fatigue pants and a white V-neck T-shirt. But for the unusual ankle bracelet, she resembled a camper standing outside her tent. Her long, thick, burnished copper hair waved unruly in the soft June breeze. She turned to glance at Eve behind her. At the sight of the weary, lumbering Eve, so out of step with the excited children and their proud parents, she forgot she was on camera.

"I'm your partner in chains, Eve," she silently told the elephant. "I'm your partner in misery for at least two of your endless lonely nights. Feel me here with you. Know that I and millions of others are here with you always. We will never stop working for your freedom."

The eyes on the newsroom wall came rushing back to her as she stared at Eve. They were all connected, all their spirits. A sense of wholeness prevailed; she was fulfilling her mission. She raised her ecstatic face hidden from the cameras up to the colors of the setting sun in gratitude. A second later she turned to her friend. "Lydia, I've never felt more liberated or more at peace, and here I am chained to a tent along Route 7! Isn't it amazing?"

"See what working for Honor will do for you? And in only six months?" Lydia returned.

They both laughed, but Eleanor gazed at Lydia with love. Lydia is always Lydia, she thought.

The woman reporter from Channel 9 was of Arabian descent and was TV camera-perfect in her cherry red suit and off-white blouse as she toted her black and silver microphone. She rushed over to Eleanor with her interview questions and announced the station's intention to do a full piece on the chaining event. Two other female TV reporters flanked her, from Channel 26 and Cablevision. But before she could pose a question, an angry young man wearing a circus uniform stepped out of the gathering crowd collected around the tent, and confronted Eleanor. He was a tall, slender, good-looking man with dark hair and eyes.

"Why are you doing this?" he asked. "We don't abuse our animals." The reporters were quick to move aside so the TV cameras could zoom in.

"It's cruel to keep Eve chained as you do," Eleanor said. "I'm only chained by one foot for a few minutes, but I feel totally vulnerable!"

"We can't let her walk around, can we?" he said. "We feed her and keep her clean. She don't get abused by nobody," he said.

"Oh, really? Then why does she look so depressed?"

"Well, you'd look like that if you were chained day and night too."

"That's the point!" Eleanor gazed straight into the camera and yanked her chain.

The circus worker vanished into the crowd after the exchange. She explained to the cameras that chaining herself was her constitutional right and a moral obligation. "For a few minutes of entertainment, Eve's enslaved for life. Such abuse should be a criminal offense." She took a couple of steps and snapped the long metal chain again, and gazed into the cameras. "We're asking Derbe residents for their support. Please don't go to the circus! Your money keeps this elephant in chains! And don't place your precious children on the back of this elephant. It might be the proverbial last straw. She might rampage. Your child could die. Captive elephant accidents occur every year, causing injury and deaths." She held up Lenore's sheet of recorded accidents. "Elephants are wild by nature. If spooked or threatened in any way, they may stampede and strike."

The media trailed off to enter the circus grounds while Eleanor and Lydia turned to their "tent exhibition." Lydia and two members of her group placed five educational posters of a herd of elephants living in the wilds of Africa along the outside walls of the tent. Lydia narrated for the curious, pointing to the photographs and comparing them to Eve's life of isolation from others of her species, traveling in trucks, enduring blaring organs and crowded tents. In her professional manner, she wrapped it up with a plea. "Please send Eve back to Eden.

When you keep your circus money in your pocket, you buy Eve's ticket back to Eden."

They watched in awe as whole families left the breezy high school field to return to their cars. After one of the many tent dialogues, a group of Derbe junior high school students, who had arrived on bikes, were converted and turned into zealots riding off and calling to families. "Don't go to the circus! They abuse their animals!" They pointed toward the tent. "Go see the chained Elephant Lady!"

After the last of the circus goers exited the field, Eve lumbered into her trailer, led by her handler and his hook, and the circus turned off its lights and settled for the night.

Eleanor and Lydia watched Derbe close down at 10 PM. Soon only the amber streetlights glowed on the highway and Oak Tree Lane, and blackness filled the adjoining woods and fields. "Eleanor, please wake me if you have to go. Don't go alone!"

The police would cruise the area all night, and assaulting her would be bad for business, Eleanor told her.

"People do strange things under pressure," Lydia said.

Eleanor agreed to wake Lydia so she wouldn't worry. They finally stretched out in their light sleeping bags, side by side in the tent. Eleanor's bag was left unzipped for her shackled leg. She and Lydia stared peacefully up at the starry sky through the screened rectangular opening in the tent's ceiling. In her effort to be comfortable while chained, she turned countless times.

"Eleanor, nobody's around. Let me take your ankle out of the chains, please."

"Not to worry, I'm used to it. I've been chained to a desk for six months, remember?"

They laughed and then soon drifted off to sleep, lulled by the chorus of katydids and the deep-bass bullfrogs croaking down in Miller's pond a half-mile away, on Old Ridgefield Road.

Two hours later, Eleanor woke. She kept the swish of her sleeping bag to a minimum as she unhooked the chain, emancipating herself. In a squatting position, she slipped one leg out of the tent, then the other, and then hoisted herself up. She stretched her body and sighed. Her spirit soared being outside in the fresh night air, free of the chains. She then realized that she was more relieved to be out of her office.

"Strange how chains can be so liberating," she thought. She sucked in the damp night air. The stars and the moon provided perfect light for her trip to the back field. But she gripped the metal flashlight as if it were a weapon.

She crossed the squishing grass and the school's back road to approach the latrine. The parked circus vehicles were only yards away in the dark field. She listened for strange noises; she could only detect the sound of herself breathing. The menacing trainer with his bull hook flashed before her. She quickly expelled the ugly vision from her mind.

The latch to the port-o-toilet was cold and a little damp. It creaked as she yanked it and pulled the door open. Once she stepped inside the small dark confines, smelling of cleaning solution, she locked the latch and set her flashlight on the commode encasement to her right. Its triangular ray illumined the green ribbed plastic walls, and the roll of toilet paper sitting beside her. When she was ready to exit and about to slide the latch open, she heard someone or something brush past a leafy branch to the left. She slid the latch and swung the door open.

But before she could exit, a dark form sprang from behind the latrine, trapping her inside. She was staring at a man's chest. The balls of her feet were perched on the doorway's sharp edge while her heels dug into the floor. She peered upwards into the face, whose features she strained to see in the glow of the flashlight that she dared not beam up at him. She had no doubt of the man's identity. The handler's alcoholic breath swept over her. She could now discern his hateful features.

He whipped his bull hook up to her face. "If you keep doing this, I'll fuck you up with this! You won't look so pretty no more!" His hatred washed over her like oozing filth.

"Eleanor, is that you?" Lydia's breathless and vibrating voice shouted from across the lawn as she ran in Eleanor's direction.

"Yes!" she shouted in the man's face. The fervent sound of her own voice surprised her. The dark form disappeared into the shadows. Lydia rushed to her. Eleanor was still poised on the threshold of the latrine. Lydia caressed her shoulders, wanting to comfort her.

"It was the handler," Eleanor said.

They rushed toward the safety of their tent and the close proximity of the highway. "He threatened me with his bull hook."

"I know, I heard every word, I just pretended not to know if you were there. You can press charges for assault."

"He was drunk. His breath was disgusting!" Again, she failed to be frightened.

When they reached the tent, Lydia declared that it was time to go. "The last thing I want is to tangle with a six foot tall drunken elephant trainer wielding a bull hook."

"But I've got to think of what's best for Eve!"

"Eleanor, after that stupid stunt, I'm sure the Tigers Club won't sign another contract. It's not the Derbe way. If Eve is your first concern, the best action is to report the threat with a dangerous weapon to the police."

Eleanor knew she had to call Honor first. Lydia withdrew a cell phone from her pocket and handed it to her. But it was 3:45 AM! she thought. Eleanor hesitated, afraid of waking her up. Then she finally dialed.

Honor sounded wide awake, verbally patted her on the head for her good work, and agreed that she should report the incident to the cops. In his small, dimly lit office, Sergeant Donald Camby assured her and Lydia that they would consider applying for an arrest warrant and charge the trainer with assault.

"Don, the circus won't hear about this until after nine this morning, will it?"

The fair-haired officer peered over his busy desk at her. Eleanor knew he was remembering that she had helped striking police officers to gain fair pay, another holiday, and adequate life insurance. He slipped the report under a pile. "I don't think anybody's going to see this till way after 9 AM."

Her remaining night's sleep lasted for one whole hour. Then she was up and on the road to the office to write and fax her press release, attempting to use the assault charges to draw CNN and others to the chaining that evening. The editor on the CNN assignment desk promised to send a crew. She also drafted a story for HOWL about the Tiger's Club bringing the circus to Derbe calculated to threaten the officials at breakfast that morning.

At 7 AM she bounded to the small variety store and smiled at the sunlight dancing on the water across the road. Life was good! The Indian owner, Nicky Kumar, was just lugging in some stacks of newspapers to sort them. Chatting, she followed him in, grabbed copies of the three local papers, and began to tear through them as she walked across the parking lot to return to PAAC's front door.

The *Norfolk Daily News*'s headline read, "They call her the Elephant Lady." "The Elephant Lady?" Eleanor said to herself. The article revealed that a couple of Derbe teenagers referred to her as the "Elephant Lady." She assumed them to be the teenage bicyclists. At 7:30 AM she telephoned Honor to describe the coverage, including the "Elephant Lady" title and CNN's promise to cover that evening's chaining event.

The diner on the west side of Route 7 was a typical rectangular diner structure with the added attraction of large picture windows on all four walls. As Eleanor entered, two men waved to her from a natural oak table in the center of the floor, just beyond the bright rays of the morning sun. At first glance it was obvious that Cleveland Downs, the Tigers Club's hefty president, would be trouble. She spotted his cynical expression from the doorway. He was dressed in beige pants and a navy blazer over a white shirt unbuttoned at the collar, looking every bit the Wall Street CEO. He was tall, with a sickening white pallor and an unhealthy, puffy face. His icy blue eyes were judgmental, and his smile was a smirk. His thin, receding, light brown hair was streaked with gray and combed back.

The Tigers Club vice president, Frank Kelly, seated at his side, was a portly, kind-faced man with the relaxed manner of a retiree and was dressed casually. Both men rose to their feet to greet her. She was surprised to find Downs's hand clammy, almost repulsive, while Kelly's was limp. Downs, being the perfect gentleman, was quick to walk around the table to pull out her chair.

"Thank you," she said. She smiled—impressed with Downs's courtesy—as she took her seat across from him and placed her briefcase on the chair next to her. She noticed his half-eaten stack of pancakes, and Kelly's one and a half oat bran muffins.

"Thanks for taking the time to meet with me. How did you recognize me?" she asked them.

"It was easy to spot the Elephant Lady. We read the papers," Downs said.

"I guessed that." She gave a good-natured chuckle.

She scraped her wooden chair on the floor, pulling it closer to the table. She was at once uncomfortable under Downs's cool, steady gaze. The chummy waitress taking her order for a bowl of oatmeal and a cup of tea offered her an opportunity to adjust to Down's condescending air.

"I know Jack related our concerns. Gentlemen, please continue eating your breakfast while I describe why no elephant wants to run away from home and join the circus."

Kelly sank his teeth into the remainder of his oat bran muffin while eyeing Downs's pancakes. Downs cut off a wedge of his pancakes, dripping with syrup, and chewed it and then sipped a little coffee, taking his piercing eyes off Eleanor for a few seconds.

"I know you have a contract with the Anderson Bros. Circus, and you can't do anything about it this year. But as a Derbe resident and the public affairs director at People Against Animal Cruelty, representing 5,000 Connecticut residents, I'm asking you to reconsider this fund-raiser for next year. I'd like to bring this issue to your full membership by giving a speech at one of your Friday luncheons. I'll include videos of rampaging circus and zoo elephants."

She remained confident as she described the deprived life of captive elephants compared to those who live in the wild.

"You're making an emotional appeal," Downs said.

"I'm making a biological appeal with emotion. I'm sure you don't think circuses are cruel, since they are an American tradition. But I hope now you're having second thoughts. Circuses are poor examples for our children. There's no educational value. The children are not observing the behavior of elephants. They're seeing a pathetic puppet." She stopped for a second and stared across at Downs. "Please, think about it, Mr. Downs, you're an intelligent man. How do you suppose they get an elephant to stand on his head?"

Smirking, Downs failed to answer. She dug out Lenore's accident report from her briefcase on the chair next to her and handed Downs a copy. He put it to the side of his dish without a glance.

"We have a record of the attacks, accidents, and fatalities that have occurred in the last fifteen years. I'm sure I don't have to explain to you that we're a litigious society, and you should have additional insurance when you invite the circus into Derbe."

Downs's look of incredulity revealed that he found her advice impertinent. Her oatmeal was served, and she ate a few small steamy spoonfuls and decided to lighten the atmosphere with casual chatter. She was a former journalist, she explained. And recently she'd conducted a short investigation of the Anderson Bros. Circus. "They'd be out of business if small towns didn't hire them."

"Yes, it's a small town circus," Downs said. He finished his pancakes.

"Then one must take some responsibility for the cruelty to animals in the circus if one does business with them," she said.

Kelly said, "I had a heart attack and my doctor recommended that I eat oat bran muffins." He told her that the fund-raiser proceeds were earmarked to purchase cell phones for the towns' shut-ins. "So if they are injured, they can call for help."

"Frank, your fund-raiser is promoting animal abuse, and I'm sure you never thought of the circus in that way. I must be honest with you. And I don't mean this to sound like a threat, but there'll be quite a circus protest tomorrow!"

"Who did you work for as a journalist?" Downs asked.

"The *Derbe Weekly* and the *Norfolk Daily News*. I won an award for an in-depth series on Vietnam veterans, and it was time to make a move. I decided to focus on the animals. I've been a vegetarian for a number of years."

Downs scoffed at the mention of the local newspapers.

"Where do you work?" she asked.

"Wall Street," said Downs.

"Somehow I suspected that," she said.

Kelly offered, "Wouldn't people go to the circus without the elephant there?"

"I don't know," snapped Downs. His eyes remained focused on Eleanor.

She leaped at this breakthrough. "Yes, there are such circuses. The shows are colorful and magical, with magicians, acrobats, dancers, and games of chance. They do very well. I'll be happy to supply you with their names and numbers."

Downs's sneer never let up as he sipped his second cup of coffee. With each passing minute, Eleanor grew more uncomfortable. "Please, gentlemen, consider that it's wrong to raise funds on the backs of suffering elephants and other helpless creatures in order to do good deeds for our town. Don't you see the irony?"

"Where do you get your money?" Downs asked.

At this moment, she realized the meeting was a farce. Downs was going through the motions. Was Kelly putting on a false front? Were they playing good cop, bad cop? she wondered.

"We have donors, grants, and bequests. I really want to address your rank and file at one of your luncheons," she said.

"I'll be glad to deliver the message to the members," Downs said.

She felt used by the men. There was only one thing left to do. She began to dig into her briefcase again. "I'm going to read you the story I'm writing about bringing this circus into town and the abuse that is obvious to caring humans," she said.

"The Anderson Bros. Circus is brought into Derbe, Connecticut, each year by the Derbe Tigers Club…" she began. She gazed up at the two men and observed the steely look in Downs's eyes deepening as she spoke. Even Kelly's eyes had turned cold and ugly. The ornery bears she had been warned about were rebelling. "Eve's pathetic life calls to arms the many who care," she continued. The tension heightened with each uttered word. Her words began to falter under their glares, and shriveled up half-spoken. "PAAC is asking that the, the Tigers…Club…and others, end such…tainted fund-raisers," she muttered. Her face burned with the humiliation as her every word slid off the icy glare of Downs's blue eyes to sink into oblivion.

What a silly fool she'd been. Did she really think that she, a little PR director of a little-known animal rights organization, could direct a right-wing Wall Street CEO?

The two men seemed to loom bigger than life, they were the winning team, and her morale was sinking and her confidence eroding by the second. Their refined hatred was as black and putrid as that of Eve's handler. She began to fear their cold, uncaring expressions. She had no desire to read the truth of them, to see the void that lay behind the icy eyes. It was in her nature to believe in the goodness of humans. But the two men supplied living, breathing proof of that absurdity! Gazing into Downs's cold blue eyes, she recognized the fearful hollow-ness where a heart should be, a heart for the animals. Downs's callousness issued the worst of presentiments for the human race. She froze for a few seconds staring into them.

Still, the optimist in her refused to forgo the search for a heart. She was worse than the most persistent saleswoman, but despite her crusader's urge, her trembling hands folded her story while she was in mid-sentence, and her voice trailed off as if losing its will all on its own. She reached down and slipped the story back into her briefcase. She felt exposed, emotionally nude before the two men. Her eyes remained on her briefcase as if hiding from the demeaning eyes across from her, abashed by her own naiveté.

PAAC's new press release poked out of the outside pocket of the briefcase.

"We'll pick up the check," Downs said.

"I guess a nonprofit should never refuse that offer," Eleanor said. She stood up. "You haven't heard this yet, gentlemen, it'll be in tomorrow's newspapers. The Anderson Bros. Circus elephant handler accosted me last night. He waved his bull hook at me and told me that he'd, using the F-word, would F me up with the bull hook. He said, 'You won't be so pretty no more.' Lydia Grant, of Animal Independence, witnessed it. We reported it to the Derbe Police about four o'clock this morning, requesting they arrest the man for assault. That's who you're dealing with, gentlemen, to raise your funds to do good deeds. You think Derbe's citizens will see the irony, even if you don't?"

She handed each of the flabbergasted men a press release. "I wrote that this morning," she said. She stared at Downs with some satisfaction.

"Why didn't you mention this earlier?" Downs asked.

"I wanted to reach you on humanitarian grounds but...you could always hire another cruel circus."

"I'm sorry this happened," Downs said. He was sincere, although accusation and anger were also present in his voice. "We'll take this whole venture under advisement now."

"That's all we ask," she said.

She avoided shaking Downs's clammy hands and went home to sit on the living room floor, taking a few minutes to pet Friday and Rusty and give her heart some solace.

Then Honor called. "Did the conservative sons of bitches choke on breakfast?" she asked.

Eleanor laughed. "They gagged on desert. Since the trainer assaulted me, they will, and I'm quoting the president of the Tigers Club, 'take the whole venture under advisement.' I couldn't convince them on humanitarian grounds, so I slapped them with the press release at the end. Downs, the president, was a bully. Last night it was the hatred of that elephant trainer; this morning it was the 'heart of darkness.' This animal rights business is very revealing, Honor. The 'heart of darkness' is what really scared me. A bull hook doesn't hold a candle to empty hearts."

"I don't want you to chain yourself tonight," Honor said. In her voice was the authority of the presidency.

"Why? It's working." she said.

"It's too dangerous. You'll be a sitting target. It's too dangerous."

"CNN is coming," Eleanor said. "We'll make the tristate area news. Even the *New York Times* promised to be there. I'm about to call Public Radio, the AP wire service, and *USA Today*. I'm going back to the office now to fax the press release about the assault! I'm sure they'll cover this! Even if it's only a blurb!"

"Well, love, you can tell them to come back for our protest tomorrow. Can't you?"

Did Honor really believe that CNN and Public Radio would be interested in a simple circus protest? Eleanor wanted to scream the question at her, but instead she silently acquiesced.

"We have to watch out for egos," Honor said. "They can get us in trouble, can't they?"

"What egos?" Eleanor asked. She was puzzled, and she plopped down on her couch as if she'd been sucker punched.

"This campaign is as much about you as it is about Eve, isn't that right, Elephant Lady?"

"Honor, this campaign is all about Eve, excuse the pun. Not my ego. People know who I am. No doubt, I've turned into the Elephant Lady. They will connect me with the circus protests. But that's what successful campaigns are about. Newspapers like a face with a story." She took a deep breath. The day's insults had no end. Honor remained resolute in her silence. "OK," Eleanor barked. "I'll see you Sunday at the protest."

She hung up and sat back on her couch, drained. There she remained for a few minutes, stunned, and a wave of apathy and exhaustion overcame her. All the work left to do for the protest was suddenly so bothersome that she again felt like a beast of burden. Could she actually do it, she wondered, without sleep or inspiration? She'd have to get the police blotter, and write a new press release and fax it. And there were so many people yet to call, while every aching muscle claimed its rightful due. Apathetic, she sank into her couch in maudlin exhaustion, flopping to her side half-sitting, half-lying down as if Honor's distrust had landed a knockout punch.

Then her reporter's objectivity clicked in: "Eleanor," the voice within her said, "here is an aging CEO, who has a dedicated gung-ho activist worker who was up most of the night chained along Route 7 and was assaulted by a circus brute. And thanks to her initiative, PAAC's name has been splashed across the front pages of the local papers and headed up all local TV news shows, and now CNN and Public Radio are knocking at PAAC's door. This was the best local PR the organization had experienced in her six months of employment. For breakfast, she single-handedly challenged and beat the muscle of the conservative Tigers Club, who most likely will not sign a circus contract for next year, a feat never before accomplished by PAAC. Sunday she will lead a circus protest that she organized with two lousy days' notice. After this jam-packed productive weekend—literally working day and night—she is expected at PAAC's office at 9 AM on Monday. Far from complaining, she is loving it! She is willing! She is able! She is the Elephant Lady!"

Eleanor spoke out loud. "It's not 'my' ego that troubles Honor!"

She sprang from her couch and raced out the door with endless calls and plans churning in her head for her virgin protest. She shouted a good-bye to her stalwart friends.

CHAPTER 8

▼

"ANIMAL ACTIVISTS"

Eleanor's exhausted body and mind drifted into a sweet sleep that night even though Eve was shackled just down the road, and the weatherman predicted monsoon-like storms for the Sunday protest. But she bolted out of bed the next morning, the forecast of 32 to 50 mile an hour gale winds sending her into a bleary-eyed panic. She turned on the lamp on her night table, her eyes flashing to the colonial windows while she slipped into her jeans. It was almost as dark as night!

In minutes she finished dressing, fed her cats, cooked Irish oatmeal, and ate while praying for sunshine before the kitchen window, as she decided to wear boots and a poncho. Minutes later, driving down Route 7 to church, it grew darker by the second as she peered through her windshield.

"What happens in the rain? I never thought of rain! You can't have a rain date with a protest," she exclaimed. "Can you? The circus goes on, so shouldn't we?" She was assured of one thing: Lydia. Lydia would show no matter what. Lydia would be there. Great, she pondered, Honor and Lydia and no doubt the oppressive Freda and the obliging Delores. "What a nightmare! There goes the damn dream job! And what about Eve? What does this mean for Eve?"

She didn't dare phone Honor, fearful of asking the obvious. At church services, she repeated her petition for sunshine. Afterward she continued with her plans as if her prayers would be answered and she drove back up Route 7 a half-mile north of her apartment to pick up the podium and speakers she had reserved for Honor's short speech. Beth Murphy and her partner, who are professional musicians, and whom she'd met during a court hearing on a dog abuse case, offered to perform gratis, with electric guitars. "Electric guitars in the rain?" she thought. Back in her driveway, with the car idling, she dashed into the house to check phone messages only to find none, and on the way out she ripped off the sign on her door and proceeded to Oak Tree Lane.

It was exactly 10:30 AM when she pulled into the pitifully empty parking lot at the end of Oak Tree Lane for the 11 AM protest. Dollops of rain had begun to fall. Umbrella in hand, she walked down Oak Tree Lane to stand across the street from the red-and-white circus ticket booth. She bent down to set her sign on the damp grass for a second in order to open her umbrella. That's when gale-force winds hit. Her umbrella was whipped inside out and her sign was soaked in a second. The giant oaks and century-old towering evergreens danced about like seedlings. A bolt of lightening flashed in the eastern sky just across the highway and over the small businesses lining the road. On the field, circus personnel scurried about securing the stakes and flaps of the huge tent. An earsplitting thunderclap followed with huge sheets of rain.

The highway thirty feet away, was a wind tunnel threatening to flood. Eleanor dropped her useless umbrella on the sopping grass under the forest overhang that bordered Oak Tree Lane. A stream of rain was flowing down the hood of her poncho to roll off her nose. Another stream routed down her right shoulder and on to the front of her poncho. When she bent down to tuck in her soaking jeans, the two streams connected, turning into a small waterfall pouring into her left boot.

She straightened up, soaked in and out. Straight ahead, Route 7 drivers inched their way guided only by shafts of headlights cutting through the sheets of rain. She held her soppy placard toward the traffic with its El Greco lettering. At the very least, she told herself, she was a yellow beacon in the storm.

With Derbe's naturally moist ground, it took only minutes for Oak Tree Lane and Route 7 to flow like shallow rivers. A car headed south came to a standstill on the highway, flooded and stalled. "Why did I tell them it was a three-hour protest from 11 AM to 2 PM?" Eleanor thought. "Three hours in this?" She had set the time to catch the circus crowds coming and going from one show to the next. It seemed like a good idea at the time.

An older woman in a black Ford drove past her and pulled into the parking lot next to her Nissan. Eleanor splashed her way back to the lot, all her foreboding disappearing at the very sight of the woman. No doubt she was one of Honor's seven activists. Maybe all is not lost, Eleanor thought. The frail woman in her early seventies stepped from her car and a blast of wind and a sheet of rain attacked her, rendering her red umbrella useless and tugging at her clear plastic kerchief. While the rain rolled down her thin angular nose and her hollow cheeks, another gust body-slammed her, tipping her fragile form toward the fender on the driver's side.

"This is too much for me," she said. Dumbstruck, Eleanor watched as her one and only activist drove back down the shallow river that was now Oak Tree Lane. Then a gentleman in a gray Bronco drove past the receding Ford and pulled into the parking lot. He exited his vehicle, and the storm drenched his blue windbreaker on contact. Eleanor rushed to him, all smiles, but he muttered something to her that was smothered by the storm while he turned to climb back into his Bronco and drive back down Oak Tree Lane. She watched, open-mouthed, rain dripping from her nose and upper lip.

"OK, savvy reporter, what now?" she asked herself. "You promised your new boss a crowd, and she's going to get a two-woman show! If Lydia shows! You'll be going back to reporting! You had to brag about the 150 new names and telephone numbers in your little volunteer box, didn't you? You did extend her pathetic seven octogenarian volunteers to a decent number. So everyone you reached agreed to come. In normal times you'd expect about 20 percent to actually show. But in this, who knows? Maybe Honor won't even show. Maybe Lydia won't show! Maybe everyone knows not to come. Maybe you don't do protests in a storm. What do I know? But the circus, it still goes on. Why shouldn't we?"

Then, to her surprise, three blue-and-green Derbe Police Department cruisers pulled up to the corner of Route 7 and Oak Tree Lane and proceeded to block off the street. One parked horizontally, while the others parked on either side. A cop in his long yellow rain gear got out of the middle cruiser to stand facing Route 7 and direct traffic past Oak Tree Lane, making it necessary to use the school's back road to park at the Oak Tree Lane parking lot or the back field.

Then five uniformed cops, all in yellow rain gear, filed out of the vehicles to form a loosely constructed human barricade from the circus ticket booth down to the corner of Route 7. It was an obvious attempt to ward off possible agitators. Most of the cops gave her a nod. She waved back at them from across the streaming road, "Hell! It looks like something big is going down! Three police cars yet!" She walked closer to Route 7, heading into the storm winds to be closer to the police car. She was grateful that she'd called them. "No doubt the selectman also had a chat with the chief of police. God! The cops must be expecting a huge turnout!"

At that moment, trudging down Oak Tree Lane from the parking lot came Lauren Grey of CFAR. She looked the activist savant in her proficient rain gear. She was wearing an army fatigue poncho, boots, and black ski gloves and was toting a large handmade placard covered in protective plastic wrap. She was of medium height and weight, with light brown hair and the smooth complexion and serenity of the Mona Lisa. She offered Eleanor a steady unruffled gaze from the depths of her protective hood, which was tied under her chin.

"My God, can you believe this rain?" Eleanor asked. "I'm so glad to see you! I thought the storm was the only one coming!"

"Where do you want me to stand?" Lauren asked.

Eleanor stared back at her dumbstruck. She'd never thought of choreographing the protest!

Lauren meanwhile surveyed Route 7 and both sides of Oak Tree Lane. "I'll go stand on the corner," she said. She plodded down the sloshing wet lawn to the corner. There were no sidewalks to speak of in Derbe. Lauren was a copy editor for the *New York Times*, and this was her day off. She stood catty-corner to the circus on Route 7, facing the sheets of driving wind and the slow oncoming traffic. It was a brilliant move, Eleanor thought. Her rain-spotted sign, which listed the deprivations of animals enslaved by circuses, was impossible to read at a distance, and in seconds the blustery wind had wrapped the three-foot poster around her body like tissue paper, while the cold rain struck her unprotected face. Yet she stood erect and tall on the side of the highway like the Statue of Liberty. All she lacked was the torch. The poignant sight so moved Eleanor that she choked back sobs, some of which were from relief. Lauren Grey was a comforting reminder that she was not alone in her efforts to free Eve.

"Just seeing this one-woman show was worth it," she told herself. She studied Lauren and was filled with pride and hope in the human race. All her doubts of the previous day generated by the heartless Downs and Kelly were being washed away in this stormy ablution.

Soon Lauren was joined by other die-hard activists who began pulling into the parking lot and lining up next to her. First there were two, then three, and then before Eleanor knew it, all of Oak Tree Lane was lined by people of all sizes, shapes, and ages wearing a colorful array of rain gear. She was preoccupied by introducing herself to those she had only met over the phone, and she recorded their names on the damp legal-sized yellow pad she dubiously shielded under her poncho.

By 11:45 AM there were forty loyal foot soldiers and fifteen of their children, including one in a stroller under a plastic cover. They lined Oak Tree Lane in a stoic show of solidarity as they protested the circus directly across the street from them. Their backgrounds were as varied as their rain gear: a nurse, a surgeon, a teacher, a postal clerk, stay-at-home moms, working moms, several salesmen and saleswomen, journalists, a bank teller, male and female college, high school, and grade school students, and a couple of law students. The strangers became family under the animal rights banner.

Lydia, never more Eleanor's stalwart friend, distributed signs covered in plastic wrap to those in need. Some simply read, "Free Eve!" Others instructed, "Send Eve Back to the Garden of Eden," "Liberate Eve," "Keep Your Money in Your Pocket!"

"Thank God Sunday is a slow news day!" Eleanor shouted to Lydia. "I was afraid to call you. I thought you'd say nobody was going to show because of the storm."

"There're no rain days in animal rights," Lydia said.

The gentleman who had dashed off earlier in his Bronco returned and approached Eleanor. "I had to get my rain gear. Here I am—ready for action."

The photographers for the two local dailies were accompanied by reporters, all of whom she knew by name. Her former editors hadn't let her down. The two TV crews from Channel 9 and Channel 26 and the newsprint reporters were presented with her flier bearing the photograph of the shackled Eve on the high school lawn. The copy listed all the deprivations of a captive elephant, including Eve being immobilized for nineteen hours.

Honor arrived at noon. By then the gale winds had subsided, allowing for umbrellas, although gusts still ambushed the crowd, periodically morphing umbrellas into missiles. Honor wore a cranberry raincoat. Freda held Honor's matching umbrella over her royal head while standing slightly behind her.

"What a turnout!" Honor shouted. "In this bloody weather!" Eleanor stood near the curb in the center of the line of protesters facing the circus. Honor smiled a glorious parental smile of approval at her. "I think it's best to forgo the speech! Don't you?"

Eleanor was relieved by Honor's approval, parental or otherwise. The musicians arrived, but their instruments remained in their van. But in an inspiring note, every few minutes, a passing Route 7 motorist honked and gave a wet thumbs-up. Chanting was useless, but the families standing along the rain-swept highway spoke louder than any mantra.

Meanwhile, Honor had boldly stationed herself next to the ticket booth, which allowed her to insult circus goers as they purchased their tickets. Two police officers had immediately requested that she keep a safe distance and join the protesters on the opposite side. She loudly proclaimed her constitutional rights to the "donut eaters," and held her position. Eleanor jogged across the street and pulled aside the officer in charge and negotiated a peace settlement, promising to contain all protesters on the opposite side if Honor were allowed her position in circus territory.

As Eleanor stood next to Honor, she viewed the jagged line of dedicated people across the road with new eyes: the adults and children with umbrellas created hills and valleys of colorful rain gear. "This is their day off," she muttered to herself. "I'm getting paid. This is their Sunday afternoon. These are the 'animal activists'!"

More often than not, they were depicted by the media as the kooky counter-culture, as rabble-rousers or left-wing wackos. They were never projected as responsible, thoughtful U.S. citizens from all walks of life who had convictions and gave of themselves for an issue that they thought was more important than their own comfort. When the second show commenced, Eleanor congratulated the exiting foot soldiers, all of whom stayed for the full three hours. Tears of gratitude streamed down her wet face more than once that afternoon. Downs and Kelly continued to fade into oblivion, like the words she'd lost in her attempt to reach them.

The following morning at eight o'clock, Eleanor rushed into the Westport variety store to purchase the local newspapers. Outside in the morning sun, and across from the sparkling Sound, she muttered a prayer of thanks. There on the front page of the *Norfolk Daily News* was a six-column photograph of the line of activists standing along Oak Tree Lane in the rain. The headline read: "The Faithful 40 and Their Children Came and Stayed for Three Hours."

"And I prayed for sunshine."

Eleanor gazed at the horizon and the water glistening under the morning sun with new luster, and offered her prayerful thanks. Then she raced into the building, up the stairs, and into Honor's office to spread the newspaper on her desk. She then began reading it to her delighted boss. Eleanor took note of the date as she read: it was Monday, June 30. She realized that Eve's rescue had moved into the realm of possibilities; it seemed the beginning of the end of "circus elephants." She knew that she'd continue to protest come that Friday night, as the circus moved north to Redding, and she'd continue to do so until Eve was out of reach.

That day and the following days of the next two weeks, Honor was a frequent visitor to her office complaining about Tina. Poor Tina was the official omega, since she was organizing PAAC's demonstration in Manhattan for Fur Fashion

Week. And PAAC would indeed be sharing the same designated protest area with the legendary RUFFFF and its leader, Leona Nesbitt. While PAAC was leafleting, RUFFFF would conduct an act of civil disobedience (CD). Tina hadn't a clue to the nature of the CD, which added to the usual tension.

But as Honor sat in her office complaining about Tina, it was Honor who Eleanor actually pitied. Leona was the undisputed leader of the movement, while Honor, in the waning days of her career, was little known and the head of a national organization that was often mistaken for a small local group.

CHAPTER 9

▼

THE FUR DEMO

On a hot, humid, and hazy Monday, July 12, the first day of Fur Fashion Week, PAAC was leafleting in front of Studio 6000 where the fashion shows were taking place instructing sweaty passersby never to wear fur. At 11:30 an ABC truck pulled up to the corner, near 35th Street and 7th Avenue. Eleanor ran over to introduce herself and invite the reporter to interview Honor, and was told they had just minutes to deadline for the noon news show. As the attractive African-American reporter and her cameraman stepped out and walked on the shoulder of 7th Avenue, Eleanor raced back inside the barricade of NYPD wooden horses to warn Honor.

Honor jumped to her feet, clicked into interview mode, and dug for the sheet of statistics in her pants pocket. Then she motioned to the approaching reporter to follow her as she walked to the opposite side of the barricade and slipped between the wooden horses to hold the interview on 7th Avenue's wide sidewalk, in the pedestrian traffic. She shot a withering look at a nearby officer who had been watching PAAC's every move.

Eleanor introduced Veta Roberts to Honor. "The fur industry claims that fur is back. Is that true?" Roberts placed her microphone at Honor's lips.

"Since fur's heyday in the late 1980s, sales have dropped," Honor began, "contrary to the fur industry's figures. U.S. government numbers prove that fur sales are not rising. It is true that there was a small 2 percent boost because of the secure economy. But included in the fur industry's sales figures are sales of cloth coats and jackets with fur trims, and leather products such as belts and pocketbooks. These types of garments were never reflected in past sales figures. According to government figures, the fur market is moribund."

Standing behind the wooden horse, Eleanor was impressed by Honor's matriarchal persona. She was as elegant as Eleanor Roosevelt.

"The fur industry spends millions on advertisement to discount the effect of our consumer outreach campaigns," Honor said. "Still, they say fur sales reached $1.25 billion last year, 1996, which was up only 25 percent from its lowest year in sales in 1991. That's the year sales dropped to $987 million," she took a breath. "That was a 45 percent drop from the $1.8 billion in the fur industry's heyday in the late 1980s. You can see that $1.8 billion was a far cry from $1.25 billion, yet they want you to think fur sales are back," she said, concluding the interview.

"Too many numbers," Eleanor whispered to Freda at her right. "I warned her against spouting so many figures. They'll cut most of them."

Honor continued pitching to the reporter in an off-camera conversation. "There are only a quarter of the trappers there once were." She handed her a printout of the government statistics.

The anchorwoman slipped them in the pocket of her dark blue blazer. "Thanks. I don't understand how anyone can wear fur."

Eleanor spotted a slender young woman dressed in New York chic black and toting a stack of anti-fur posters. By the haggard look on her face and her hurried step, she had no doubt that it was Tina.

"RUFFFF screwed up," Honor told her. "I just did an interview. We'll be on ABC's noon news show!"

"Hurray for us!" Tina shouted. "I'm sure you were terrific!"

"Thanks," Honor said. Eleanor noticed sincere affection for Tina in Honor's tone. Tina walked to the end of the barricade to slip the flapping posters under the card table at the end. Honor followed; she had been seated there under the umbrella to avoid the scorching sun.

"What a coup," Tina said. "I'm surprised Leona slipped up on this one!" She gazed toward 35th Street, as if she expected they'd pull up on the side street rather than traffic-jammed 7th Avenue. "Maybe their plane was delayed!"

Eleanor stood by waiting for Honor and Tina to finish chatting before she tapped Tina on the right shoulder.

"Oh," Tina said, "we meet at last!"

Eleanor hugged her briefly. Tina had held a maddening schedule to accomplish all that was required of her to organize a demonstration in the city. She had arrived just three days previously, although the preliminary work had been done electronically from Boston. Her contacts were numerous, since she had grown up in the Bronx, but they were all working. Eleanor had managed to bring a carload of people for the occasion.

As they chatted easily with Honor, Eleanor noticed Tina becoming uncomfortable under Freda's gaze. Freda stood at Honor's left and facing Tina. Tina's hands shook from the lack of sleep and tension, and from the added knowledge that Freda was no doubt pumping suspicion into Honor's ear, accusing her of acts of subterfuge. RUFFFF's CD had been the best-guarded secret. The media had been alerted that arrests would take place, and that remained the extent of PAAC's information.

"Tina, are you sure nobody leaked anything about RUFFFF's plans?" Freda asked.

"Of course I don't know! You can bet my salary on that! If I knew the CD they planned to use or the theme of their campaign, I'd divulge that to Honor in the proverbial New York minute!"

Honor shot a disapproving side glance at Freda. "I know, I know, you would tell me," she uttered. Honor moved to stand next to her and stroked her gently on her left shoulder. Tina heaved a sigh of relief.

Eleanor surmised it was the TV interview that had defrosted Honor's heart. It was obvious that Tina wanted to escape when she volunteered to circle the block looking for signs of RUFFFF.

Eleanor resumed leafleting. She stood next to the blue-and-gold NYPD wooden horses and reached out to an approaching African-American male. "Sir, whatever you do, don't let them talk you into buying a fur coat!"

Her words stopped his racing steps. She felt the message slipping from her hand to his, and the feeling made her catch her breath.

"I can't afford a fur coat," he said. He gazed down at the flier and than back at her.

"Well, sir, the fur retailers are clever. The movement has stigmatized fur, so they've lowered the prices to market fur not only to the rich, but to regular consumers such as you and I. If you ever do think you can afford a fur coat, please don't buy one. It's a garment made from cruelty and arrogance."

The animals lived all their days in fear and loneliness, she explained. On their last day they finally were allowed out of their cages only to be anally electrocuted, or when bare hands snapped their necks. "So please, sir, don't ever buy a fur coat."

"I won't," he said. As he walked away he opened the flier and gazed at the color photographs of innocent faces staring at him: a baby seal, a mink, a lynx, a red fox, and a raccoon. He shouted, "I won't buy a fur coat, you can count on that!" He shook his head as if repelled by the thought.

She gazed up at a patch of heaven above the concrete canyon and asked God what she had done to be worthy of such privilege. She watched the gentleman fade into the sea of strangers, sweat running down her forehead unnoticed.

She was exhausted from three weeks of nonstop work, with weekends that began only after fifteen-hour Fridays. Then she had faced the brutish handler and the craggy faced trainer who glowered at her every step. Ambling around Manhattan in her exhaustion was sheer pleasure. Thank God the gig wasn't hers, she often thought, pitying poor Tina. As she leafleted, it was refreshing to welcome strangers. It was a liberating moment; she was free of the Westport office where Honor invaded every inch.

She saw Tina approach from 35th Street, finishing her search for signs of RUFFFF. "Tina! I had no idea you looked like Winona Ryder! I am accused of categorizing people's looks according to stars. But no kidding, you do! You look just like her!"

Before another word was spoken, they turned out of Honor's line of vision at the north end and walked to the far south end and across the barricade to avoid being observed. They faced 7th Avenue and talked into the three lanes of steadily honking and brake-hissing traffic. Standing at Eleanor's left, Tina smiled only briefly at her Winona Ryder comment.

"I'm so afraid of what RUFFFF will do! They'll be spectacular as usual! And I'll be the scapegoat!"

"Tina, they've got a few million dollars more a year to play with, and a dynamic management team! Leona Nesbitt has a genius for timing and publicity. Look, Honor already did one interview with ABC! At least we got that much! I'll make sure we cash in on RUFFFF's PR machine, Tina. You can count on that!"

"But, Tina, the big boys are not coming here for our little demonstration! Or to see our little video. I don't mean to insult you. The circling truck thing with the educational video is a benefit to the public, but it's unsexy, and our fox farm exposé is two years old."

"I was told my other ideas were too 'fucking' expensive," Tina said. "I hate her! Fuck her! How I hate her! RUFFFF's PR director, Struthers, does nothing but wine and dine celebrities. Why doesn't she hire a well-connected Struthers type if she wants celebrities and headlines?"

"You know she hates celebrities," Eleanor said. "She doesn't like catering to them, and they change with the fads! They're unreliable!"

"There are great stars who have supported the movement for years," Tina said. "She just turns people off! We have no damned friends anymore, thanks to her! That's why we stay small! Last week, at the eleventh hour, she tells me to find a celebrity! We have no connections! And little money! She waits until you need a miracle so you can fail her!"

"What? You mean like PAAC should have a plan? Like a five-year plan, or how about a one-year plan, or just any plan? Or actually have winnable campaigns, targets that you work year round on—stuff like that? It shouldn't be seasonal work? If it's fall it must be hunting, if it's winter it must be fur, if it's spring it must be spay/neuter and animal laboratories, and summer, well it should be circuses, but it isn't even that! Oh, come on!" Eleanor waved her arms to Tina's amusement. "You ask too much!"

"I'm getting burned out being the omega," Tina said. "I hate her! I shouldn't take her abuse!"

"Of course, you're the omega," Eleanor said. "You're doing a demo. Honor's success or failure is in your hands! Tina, you know better than I, she's plain scared!"

"She was calling me constantly, writing insulting memos telling me I'm not organized, I'm not this, I'm not that! I hate her for it! With all the work entailed, the PR, renting the monitor, finding the truck and a driver, getting the video programmed, finding the volunteers, she wanted me to list the assignments and times for each member of the staff here today, creating busywork for me—just to harass me!

"Just when you require her trust the most, she stabs you in the back. I'm no longer the director. Friday, she demoted me to the Boston outreach coordinator, and entry-level position! Again! I took Thursday off. That's what triggered it. I was sick from being humiliated daily by my boss. I keep asking, how much of this should I take?"

"I'm so sorry," Eleanor said.

Tina had been a well-respected editor of *Women's Day Daily* before her employment at PAAC. "I willingly accepted a reduction in salary to work for PAAC. And I still don't like raises. The money should go to the animals! But I never dreamed I'd have to eat dirt! Since Friday, Honor has refused to speak to me. I was forced to communicate through Freda! Still, who wants to work for a commercial firm? But how much more humiliation should I accept? Working here makes you sick."

Just two Mondays ago, Honor had sat in Eleanor's office on her corner chair complaining about Tina, who at the time was near exhaustion from trying to please her. "Actually, I'm bored," Honor said. "I feel like punishing someone! I'm going to send Tina another fax!" Try as Eleanor might to dissuade her as she trailed after her, Honor pounded her feet back to her office like a petulant queen thirsting for revenge.

"Tina, now Honor is my buddy. So hurray for me, I get to watch you being abused! It's another kind of hell. Believe me, I try to come to your defense! But she hates it when I do that. I wind up making it worse for you!"

"I hate her!" Tina said. "If there was another national to go to! But they're all abusive in their own unique way!"

"Not to worry!" Eleanor retorted. "I'm the official in-house whipping girl, remember? I'll be relieving you of your omega duties forthwith!"

Tina chuckled at the thought and even took some solace in Eleanor's words for a weary second, but caught herself. "I hate her!"

"Get a life!" shouted the driver of a florist truck stuck in the middle lane of traffic on the noisy, congested avenue.

"Get a heart!" Eleanor said.

"That's a great response!"

"Thanks! At every demonstration there's some meathead ready to shout that tired line!"

They chuckled. Then the howl of a wolf pierced the city's din. Eleanor's eyes darted toward Honor, who seemed to sink into her chair. She grabbed Tina's arm, hell-bent to rush to her.

CHAPTER 10

▼

HOME AT LAST

Eleanor never reached Honor. A dump truck pulled up the avenue, blasting the sound of wolf howls and carrying a cargo of standing people, their heads and shoulders clearing its sides. It stopped between the two barricades. While the driver jumped out and ran to the rear to lower a ramp, a fleet of the NYPD arrived in cruisers, motorcycles, and patrolmen, followed by swarming reporters and cameramen.

The superstar Paul Phillips, with his choirboy looks intact, was the first to descend the ramp, his guitar strapped about his chest. His band and his wife, Liddy, followed, and what appeared to be a chorus line of men and women that Eleanor surmised were RUFFFF employees, along with a couple of familiar New York soap stars. Leona Nesbitt and Donald Struthers, her PR director, were the last to hit the pavement.

The patrolmen formed a crescent-shaped line in front of the Studio's gate, while the police cruisers lined 7th Avenue and the motorcycles double-parked alongside them.

Tina began shrieking and jumping as she squeezed Eleanor's hand. "Oh! Oh! Paul Phillips! And Liddy! Oh! How I love her! Can you believe this? Of course! Phillips played Radio City Music Hall this weekend! You have to hand it to them! That Leona, how I love her! She knows how to work it! You have to hand it to her! Look at them! They look great," she said of the chorus line. "Ha, Ha!"

Eleanor watched starstruck as Paul Phillips, looking like an animal rights troubadour in a T-shirt and jeans, began to sing "Let 'Em In." He faced the line of cops. At his side were his wife with her tambourine, his drummer, guitarist, and sax player. Behind him swayed the chorus line of young men and women. The women wore fur coats smeared with fake blood, red bikinis, black fishnet stockings, and thigh-high, black boots. The male counterparts sprinkled among them were similarly clad and wearing sandals.

Eleanor noticed that Nesbitt, in the same costume, stood off to the far right side on the sidewalk, facing Phillips, like a director observing her actors. She was a petite woman with pleasant but ordinary features and plainly styled, light-brown hair. She was known to blend into the crowd. Of course, face recognition was not healthy at her level of activism.

In seconds, Phillips's familiar tune transformed pedestrians into smiling fans huddling in scant spaces along the sidewalk. Some filed into the designated protest area as if they'd been given front row seats to an off-Broadway musical. Other pedestrians pushed past, anxious to escape. In seconds, two Big Apple tour buses triple parked and towered over the motorcycles and cruisers. Tourists hung out the windows of the yellow-and-green double-deckers clicking away, while those on the top draped over the sides.

Some of the fashion show participants exited the building, no doubt for a glimpse of those who seemed determined to ruin them. They soon flooded the small twelve-foot-square garden area between the Studio's front door and the wrought iron fencing. Their angry fingers gripped the black shiny bars, and their enraged faces poked through and above the fencing.

When Phillips finished his song and turned toward the barricade, the media frenzy ensued. After five minutes of questions, the police captain, a dark-haired man of medium height, stepped out of the line of officers and addressed Phillips in a commanding tone.

"Sir, please have all your people move inside the wooden barrier. I warn you that once inside, if any of you walk outside the barricade, except to leave, you will be arrested. We'd like your cooperation to keep tempers cool," he said.

"Let's go, ladies and gents, let's be 'cool.'"

Phillips waved both arms good-naturedly as if he were leading a parade and marched his followers into the designated protest area.

The sixty-by-thirty-foot space that had previously held PAAC's few demonstrators shrank in minutes. A number of New Yorkers, including two smiling mothers pushing strollers, joined the entourage. The euphoric smiles of newcomers faded, however, with one glimpse of the posters of rows of skinned wolves hung by their skin on steel hooks, which had been handed to them by a RUFFFF representative.

Eleanor stood to Betty and Carla's left as they held PAAC's six-foot-long banner in front of the barricade. They moved back to make room for the superstar and his wife and band, but when the chorus line attempted to push them aside, Eleanor instructed them to resist.

"Fur on your back is blood on your hands! Fur on your back is blood on your hands!" the activists began to chant, spurred by the hateful faces behind the fence and the pathetic images on the posters.

"Compassion is the fashion! Don't wear fur! Compassion is the fashion! Don't wear fur! Compassion is the fashion! Don't wear fur!"

The simple words were easy to grasp, and the newly enlisted and the veterans boomed their message to the fur people. "Compassion is the fashion! Don't wear fur!"

Together they pandered to the greater stage, chanting to the TV cameras televising their anti-fur message to millions of viewers across the United States, Japan, Germany, England, France, and China.

Eleanor and Tina squeezed together in the center, baking under the overhead sun and swimming in the humidity. Inches in front of them stood fur-clad activists whose body heat burned like roaring furnaces and bounced off onto Eleanor and Tina.

Eleanor failed to notice. She was too busy joining her fellow activists as they were lifted to the outer limits of their devotion. All partisanship was evaporating between PAAC and RUFFFF's employees. They were one; united against the common enemy of greed and animal exploitation. As they chanted, they bounced their posters of various sizes and colors, some handheld, others on wooden posts. Some were wearing crisp white T-shirts, and others wore fur-clad bikinis. It didn't matter; they formed one compassionate chorus, entranced by the moment of camaraderie.

In that moment, Eleanor realized that she stood among her people, not competitors. She clutched Tina's thin, clammy hand to her left, her heart pounding with satisfaction as she realized that she stood in the center of the citadel of good, surrounded by people joined together attempting to do good, those she knew and those she didn't know. That was the beauty of it; they were a show of solidarity united by one commonality: universal good—not by family, friends, or country. And among them was a legendary singer, a shining star, a man who chose to use his fame and fortune for good!

Tina squeezed her hand in return as if she read her mind. "What you think is all true," she said with her eyes. "This moment is no aberration, this is purity of spirit! Celebrate it! Here on the streets of Manhattan, the most powerful city in the world, there is proof that some humans understand! And we are part of it!"

"Compassion is the fashion! Don't wear fur!" the chanting continued. "Compassion is the fashion! Don't wear fur! Compassion is the fashion! Don't wear fur!"

Eleanor soon became fixated on the matted fur coats staring at her. The stringy gray and white hairs formed rows of small triangles, their points sticking together from accumulated filth. These furs foretold the future of the furs adorning the models inside the Studio. They evoked the infinite number of innocent lives taken for vanity. Trying to shake off the depressing thought, Eleanor stretched her neck for a glimpse of the inspiring Phillips a few rows ahead of her. At that point, she saw several of RUFFFF's staffers spraying fake blood on the sidewalk and wooden horses, and others pushing Carla and Betty.

She left Tina's side to plow through the rocking crowd to reach Coretta, who stood in front of the card table. "Come with me!" Eleanor said. Holding Coretta's hand, she plowed her way back to the two women.

Carla and Betty stood behind Phillips and Struthers with their arms outstretched to hold the banner above their heads. Besides their aching arms, they were losing patience with RUFFFF's pushy protesters.

Eleanor slipped the pole of the banner from the less aggressive Carla's hand into Coretta's. "Carla, I need you to guard Honor," she said. "You make sure Honor is OK!"

"Me?" said Carla. "I've never even spoken to her! She hates me!" Tears sprang to her eyes.

"Now she'll love you!" Eleanor said. "Keep RUFFFF's sweaty people away from her highness! She's over there calling them 'sweaty RUFFFFians!' and 'RUFFFFage!'"

Eleanor turned her attention to Coretta and Betty. "You remember, we were here first! Hold our banner behind the person on camera! PAAC's banner has to be the backdrop. Tonight and tomorrow when people watch CNN, we want our banner in their faces. Phillips will look like he's with us! Honor will love you for it!"

A new round of chants began. "Forty dead animals for one fur coat! Forty dead animals for one fur coat!" Eleanor began to mingle among the groups of reporters and cameramen outside the barricade. While she distributed her press release, she led them to believe the protest was a joint venture between RUFFFF and PAAC. "And lucky for you, PAAC's president is available for questioning!"

In the middle of her pitch, she saw Struthers bogarting Coretta and Betty. At the first opportunity she rushed back to the table for Lisa and Mary, bringing them to the front lines to help Coretta and Betty.

"Let them stand in front of you. It's OK," she said. "They only have handheld signs! You keep your arms up; the cameras will eat up our banner!"

Lisa and Mary began to brace Coretta and Betty's exhausted elbows, all four finding it a challenge to maintain their position in the shrinking area. Eleanor shouted as she walked away, "Hold on! Don't you worry about Struthers coming back! In a second he'll be too busy posing for the cameras! I promise!"

Eleanor fetched Honor to escort her to the primed reporters. Of course, CNN was first. The thin blonde woman was duly impressed with Honor's command of the subject. Other reporters followed CNN's lead, and lined up for an interview.

The reporters were keeping busy while waiting for the arrests, Eleanor realized. As the protest area bulged to an alarming degree, the police captain issued a new warning, reminding people that arrests would take place if anybody moved from the barricade. The police seemed to be waiting and watching. A wayward hand or foot slipping outside the barricade was all it would take.

Meanwhile, with one eye on the police and PAAC's banner, and with interviews lined up for Honor, Eleanor resumed her leafleting. "Don't ever buy a fur coat, miss," she said to a beautiful Asian woman. "It'll make even you look ugly!"

"You mean, *please* don't ever buy a fur coat, miss. Don't you?" Eleanor turned, annoyed by the correction. But staring at her was a young RUFFFF employee with the most honest, devilish eyes she had ever seen. His bare chest was exposed under the open lynx coat. "Aidan Quinn," she thought. Even his husky voice resembled the actor's. His sleepy turquoise eyes were under feathery arched eyebrows.

"I'm Hank Cagney," he said, holding out his hand.

"Eleanor Aquitaine Greene," she said. She managed to gracefully switch her fliers to her left hand for a handshake. "I said 'please' all day, I just forgot this once," she said. "Any relationship to James? You know he lived right here in New York, in Gramercy Park."

"No, I didn't know that."

It was obvious that Cagney was captivated by her, but more importantly, she was attracted to him!

"Eleanor, if I may call you Eleanor…let me tell you confidentially, the CD will go down in one minute."

"Well, what is the CD?" she asked. "What's the big secret?"

He hesitated as if stunned by his own actions. Just as he caught his breath enough to speak, six RUFFFF staff members, three men and women, stepped out of the barricade to stand in front of Phillips. They dropped their fur coats to expose nearly nude bodies. The young nymphlike women wore thick garlands of yellow daisies to cover their breasts and black bikini bottoms.

"RUFFFF in the BUFF! It's the RUFFFF Collection!" A RUFFFF employee with a bullhorn stood behind the wooden horses narrating. As she spoke, the six activists mocked modeling poses. The police converged. The six dropped to the hot concrete and concealed their hands, engaging a cadre of officers who struggled to handcuff them.

Leona Nesbitt, two men, and three women slipped under the barricade on the 7th Avenue side and ran to the Studio's entrance. The few officers left guarding the gate were staring at the nude women, allowing Nesbitt's crew to sit before the gate in a lockdown. Their arms, hidden by the fur coats, were encased in double-reinforced steel pipes.

Eleanor watched it all go down: once the locks between the pipes were secured and the activists locked down, the area was officially a crime scene and the Studio would have to shut down all intercourse coming or going. The objective was to hurt sales and give furriers, models, designers, ranchers, and buyers a taste of being trapped for a couple of hours. She gazed at the fur people behind the gate.

When the diversionary tactic took place, Hank leaped over the wooden horses and raced to Nesbitt's side. Obviously he was her caretaker. Nesbitt leaned her back against Hank's, preparing for the long haul. Hank turned to glance at Eleanor, who plowed through the throng to the front, wanting to make eye contact with him. He could be sent to the Tombs, she thought. In seconds Tina was standing to her left, looking a sickly green. Eleanor slipped her arm around her for a quick hug.

"We all belong to the same cause," Eleanor said.

The cops had surrounded the lockdown and were stringing crime scene tape, but Eleanor was watching Leona being interviewed by a CBS reporter as she squatted on the hot sidewalk. The reporter was stretching her arm to reach Leona with her microphone.

"It's ninety-eight degrees and the humidity is the same. Your face is beet red; don't you think it's pushing it being in fur coats?"

"Just think of what the animals go through," Leona said. "We can take this for a few minutes. Think of the minks, beavers, foxes, and wolves trapped…alone…in the dark, exposed to all predators and weather, without food or water, not knowing what will happen to them. Not knowing if they'll ever be free again to return to their families. Many of them are caught while searching for food for their young. Their babies left behind starve; they freeze and starve to death waiting for their mothers to return. Please televise the discarded coats we're wearing. The lives of those whose skin we wear were taken, and now their magnificent coats are nothing more than rubbish."

Hank reached around and with a white tissue wiped the sweat that poured down the sides of Nesbitt's brow.

"Some say your views are extreme, radical. Do you have an answer to that charge?"

"Our beliefs are far from radical," Leona said. "It's reasonable to be compassionate to others with whom we share the planet. It's reasonable to respect other life forms such as fur-bearing animals. Don't you think they have every right to their own skin? We don't need fur, to exist. After all, they live in the wild. One day our beliefs will prevail. We're attempting to accelerate the evolutionary process." She smiled charmingly at the reporter.

"She is a hero!" Eleanor said. "Certified right there!" She shook her head in awe of the inspiring leader, proud to be associated with the ethics and courage she represented.

"She's forty-six!" Tina said. "This is an action is for a much younger person. She's risking heatstroke in this weather!"

"I wish she'd die!" Honor said.

She had plowed through the crowd with Carla trailing after her like a trained puppy. She stood between Tina and Eleanor. Her voice was so bitter that Eleanor shuddered as she turned to gaze up at her. With a roll of the eyes, Tina registered her disapproval to Eleanor but said nothing. At that moment a Connecticut college student, an activist who had ridden in with Eleanor, approached her from the back and whispered in her right ear so Honor couldn't hear. "I'm handing out RUFFFF fliers. We've run out of PAAC's."

"Go for it, we're all brothers and sisters of the movement."

Among the circle of locked-down activists, Eleanor noticed an apprehensive young woman with light blonde hair. She was positioned directly opposite Leona. Leona's back was to the Studio's gate. The young girl wore a beat-up beaver coat which dwarfed her petite body. Underneath the coat she wore a red bikini, stockings, and boots. Her eyes were tightly shut as if she dreaded the inevitable.

A policeman dressed in yellow protective gear approached the ring of activists, carting a huge unwieldy saw and a fireproof blanket. A thick, long orange wire trailed behind him, which was connected to a generator in a silver truck double-parked alongside the motorcycles and cruisers. Without ceremony, he threw the silver fireproof blanket over the young girl and the others at her sides, allowing her left arm to be exposed.

The crowd was hushed by the actions. The officer donned a protective mask and gloves, and like a mechanic about to work on an automobile, he squatted down, braced his arm on his bent knees, and struggled to control the heavy electric saw before it was turned on. He held it a few inches above the girl's left arm covered by the pipe. Then he turned it on, and lowered it to make contact with the pipe.

The angry men and women who peered from behind the wrought iron bars were also spellbound. An officer shouted at them to stand back. When the saw made contact with the metal pipe, it shot sizzling red sparks several feet above the ground and backward in the direction of the fence.

"Ohoooo!" swooned the entire New York audience. Those behind the fence bolted backwards.

Eleanor knew that the girl had been warned of the danger in CD training sessions, but sitting under the blanket was another story. It must be dark, she thought, and the heat of the saw must grow in intensity as it runs. Then there was the smell of burning metal. It was no exaggeration to worry about one slip of the heavy blade. It could result in cuts, burns, or even worse, the girl could lose a finger, a hand, or even a limb.

The young girl began to screech hysterically. Her high-pitched cries stood out above the city's din. The screams of the innocent young girl seemed to echo the screams of those killed for their fur. Eleanor fought her instinct to run to the girl's aid, and even to take her place if she allowed.

"What stupidity!" Honor said. "What did she expect, a bloody tea party?"

To comfort the girl, Paul and Liddy Phillips began to sing, "We Shall Overcome." The band joined in and the crowd sang along. In seconds, the girl's nerves were soothed.

Eleanor handed Tina her pamphlets and sign and slid between the horses on to the sidewalk, walking toward the Studio's gate to pose as a pedestrian longing to get an objective view of the scene.

The numbers of those behind the fence swelled as the fashion show ended. Eleanor noticed a handsome middle-aged man outside the gate and standing alongside the crime scene tape that roped off the whole area of the lockdown.

"Arrest every damned one of them in or out of the barricade!" he shouted. He was addressing a couple of patrolmen standing a few feet to the left of him. He had thick black eyebrows and graying sideburns, and despite the insufferable heat he was dressed in a suit, shirt, and tie and a fedora. "Put all the freaks in jail! Pick up the freaks! Don't saw them apart! Drag them away from the gate!"

"Who are you?" Eleanor asked. "Or I should say why are you here?"

"I'm a fur farmer," he said.

It startled her to think that she was standing next to a person who actually strangled minks with his bare hands.

"These women are Joan of Arcs!" Eleanor said. "All of them! And the men are like Gandhi and Dr. Martin Luther King! You should be put in jail for killing animals, wild creatures, just to make a fur coat! How many minks? Sixty? Sixty of those poor helpless creatures? Little children of the earth! To make one coat? Shame on you! Fifteen lynx for one coat! How despicable you are! All you care about is money!"

He bounced sideways away from her looking askance at her, as if each of her words were stones that had struck their mark. He stared back, horrified by her accusations. His eyes and mouth perfect circles of shock and disbelief. He screamed and waved his arms in the air, bolting toward her, towering over her.

"What kind of shoes are you wearing?" He pointed down at her Saucony shoes, his eyes bulging, his face contorted in fury.

"The material is man-made, sir."

"I use everything natural," he shouted. "I bet you don't have any animals. I have many. Do you? Do you have any? Do you?" The man looked feverish, beside himself, even deranged.

"You kill mink with your bare hands, sir! You electrocute foxes and lynxes, holding them while they squirm in fear and pain until the life is burned out of them. You raise pathetic animals in small cages, who suffer and run in circles endlessly because their instincts are denied them! You place their cages in their natural habitat! They can smell the scents that drove their ancestors to run; they can see their natural paths around them, but it's all on the other side of a wire fence! They go mad in front of your eyes and you dye their coats blue. You hold them in your arms and kill them. No wonder your hands are so strong; they killed defenseless creatures for money. How do you live with yourself, sir? Money! It's all you are about."

A strawberry blond patrolman with a handlebar mustache rushed over and stood between the two of them and issued orders to Eleanor. "Get behind the barricade!"

"Send him behind a barricade!" she said. "He should be behind bars for murdering defenseless creatures for profit! Make cloth coats! That's a decent business! How do you look at yourself in the mirror?"

With those words, Eleanor slipped between two wooden horses escorted by the police officer, with Honor standing nearby having heard every word. But Eleanor never acknowledged Honor. She was pondering the reality of her situation. For the first time she understood that the Tigers Club officials, the circus people, the fur farmer, all those who were victimizing animals viewed themselves as victims of the animal rights movement and despised "activists" such as herself. She gazed around her at the New Yorkers fresh off the street who had joined them, and she recalled those families that had left the circus grounds to go home. "They get it!" she assured herself, gazing at the mothers and the children in strollers. "They get it! I bet if they saw a slaughterhouse, none of these people would ever eat meat again!"

Paul's plaintive singing stirred her to the present moment. She glanced to her left over the crowd to see the back of his dark head. He was accompanied not only by his band, but also by the constant roar of the chainsaw.

He sang the song, "All You Need Is Love."

Eleanor heaved a sigh, swallowed, and fought back the tears.

A cheer rose from the crowd as the young woman was retrieved from the pipes and refused to be arrested. Two policemen dragged her to the paddy wagon. As they sawed the others out of their pipes and dragged them off, Eleanor envied each one. Even if the Tombs was their final destination, such deprivation would only serve to fortify their resolve.

Honor, Freda, and Delores left at 4 PM, hurrying to board the air-conditioned bus that was waiting for them at the corner of 35th Street. Honor was "totally bored of the tiresome ordeal of cutting the activists from the pipes" and wanted to avoid the commuter traffic. An hour and half later, in Westport, Eleanor watched Honor disembark from the bus while also thinking that Leona Nesbitt was in a steamy paddy wagon, handcuffed and huddled with ten others, still in their fur coats, headed for the Tombs, and loving it.

Twenty minutes later, however, she was grateful to arrive in Derbe. It was refreshing to drive into her short driveway and view the little colonial with the gingerbread porch and its virgin woods.

As she turned off the motor, a strange feeling took hold of her. Everything was familiar and yet everything had changed. She stepped out of the car. The air had never felt so cool and refreshing. "I feel like I've been gone." She wasn't referring to her day trip into the city. "I have been gone," she thought. Hank Cagney did not come to mind, but the encounter had been nothing less than cataclysmic.

She held the front door's brass doorknob in her hand as she placed the house key into the lock and turned it, still preoccupied. When she stepped into the living room and bent down to greet her circling felines, it was as if she hadn't seen them for years. She cooed words of love to the two and petted their silky coats, which seemed silkier than she remembered. She promised to play and feed them in a second, and then headed for the phone as if she'd burst if she didn't share the news.

The room glowed with love. Her grandmother's cherry wood dining table in the rays of the setting sun beamed with new luster. She scanned her home, its ambiance, its occupants. It was as though she viewed the whole of her life for the first time, and it was good. It was uniquely her own, and she was satisfied to claim it.

She reached for the phone on the lamp table and began dialing. "Mom, I'm back!" She could hear her mother's startled breathing. It took a second for her to speak.

"It's been a long time, Eleanor, more than nine years since I heard that kind of music in your voice." She sighed with relief, and than laughed. "Welcome 'back,' darling!"

CHAPTER 11

▼

HONOR'S NIGHTMARES

A night rain broke the heat wave. In the morning, as Eleanor drove along the shoreline, the fresh rainwater added a mesmerizing sparkle. She heaved a sigh of relief gazing at it; perhaps the conference call wouldn't be that bad. Maybe Honor would be in a benevolent mood and she could avoid getting fired for coming to Tina's defense.

Two hours later, when she entered Honor's office, Honor was sitting ramrod straight behind her desk, once again the calm and collected CEO. Her red silk scarf had gold crescent moons and indigo stars. The vertical blinds allowed a soft yellow brilliance to filter in, and three chairs waited in front of her desk.

All the signs were good.

Delores sat in the chair farthest from the door. She smiled a "hello" and sat down in the middle chair, leaving the other for Freda, who was arranging the conference call. Seconds later, Freda charged in.

"Struthers must be turning over in his cubicle this morning," Honor began. She spoke into her phone set in the middle of her desk. "Compatriots, I'm impressed with you! I really am! We capitalized on Leona's ridiculous theatrics! I wouldn't trade in any of you for any of her managers! Eleanor's aggressiveness with reporters and the placement of the banner...." Honor said, and stopped. She shook her head as if words failed her. "And we distributed 5,000 anti-fur fliers in the process! I'm also proud of Eleanor's argument with the fur rancher and her bantering with the public."

"We all know that they're headline grabbers!" Eleanor said of RUFFFF. "And we can't afford their PR machine! So we used their PR machine for our own purposes! And guess what? ABC's five o'clock news show had 'technical problems!' So the station reran Honor's noon interview! We cornered all the coverage on ABC!"

"Yeah!" rang a chorus of ecstatic-sounding cheers from the speakerphone.

"During the CNN interview Struthers looked like he belonged to us, didn't he?" Honor asked. "Not that I'd have the peacock! He supplied CNN with a fur-trapping video and did the voice-over…that segment could have been ours. That was a good piece of advertisement for RUFFFF. But it's OK. We'll remember next time."

"Who knew the networks would run trapping footage!" Tina said. "They've always said it was too gruesome! Actually, this is progress! From now on, we'll note that videos are available on our press releases. That's all! I bet that was the same trapping video they used to convert Hugo!"

Honor bolted upright in her executive chair as if she'd been attacked. "Our damned activists handed out RUFFFF's fliers!" she said. "If they don't know whose bloody camp they're in, we sure as hell don't want them!"

Eleanor sat petrified in her seat. She had seen it coming. She steadied herself for the next torpedo.

"Our people were physically moved by RUFFFF's thugs," Honor said. "This was totally out of line! Some of our volunteers and staff were even sprayed with fake blood! Next time I want bouncers with us. Remember that! Write that down!" she told Freda. "I'll pay to keep their sweaty muscle off us! I won't be treated with such disrespect!

"Our activists have to wake up!" Honor continued. "Penny refused to represent us! She was interviewed by the *New York Times* reporter as she stepped off our bloody rented truck! Stupid cow didn't give our name! I hate volunteers!"

She continued in a calmer voice. "She was dressed in our T-shirt, riding in our rented truck. Doesn't this constitute a PAAC action? Does the woman understand that it took time and money to produce our demonstration? Did she think she was representing both RUFFFF and us? Is that what this is about? Don't that idiot and her sister know that it's only good business to get credit for our actions? This is a business! A not-for-profit animal protection business! Our customers are our donors! They expect results!"

Under the piercing eyes and indicting words, Eleanor's stomach shriveled to a raisin. What made it worse was that Honor's expectations were reasonable. Penny was acting as PAAC's volunteer, at Eleanor's request, and should have identified herself as such to reporters. But newspapers are notorious for cutting quotes. Honor was aware of this.

"What good are these volunteers anyway, if they don't give our name to reporters?" Freda asked. She shrugged her thick shoulders. "They should have stayed home! Somebody else would've done it and given us the credit!"

"Right," Pamela added.

"What fools," Honor said. "She and her dumb sister volunteer to ride around the city in the back of a truck during a heat wave! How dumb are they? I hate them! I hate volunteers!"

Eleanor sat back in her chair disgusted. Jane was a lawyer, and Penny was a physical therapist. Both had rearranged their busy schedules to accommodate PAAC, responding to Eleanor's call. She inhaled a few deep breaths to steady her nerves, and reminded herself not to defend them.

"Honor, you have to know that Wally, Struthers, and Hugo are gay!" Larry said.

"Really?"

"Sure. That's how Struthers got into Hugo's studio in the first place! You didn't know? They travel in the same circles! Didn't you think it was strange that Hugo, a world-famous designer, didn't file any charges after being kidnapped in his own offices and held hostage and forced to watch the trapping videos? Even if he was converted? And there was also some damage done to his office!" he added. "Come on!"

"I hate the criminals," Honor said. With hands clasped on her desk, and still staring at Eleanor, she said, "The national organizations spent twenty fruitless years campaigning against the leghold trap. We campaigned in Connecticut a couple of times. In the last attempt we lost the vote by one point. We also attempted to reach trappers and farmers at state hearings. Ten years ago, we finally targeted consumers. They made the difference," she concluded. "They deserve the credit.

"They want to see us out there. Our contributions rise in the next mass mailing after we've been on TV or in the newspapers. And our membership rolls get a nice little bump. It's not magic. It's advertising. It's not cold business that drives us, either. How many times are we the sole voice raised for the animals at small public hearing rooms far from national coverage? When we have worldwide media focusing their cameras on us, we damned well better dance. PAAC and

RUFFFF and every other national organization compete for the same demographic: the 400,000 to 500,000 animal advocates. Eleanor, I think, understands this better than anyone that's held her position thus far."

Eleanor heaved a sigh of relief. At least she wasn't an outcast because of the actions of her volunteers.

"No more Penny and Jane!" Honor said. She slammed her fist on her desk, as if she were literally breaking a bad habit. "From now on, Penny and Jane are prohibited from entering PAAC's offices. Write a memo to that effect for the office staff," she told Freda. "They're composing their own animal rights ads now? Walter Sharp, that idiot, is teaching people 'how to!' So they placed an ad in the local paper and were so thrilled with the response that they're writing another! Next thing we know, the bloody fools will be tax deductible! All we need is another unprofessional group! How do we know that they aren't nipping our members' names, addresses, and telephone numbers when they come in here to volunteer! I hate volunteers!"

Eleanor remained stiff, prepared for more as Honor glared across at her.

"RUFFFF's on the downslide," Honor said. Her eyes were still locked on Eleanor. "RUFFFF's emphasis is on youth, sex, trends, and sensationalism…but their hype is petering out. They have to keep raising the bar. Each action must be more bizarre than the last. There is a backlash within the movement."

Her eyes turned toward the speakerphone as if she were now directing her remarks to Helen. "Even Leona's fans question the wisdom of these sensational campaigns! Are they advancing the movement with campaigns featuring weirdos like heavy metal rock stars and transvestites, using women as sex symbols, and throwing parties on Hollywood lots and hobnobbing with models and politicians?"

She paused for a moment and gazed at the small manila lined pad sitting in front of her. "Last year supermodel Tabitha Coleman promised never to model fur again, right? Her bare ass was pasted on billboards from Times Square to Rodeo Drive. Now guess what the skinny cow will be doing this November?"

"No!" said a chorus of squeaky, shocked voices.

"Yep! This time from Times Square to Rodeo Drive she'll wear a full-length lynx coat and say, 'Fur Is Back and So Am I!' Compliments of the Fur Council!"

"No," rang another chorus.

"And you ask me why I hate celebrities?" Honor said. "You cater to them, supply limos, hotel rooms, and costly, upscale munchies, then a new fad blows into town and they make a damned fool of you! I hate them! I hate Leona!"

Eleanor squirmed in her chair at Honor's expressions of hatred. Why does Honor hate her own kind, she wondered. Why did she hate at all? Of course, no one could deny that Leona was the unofficial "spokesperson" of the movement, the go-to woman for the media. That undeniable fact seemed to be at the very heart of Honor's jealousy. But why hate Leona for it? Wasn't she helping the animals?

Helen ventured, "We're all guilty of pulling outlandish stunts to attract reporters. Public service announcements cost $35,000 to produce, and then they're played at the odd hours donated by the networks. TV networks can't risk losing meat, dairy, and fur advertisers on account of our very few advertisements. Newspapers and TV throw up roadblocks by asking us of for proof of our statements. I don't think they do that to the pharmaceutical companies.

"I remember a woman who took Premarin calling me saying that every time she sweated, she smelt like horse urine. She was grateful to learn from our magazine article that she wasn't imagining it. She was also appalled to learn that Premarin was derived from the urine of pregnant mares, and that the horses were tethered for months during their pregnancies for urine collections and their foals were killed for horsemeat. Yet we couldn't get ads in women's or physicians' magazines."

Honor didn't respond.

Tina said, "Our PAAC signs are clear in the *New York Times* photograph where the cops are dragging Leona into the paddy wagon. And Honor, your quote was great! Your fur stats were so encouraging!"

"Thanks," Honor said.

With that comment, Honor closed the meeting with a smile of satisfaction. Eleanor, on the other hand, wondered why she worked for such a hateful woman. She gravitated to her office dazed and befuddled, like someone who found herself washed up on some strange shore, staggering around and wondering how she got there. That evening she took a four-mile run on the back road in the light of the moon, gazing up at the bushes and trees silhouetted against the sky while she attempted to dismiss or discount in some way, any way, Honor's vilification of Leona, Jane, and Penny. Even with the help of every soft step on the macadam, every caressing summer breeze, every frog that croaked, every rustling leaf caused by scurrying wildlife, she could find no justification to ease her own guilt for having brought volunteers to work for the malicious Honor. She returned home believing that the only honorable act open to her was to quit.

When she reentered her home, she turned the TV on and CNN was reporting on the Paula Jones case. She had no interest in it. She reached for the cordless phone on the lamp table, knowing it was probably fruitless to call Helen, but there was nowhere else to turn. To her surprise, Helen answered.

"My job is to get new members. How can I do that in good conscience?" Eleanor asked her. "I can't be a party to the abusing and disrespecting of good people like Jane and Penny. It's unethical. Helen, what is going on? Honor hates everyone! That's what it seems like. This so-called animal protection organization is led by a woman who hates most humans? Don't you think that's ironic? Helen, I don't think I can work for this 'charity' any more!"

"Frankly, I think she's burned out. It's been forty years!" Helen said. "I hesitate to talk about her because she's also a good friend. She hates Leona for 1982 and 1985, Eleanor, for the defeat of her legislation. Tens of thousands of animals could have been saved from laboratory experiments if the movement leaders had backed her bill—that's her belief. She blames herself for failing to lead at this crucial time."

Eleanor went to the kitchen and made a cup of tea, and returned to her couch while clinging to Helen's every word. Helen explained that Honor's focus was always legislation. In the 1950s, during her first year in business, she had argued at the Capitol against the Humane Slaughter Act, contending that mass slaughter would always be cruel and the government should promote vegetarianism. Those in the movement who worked to promote the bill relegated her to the "radical fringe."

During the 1960s she, Alison, and Gertrude Sandler had argued against the Laboratory Animal Welfare Act. Again it was impossible to take the cruelty out of the lab, she contended. Worse, the humane law would advance animal cruelty because the public would be led to believe that, because of the law, the animals had to be treated kindly in laboratories. She urged legislators to demand research for alternatives to animal testing.

In both instances, humane groups developed and promoted the "humane" bills, and Honor labeled the movement leaders "inhumane." But the animal welfare community believed that humane legislation was better than none. And if animals were humanely killed, it was acceptable to eat them. Honor called them all "cannibals."

By 1975 the movement seemed just about dead, as dead as it is now, Helen continued. The core issues such as spay-neuter, fur, hunting, and circuses with animal acts seemed like tired messages. The membership was aging along with the national companies. "But that year the movement began to change."

The Animal Liberation Front, ALF, based in England, rescued laboratory animals and destroyed equipment used in animal experimentation. They were rescuing tortured animals in experiments that were against the laws of nature. But breaking society's laws was totally out of character for Honor and her membership. The groups of Honor's generation thought it necessary to obey the law in order to gain acceptance and credibility with the general public. But that year U.S. environmental groups began to use direct action which took place close to the scene of abuse, such as sitting on top of ancient redwoods. Some animal activists began to adopt these practices.

The media that had been preoccupied by the Vietnam War began to pay attention as the war wound down, Helen continued. Exposés on factory farming were finally finding their way into major newspapers. All of a sudden, editorials debating the morality of speciesism and linking animal rights with other social causes, such as feminism and racism, were published. It was in 1975, when an Australian named Peter Singer wrote *Animal Liberation*, that the movement matured. He labeled society's use of animals as "tyranny." He espoused "utilitarianism." He said that animal experimentation must only be allowed when "the benefit to humans (or to humans and animals) clearly outweighs the pain and suffering experienced by the experimental animals." Singer's book featured graphic photographs of animals suffering on factory farms and laboratories. "People were shocked by them; nobody had seen such pictures before."

A group of a physicians formed TTPFEM, Three Thousand Physicians For Ethical Medicine, which espoused compassionate medicine and denounced animal experimentation as useless, expensive, and the cause of great suffering. Veterinarians formed their own group, Veterinarians For Responsible Medicine, VFRM, and they condemned animal experimentation and the accepted practice of training veterinarians and students with live animals. Psychologists dedicated to responsible medicine created Psychologists For Animal Welfare, PFAW, and condemned psychological testing on animals, calling it cruel and a waste of taxpayer funds. Lawyers formed the Legal Defense For Animals, LDFA, which offered legal advice and charted a new course through the courts for justice for animals. High school students got into the picture by refusing to dissect frogs, with the help of the movement.

Tom Regan, an American philosopher, developed a series of articles forming *The Case of Animal Rights*. "His words crystallized the movement for many, including me," Helen said. "'The harm done to animals in pursuit of scientific purposes is wrong. The benefits derived are real enough, but some gains are ill-gotten. All gains are ill-gotten when secured unjustly.' I'll never forget those words because they represented my beliefs.

"At that time, I was very impressed with the morality established by Singer and Regan. We were no longer women in sneakers rescuing dogs and cats. Philosophers like Singer and Regan and respected professionals like physicians and veterinarians and lawyers were validating us. They raised the level of the animal rights movement to a legitimate social cause."

Schoolchildren boycotted major tuna companies, which were brought to their knees and promised to end the use of drift nets that caught dolphins, considered to be one of the most intelligent animal species on the planet. Helen explained that Honor, Alison Barrington of People for Animals, and Rutherford Gee of the Animal Trust had led the campaign. With the help of Rutherford, an environmental group called Blue Spirit launched its first ship to fight pirate whaling ships that invaded breeding grounds considered off-limits by the international community.

"Health gurus promised that vegetarianism was the fountain of youth," Helen said. "Albert Einstein had recommended vegetarianism as the one single lifestyle habit that could do more to save the planet than any other. People dragged up famous quotes from other vegetarians of the past and present, including Gandhi, George Bernard Shaw, Tolstoy, and others.

"It was a movement growing in stature daily, but Honor went ballistic when the ALF received praise in 1977. That's when its American chapter broke into a Hawaiian research lab to rescue two dolphins swimming in a two-by-four tank. It was all over the papers and TV. She announced that PAAC would never stoop to break the law; doing so took the issue off the animals and focused on the 'rebels.' She and others still hold to that belief.

"It was in 1979 when Honor began to doubt herself. Stray cats, we found out, were being used by the Museum of Natural History in sex augmentation experiments in their laboratory. Honor had been in the movement for twenty years by then. But it was Walter Sharp, a New York City social worker, who exposed the museum. Yet Honor had the same information, with photographs sitting on her press release the following day. Sharp's exposé made the front page of the *New York Times*. And network news shows carried the sensational story about poor city cats being mutilated by the respected Metropolitan Museum of Natural History. The museum was removing and adding sex organs. And the NIH, the National Institutes of Health, our very own government, was using taxpayers' money to do it. The exposé placed Sharp at the epicenter of the emerging protest movement and right where Honor wanted to be."

"Oh, now I get it," Eleanor said. "That's the same Sharp she was talking about today? The one who showed Penny and Jane how to write ads? No wonder!"

"The very same! Sharp led a boycott. He also organized a parade in Manhattan of museum members and others. The museum's benefactors threatened to pull their support, and the mayor and 120 members of Congress voted to investigate the issue. As a result, the National Institutes of Health cut off its funding and the museum's laboratory doors closed forever. Of course, Honor joined the protests, but the issue and the exposé went down in modern animal rights history as belonging to Sharp.

"Eleanor, can you imagine how this successful boycott inspired us? I was working in California at the time with the Animal Rights Coalition of California, ARCC. We were jumping and screaming when we heard. Boycotts were our new weapon. They had worked with the tuna companies, and now with the museum. There was a sense of new beginnings. For Honor, however, it was misery. She missed out on making animal rights history by a day. I, frankly, don't think it was in her nature. And then Sharp beat her again by just one day. This time it was Trite Cosmetics headquartered in New York City, which used rabbits to test for a new shade of mascara. Sharp faxed his press release one day sooner.

"And again ordinary consumers, women not involved with animal rights, materialized on New York City streets led by Sharp. So consumers were again transformed into protesters demanding an end to the experiments and boycotting Trite's products."

"Rabbits were locked in stocks with their pink eyes oozing and blinded by cosmetic tests. There were descriptions of screams of pain when the chemicals were applied. The rabbits proved to be perfect test subjects because they had no tear ducts, so it was impossible for their eyes to wash themselves clean when smeared with eye makeup." "The tests continue today," Helen added. "Rabbits are used to test shampoos, skin creams, hair spray, and mascara. They suffer from corneal ulcers, hemorrhaging, and blindness. Chunks of lipstick are placed under their eyelids.

"Then Trite agreed to reduce the numbers of animals used in experiments and to search for alternatives—a success again attributed to boycotting. Can you imagine Honor's envy? Since the beginning of the Laboratory Animal Welfare Act in 1966, she's been promoting the issue of alternatives to animal testing, and here's this relative newcomer, Sharp, a social worker, succeeding where she failed. And he didn't break any laws to achieve his goals, or fight the powers in Washington to change federal laws. He found a way to circumvent our political system.

"This was the beginning of the protest movement, and Sharp was its leader. Honor seemed stuck in the days of polite demonstrations. She hates Sharp for it! Then Leona and Tony's exposés created what historians labeled the cornerstones of the animal rights movement. Honor hates Sharp, but not like she hates Leona. She views her as her archenemy. Leona is a good friend of mine."

"She is?"

"Yep."

"But how do you keep from defending her to Honor?"

"It's just good politics. Besides, it's like throwing fuel on the fire to defend Leona. Eleanor, you should read *The Animal Rights Crusade*. It gives the basics, and *Monkey Business*, and Gary Francione's *Rain without Thunder*."

Leona Nesbitt and Tony Pesco had been lovers, Helen revealed, when they incorporated RUFFFF and placed a homemade sign in their apartment window. The apartment was a short distance from a Dr. Herbert Schmidt and the seventeen monkeys he experimented on, the experiments financed by the NIH.

Tony applied for a job and was hired by Schmidt, and was even given a key to the premises. The monkeys had lived in the Philippine jungle before they had the unfortunate luck to be caught and sent to Schmidt. For years, they lived in his roach-infested basement isolated in small filthy cages. Tony said that the monkeys cried like babies abandoned by their mothers. He became their surrogate parent in Schmidt's absence. The cages were caked with feces, and the monkeys' food was laced with it. Tony talked about the barrels of dead monkeys Schmidt had killed with his experiments who were floating in formaldehyde. He could never forget the stench.

"Schmidt was a 'physiological psychiatrist,' not a veterinarian, and not a medical doctor or a surgeon, yet he operated on the macaque monkeys and paralyzed some of the limbs of twelve of them," Helen said. "He then starved them to force them to use their paralyzed limbs.

"Tony took photographs of the tortured monkeys. One became RUFFFF's signature poster. You probably saw the poster of the crippled, screaming monkey who's in a restraining chair? That chair is Schmidt's old refrigerator."

"Oh, my God," Eleanor said. "I'll never forget it! I had never seen anything like it! I did not believe my eyes at first! He was stretched out as if he were standing. But he's strapped in this contraption; his thin arms and legs are stretched out in weird positions for a monkey. He's crying, and even choking from the tight strap around his throat."

"That's the one. The macaques are very small, and his little face resembles a baby crying. His legs are spread-eagled grotesquely in a position so unlike a monkey. Tony revealed to the public that Schmidt clamped surgical pliers on the monkey's testicles to test his ability to feel. The monkey screamed and tried to free himself from the chair. Such 'acute noxious stimuli tests' were done with cigarette lighters as well."

"'Oh, my God!'"

"Then Tony took a photograph that showed Schmidt laughing at a starving monkey in the same chair. The monkey couldn't pick up raisins even though he was starving because he'd chewed off his numbed fingers, reducing them to nubs. The point of the experiment was to force the monkey to reactivate his numbed areas. But the monkey couldn't grasp the seven raisins because of his stub fingers. Tony caught Schmidt laughing at the monkey's futile efforts. The photograph outraged ordinary U.S. citizens. RUFFFF's posters and advertisements turned meat-eaters into animal rights activists. People joined the movement to hold RUFFFF's posters of the monkeys and protest outside NIH's Maryland building, demanding an end to Schmidt's experiments. Others from across the country called their congressmen and women.

"Eleanor, you should see RUFFFF's videos of this and other animal experiments. And Leona's book on the subject, I forget the name.

"Eventually, Schmidt was found guilty of six counts of cruelty under Maryland state law for the filthy conditions and the handling of the monkeys in his laboratory. This was a major turning point, not just within the movement, but also for the general public. Now the doctors once hailed as miracle workers in Honor's time, and for the last three decades, were being labeled 'monsters.' It was our window of opportunity, and Honor had nothing to do with it.

"Honor came from an era when hideous pictures were offensive. She worried that her members would cancel their membership if she published such photos. So Honor watched dumbfounded as Leona used raw truth as proof of atrocities and became the center of the modern animal rights movement. I think it was about then that Honor began to think that she was hopelessly out of step with the times.

"Then Leona adopted the civil rights movement's tactics by adding civil disobedience to her protests. Far from her membership being turned off by arrests, people flocked to her, begging to be a part of it. At this time, Leona was fresh, smart, and courageous and in her early twenties.

"Tony and Leona, at one point, even kidnapped all of Schmidt's monkeys. But their lawyers convinced them that the monkeys were required as evidence in the trial to convict Schmidt. As a result, the monkeys remained the property of the NIH, still captive, and isolated in small empty cages. Even Honor felt pity for the pain and regret Leona and Tony suffered over the following years."

"The monkeys at this time were of absolutely no use to the NIH. But to surrender them to a sanctuary at this time would have appeared as though they had buckled under the pressure of the movement. This period was viewed as a pivotal time for the biomedical organizations. Schmidt's conviction, the museum closing, Trite Cosmetics' reduction of animal experiments, and the morality issue raised by respected philosophers. These were movement successes in which they had no power. But the monkeys, that was another case.

Tony and Leona took the monkeys' case through the court system right up to the Supreme Court, Helen explained, and won the right to represent them. At least five of the monkeys were finally released to a sanctuary, but the rest were destined to live out their lives in small isolated cages stacked in rooms. Some were operated on again for the last time and then put to death, while others remained helpless captives of the politics of the NIH.

Schmidt was only convicted for the brutal handling and neglect of the monkeys, not for the experiments themselves. The NIH still defends the experiments. The Maryland Court of Appeals overturned Schmidt's conviction because Maryland anti-cruelty statutes didn't apply to federally funded facilities. But the NIH cut off his funding permanently. Three years later, the NIH would state that the monkeys' poor conditions were not the consequence of Schmidt's paralyzing operations. The NIH resumed the experiments using guinea pigs.

"Honor will never admit that PAAC benefited from Schmidt's conviction, but it brought hundreds of thousands of people to the animal rights movement, including new members to PAAC. Schmidt's conviction was a blow to the medical research community from which it would never fully recover. Researchers came to Schmidt's defense, testifying that he was honorable and his laboratory was up to standards. But as I said before, the photographs turned the 'miracle' worker into a 'monster,' and RUFFFF's spectacular exposé is considered one of the cornerstones of the modern animal rights movement. You need to read about it. It's basic education. RUFFFF then went on to expose military and commercial animal testing using graphic photographs, and it promoted the use of cruelty-free products.

"Only three years after putting up a handmade sign in their apartment in DC, RUFFFF was attracting world-class stars to the movement, and even kids wanted to join, thinking it 'cool,'" Helen said. "The face of the movement changed with Tony and Leona. They are from the middle class. Honor's ilk were from the upper classes and the privileged."

People across the country were calling for new laws to harness the "monsters," Helen revealed. It was 1982. This was Honor's forte. She wrote and had introduced into the U.S. Senate the New Biomedical Research Act. The act would have prohibited the NIH from financing experiments that caused pain that could not be controlled by "painkillers," such as psychological deprivation tests, head trauma tests, and more.

"This was revolutionary animal rights legislation," Helen said. "This was the moment she had waited for her whole career. Rutherford Gee agreed to support her."

Helen's voice was hesitant. It was obvious that she found no joy in revealing Honor's painful history.

"Then Allen Dey, the founder of NAHS, joined Honor and Rutherford. NAHS had 500,000 members at the time. It was and still is the largest animal welfare group in the country. Honor hates Dey for this! Of course, Alison and Gertrude Sandler were also part of the campaign.

"I was working for Leona at the time," Helen said. "She considered Honor's bill politically doomed and refused to support it. When I relayed the message to Honor, she wrote a press release that called Leona 'a coward.'"

"That sounds like our Honor," Eleanor said.

"Honor's bill was condemned by most legislators and the research community including the NIH, as Leona had predicted. 'Lawmakers have no business interfering with the progress of medical science': that was the position of most legislators then and now. Medical research is 'sacrosanct.'"

Helen explained that scare tactics were used in the Beltway to bully Allen Dey and Rutherford, who were threatened with losing their insider status. As a result, both men withdrew their support from Honor's bill. Both of them believed that influential DC relationships were required for significant change. Furthermore, Rutherford revealed that he and Dey believed in some animal experimentation if "humanely done."

"Lucifer's henchmen" is what Honor, Alison, and Gertrude called Dey and Rutherford in a press release. The memo revealed the fracture within the movement. No bill was passed that year. And Honor, Gertrude, and Alison were blamed for the failure. Honor was condemned for being uncooperative, self-righteous, and damaging to the cause, basically because she had refused to fold under pressure. But Dey and Rutherford had withdrawn their support of a valid bill. "They joined the forces we were fighting: the biomedical researchers."

Eleanor shook her head in disbelief and pondered. "No wonder Honor felt like the victim—she was! Honor seemed the 'problem child' of the movement. She was the lightening rod that drew all wrongs to her, placing all the blame for the movement's failures at this crucial time at her feet."

The legislative setback failed to stop the growth of the movement, Helen added. "New national organizations were being formed, and memberships in PAAC and other animal protection organizations continued to multiply. RUFFFF had inspired a nation, and people across the country began to rescue abused animals in their neighborhoods. They turned to RUFFFF for direction, of course. Overwhelmed by all the calls, Leona decided to form chapters in each state and more, and her organization also operated training camps for novice demonstrators in major cities. I ran a couple of those. After a while they closed the chapters, finding them too difficult to control, but the nationwide chapters expanded animal rights throughout the country. Some defunct chapters continue on their own steam.

"Then Leona broke the story about baboons being injured in head trauma operations at the laboratory of the University of Pennsylvania: the very experiments Honor's legislation would have outlawed. We saw horrible films of fully conscious, anesthetized baboons strapped on an operating table, their heads encased in cement while a heavy hydraulic machine damaged their healthy brains. It was Thomas Gennarelli's laboratory, and the ALF raided it, stealing forty-five hours of videotapes, some of which show Gennarrelli and his lab technicians making fun of the baboons. One technician even lifts a baboon by his shoulders after saying that his shoulders were most likely dislocated. Another video reveals two doctors operating on the brain of a restrained baboon who is fully conscious and in obvious pain.

"Again our government was financing the experiments. Leona and Tony acted as one of the PR arms of the ALF, igniting interested parties. In another videotape, the researchers mocked one of the brain-damaged baboons by waving his hands as if he were saying good-bye, much like a mother would with her infant. One video of a head-bandaged baboon who was a victim of brain trauma experiments showed lab technicians laughing at him because he was pleading to be freed.

"I was with Leona when RUFFFF and other groups invaded the NIH's Maryland building," Helen said. "We occupied the director's offices for four days, demanding an end to the head trauma experiments, and we had no intention of leaving until the experiments were stopped. It was the most satisfying moment for me as an activist. It still inspires me. I owe that to Leona and the Animal Liberation Front."

It was on the fourth day of the occupation that President Reagan stepped in, Helen explained. The Health and Human Services secretary, in the president's cabinet, stopped the experiments. This action insulted and embarrassed the scientific community; they were getting slapped on the wrist by the president himself. At last the government was working for the movement. "Thanks to Leona's actions! This was again an incredible feat, another first."

"Eleanor, you can see, when Honor calls Leona 'all hype,' just how ridiculous that statement is."

The last straw was the discovery of an infant monkey with her delicate eyelids sewed shut with course black thread, Helen explained. The ALF broke into a California laboratory, freeing a thousand animals along with the isolated baby monkey. It was another NIH-sponsored horror. The monkey had a grotesque cube-shaped apparatus taped to her small head emitting grating and shocking sounds that caused her arms, the size of a baby's, to jerk out with each sound. The video outraged everyone who viewed it. The American Council of the Blind condemned the treatment of animals and the waste of funds. But the NIH again defended its experiments. Other associations for the blind condemned them, labeling them worthless and saying such ill-gotten information was 'morally unacceptable.'

"At this point, it became obvious to the public that the scientific community couldn't regulate itself," Helen said. "Its cruelty didn't begin and end with Schmidt's seventeen monkeys. The baby monkey whose eyelids had been sewed together was adopted by another monkey and now happily lives protected in a sanctuary. The movement learned from Schmidt's monkeys never to return anyone who was rescued."

Leona and Tony organized ongoing protests outside the NIH building, demanding legislation to control the research community. They drew the leadership of the animal advocacy community together, including legislators, Rutherford Gee, Frances Garnett, and most other movement leaders. In 1984 Congress held public hearings on the issue of animal experimentation.

"Eleanor, the movement had never been as strong or influential as it was at this moment. Animal rights became a household word. People were clamoring, as they say, for change.

"Again, Honor saw an opportunity for strong federal laws. She proposed, and by some miracle managed to get introduced into the Senate, her Alternatives to Animal Research bill. She was now forty-eight years old, and dynamic. Alison was again at her side. If the bill became law, it would establish a center for alternative research to animal experimentation, just as she had proposed back in 1966. Its budget would come from the money appropriated to the NIH. Part of the center's responsibility would be to disseminate the information obtained from alternative testing. Honor and Alison would establish their own research center and route all information to the government center.

As a result of Honor's proposed legislation, Washington resembled a war zone, with every vivisector and his or her affiliate institution flooding the Capitol prepared to defeat Honor's bill. If the bill was passed, the political landscape could be redefined, with some money and power placed in the hands of animal advocates for the first time. Information relating to alternative testing would link rights advocates to influential legislators, a relationship that would no doubt grow."

The research community responded with scare tactics. "Scientists must be free to use animals if they are to find cures for heart disease, diabetes, cancer, and other disorders. If their ability to use animals is restricted, their research will virtually stop," predicted a leading NIH scientist before the House subcommittee Science, Research, and Technologies .

"It was the money," Helen revealed. "Allen Dey, who attended countless meetings, reported back telling us that researchers didn't want to sacrifice the federal funds necessary to research for alternatives which, they claimed, would decrease the amount of funds available to them for their research. And the government would be dictating when and if researchers could use 'their own' animals in research. Dey was told to distance himself from the alternatives bill, that it hadn't 'a snowball's chance in hell.'"

Dey took the threat seriously, again prizing his insider status with the research community, Helen explained. Dey joined a committee formed to create a friendlier bill. It was comprised of vivisectors, legislators, a couple of veterinarians, and animal welfare advocates. They created another amendment that proposed on-site animal care committees to monitor each research site financed by the NIH. The committees would consist of the same mix: a licensed researcher, a veterinarian, and, at least one person from the animal welfare community to monitor experiments. All the members of the committee had to believe in vivisection.

"By the first day of the 1984 Conference for the Animals, Rutherford was still sitting on the fence, but Honor was convinced that this time she'd reel him in. Of course, she totally rejected the Animal Care Committee Act, because it supported vivisection and it also imposed criminal penalties on whistle-blowers. Any committee member who revealed 'confidential information' would be penalized. She believed the amendment actually added very little to the present Animal Welfare Act and would set the movement back with the whistle-blower clause. She pointed out that the NIH already had committees that were supposed to monitor their experiments.

"That year the Conference for the Animals was held to decide which of the two amendments to the Animal Welfare Act we'd back. Again Leona viewed Honor's bill as doomed, but Honor wasn't taking no for an answer. The bill would begin to turn thousands of animals away from being automatically funneled to commercial and medical research laboratories, she told me. 'It would turn the tide,' she said. At the conference she whispered to me, 'This is the time. This is the issue. This is the bill!'"

Helen's calm voice turned somewhat tremulous, and Eleanor's stomach tightened.

"It was a beautiful April morning, and she was dressed like Easter in her powder blue suit. You know how beautiful she can look. And she was so optimistic and enthusiastic. You know how she gets, just like a teenager. We were at the Washington DC Sheraton. And, of course, she understood that Allen Dey was pushing the less controversial amendment, but she was totally confident that Sharp, Rutherford, and especially Leona would support her bill.

"We were on the brink of a technological revolution, she said in her speech appealing to everyone present. There were alternatives, now far less expensive than animal experimentation, such as computer replications, simulated body and tissue fluids, and live cell cultures. Alison's organization would begin a worldwide search for alternatives and citations of recorded experiments demonstrating their successes, and would feed them to the government center for dissemination. She hoped that, eventually, as it is done in Britain, animal protection organizations would receive grant money for the collection of research data.

"Grumpol suggested that Britain's system of monitoring animal experimentation could act as our model. In Britain, alternatives must be used if they are available, despite the researcher's opinion. So the researcher is not God. If great suffering is taking place, the animal must be put out of his or her misery or the experiment stopped whether it is finished or not. Two people are legally responsible along with the licensed researcher in each experiment. As you may know, all experiments are licensed in Britain and are graded for the degree of suffering involved.

"Grumpol explained that Britain's animal researchers are monitored by the home secretary and his team of inspectors, and there is also an Animal Procedures Committee, similar to the proposed on-site committees but with a huge difference. It is endowed with independence and authority, Grumpol explained. The committee is independent of the home secretary and publishes its own report to Parliament. Two thirds of the committee must be doctors and surgeons, and at least three of its members must come from the welfare groups, and two must be lay people. Only half of the committee's members can hold licenses for experiments.

"The home secretary must explain his decision to Parliament if he refuses to accept the committee's advice. Applications for particular tests such as cosmetic testing, tobacco research, and gaining manual skills in surgery techniques are referred to the committee.

"Honor lost the vote and it wasn't even close. The animal rights leadership instead backed the Animal Care Committee Act written in conjunction with the biomedical community. It was a case of wanting to return to their membership with something after all the clamor for change. They had failed in 1982; they couldn't afford to fail again. Leona had faith in the animal care committees because they would be bound by law to protect the animals.

"Dey said that the Animal Care Committee Act would ensure that multiple surgeries on animals would be prohibited except for 'scientific necessity.' It also included exercise for dogs, and at least some sensitivity to the needs of primates by enhancing their physical environment for their psychological well-being. And no paralytic drugs without anesthetics for surgical procedures would be used. Alternatives had to be used for painful procedures, if they existed. The researcher would be required to prove that no alternatives existed. Then the animal care committee would inspect the facilities and register reports semiannually with the Department of Agriculture.

"Grumpol argued against the bill, saying it allowed the scientific community to continue to monitor itself. And it allowed continuous and severe pain, multiple surgeries, the rejection of alternatives, and vivisection without anesthesia if the researcher 'deemed it necessary.'"

Helen hesitated for a second. "Eleanor, I believe that Honor had a breakdown right after they took the vote. I was sitting right in back of her. After the vote, she stood up and accused those who had voted against her bill of 'making a pact with the devil.'

"After she said those words, she looked like she'd seen a ghost. I nearly ran to her to support her. Later she told me that she had a vision of the animals she'd seen in her travels in Kenya and other countries. They flashed before her, triggered by the realization they, or others just like them, would fall prey to animal experimentation. She was blinded by a vision of the faces of primates: macaques, rhesus monkeys, lemurs, langurs, orangutans, baboons, and chimpanzees of all shapes and sizes. They were scared and watching her. They peered at her from a wall of green jungle growth, a steep leafy green that faded into the infinite distance as far as her eyes could see. All those frightened and accusing eyes!

"She had a second vision. This time she turned white, again seeing rabbits, romping pigs, thousands of mice, and endless numbers of dogs and cats. Some of the faces, she said, were those of animals she'd met at the shelter where she first began. The familiar faces thundered past her, all gazing at her as if they believed she'd protect them. Her body began to tremble when she realized they were all charging into a bottomless abyss, and all the while their eyes were locked on hers.

"I saw Grumpol catch his breath at the sight of her. The room was totally silent, with everyone thinking that Honor had finally lost it. I was seated behind her, and I remember pushing my hands against the soft seat cushion, ready to spring if she collapsed. But she snapped out of it and looked at all of us as if we were strangers. She...well, she asked everyone in the room who they were. She held up a copy of Dey's bill in her outstretched hand, which was really shaking. I'll never forget this: she asked them if they were animal exploiters or rescuers.

"She said, 'From this bill, this bill that both you and the scientific community created, it's impossible to tell who's who. You approve a bill written by the vivisector's hand! Then I ask you, who are their exploiters and who are their rescuers...can someone point them out to me on this paper? Where do you begin and end and where do they begin and end?'

"The bill slipped from her hand with all eyes on it. The two pages seemed to be suspended in the air miraculously for a second, and then slowly sailed this way and that over the table and landed next to a half-filled water pitcher like a silent time bomb. There was so much truth in her words.

"Very erect, as usual, she walked to the door, but we were all wondering if she'd make it. Grumpol followed her. Honor later confided that it was the first time that they became lovers. They cried and made love. She cried for the animals because she had failed to lead and therefore failed them. Since that day, she has nightmares at times of stress. In these dreams, she's always in a laboratory trying to get the animals out of the cages. Sometimes she has a huge ring of keys in her hands, and she's trying each one in an attempt to unlock the cage doors. She's terrified because she hears footsteps coming. And she wakes up terrified. But waking up brings no relief.

"She required triple bypass surgery six months later. Her family has a history of heart failure, but I'm sure this helped it along. She believes that if her bill had prevailed, countless animals would have been saved. I think the leaders voted judiciously. I don't believe Honor's bill had much of a chance. But some still agree with her today that, at that point, with the public demanding change, they should have at least pushed for more, especially since animal experimentation was the issue that had stirred the country.

"Leona went on with exposés that did end up reducing the amount of animal experimentation, in the same way as Sharp did. But no doubt tens of thousands of animals are suffering right now for lipstick and detergent, as well as questionable medical studies."

This enlightenment was an unwelcome one for Eleanor. It was an abomination. Thousands of animals might have been saved from the hands of vivisectors if the leaders had been tougher? Could this be?

After a few numbing seconds, Eleanor managed to whisper, "Thanks, Helen. Wow." She muttered softly, as if not wanting to disturb the ghosts of the past, as if it would be better not to even contemplate the awesome loss. With zombie-like movements, she put her mug on a coaster on the lamp table and stood up while the depth of the loss continued to astound her. Her little ethical problem seemed of no consequence in the larger scheme of things. They said their good-byes.

CHAPTER 12

▼

"ONE TRUE SANCTUARY."

Helen's tribal tale had so inspired Eleanor that the next morning she awoke with even more determination to contribute to the movement by following Eve through Connecticut and Massachusetts. She pursued the case nonstop for two months. When the Anderson Bros. Circus continued to Rhode Island, she contacted activists there to hound the circus, and took a week's vacation primarily to sleep. Back at her desk, she added undercover work to her clerical and writing duties. Assuming a different name, she pretended to be a primary school teacher interested in hiring the Anderson Bros. Circus as a fund-raiser. They didn't fall for it, but she proceeded to appeal to another larger circus with seven elephants that also traveled through Connecticut, and to her surprise she was sent a list of ninety clients that would act as recommendations for them. Names, addresses, and telephone numbers were included. It was manna from heaven.

She wrote each one, which resulted in two political groups and two volunteer fire departments canceling their circus contracts. Another fire department accepted her invitation for a luncheon talk, and Lenore's video of rampaging elephants resulted in a debate among the firefighters. Tina, Helen, and Larry congratulated her. Her office family cheered each canceled contract.

Honor shunned her, however. Again, without explanation, Eleanor was out of the loop, cut off from the daily commerce of the office. Sitting at her desk, she encouraged herself to feel inspired by her empty in-box, telling herself that less official work allowed more time for Eve. But after four more humiliating weeks of spying, doors being closed in her face, and Honor grimacing at her, her spirits hit bottom.

Then Eleanor was demoted. It was the beginning of November when Honor's memo, delivered by Freda to her in-box, described her "new position." She was now supervisor of the Westport staff, and was confined to answering donor complaints. In the same memo Larry Knowles was named PAAC's "Media Contact Director." No explanation was offered for the demotion. The good part was that she'd remain responsible for requests from her activist cousins. Again, Eve benefited because Eleanor had more time to devote to her case.

But still, the demotion gnawed at her. In any sanely run organization, the local TV and newsprint coverage, her quotes in the *New York Times* and *USA Today*, and her countless hours of overtime would have garnered her a raise or a promotion. As the days of vilification slogged on, she began to ask herself: "What did I do wrong?"

Honor required a scapegoat and it was her turn, her colleagues assured her. "Hold on for them," Tina pleaded over the phone numerous times daily. "This is just another temporary storm! Hold on to the rocky ship! Please! You're a great activist! Look what you've done for Eve! Remember the canceled circus contracts! Remember the Colorado wildlife!"

"Whatever you do, don't quit." Helen said.

Meanwhile the Westport office staff avoided her as if she were tainted with *E. coli* bacteria. It was the middle of November, and nearly four months had passed with little or no contact with Honor. That Monday morning, Eleanor searched the sky from her office window and again placed her life at PAAC in God's hands.

Minutes later, Honor stomped down to stand in her doorway. "The yahoos are proposing to kill 233 deer in Denmark Cliff State Park unless we stop them," she said. "I want you to write to the legislators on the Legislative Review Committee to tell them to vote 'no' on that bogus piece-of-shit Deer Management Plan."

The photograph of the three-legged deer on Eleanor's newsroom wall flashed before her. From behind her desk she gazed at Honor, thinking that it was almost one year ago that the threat of a Denmark Cliff hunt had prompted Honor to hire her. Then and now the urgency in her voice was real.

Honor told her that she had received a telephone call from her state capital contact that morning. The committee was to vote on the Deer Management Plan in two and a half weeks. The "plan" was a pseudonym for a hunt that would cull

233 deer from the herd, leaving just 25 deer. If approved, the park would be the site of a new yearly hunt. "It's a wet kiss from the governor to the NRA!"

Eleanor remained seated. Relief flooded her. Honor's presence meant that her punishment for crimes unknown was over. And her soul heaved a sigh of contentment at being called upon once again by a movement leader.

The letters were the deer's last chance, Honor said. The bogus management plan had been introduced two years ago at a public hearing. She, Alison, and others had testified on behalf of the deer and had represented 30,000 like-minded Connecticut residents, but to no avail.

When Honor left, Eleanor was far from overwhelmed. She believed PAAC could save the deer even if she had only twelve working days in which to do it! Wasn't she where she was supposed to be? Hadn't she once again turned her life over? Wasn't this the same dynamic at play when she discovered Eve? Her gut was also telling her that her job depended on the success of the mission. Overdrive, she shifted into overdrive.

After an urgent request to the state clerk for a fax of the committee member's names and address, she turned to her computer and began to punch out a letter. When she received the addresses, she faxed the letter while Lisa e-mailed it. Then she hopped in her car for Hartford, an hour and a half away, to slip a copy of the letter into each legislator's mailbox. The following day, she began her marathon of calls to them, bombarding them with information. And after calling the Westport state representative, Michael Whitcomb, the Democratic chairman of the committee, day and night in his two offices for two weeks, he agreed to meet with her at the Norfolk Diner.

The meeting with Whitcomb wasn't until the Monday evening before the Wednesday vote. When she rushed into Honor's office and announced her upcoming meeting with the deer's possible savior, Honor seemed astounded. And without a word spoken, Eleanor knew she had her old job back.

The frigid, blustery weather was severe that Monday night, and most people had stayed home to keep warm. Whitcomb entered the Norfolk Diner fighting the north wind for the door. Eleanor and Andrew Dewhurst were seated in the first booth only a few feet away. She had invited Dewhurst, a wildlife biologist, to present the biological argument. In the virtually empty diner, it wasn't a problem that they had never set eyes on each other before. She had met Dewhurst only a few minutes earlier. They stood up to welcome Whitcomb—the deer's last hope. The veteran legislator was reputed to be sharp witted and responsive. She was counting on that.

Whitcomb was heavyset. He strode toward them, his walk revealing that it was the last appointment of a long day in a season of long days. On his beaklike nose sat thick horn-rimmed glasses. He had a full head of wavy salt-and-pepper hair and a matching walrus mustache. His weather-beaten, watery eyes stared at them as he approached, and he raked his cold stiff fingers through his windblown hair.

Eleanor shook his hand and introduced Dewhurst. Whitcomb struggled out of his dark wool overcoat, and as the smell of fresh air sprang from its folds, he muttered about the bitter cold night. He slid his wadded coat into the booth and sidled up to sit opposite Eleanor. With an effort he crossed his heavy legs. His exhausted eyes were all business.

A petite waitress rushed over to their booth and smilingly took their order for two coffees and an almond herbal tea. Andrew passed on the dessert, saying he'd indulge later, when, he hoped, there'd be something to celebrate. Eleanor guessed that Andrew was in his early forties. His blue eyes were thoughtful, and his light brown hair was carefully cropped. His turtleneck sweater and jeans revealed a lean, healthy body. He probably worked out, she thought.

Dewhurst told Whitcomb that he worked for the state and that he was voicing his personal opinion and not that of the state. "Hey, I have to say that to keep from losing my job. I work in the Department of Waste Management."

"The Wildlife Department called in six independent federal wildlife resource officials," Whitcomb began, "who as you know have supported the state's contention that Denmark Cliff should carry only twenty-five deer in order to ensure the survival of the rare flora of the peninsula. I kid you not; the six opinions will serve to highly influence the legislators. They have honest concerns about the rare flora being destroyed by the unusually high number of deer. I and every other legislator consider this an authentic and indisputable concern. Blott, the deer biologist, will be giving us a tour of the Cliff Wednesday morning before the vote."

"With all due respect, Rep. Whitcomb," Eleanor piped in, "ask your constituents if they think deer should be killed to save a plant."

Whitcomb heaved a weary sigh and repeated his concern about the Special Act protecting the peninsula's rare flora. The waitress served the hot beverages. Eleanor watched Andrew, waiting for his response, as he calmly poured some soy milk and a little maple syrup into his coffee before he began.

"Sir, with respect, I must remind you that the Special Act was originated at the behest of the owners of the property, the Johansens," he said. "They donated the land to the state primarily to protect the deer and their habitat. So a hunt would be an act of betrayal to them and the deer. You know the Johansens are buried on the land?"

Whitcomb shook his head. He had no idea.

Dewhurst than explained that the state's six "independent" experts were far from independent. They were schooled in "wildlife management" and worked for other state departments. He pointed out that the state hired wildlife managers, not wildlife biologists. "I'm a wildlife biologist. I studied zoology, biology, and other sciences as a student. The state wildlife managers study forestry and wildlife management. These are not sciences. Basically, you learn how to manipulate herds to provide game for hunters, which results in revenue for the state."

Eleanor, already grateful for Dewhurst, sipped her warm tea and listened while the cold wind whistled outside the picture window, just inches away.

The Wildlife Department contended that the understory of the oak trees on Denmark Cliff was being depleted by the deer because they grazed on acorns, Dewhurst said. But he pointed out that oaks could hardly be classified as rare in New England. "There are rare plants, however. But ask them for their studies on the rare plants, and you'll find that they can't produce them. And when you hike Denmark Cliff on Wednesday, inspect the dense greenbrier areas where the deer don't forage. You'll see new oak seedlings growing there."

Whitcomb shook his head in agreement, and dug for a small notepad and a pen from his pockets and made a notation. Dewhurst suggested placing fencing around the rare flora as a solution, rather than destroying an entire herd of deer. He tapped the index finger of his right hand soundlessly on the table as he continued.

"Even if there's just one deer left on the peninsula, he or she can destroy rare plant life," he said. "They'll be leaving twenty-five deer to survive after that devastating hunt. I will gladly organize a team of people to fence off the flora, if that's the issue," he said. Dewhurst gazed down modestly at the table. "I'll get the volunteers and some donated fencing. It's no problem."

Eleanor's eyes bounced from the slender biologist to her right to the scribbling Whitcomb across from her. Studying his reaction, she was so grateful for Andrew's calm delivery. Dewhurst was as new to her as Whitcomb. But what an enormous pleasure it was to do business with both of them. Even with the lives of the deer at stake, she was more comfortable at this moment with them than she had been since she left the newspaper; they treated her as their equal. Oh, how reminiscent the respectful atmosphere here was of her more normal situation at the *Norfolk Daily News*!

Dewhurst continued. People, he explained, understood starvation. Natural selection was too scientific a term for it. They also understood Lyme disease, and deer-car collisions, and deer eating ornamental shrubs. "I don't know how they got the name 'deer' ticks, but if they didn't have the deer to use as a host, the ticks would tend to jump on people even more. If you removed all the deer in Connecticut, you would still have Lyme disease. They're part of our ecology."

He took a second to gaze down at his cup and then returned his gaze to Whitcomb. "Like any other exploitation, propaganda is part of the department's business…like big business which distributes propaganda so the public will tolerate environmental abuses such as drilling for oil in wildlife reserves. So the department first used starvation to justify a Denmark Cliff hunt. Then when some questioned that rationale, they came up with this dubious theory about damage to the park's rare flora. Clearly, they want to provide more hunting occasions to their customers. Hunters purchase licenses and permits, which sets the department's yearly budget and pays their salaries."

Whitcomb was sitting straight up in the booth, rapt with attention. Dewhurst explained that as a state employee, he knew very few within the Wildlife Department who supported the hunt. He lowered his head while his eyes telegraphed that he was about to share confidential information. He revealed that Rick Delaney, the director of the Wildlife Department, was expected to quit because of the controversial hunt. Rick and many others in the building, from managers to secretaries and clerks, opposed the hunt because Denmark Cliff was a state park, and they morally objected to the propaganda.

"You know Rick told legislators in 1993 that the herd and the flora were well balanced," Dewhurst said. "That there was no reason to hunt the Cliff. This will come back to haunt you. And Rick managed to stop the hunt last time, saving some of the deer. So I'm not surprised that he's ready to quit. He doesn't want to be part of the lies told to the public."

Eleanor observed the legislator's eyebrows knitted in skepticism as he stared at Dewhurst while he waited for more. She was stunned by Dewhurst's candor. Dewhurst took a quick sip of coffee, with his eyes on Whitcomb as he set his cup back down.

"To keep the herd to 25 individuals is ludicrous," he said. "If the land had enough food to produce 258 deer, then that, in fact, was the land's carrying capacity. Of course, that might change. But no mass starvation would take place as a result of the present population. In fact, the genetic health of the population would suffer by reducing the herd to only 25 individuals. Generally, breeders of domestic animals know that it is a dangerous practice to allow breeding populations to fall below 50 individuals over the short term, and they ideally seek breeding populations in excess of 500. Keeping the number to 25 individuals would be impossible anyway. Migrating deer would move into the choice habitat—that's nature's way. The 1993 hunt was the reason the herd's numbers were so high now. The deer numbers were kept to 160 when the land hadn't been hunted for 20 years. They killed 100 deer, and now, in just six years, the numbers allegedly were up to 258 individuals."

He continued to prove the fallacy of the department's argument for the hunt by pointing to the stability of the deer herd's population for the 20 years in which it had remained intact. The peninsula was not defoliated in those 20 years either, he advised. Nor did biodiversity suffer, nor did all the deer starve to death as the department would mislead the public into believing, in order to manufacture consent for hunting. Dewhurst took a deep breath, wanting to remain calm as he stated his objections, but his anger flared again. "As members of a herd die, they are replaced by births; that is the natural order. But with a hunt there is carnage. If anything, the department's previous hunt proved that hunting promotes increases in the reproductive potential. And the hunt will be nothing less than a massacre because the deer live side by side with people. It is a state park, after all, sir. They're used to people. My girlfriend and I hike and jog in this park weekly. In the many times we've been there we never once witnessed a starving deer."

He explained that if there was an overpopulation problem, nature through natural selection, disease, scarcity of resources, weather conditions, genetic inheritance, and accidents would serve to thin out the herd. "Of course, the weather is a major factor. But whatever occurs, nature won't kill 233 deer in one winter season. It will take a number of years, no doubt, for the herd to reduce to 160 or so deer."

"The department found ten deer that died of starvation last year," Whitcomb said.

"But you are accepting the argument that because ten deer died, it is then merciful to kill 233?…Most of whom are healthy and thriving?" He didn't wait for an answer. "I see healthy, fat deer that I know will be taken for trophies by hunters if this so-called Denmark Cliff Deer Management Plan is accepted on Wednesday. Remember, hunters don't take the emaciated deer; they cull the trophy animals, the big and the strong. That one healthy deer should die because another may starve is an abomination."

Eleanor sat back, grateful that Andrew was handling this part of the session, and recalling how she had been accused of being emotional during her breakfast with the Tigers Club officials. Whitcomb had to be impressed.

"Now people who use the park are rightfully disturbed by the sight of a starving deer," Dewhurst said. "It's a humane and worthy reaction. But, sir, a death by starvation is not nearly as tragic as killing a healthy, fit deer for a wall trophy."

At that point Eleanor decided to talk about her experiences as a reporter when she called the department for roadkill stats. "I thought they were protecting wildlife, only to discover that their job was to protect the state's 'resources' in order to sell hunting licenses. I was shocked when I requested a yearly report and found it filled with 'harvest' numbers: the thousands of deer killed and harvested! I remember thinking, 'Are they really using "harvest" for the word "kill"?' We harvest wheat or vegetables, not individuals. I thought they were 'protecting the environment.' To me that meant wildlife."

As she talked, she noticed that the legislator's expression changed as if her experience enlightened him. Dewhurst added that filling the woods with deer had a long history that dated back to feudal years, when the king's men were obligated to keep the king's woods filled with "game." The same process was at work in modern times, he explained. On the state level, it was the department's job to keep the woods filled with game, while the Pittman Robertson Act, on a federal level, was created to assist in that endeavor. "Eleanor's right. The animals are not considered individuals. They're viewed as a 'natural resource' to be used and exploited."

"Legislators think the department's wildlife managers are the experts and accept their opinions without question," Eleanor said. "Well, you should question them!"

"No, we don't," Whitcomb said. "But I don't think they're out to kill all the animals just for the sake of pleasing hunters." He shook his head as if the notion were ridiculous.

At this out-of-hand rejection of her and Dewhurst's opinion, her heart sank. She glanced at Andrew, registering her alarm. Then Whitcomb invited her to tour Denmark Cliff Park on Wednesday morning before the vote. "I'll call you after I speak to Franklin Blott tomorrow. To see if that's acceptable."

She was relieved by his invitation. "Our lines don't pick up after five. I know, we're archaic," she said. "Please call my home phone, I have an answering machine. Of course, I've walked the Cliff. I came face-to-face with a doe who darted into the bushes just a few feet away from me for cover. She was so beautiful, round and full. She'll make it through the winter if she's not shot. I couldn't help thinking that if she were really wild, she would have flown into the woods and disappeared. But she was so used to people that she just started eating again farther in the woods."

Dewhurst warned Whitcomb that a vote for the Deer Management Plan was actually a vote to allow hunting each year, because it would take yearly hunts to maintain the artificially low number of twenty-five deer on the land. He dug into his briefcase for several copies of his treatise for Whitcomb to distribute to other committee members.

As Eleanor prepared to offer her final pitch, the howling wind seemed to issue an ominous warning.

"We are urging you, sir, to do your best to save the park deer from an act of betrayal that will devastate all of us. You must know that hunters comprise less than 3 percent of Connecticut's population. We're sure that the Denmark Cliff hunters are not hunting to save their families from starvation or to feed the poor in homeless shelters, nor are they hunting to save the deer from starvation, so that leaves trophy hunting. Nationwide 86 percent of the population objects to trophy hunting, according to a recent North American Humane Society survey.

"If we are forced to tolerate hunting, at least let there be one true sanctuary in the beautiful state of Connecticut where the deer may run free. If Denmark Cliff fails to be that safe haven for deer, given the passage and the intent of the Special Act approved by legislators such as yourself to allow the land to remain free from human interference, then no deer anywhere in the state is safe. And we, the vast majority, are without representation at the capitol!"

The silence that followed her words amplified the howling wind, as if nature itself were underscoring her message and reminding Whitcomb of universal laws. He stood up and offered her his hand as if to seal an agreement. "I'll support your stance," he said in his sputtering machine-gun fashion. "You must understand I'm not against hunting as a tool to control populations. But I am disturbed about this hunt because of the Special Act. I do believe something must be done to lower the numbers there. I will, however, support your proposal to allow nature to take its course. I don't see the need to rush into this and slaughter 233 deer." He lowered his head in contemplation and stared at the restaurant floor. "I share your concern about representation. I'll call you tomorrow about touring Denmark Cliff with us."

He shook their hands and began to put on his heavy coat. "Mr. Whitcomb," Andrew said, "be sure to ask about the new oaks growing near the thick greenbrier in the meadows."

Eleanor stared at Andrew dumbstruck. They both watched Whitcomb exit the diner, sucked into the darkness by the wind. Then she turned toward Andrew. "We did it!"

"Now I'm going to have a piece of that vegan chocolate layer cake," Andrew said.

The following morning, Eleanor woke once again awed by the influence of the animal rights community. Honor seemed equally stunned by the outcome. That evening Whitcomb called as Eleanor finished dinner, informing her that she would not be allowed to join the legislators' tour of Denmark Cliff. He then revealed that there were six newly elected legislators. "They're looking for direction. So I have some chance of reaching them. And the three senior legislators I spoke to, I'm fairly sure will cast their votes against the hunt."

As Eleanor sat on her couch talking to the legislator, she counted the votes. Honor's Norfolk contact promised a negative vote, but on the strength of Whitcomb's influence alone, it looked good. "Four and six are ten, and if we receive ten votes, we have a decent chance to defeat it," she said. "There's only twenty-one legislators on the committee! And some are sure to be absent, and with others who will abstain from the controversial vote, getting ten votes could definitely swing the vote our way."

"There are no guarantees," Whitcomb warned. "I know I won't convince all six of them—three of them are Republicans, and Rummick is the Republican Senate chair. Then we have the influence of the 'six experts' to contend with, and the pressure from the governor and the NRA."

Whitcomb thought they had a chance, despite his cautionary words. Eleanor telephoned Honor with the news. "Great!" Eleanor noted the skepticism in her voice.

The following afternoon, Eleanor returned to Hartford. She hurried into the Legislative Office Building to witness the vote. Daylight filtered through the three-story atrium. She crossed the marble rotunda. Her heels clicked along the black-and-white peppered floor as she floundered, not knowing where the hearing rooms were. She spotted numbers over the one-story-high ornate doorways circling the area. 1-A was to her right. She spun around and hastened her pace. The meeting was about to commence. The enormous carved doors, trimmed in gold leaf, appeared impossible to open, but it took only a touch on the oversized brass doorknob. She felt like Alice entering Wonderland.

The hearing room was quiet and looked like a theater in the round. It had blood-red carpet and seats that matched. The room slanted to a huge oval table where the legislators sat. At the head of the table were Whitcomb and Rummick seated side by side, and other legislators were scattered around the wide table.

A small group of well-dressed people sat in the front row. She assumed them to be animal advocates and joined them, occupying the first seat. Several men who were seated on the opposite side appeared to be department officials, and then there were people scattered here and there, no doubt waiting for other bills to be considered. With her parka folded over her arm, Eleanor pushed down the suspended red-upholstered chair seat.

The two women next to her introduced themselves as Alison Barrington and Roberta Steinway; her husband Richard sat next to her and offered a smile of encouragement. Eleanor's eyes lit up knowing that the Steinways were friends of the Johansens, who had helped draft the Special Act. And it was her first glimpse of the PFA founder, Alison Barrington, in person. Her haughty, aristocratic manner immediately called Honor to mind. Across the aisle to her left was a tall, sandy-haired, well-dressed gentleman. Alison told her that he was Allen Dey and he represented the North American Humane Society. Honor's description of him was on the money, Eleanor thought while gazing at him. And it appeared as though Dey didn't want to be associated with the more extreme factions of animal advocates present.

Standing, Whitcomb brought the meeting to order and began to read slowly and clearly the proposal of the hunt included in the Deer Management Plan. Eleanor's breath became shallow as he read, her heart pumping in her throat. She had covered enough public meetings to know that it could be over in seconds.

"It is my opinion that Special Act 35-78 was deemed to put the land aside to remain untouched," Whitcomb announced after reading the proposal. "I'm not satisfied with this plan, as it will require that hunters invade this property almost each year to keep the herd to the artificially low number of twenty-five deer. The founders never wanted this to be a hunting ground. I'm not adverse to an initial hunt to lower the numbers. But this management plan is nothing more than a hunting proposal, since no other follow-up measures other than hunting are proposed. With regard to the rare flora being compromised by the overpopulation of deer, little data on the destruction of the rare flora is provided, and from my tour of the property, it far from warrants such a drastic measure."

"That was perfect," Eleanor thought. But she continued to hold her breath.

The Democratic representative from Fairlawn, Rep. Hannah Brooks, spoke. "I agree that no plan should be approved that calls for annual hunting. I know we had federal experts in who supported the number of twenty-five deer, but we all have to understand, the founders didn't place any number on how many deer should live on the land. I'm not satisfied that opening the land to hunting is appropriate. But I'm also not averse to opening it for hunting to originally reduce the herd. No doubt there is overpopulation. But then it should remain untouched once the herd numbers are dropped. I'll never support the Wildlife

Department coming back each year to hunt this land. I will not vote for this plan as is. Basically, it will give control to the department to hunt at any time it deems necessary. This alone violates Special Act 35-78."

"Yes. This is a convincing argument," Eleanor thought. "Yes! Yes!"

"Eleanor," whispered Roberta Steinway, leaning across the lap of Alison Barrington. "I've heard that only two legislators will support a ban on hunting on the property. That means this plan will pass." She frowned.

Eleanor whispered that Whitcomb had been lobbying for them and that he thought some of the six new legislators would vote against the plan. "We have a good chance."

The Senate Republican chair, Sen. Charles Rummick, spoke. The senator, whose office sported a huge stag with antlers, was an ardent NRA member. With an impatient jerky wave of both arms, he bellowed: "It's simple math! We've had six federal wildlife experts come in here and support the department's number of twenty-five deer! They say that's the carrying capacity of the land. If we want healthy deer, that's the number. We have ten times that number, 258 deer. It's simple math. We asked for a management plan. We got one. We've all had time to study it. Let's vote on it."

Rummick had the attention of the six novice legislators: four women and two men. Eleanor saw the uncertainty in their eyes as they weighed the two differing opinions. In seconds the vote was called. They raised their hands, and the clerk counted the votes: nine voted for the plan and four voted against it. Four abstained, and four were absent, Jefferson among them. Jefferson was Honor's associate who had assured her by phone that he would vote against the proposal. The wildlife department was now independently operating Denmark Cliff State Park, and the hunt would proceed.

Eleanor was stunned by the swiftness of the vote and the lack of debate. Her eyes were still fixed on the legislators around the table in the center of the ring, as if she expected some kind of reprieve. Although she was no stranger to public hearings and their quick and cryptic actions, this was final. There was no court of appeals for the deer. This was done!

A woman rushed up from the opposite end of the aisle. The intense, thin, middle-aged woman knelt, in the aisle, next to Eleanor. Her jittery black eyes stared into hers as she whispered in a rapid fashion. "I'm Patricia Keel, a lobbyist for the Animal Trust. We got four votes, the most I've seen at the capitol against hunting in the four years this governor has been in power. Congratulations. I know you lobbied Whitcomb."

Eleanor nodded her head in the affirmative and stared at her while still perplexed and in shock, finding it difficult to make sense of the strange woman's message. "Is this woman saying the outcome was good?" she asked herself. "The four votes were good?" She collapsed into her cushioned seat and continued to stare at the committee under the dim lights in the center of the room, not answering the nervous, admiring woman kneeling next to her.

Roberta, seated at her right, flashed her a look of sorrow for the deer. But Eleanor was focused on the legislators. Then Whitcomb left his seat, walked up the aisle, and disappeared out the giant doors. She sprang up and rushed after him. He stood just outside the door in the rotunda waiting anxiously to speak to her.

"I tried," he said. "I just didn't get any support." He uttered these words with a slight accusation in his voice, as if she had failed to deliver.

It was a thunderclap of realization, lightning that struck her to the core. She froze with the damaging accusation that she had somehow failed Whitcomb and the deer. She was speechless and just stared into Whitcomb's eyes. He shook his head in compassion for the deer and then returned to the hearing room. She had mistakenly aborted her campaign to win over the legislators, believing that Whitcomb had more influence than she. She watched his back as he disappeared into the auspicious room that was now like a death chamber. "I should have hounded them!" she told herself. She had requested audiences with all of them in her letters, but of course that wasn't enough. She'd only succeeded in seeing Whitcomb because she'd called him nonstop! It was now crystal clear.

What a fool she had been! She had overrated Whitcomb's influence. That was the fatal flaw in her plan. How much time had he to expend on this one issue? He had hundreds of bills. She had one! People rushed by her as she began to sweat. She was wet with perspiration in seconds. The lapse in judgment was so unlike her. The words of Patricia Keel kept replaying. "She said it was the most votes we had gotten against hunting in four years," she told herself. "She actually congratulated me. For failing!"

Eleanor headed for the door, putting on her parka as she walked, wanting to escape the cold rotunda and the capital city. She raced past the information desk, through the double glass doors and stepped out into the brisk, unseasonable November air. She allowed it to whip her hair, wanting it to comb through the thick strands to help rid her of the political pollutants clinging there. She wrapped her parka around her as she scudded past the Legislative Office Building to the corner and anxiously peered at the four lanes of heavy traffic on Capital Boulevard, eager for an opportunity to dart across, unable to reach her car fast enough. Patricia Keel rushed up behind her again, she shouted to be heard above the roar of traffic and wind. The hood of her dark green wool jacket was wrapped tightly around her face.

"Rummick traded for the votes, you can bet on that. Besides, he's powerful, it's hard to get past him, and he wanted this thing! He hates Barrington for fighting the last hunt. And don't forget, it's common knowledge that the NRA hired the best lobbying firm in the capital! And this vote was a priority to them. With this governor, the cards were always stacked against us!"

Eleanor nodded and sincerely thanked her for giving her the skinny on the whole affair. She kindly invited Eleanor back into the Legislative Building for coffee, but Eleanor refused and continued her hasty retreat from the scene of the crime. She was so disappointed with the legislators and Connecticut's state government that she was actually trying to escape her own relationship with any of the humans that had participated in the miscarriage of justice. She continued along the boulevard to reach her car, which was parked in the basement of an office building a half-block away. Whitcomb's slight accusation still plagued her. "But we changed Whitcomb's mind!" she told herself. "We could have changed others. I should have worked harder! That's all there is to it!"

She walked up the street and made a right to continue down a half-block to the entrance of the building. She blindly walked into the lobby and past the receptionist desk, which had a man in uniform behind it. She headed to the elevator as if in a trance. In all honesty, she thought, it was her first episode in state wildlife politics. Hadn't she followed Honor's instructions? Honor was supposed to know. But Honor had never told her to call Whitcomb day and night! She'd figured that out all by herself!

She pressed the silver circular button marking the garage on the second level. The doors closed and the elevator started its descent. "I thought we had done great by getting Whitcomb to lobby for us," her mind raced. "Damn, I thought we had it. I should have known better." She was never sloppy in her work. She made sure; she made double sure. And she'd always found a way with the help of prayer, even when "they" said there was no way. Now this. She was not used to losing once she'd put her mind to it. Look how good the Colorado campaign had turned out! Honor and even Mary had thought it was hopeless, but she'd found a way. A positive way. How about the forty people bearing the summer storm for Eve for three hours? Look at the circus cancellations! She just couldn't accept this defeat!

There had to be a way; there always is. She'd just never found it! "How much time did you have," she asked herself, "for this monumental task? Excuses!" Why hadn't she hounded the six new legislators once Whitcomb gave her that info? Why hadn't Whitcomb advised her to lobby them? He'd just assumed that she would! That's "why," she said, answering her own question that now seemed apparent from his accusatory expression.

She exited the elevator to the parking garage and walked to a wall phone to her left. She eyed her welcoming gray Nissan, which was six cars down the slanted drive of the parking lot, as she dialed Honor, and related the bad news. "It was nine to four with four abstentions and four absent. Whitcomb got us three votes, and one, Jefferson, your contact, who said he'd vote for us, never showed."

"So we got four votes and Jefferson never showed?" Honor said, sounding grateful for the four votes. "So if he'd showed it would have been five to nine?"

"Right. We would have five votes and then it would have been five against nine. Rummick was too powerful, and he pointed to the 'six experts' as swaying evidence to the six new legislators."

Honor was silent.

Eleanor told Honor that Whitcomb said he had no support, and that Patricia Keel said it was the first time in the four years of this administration that there had been four votes cast against hunting.

"Oh, really. That's good. Well, animals are not a priority. They don't vote. I think we did great getting the four votes. This governor had it tied up. I'm proud that we got Whitcomb to work with us. The legislators always defer to the department on these issues. I'm sure it's been lobbying them for two years. And Rummick is a bloody old hunting warhorse! Cheeky bastard! This was always stacked against us! But I'm the eternal optimist. I thought we had a chance."

But not enough of a chance to spend money on a professional lobbyist, Eleanor thought, as Honor continued. The whole lousy picture started to crystallize. Why hadn't Honor paid for a professional lobbyist? Why hadn't she given the NRA some stiff competition early on? "She could have at least set me on this thing earlier," she thought. "I've spent so much time in my office conjuring up things to do because of her ridiculous and inexplicable banishment! It was down to the wire when she threw it in my lap, and by then we were short of time and money! This lobbying should have started two years ago, after the public hearing when they proposed the hunt in the first place! Dewhurst would have accompanied me every time!"

"Public opinion is our next target," Honor was saying. "If it's bad enough, it'll stop the hunt! It's not all over yet! We'll send letters to the editor! We'll also have ads prepared to be published after the bloody massacre begins aimed at the department and the governor."

Eleanor's hands hung like dead weights on the steering wheel, and she stared blankly ahead for the hour-and-a-half ride home on Interstate 95 with eighteen-wheelers barreling past. What a losing game she had been playing! But she had no idea! Honor was unrealistic, childish in her optimism. She had given her false hope. The political realities were that they were losing right from the get-go. But the novice legislators had been fair game...no doubt Dewhurst could have reached them with his biology lesson! She had seen some of their faces, especially two women who seemed to know nothing about the issue. They took their cues from Rummick. When he talked about the "six experts," she'd seen the light come into their eyes. After all, weren't they the official wildlife "independent experts" brought in by the department? What more proof did they need that 258 deer was ten times the carrying capacity of the land? "It's simple math! The land can only support 25 healthy deer! What's the problem here? It's simple math."

"Simple math," Eleanor said out loud. The faces of the innocent deer flashed in her mind's eye. "Simple math," she repeated.

PAAC's effort to save the deer had been a last-minute scramble rather than a calculated plan. What the hell had Honor been thinking of? The more Eleanor thought about it, the more it seemed like pure madness! Even an embarrassment. And next to come would be the demonstrations, she thought. "No doubt, I'll handle that and somehow we'll have to stop the hunt!" she thought, grasping at the very last hope. "Through public outcry, we'll stop them! They can't kill the deer!"

Since she'd begun at PAAC her duties had been basically clerical. Except for the Colorado campaign. Calls and letters slowed up in the summer. If not for her own initiative with the circus campaign, she would have been half asleep. She recalled Tina's remark that lately PAAC's corporate office was run like an insurance office rather than an animal rights organization. This comment was beginning to make sense. Then came fall and Honor's mysterious banishment of her, and if not for her impetus to rescue Eve, her days again would have been spent on clerical duties.

"And yet the Denmark Cliff deer were doomed by a public hearing two years ago!" she thought. "Why wasn't PAAC on the case?"

So Eleanor's thoughts spun all the way back to Westport. As she hung up her beige parka on the wooden hanger behind her door, it was past 5 PM, and she prayed to be spared a session with Honor. No way did she want to lay eyes on her. She felt used: tossed to ruthless politicians in a mere show of resistance at the capital. Honor arrived just as she was hanging up her parka.

"We're opening an office in New York, and I hired another disgruntled RUFFFF employee, Hank Cagney," Honor said. She stood in the doorway for a second before rushing in to stand just inches from Eleanor.

Eleanor's blank stare didn't change at the mention of Hank Cagney's name.

"You remember Hank, he wore a bloodied fur coat in New York and was part of the lockdown. Leona's caretaker. I was impressed by Hank, but due to budget constraints I had to wait. Anyway, the timing's bloody perfect. He knows CDs are usually no part of our protests, but we're forced to take drastic measures. Two hundred thirty-three deer will be taken."

Honor was rattling on about the deer while one thought kept circling in Eleanor's mind: "How accepting will Whitcomb be the next time?"

Honor stood inches away telling her that Hank was setting up an office in his apartment in the city until Freda could find reasonable office space. "When they finally allow us to know the dates of the damned hunt, we'll have only days, and he'll work from here. I want you to set up a meeting with CFAR as soon as possible," she ordered. "CFAR will sabotage the hunt as they did in 1993. And Hank will be involved. I want photographs of a dead, healthy deer to prove the fallacy of the wildlife department's claims that all the deer are starving. We could put an early end to the hunt and save some of the herd. It's now November 28. The hunt could start as soon as Monday, December 4. They always pick a weekday because they know activists work."

Eleanor wished Honor would just go away with all her new demands and Hank Cagney. She was exhausted. And now Hank! His handsome, gentle image had never left her mind since that day in the city. But she couldn't feel anything! She silently stared at Honor. "This is a crazy kind of coincidence, her hiring him," she told herself. "Weird coincidence! Well, maybe not. Helen said the activists drifted from one company to the other."

"Why don't you run an ad before the hunt?" she asked Honor. "If you think public outrage could stop it?"

"You're right! One before and one after," Honor said, studying Eleanor's grim face for a few seconds before she charged out of her office.

Life began to flow back in her veins with the thought that PAAC could save *some* of the 233 deer. She called Lydia, whose calm voice soothed her. Barrington had spent $10,000 trying to stop the 1993 hunt with an injunction and had failed, Lydia explained. If Honor repeated the action during a reelection bid, it would be a waste of money.

"Don't forget, we still have the opportunity to scare the deer from their home range the day before," she said. "And I intend to join Steve Roberts of CFAR, who will sabotage the hunt. He was the only one out there in 1993. I'll be arrested, no doubt, and my husband will have to feed my cats! Ha, ha, ha. He doesn't mind."

After processing Lydia's information, Eleanor felt convinced that PAAC's feeble attempt to stop the plan should not have taken place. Honor had known the cards were stacked against the deer; she should have either enlisted Eleanor's assistance on her first day on the job or hired a lobbyist. "If Honor is defeated before she even begins a campaign, then it's time for her to retired," she thought.

That evening she had never felt so grateful to step into her home. As she entered, her phone was ringing. Rusty stood in the middle of the living room, his tail straight up like a welcoming banner. She rushed to answer the phone while struggling out of her beige parka, and threw it on the couch. It was Hank Cagney. Just what she needed. After a brief update on the deer situation, she excused herself, mumbling that she was exhausted. With that she stumbled to the kitchen to fill the cat dishes and then escaped to her bedroom and finally allowed the tears of frustration, grief, and guilt to flow. Then she drifted into a long-awaited sleep. About 10 PM, however, she woke with a start to sit straight up and stare at her alarmed cats.

"I didn't even welcome him to our madhouse!" Then the horror of the impending deer hunt rushed back. She heaved a heavy sigh and fell back down. The following morning she abandoned her workout and called the wildlife department at 7:30, knowing the wildlife managers started early. The hunt would begin Monday at daybreak, December 4, as Honor had predicted. Next she managed to reach Steve Roberts. He agreed to meet her at PAAC's office that evening.

She rushed through the lobby past the quizzical Ellen and was met with the unexpected sight of Hank Cagney. He was leaning against her office doorway chatting with Coretta. Gone was his casual look and the dark stubble. He was clean shaven with his hair combed back looking very GQ, wearing a dark navy suit, a light blue-and-white striped shirt, and a tie with horizontal stripes of gold, blue, and black.

"I wanted to come in just to touch base with Honor," he said. He rolled his eyes devilishly. "I brought her some flowers."

"Oh, I'm so sorry I didn't welcome you last night!" Eleanor exclaimed. "Welcome aboard!" she said. Then she whispered, "I think."

"You got that right," Coretta mumbled.

"Can we get together after work?" he asked. He leaned over to speak softly into her left ear, revealing the true inspiration of his unexpected visit.

"Yes," she said.

"Eleanor!" Honor shouted demandingly. She was clamoring toward them while slamming her feet, and was dressed in cocoa brown from head to toe. "Call Steven, tell him we have to meet ASAP," she demanded. "Call the bloody department to see if they've announced the date! Try to pull it out of them! I'm sure they'll give us two or three days. If you can get Steven to meet tonight, Hank, you'll stay. If not, you'll hop a train back to the city after lunch."

Hank shot Eleanor a glance.

"Honor, I called the department already," Eleanor said. "Before I left the house. The hunt starts Monday at dawn." She checked her tone, annoyed that Honor issued such simplistic instructions.

After a few groans were emitted, everyone was numbed into silence. Honor sighed, and fell quiet and moved closer to Eleanor, actually leaning on her for moral support. Eleanor stood next to her open door, her hands clutched in front of her, her parka thrown over her right arm and her black shoulder bag hanging from her right shoulder, with Honor on her left staring at her. The two women knowingly gazed into each other's eyes just inches apart, silently sharing their grief for the innocent deer.

"I spoke to Steve before he left for work. He'll be here about 6 PM," Eleanor said. "Today I'll write and fax out the press release and contact the assignment desks of CNN and the local TV and cable stations."

Honor offered Hank's assistance to create signs and alert activists, again mentioning that Monday was a workday and fewer people could protest, which was the objective of the department.

"I know some loyal activists. They'll be there," Eleanor said. "You can bet on it."

The activists would rise three hours before dawn to arrive in Seaview to harass the hunters. "We'll be waiting for the yahoos to cart the dead deer out of the park in the back of their pickup trucks!" Honor said.

Eleanor raised her voice so the office could hear. Most of PAAC's employees would be required to stand on the freezing strip of land before daybreak, exposed to the elements.

"Honor, I guarantee CNN!" she said. "Guns, blood, dead bodies, and arrests!…It's perfect!" Everyone chuckled at the macabre humor. "We can't lose on this one! This is news they die for! Honor, I hope you can get the ad in the newspaper for tomorrow. It may work; the governor's been in the papers these days with a couple of shady deals regarding the environment. People might be getting sick of these environmental crimes."

"I'll promise you one thing," Honor said. She stood up, her head held high. "This carnage will not occur in the shadows of Denmark Cliff hidden from the public! The bloody massacre, yes, I'm sure will be on CNN! In people's living rooms! And more!" she said. She searched Eleanor's eyes, depending on her to deliver.

"We'll make them pay for the death of each and every one of the 233 deer with the price of bad publicity! We'll tell the world 'something's rotten in Denmark'! That'll nip the bastard boy scouts in the butt!" Honor exclaimed. The state spent thousands yearly on ads in newspapers, running children's essay contests, and printing a magazine. "Nobody knows they run a bloody wildlife factory for hunters! They cut down trees to clear the woods in our forests so that the land will produce low-growing shrubs to feed deer who have become nothing more than game for hunters. I hate the bloody bastards! Damn it, I hate them! They'll pay dearly!"

While Honor inspired Eleanor and Hank, they gazed at each other, sharing their mutual admiration for her. Eleanor rethought her doubts about Honor's loyalty to the deer. Perhaps Lydia was right, and Honor had been shrewd not to waste money on a losing campaign. And maybe Honor truly believed that a last-minute attempt could have made the difference.

Hank mentioned that his upstate activist friends, about fifteen in number, most of them college students at Syracuse University, were willing to drive down to participate in a CD. He suggested doing a second-stage invasion, one that followed Steve's group into the woods hours later, at about 9 AM. "That'll keep the cops chasing after us and divert their attention from Steve and his crew until they can get a picture of the killing of a healthy deer…If they haven't been arrested by then, that is." His eyes were on his boss as he respectfully explained, "Honor, you can offer this plan at tonight's meeting. If anything, it'll give us options."

Oh, how Eleanor craved to be one of the saboteurs led by the self-effacing, charismatic Steve Roberts as he spoke about their plans that evening in PAAC's conference room. The saboteurs would approach the hunters, speaking to them in hopes of throwing off their aim. But Honor would hear none of it; she required Eleanor's assistance on the street, organizing protesters and the media. But when Steve, who was in his late forties and was a twenty-year animal rights veteran, requested a ride from the Seaview Motel to the park at 3:30 Monday morning, Eleanor jumped at the chance despite Honor's disagreeable glance. She and two CFAR members would rendezvous with Steve and his crew of infiltrators, including Lydia, at a local hamburger joint in Seaview, far from the park entrance. Eleanor's passengers would take Steve's car, while Eleanor would drive Steve and his crew to the dead-end street that bordered the park grounds.

Steve rejected the suggestion that they scare the deer away from hunters during the hunt. That might force the jittery creatures directly into the hands of their enemies, he explained. And chasing them the day before with clattering and clashing pots might render them less responsive to gunshots the following day; besides, they'd only return at night to their home range. But they all agreed that a telling photograph of the bloody massacre captured early on, and placed as an advertisement the following day, was the best hope of survival for some of the herd.

Was it the doom of the horrible hunt or just the right moment in life that drew Eleanor and Hank together in just hours? Like a comfortable stare between old friends, their eyes often rested on each other during the meeting with CFAR. As they exited PAAC's conference room, Eleanor offered to drive Hank to the Westport train station to catch a nine o'clock train. He planned to return the following afternoon with the basic necessities and stay at a nearby Holiday Inn for the duration.

As she drove through the parking lot toward Compo Beach Road, Eleanor asked if he'd like a veggie stir-fry at Jimmy's Seaside Café. Hank jumped at the invitation before she could finish. Even with the Cliff hunt looming over them, the two were so drawn to each other that they attempted to suppress their smiles of delight when they caught each other's eyes on the ride to the restaurant. A waiter showed them to the enclosed sunporch overlooking the water. Their narrow table with a white tablecloth was right next to the multipaned window. The view included a full moon shining on the water like a postcard. The hurricane lamp in the center of the table was the only light in the dining area.

Once they settled into their seats, the strands of Eleanor's hair turned a metallic gold in the hurricane lamplight. Her beauty made it necessary for Hank to turn away to peer out the window to gather himself, pretending to gaze at the Long Island Sound. But alas, there above the dark waters was the brilliant full moon, its rays shimmering on the water. "Look at that moonlight," Hank whispered.

After grilling the waiter about the vegetarian contents of their foods, they ordered and the two easily chatted like close siblings. Often they stared in comfortable silence at the full moon, each time stunned anew at its beauty. As they talked, Eleanor gravitated toward him physically and mentally, as if his strength and warmth could protect her aching heart and the grief to come. His black thatch of hair caught the light and draped onto the wide forehead of his diamond-shaped face as he spoke. He was always smiling at her, brimming with gentleness and quiet intelligence.

They talked like brother and sister who shared similar educations specializing in literature and English. Both were Knicks fans and film buffs. He told of his experiences as one of three sons of an Irish mother and an English father, and of his childhood in Queens. After college, he'd made it his duty to see as many Broadway and off-Broadway plays as he could afford, he revealed. She related to his daily routine as a staff reporter for *Newsday* in Long Island, where he was employed for five years after graduating from college, and she empathized with his reluctance to "get the story at any cost."

He had joined the movement after a glimpse of RUFFFF's pictures of the tortured monkeys. "That converted a lot of us," he said of his high school mates. "I quit *Newsday* to join RUFFFF as a staff writer. I was an editor by then, and the money was good but something was missing." He had worked for RUFFFF for the last year and a half. "If this doesn't work, I'm back at *Newsday*."

While the waiter served their dinner and refilled their water glasses, he mentioned that he had met Helen at an LA demonstration. "She recommended me to Honor," he said, having just chewed a healthy forkful of the tasty dish of stir-fry vegetables and coconut on a bed of rice. "When I returned to the city for a fur protest, I wanted to stay." He didn't reveal that his decision was partially a result of their encounter.

Eleanor, however, knew.

"But it wasn't until a few weeks ago that I called Honor, and then contacted Helen to put in a word for me. I was pleasantly surprised by Honor's speedy decision."

During a welcoming dinner at Honor's home, Hank had caught no hints of superiority. "I hear she's different in the office. Poor Honor. Anyway, I decided to ignore all the warnings and take the job. So she becomes intense? But so what? I think she's earned the right after forty years."

Eleanor empathized, relating to her own eagerness to forgive Honor's transgressions. "A warning, Hank: she knows how to hurt."

Suddenly two pair of hungry mallards drew Hank's attention, and he pointed to the window behind Eleanor. The ducks scrambled for bread being tossed into the dark, rippling water by a waiter on a cigarette break. Eleanor glowed at Hank, delighted that he'd be drawn to the endearing scene. In her mind, the big switchboard in the sky lit up as they connected on endless levels, and at that very moment she knew that the special night marked the beginning of a lifetime relationship.

"Hank, do you know that my full name is Eleanor Aquitaine Green? When my mother was pregnant with me, she had a dream of a young woman in armor wearing a red cross and sitting upon a stallion. When she woke she was sure she was carrying a girl. It was a premonition. She knew that Eleanor of Aquitaine had led a band of women to the crusades, and she always admired her for her independence. You know that she led troops of men into battle in her eighties. So my mother named me after her. Not that she believed in the crusades and the killing, of course! But in Eleanor of Aquitaine's incredible independence."

Hank began to recite:

"Were the world all mine,
From the sea to the Rhine,
I'd give all away,
If the English Queen,
Would be mine for a day."

Eleanor began to laugh.

"That was written by a German poet for Eleanor of Aquitaine," Hank said. "I don't remember his name. But everyone at the time, it was said, was in love with her. I worked for a historical magazine straight out of college for a few months, and my first assignment was to write a story about her. The poem reminded me of the TV program *Queen for a Day*, that's why I remembered it…Better be warned that I'm not a romantic, it's not in my nature."

"You could fool me," Eleanor said. "Although the poem was kind of lame."

"That's why nobody bothered to learn his name."

"Isn't Hank a nickname?" she asked.

"Was there some other significance to this Aquitaine name?" he asked.

"Well, isn't Hank short for Henry?" she said.

"Yes, my full name is Henry William Cagney. The William is after my father. It's all very English," he said. "My mother's father was born in London."

He leaned across the table, inches away from her incandescent face. "Not to worry, Eleanor, no matter what happens to us, you have my solemn promise that I will never, never lock you up in a tower!"

She burst into laughter, tickled that he'd played along. "Henry II was a pretty obnoxious husband. I just thought it strange…that here we are, about eight centuries later, Eleanor and Hank…Without title, land, or money, that is."

The waiter arrived with the check and Hank was quick to grab it. Eleanor fished into her shoulder bag, which was hanging on the back of her seat. "I insist we split it," she said. "Don't argue with a queen."

They stood up to put on their jackets. "You must be exhausted! I am! I'd hate to have to take the train all the way back to the city and then travel to Queens. You could sleep over, go back in the morning!" She was speaking as if she were talking to a friend, and she surprised herself by her spontaneity. "I have a comfortable couch."

"Sure, why not?" he said. He smiled gratefully. "How far is it to your apartment?"

"Twenty minutes away. It's in Derbe."

She'd drop him off at the Derbe train station down the road from her, just off Route 7, at 6:30 AM on her way to the YMCA next morning, she told him; it was no inconvenience. "You'll be back in your apartment in time for Honor's check-up call at 9 AM! Ha, ha."

Hank was comfortable in Eleanor's apartment. He relaxed on the couch, smiling with pleasure as he petted Rusty, who purred in his lap. Friday studied him from a safe distance on the floor next to the fireplace, while Eleanor sought a set of spare sheets. She sighed, haunted by the prospect of the hunt, as she spread the checkered lilac-and-white sheets over the cranberry cushions with Hank's assistance.

As she passed the lamp table to go to bed, he reached toward her small waist, gazing at her moist lips. He closed his eyes and kissed her. When she responded in kind, he was moved. Eleanor had waited for someone like Hank all her life, since her father, since her husband; that message was delivered in the kiss.

She led him toward her bedroom, not wanting to neck like teenagers on her couch. She folded down her mother's quilt, placing it on the closet shelf, and undressed behind the closet door. As she slipped into her beige satin-and-lace nightgown, he took off his clothing and placed them on the chair in the far corner next to the window. Then she put on the Dells tape in the boom box on the floor under the window. The first song was "Oh, What a Night." She turned off the light on her night table, and they slipped between the sky blue sheets together in concert, smiling at each other in the moonlit room.

The sultry, sweet tones rose from her boom box, and the small bedroom blurred in their desire and their wish to escape the tragedy to come. The Dells' earthy rhythm and blues did what Eleanor wanted. The passionate voices wove a romantic web that embraced the large brass bed, allowing them their moment. The celestial bodies outside her window, the brilliant full moon and stars, shone through the sheer, white-dotted Swiss and cyan blue ruffle café curtains filling the space with their magic. The couple lost themselves in each other in a dreamy, moist love cloud drifting slowly to their primordial selves.

Their desire uncovered urges planted in their minds eons ago, before the intellectualization of sex, the sexual revolution, before erotic doodads and porno films, before the study of form or the liberation of women, before the pill. They were a man and a woman loving with the ardor of their craving bodies, and with souls searching for the comfort of peace and kindness in each other.

She swept his body with her own, touching each sacred part of her mate. Her passion followed her heart. Coming to the love feast was every hidden and pent-up emotion in her body that had waited for this moment. In the dark without his knowing, she buried her face in the soft bed, while a silent primal scream ripped through her body born from the ecstasy and agony that was turning her inside out.

He groaned as his hands ran along the curves of her hips. The music faded as their bodies clung and caressed until passion overcame them. Together at last, they groaned in ecstasy, the heat building to an agonizing pitch. Afterward they were as natural and peaceful as songbirds in a forest glade, sighing, petting, drifting, petting, drifting, sleeping—ah, the precious sleep of lovers, fast and safe in each other's arms.

The winter morning light was made brighter by the brilliant snow. Eleanor, in dreamy comfort, gazed at the sleeping face that was a miracle to her as she listened to the commuter traffic.

"We're more than animal rights soul mates, we're soul mates," she thought. "Jane always knew love could be like this," she thought, laughing at herself. "But Jane just didn't know if she'd ever find it." Tears of gratitude brimmed her eyes. It was finally the end of the sadness, the pain of betrayal that had haunted her. "God, thank you," she thought as her lips grazed Hank's wide brow.

Hank awoke and whispered, his mouth close to her right ear, "It's such a simple act." And he stopped there, obviously awed at what had taken place. He glanced about the homey room and listened to the hum of the traffic. "There are three things going on: I don't want anyone else to have you; and you make me feel like a man; and then there's this incredible feeling."

Her satin strap hung off her left shoulder as she faced him, her alabaster skin held a hint of yellow. He lifted the strap up gently, smiling, and set it in its rightful place on her shoulder. "When did you become a woman?"

"I really don't know. But I've never really felt very young."

His arms tightened around her, pulling her soft, silky body even closer. He closed his eyes. "Vegans taste better."

She chuckled. "We ought to put that on a valentine card. Hank, let's keep this our little secret. I don't want Honor to know about 'us.'"

Hank sighed at the sound of "us." "You're right. Let's be secret lovers," he said. A few seconds later, he opened his eyes again and was surprised to see a frown on her face. He sat up and hugged her. "The deer?" he asked. "It's not over yet! We can chase them from Denmark Cliff the day before the hunt—walk the park clanging pots to chase them! Even if Steve thinks they'll return, it's OK. So maybe some won't!"

"Hank. Think about it. Only 806 acres and 25 hunters swarming the place? You have to promise me not to take any chances." She turned to peer at him, the strap falling off her shoulder. "You'll be rushing into the forest to foil hunters with bullets flying!"

CHAPTER 13

▼

THE MOVING FOREST

That Friday evening, a northeaster blew in six inches of snow, followed by subzero temperatures on Saturday. On Sunday an arctic storm contributed another five inches. The severe temperatures continued into the predawn hours Monday, plunging the region into severe weather conditions. That morning the wind whipped the shoreline of Denmark Cliff, threatening to cripple anyone who dared to challenge it. At 2:30 AM, Eleanor dressed for the weather in her room at the Groton Motel.

A half hour later, two CFAR activists arrived for the trip to Seaview. At 3:45 AM they arrived outside a hamburger joint where they picked up Steve's car. Lydia, Steve, Lindsay Brenner, Nathanael Grant, and Bob Fiore jumped into Eleanor's car for the ride to the park. The five were dressed in black. They sat on the floor in silence as she drove past the park's entrance and the two police patrol cars parked in front. Gazing into her rearview mirror, she continued down the dead-end road. Then Bob, who was seated next to her, ordered, "Turn off your lights!" She continued in the dark, peering over her steering wheel in order to see as she drove to the end of the unlit block to a dark building that was a defunct train station. The five scrambled out, and Eleanor watched as they scampered like chimps, their eyes squinting to bear the gusts of frigid wind. They faded into the shadows of the low-growing coastal underbrush that grew between the road and the railroad tracks. One by one, the huddled forms crossed the tracks and crept and slid down the icy embankment.

Eleanor circled back down the street, turning on her lights. "As far as the police know," she told herself, "I drove up this street alone and I'm driving back alone." But her heart skipped a few beats as she drove past the two patrol cars, the rays of the headlights intermingling as they faced each other. Back at the motel, sleep was impossible. Instead, she faxed her press releases one more time on the motel's fax machine. A half hour later, she met Honor and Hank for a quick breakfast. At 6:30 AM she drove them while Freda followed her car with the rest of PAAC's staff to Denmark Cliff. A line of grumpy and cold policemen stood at the left of the park's driveway, lining the tracks to block access to the park grounds.

During the next couple of hours, local activists and neighbors arrived. Most were bundled up, leaving only their eyes exposed to the stinging cold. They lined the driveway to the entrance of the park and shouted at arriving hunters, urging them to go home, and then took turns defrosting in cars parked at the curb of the dead-end street.

At 9 AM Eleanor heaved a sigh of relief to see CNN and other local TV stations arrive. Minutes later, the upstate college students arrived with tattoos and an array of outfits. She then alerted the reporters, who had remained waiting in their warm trucks, about Hank's civil disobedience about to commence.

She and Honor stood next to the curb watching as the students walked to the tracks for a face-off with the police, some of the neighborhood activists joining them.

"What do we want?" they chanted. "Animal rights. When do we want it? Now! What do we want? Animal rights! When do we want it? Now!"

They seemed impervious to the cold, and unapologetic to the police. Eleanor was filled with pride watching them. And she was grateful for the diversion from the nagging questions about Steve and his crew. She wondered if they had gotten the video yet. Would they get the video before they got arrested? Her foot warmers were working overtime. "They must be freezing!" she thought. "It's five hours now. When will they call?"

Just at that moment, Honor's cell phone rang, and she fumbled with her cold fingers to unfold it.

"Eleanor?" Nathanael asked.

"It's Honor. What's going on?"

"Honor, we got it! We got the video! They're coming! They're coming! You gotta stop this! Anyway you can! You gotta stop this! Steve and the others are still out there. Tell them people could get killed! Tell them anything! We can't let them all die like this! They can't all die like this!"

"We'll do it!" Eleanor shouted into the phone, gazing at Honor. "Don't worry, Nathanael, we'll do it!"

She didn't know how, but she was going to try like hell. The phone went dead. Eleanor looked into Honor's eyes. Without a word spoken, they marched to the police sergeant standing in front of the tracks. Honor approached the short burly man, asking him to join her for a private conversation. They took a few steps away from the track. She looked down her nose at him as she spoke.

"Sergeant, you must call off the hunt. Activists are now in the reserve with the hunters." She summoned her most demanding regal voice, her most elitist and imperial tone. "I insist you call this hunt off right now!" Her neck stretched to its fullest, her shoulders were squared. "You are endangering the lives of humans!"

"I have no authority to do that." He shuffled his feet and gazed away from her.

The media, waiting for Hank's CD, circled them.

"Sergeant," Eleanor said, "please call Rick Delaney or the commissioner! If someone gets killed or injured, you'll be responsible. This is a warning. It's dangerous out there!"

"I'll try to reach someone." He plodded straight ahead to his cruiser parked along the curb, close to the entrance, and ducked inside. Eleanor followed him and heard him call Rick Delaney. Seconds later the sergeant got out of the car. "Delaney's at the tagging station. He'll be right out."

Seconds later, a tall, thin, attractive man in his forties with leathery skin walked up from the tagging station, which was just a few feet into the park. Eleanor knew it was Delaney. She even knew the name of his kids: Noah, Joy and Faith. He was a good man. He looked grave. She introduced herself and Honor.

"You need to tell us where your activists are," Delaney said. "I only want to protect your people. If you reveal their location and number, there'll be less chance of injury."

"There's too many to count!" Honor said. "We have no idea where they are!"

It was then that Delaney quoted the commissioner verbatim. "The State Wildlife Department four weeks prior to the hunt advertised the closing of Denmark Cliff State Park to allow the hunters to mercifully end the lives of the starving deer," he said. "We are grateful for their help. Any intruders are breaking trespass laws and are at their own risk. The commissioner insists that the hunt continue until the target number of 233 deer are taken. I'm sorry, but that's it."

Eleanor touched his sleeve, almost out of pity for him as well as the deer. "I know you stopped the 1993 hunt, and I banked on your stopping this one. We understand you are following orders, but this is a disgrace to your department and to the state of Connecticut."

That's when the shrill cry of a young girl pierced the air. In the middle of the park's entrance road, a college student dressed in a black jacket and blue jeans was on her knees, crouched over holding her stomach. A young man rushed from the tracks to her aid, followed by the media and the police.

Hank led the new wave of twenty infiltrators over the railroad tracks and down the icy embankment. One officer turned in time to discover their fading backs and shouted to the police sergeant. Eleanor's fears for Hank's safety disappeared in the action. The police would arrest them in minutes, it seemed, and she heard no rifle shots in the vicinity.

"I doubt you'll catch them," Honor said to the sergeant. "Too many donuts!"

He dashed to his cruiser to request additional cars and another paddy wagon. Honor opened the door on the passenger side and stuck her head in. "Sergeant, what will you bloody do? Wait until someone gets killed? Put an end to this sad excuse for a hunt, why don't you? Your hunter slobs could be injured too!"

"You already have our answer."

Rick had walked back to the tagging station when the CD ensued. Alison Barrington and her staff of five drove up the street to the park minutes later. They soon stood with Honor and PAAC's employees lining the park entrance, harassing hunters who were still arriving. Barrington positioned herself next to Honor. Eleanor stood on the other side of the entry road, fascinated as she observed the two aristocrats who seemed a world apart from most of those present.

Ten minutes later, the first paddy wagon exited the park carrying Lindsay, Nathanael, several of the college students, and Beverly Lawson, a seventy-year-old woman who was being arrested for the first time in her life.

Waving proudly, Honor and Alison led the protesters in a victory cheer. It seemed strange to see the two women cheering. Then it came to Eleanor: "Honor and Alison are content to be cheerleaders; Leona would be inside the truck," she thought. "What a difference an era makes."

An hour later, with activists still hidden in the park, Eleanor went to the Seaview Police Station, driven by the urge to get Nathanael's videotape to the media. The police station was situated at the top of the wide snow-plowed avenue that ran through town. A few feet from the front door, an officer sat behind a protective, glass-enclosed booth. To the right was a waiting room with benches where several of the college students sat waiting for their friends to be released. One smiling college girl was milling around serving her home-baked vegan cookies.

Lindsay sat on the floor to the right. With one look at her downcast eyes, Eleanor knew that it was she who had filmed the slaughter.

"Nathanael left with the tape," she told Eleanor. "He's bringing it to the CNN reporter. He wanted to handle it. He knows what needs to be done to have it converted."

Eleanor unzipped her parka and settled down on the floor next to the dazed girl with the dark eyes and hair. Honor and Alison arrived forty minutes later, all the infiltrators having been arrested. Minutes later, Lindsay was asked by several reporters to step outside in front of the police station for an interview. Honor and Eleanor trailed after her. Large snowflakes began to fall as Lindsay spoke. Eleanor was surprised by her strong voice and composure.

"I'm a third-year law student at Yale University, and this morning I witnessed a healthy doe being shot by a hunter," she began. "She died violently for absolutely no reason. I assure you that she was no more starving to death than you or I. But she didn't have a shield to protect her from hunters' bullets." Her body heaved a sigh. Tears filled her eyes. "Her fawn is still roaming in the park looking for her."

"Where was she shot?" asked CBS's female reporter.

"She was shot in the right side of the neck. She began to bleed immediately, but she was still standing. She was shot again, this time in the abdominal cavity. Her entrails slipped out of her body as she attempted to run from the hunters. Then after running about a hundred yards, she was down. And after several minutes of struggling to rise with her fawn licking her, she died. One hunter laughed as she began to run. He said, 'She's dead, and she don't know it!' The other hunter tied a rope around her neck and dragged the mother through the forest. The fawn followed his mother to the tagging station. Hunters were shooing him away. But nobody killed him. They left that baby alone to starve and freeze to death, ironically."

As she watched Lindsay, Eleanor became jittery. There had been no word from Nathanael. Honor stood to her right. "I've got to go back and find Nathanael and make sure the videotape gets to all the TV stations."

"Why don't you just call them?" Honor said.

Stunned by Honor's faulty advice and knowing well that she'd view any suggestion as an act of high treason, Eleanor's heart sank; she stared at Honor stymied realizing that she had no heart to buck her. Lindsay, who had just finished the interview, overheard the exchange as she approached.

"She should talk to them in person!" she said.

"You're right," said Honor.

Eleanor raced out of the police station like a prisoner set free. "Thank God for the independence of volunteers!" she thought. She jumped into her Nissan parked right out front. It was as cold as steel. She gunned the gas to heat it up. She pushed the speed limit down the hill through the busy avenue. The snow was thicker now and sticking. With her fingers grasping the cold steering wheel, she realized that for the first time in her employment at PAAC, she had actually backed down from Honor.

"Where is the savvy reporter who will get the truth if it kills her?" If Honor's behavior prevented her from doing her job, she'd be forced to quit, she concluded. She'd fulfill her mission by some other means!

As she approached the park and made a right on to Denmark Cliff Road, to her relief, the CNN truck was still there. She uttered a prayer of thanks. The rest of the media were still there too, no doubt waiting for the exiting deer carcasses dumped in the back of pickup trucks.

Nathanael was slumped in Steve's idling Camry, which was parked behind the white-and-navy blue CNN truck. He held the videotape in his hands. Eleanor pulled up alongside.

"They can't convert it," he said, rolling down the window. His voice sounded dead. "It's no use," he said. He shook his head in hopelessness. "They're missing some kind of hookup. And the Kodak store can't do it either." He shook his head forlornly, as if all their desperate efforts to save the deer had been for nothing.

"Nathanael, you've done enough! Don't you worry about this part! This is my baby! I'm the PR person!"

She made a U-turn and parked behind him and jumped out. Without a word spoken, she reached into the open window and took the tape from his limp hand. "Go to the police station. They have some home-baked vegan cookies. You need to get away from this place!"

He failed to move as she mounted the steep metal steps and pounded on the door of the truck. She introduced herself to the pudgy young man who greeted her with a smile of amusement. He resembled Jack Black, she thought. She waved the videotape before him.

"This shows a hunter laughing as his partner kills a healthy mother deer with her fawn at her side," she said. "This is *Bambi* all over again! The orphaned fawn follows his mother as the hunter drags her dead body through the snow. You've got to convert this! Your viewers will be shocked at this! This footage proves that this was no starving deer!"

She paused, staring into the smiling eyes. "Let me know what you need. I'll find a store and get it for you. Or get the film converted somewhere! And we'll be happy to pay you for copies to give to the other stations if you can do it."

His eyes lit up. He shot a smile of confidence at Eleanor, and without a word uttered, he whisked the tape from her hand. As he was about to reenter the truck, he turned. "Oh, I just thought of how we can do it. Don't worry, we'll give it to the others. We're sister stations."

"Will it be on the six o'clock news?" she asked. "You'll give us that tape back?"

"Definitely. It'll play every hour on the hour throughout the night and then on the following day until noon. We'll give you your video back, sure, wait here." With a smile, he disappeared inside the truck.

Nathanael finally left, not looking much better. An hour later, the man reappeared to return the videotape and offering a thumbs-up. Eleanor rushed back to the Seaview Police Station. The snowfall was heavier now. It was after 4 PM. Hank, Steve, Honor, Lydia, Lindsay, Lauren, Beverly, Nathanael, several of the local neighbors, and Andrew Dewhurst sat on the waiting room floor, chatting easily and waiting for others to be released.

Eleanor ran in and came to an abrupt stop in the center of the waiting room, raised her hands in a victory sign, and announced, "We did it! All the channels have it and it will play tonight! CNN will show it on the hour from 6 PM tonight until tomorrow at 12 noon! Congratulations!"

A ringing cheer rose from the floor and there was applause. All the work and effort had at least garnered a spotlight for the betrayed deer and the Johansens. As Honor had promised, the deer would not die in the shadows of Denmark Cliff but before millions, Eleanor thought. While everyone was cheering, Steve, who sat next to Lindsay and Nathanael, raised his weary eyes to meet hers and transmitted his grief. It was a sobering moment.

The death count was at forty-five deer, she learned. The arrest count was high: twenty activists and neighbors, most of whom had been arrested for the first time in their lives on behalf of the deer. It would be a black eye for Connecticut's Wildlife Department

That evening, with Rusty and Friday at their side, Eleanor and Hank sat in the living room leaning against the couch and anticipating the news. CNN played the tape as a teaser and then presented full coverage of the deer being shot, others being hauled out in the back of pickup trucks, and protesters being carted off in paddy wagons.

Sue Simmons on the CBS news show announced that "the controversial hunt drove local residents to be arrested in protest." People For Animals signs and

PAAC's protest signs advertised their presence in both shows. Simmons continued in her upbeat manner. "The state contends that it is necessary to hunt the deer because they are starving, but the residents object, saying the deer are healthy and hunts should not take place in state parks. So there!"

They flicked to other channels and managed to catch Dan Rather and Tom Brokaw, both of whom touched on the "controversial hunt" and used the wrenching footage. With each showing, Eleanor shouted in hopeful screams. With each viewing of the mother deer and her orphaned fawn, her hopes escalated.

"I don't recall ever seeing footage on a deer hunt on network news, do you?" She peered into Hank's troubled eyes just inches from her.

"It's good. This is very good."

Hank told her that he had witnessed hunters dragging the bodies of the healthy and innocent deer to the state's pickup trucks to be driven to the tagging station. But he had also met Steve and was inspired. "I'm sure right now there are people watching this and wondering why they ever hunted, or why their fathers hunt."

On the following day, Eleanor could barely wait to go to work. She rushed into the large office an hour early and met Honor racing toward her.

"Eleanor, you did a brilliant job! You were calm and collected. I would have been a maniac under such pressure. This TV coverage will be legendary for PAAC. Come to my office, I have the prints for the ad. The studio did a rush job for us last night."

Spread across her desk was a blown-up copy of the advertisement with two pictures. The first was of the fawn licking his dying mother, who appeared to have been a fit and healthy doe. The second picture was of the two hunters aiming at the doe and her fawn in the first photograph. In bold letters underneath the photographs was written: "Your Telephone Call Can Stop the Slaughter." The fine print explained PAAC's position on the "Massacre of healthy state park deer."

Now there was nothing to do but wait. When Eleanor arrived at work the following day, Wednesday, the third day of the hunt, she paced as if she were a large cat in a cage. Finally, at three o'clock she called Andrew Dewhurst.

"Eleanor, the phones are ringing and the secretaries are happy about it," Andrew said. "They're telling the governor's assistant as fast as the calls come in. But I'm afraid it's helpless. The governor's getting the same amount of calls from hunters. He's got to keep on course with the NRA. It's politics. He wants to be reelected."

It was dark for a second as Eleanor took in Dewhurst's assessment. "What a stupid pie-in-the-sky optimist I've been! I really thought we could save them."

"Hope is the engine of the movement. Without it, we'd get nowhere. Your and Honor's optimism engineered the interview with Whitcomb. Thanks to your optimism, I can live with myself. I know we did our best."

Eleanor hung up and recalled Honor's bizarre behavior during her job interview: her display of fury regarding the Denmark Cliff Hunt. "I had no idea."

Her eyes clung to the seagulls busy in their daily pursuits outside her window. She stared ahead at Coretta and Betty who were discussing a piece of correspondence from a member, and wished her own job was as uncomplicated.

It occurred to her to turn on her radio to hear the reaction. She was lucky to catch a talk show host saying, "Why should we become outraged about killing a few healthy deer, when after all we go to the supermarket every day to buy meat, healthy meat from healthy animals, to eat it? So what's the big deal if hunters kill a few deer?"

In six days the entire 233 deer had been killed. On the seventh day, Monday, December 11, Steve and Nathanael searched the Cliff for orphaned fawns and discovered two small bodies shot and left to die. They telephoned Eleanor. On Wednesday, Roberta Steinway called first thing that morning to report witnessing a small herd of deer migrating onto Denmark Cliff from the mainland. It was just as Dewhurst had predicted: if there's a niche, nature will fill it.

Eleanor stared at her door, again envying the calm Coretta who was peacefully punching in numbers. Andrew called her later to report the outcome of the necropsies report. If the 233 deer hadn't been killed, they would have multiplied to 346, because 112 of the does were pregnant. Twenty of the pregnant deer carried twins, proving that the land was sustaining the herd numbers. If she is in a state of starvation, a mother whitetail deer is able to ingest her fetus to survive, and starving stags are too busy foraging for food to mate with numerous does. Although the report determined that the deer were smaller than typical deer and had less body fat, the pregnancies were at odds with the starvation predictions. If resources are low, fewer does bare offspring and they don't bare twins, Dewhurst explained. And, he added, shoreline deer weigh less than inland deer anyway.

"Delaney resigned," Dewhurst said. He related the department's scuttlebutt about the resignation. Blott, the arrogant wildlife manager who was known to laugh at animal activists, walked into Delaney's office with the necropsy report. With a smirk on his face, he said, "I guess we'll call an annual hunt to keep the deer number down to twenty-five."

Delaney said, "I've had enough."

"What do you mean?" Blott asked.

"Denmark Cliff's what I mean. I'm sick of the lies."

"Are you forgetting who pays our bills?" Blott asked.

"That's just it, I'm remembering."

"Eleanor, that's the story, Delaney is a hero around here. Everybody knows he's leaving because of Denmark Cliff."

Eleanor remained driven, as if huge doses of hard work were a magic elixir that would kill the constant pain in her heart. At Steve's direction, she organized a candlelight vigil for Friday night, to be held outside the governor's mansion in Hartford. The single-digit weather continued. Would people bear such weather and interrupt their Christmas shopping in memory of the deer?

The governor's white colonial mansion had black shutters and sat behind a black wrought-iron picket fence. It was unobtrusive in the quiet suburban neighborhood. The sidewalk that ran past the mansion and the entire block had been shoveled, and a four-foot high border of shoveled snow ran between the sidewalk and the curb. Eleanor, standing directly in front of the mansion, lit the first candle, pushed it through a small, white paper cup, and placed it on top of the snow mound facing the mansion's front door. She continued the process five times. With each candle she lit, she remembered the innocent faces of the deer. With each one her heart felt the grief it carried.

She was satisfied that arriving mourners would recognize the fiery landmark. One by one they arrived and slowly approached, seeming grateful at the sight of her and the candles. She directed them to parking places on the side block. When they returned on foot, she handed each of them two white candles from the many boxes she had stacked up on the sidewalk, and then lit them. Soon a small, steady line paced in silent vigil in single file from one end of the mansion to the other and circled back around, like a candlelit moving forest. In a half-hour, eighty people in all paced with their candles illumining their sad faces.

The arctic cold front made the attendance all the more poignant. Most were strangers who had been alerted to the vigil through radio and TV announcements as a result of PAAC's press release. Some resided in Hartford, and others had traveled from all parts of the state. Some came straight from work, some brought children, and some were high school or college students. It was the first vigil for some, while others were veteran activists.

Grief became the common bond that united all present. Grief, along with a need to commune with like souls, those who offered encouragement. The 233 deer were honorably laid to rest. And the vigil, Eleanor prayed, offered some peace to the Johansens.

Honor in her bereavement appeared a credible and heroic figure bearing the freezing temperatures to respect the deer, as she was interviewed by a local TV station. It was apparent that the single-digit temperature made it difficult for her to speak. "Two hundred and thirty-three park deer were killed to entertain 75 hunters," she said. "Federal statistics show that 200,000 fewer hunters fill the country's forests each year. As we remember the deer, we are encouraged by this statistic."

After twenty minutes of the procession, Steve stood in the driveway of the mansion before the locked gates to address the mourners. The candle in his thick hands flickered robustly and with a brilliant yellow light, as if the spirits of the deer were present. As the crowd gathered in front of him, Eleanor couldn't help but think Steve's humility was prevalent, even now. It was there in his sloped shoulders, his bowed head. But in his humble bearing there was a strength that refused to buckle.

"We're remembering," he said. "We're remembering those families of deer at Denmark Cliff that died for no reason. We're remembering the elders who taught the young the code of the herd. We're remembering the mothers who protected their young and taught them how to survive. We're remembering the families that lived within the herd, and the roles they played. They were a nation. That nation is gone. We in our respect will keep them alive forever in here," he said pointing to his heart. "And in here," he said, pointing to his head. "They live on."

Steve finished and rejoined the semicircle of people. Honor propelled out of the crowd, as if Steve's words had inflamed her. In one full swoop she stabbed her candle in the mound of snow along the sidewalk as if she were stabbing the governor in the heart. She streaked toward the black gate to grip the bars, staring with contempt at the lighted windows where no doubt the governor hid.

"Face us like a man, Governor!...You coward! You're as much a coward as those so-called hunters who mowed down the deer!"

The shocked mourners—men, women, and children—stood frozen in place watching this irate woman, their candles highlighting their stunned faces, her identity a mystery to most of them.

"We know you're watching us!" Honor yelled. "Why don't you show some guts and come out here! Can't do it, can you? You can't face us like a man! Your election cost the price of precious wildlife, and you don't care! You're not a man! You're a bloody asshole! That's what you bloody are, a bloody asshole!"

With that Honor pounced off the scene to her car, which was across the street and up a side block. Eleanor watched as Freda trailed close behind and Steve gazed at her smiling with open admiration.

The mourners placed their burning candles in the snowy altar before departing for their cars. Eleanor lit the remaining candles to be sure there were 233 of them. Alone again in the silence on the dark street, she lit the 234th candle and stretched across the mound to set it in the center of the snowy altar. The last candle was in memory of the three-legged deer on her newsroom wall.

"I did my best to save *all* of them, but I failed. I did my best to save *some* of them, but I failed. But thanks to you, I did my best," she said.

It was exactly one year to the day since Eleanor had entered PAAC's premises and was promised her dream job. In the painful grief-filled weekend, she called Steve and told him she didn't know what to do with her grief. He had no answers. She called Lydia saying the same, but Lydia had no response. On Monday, Honor sped past her as if she weren't there, no doubt beginning another season of banishment for crimes unknown. But Eleanor was so numbed by grief that she felt nothing. Her mind dwelled on the suffering of the surviving deer, and those who had lost their lives for no reason.

She returned to her office to gaze out her window at the Grandma Moses scene below and began to meditate on the deer. In that moment, she found the comfort she needed in a vision of the deer. They were at peace, she discovered. It was she who suffered. She realized that her suffering resembled that of a family member of a deceased loved one. It was such a relief to think of the deer in peace and to realize that her pain originated from her own grief, that she at once became tranquil. Why hadn't she turned to God sooner for the answers, she chastised herself.

When she turned from the window and viewed her desk, it seemed such a hostile place. To her relief, the telephone rang. It was Lydia. Grumpol had federal statistics that proved the 1985 legislation was a failure, she revealed, and he was to present the findings at the Conference for the Animals at the end of January. The results were not surprising to anyone, given the present status of laboratory animals, Lydia added, but to have concrete evidence that proved Honor right was another thing. All the main characters in the movement's history, from pioneers such as Rutherford Gee to protest maven Leona Nesbitt, would be present.

"Lydia, I'm going to squeeze an invitation out of Honor somehow," Eleanor said. "Perhaps with justice being served, and by her lover, no less, Honor will finally mellow. And just think, Grumpol and Honor could recharge the dying movement!"

Lydia groaned, as if Eleanor's optimism was too much.

"You said it was dying! I agree! Lydia, we have yet to address the eight billion animals slaughtered every year for food! That issue's been the forbidden fruit of the movement. Not anymore, thanks to pioneers like Honor! Times have changed! Even if Honor can't change! That's the issue! That's the issue that will galvanize and unite your dying movement, Lydia! I know it!

"Lydia, think about it. If people eat the animals, why not do everything else to them? Hunt? Laboratory experiments? What's the difference if they eat them every day? That's the issue!"

Only minutes later, Eleanor was shocked into silence by Hank's call. He was writing his resignation. Since the end of the hunt, he had been working with Tina in organizing PAAC's first official CD, which was to be part of FFAD, Free Fur Animals Day, on December 26.

"I told Honor, after several harassing telephone calls and faxes, that abuse wasn't part of my job description. She refused to admit that she was being abusive. That was the end of our conversation."

Hank would begin working for *Newsday* in a couple of weeks, giving Honor the two-week option. Eleanor told him to pack all his belongings at once. As far as FFAD was concerned, PAAC would join Alison in her usual anti-fur parade in the fur district.

Honor stood in the center of the Westport office that afternoon and ordered her employees never to speak to Hank again; their jobs seemed to hang in the balance.

CHAPTER 14

▼

GRUMPOL

It was Tuesday, January 28, the first day of the Conference for the Animals. Eleanor sat with Helen against the wall on chairs reserved for guests. Although Leona Nesbitt wasn't present, Eleanor was far from disappointed. She focused on Honor and the spacious conference room packed with people who represented the movement. Honor sat at a large rectangular table in the center of the room among the sixty CEOs and other top brass from national animal advocacy organizations. Their attire ranged from business suits to casual wear. They were talking in hushed tones, still catching up, and were settling back into their seats after a brief lunch break. They sat on dark carved Spanish chairs at a table that was covered with a white tablecloth and set with Spanish cobalt cut-glass water pitchers and goblets, and pads and pencils. On the walls of the large room were Native American portraits, and sitting on the Native American carpets were huge pottery filled with cacti. From the surrounding windows, Eleanor could see the whole of Tucson clear through to Nogales. And the colors of the surrounding mountain ranges that changed with the sun.

Grumpol pushed his chair back to walk a few feet to the head of the table, leaving Honor's side. He was a cross between Antonio Banderas and Clark Gable, Eleanor thought, unable to take her eyes from him. Helen whispered to her that Grumpol was only one of three or four of the many people present that Honor hadn't alienated. Eleanor saw him flash Honor a glance of assurance as he approached the podium set at the head of the table. Alison Barrington, the chair-woman, sat at the head with Gertrude Sandler of Animal Rights of America at her side. Honor sat at Gertrude's left.

Rutherford Gee, now in his mideighties, was hobbling back to his seat next to Alison. It was one of many trips to the restroom. He walked tipped forward and leaning heavily on his cane. Allison and Gertrude adjusted their chairs to face Grumpol and the blackboard behind him, waiting for Rutherford to sit down.

Helen pointed to Frances Garnett, the animal rights lawyer, educator, and writer who supported Honor's bills and who considered her a true animal rights advocate, a tribute he gave to few in the movement.

"I know who he is," Eleanor whispered. "He looks like Al Pacino. Are you sure he didn't star in *The Godfather?*"

"Talk about fathers, there's Walter Sharp. And there's Dey next to him."

The dark-haired and perky Lenore Davis of TUSKS was present, and Eleanor couldn't wait to commiserate with her after the meeting. Welfare representatives from humane societies, animal protection organizations, and animal rights orga-nizations were there. They ranged from those operating sailing vessels that moni-tored protected international waters to cat and dog shelters. The animal advocacy organizations present also represented psychiatrists, doctors, and those in the business of protecting captive animals, performing animals, mammals, fish, and poultry. Women for animal rights, vegetarian organizations and magazine edi-tors, and more were represented.

Once Rutherford was seated, Alison tapped her goblet to quiet the room for Grumpol, who was dressed casually in a beige knitted shirt and charcoal slacks, looked calm and collected.

"My brothers and sisters of the movement," Grumpol began, "your donors send you their dollars to do right by our nonhuman friends. They offer their money so that you may disclose the horror behind a society that chooses to ignore suffering. Your donors want their dollars to help free those tortured within our laws. And with their dollars you have at times disclosed, exposed, and reached for the stars! But in Washington, you are met with steely political resistance and must often compromise; thus your efforts turn not to stardust but to sawdust!"

Eleanor's eyes popped open at this negative remark and she glanced at Helen, who continued to calmly gaze at Grumpol.

"My brothers and sisters, animals are worse off now than they were forty-five years ago, despite all your hard efforts, simply because eight billion alone are slaughtered for human consumption yearly and the number continues to grow. I question the movement's success. Our federal laws have not moved one inch closer to animal liberation. For the sake of greater profits, our farmers are allowed every liberty at the expense of nonhuman animals.

"You raised the issue of animal rights and it became a household word. Millions would rather give up meat and dairy products than support the cruelty of the meat and dairy industries with their dollars. Millions march in Europe and here, unpaid and in their free time for the cause. You've impeded the growth of the fur industry, saving millions of animals from suffering each year. You have a great deal to pat yourselves on the back for, not the least of which is conscience-raising on the issue of animal rights, which has led to a rise in vegetarianism. But at least 70 percent of the nonhuman animals slaughtered for food today are raised on factory farms that are infamous worldwide."

"Oh God, why isn't he our president?" Eleanor thought.

Grumpol explained that U.S. politics led to corruption. Legislators were too influenced by campaign donations from industries to follow their conscience. The cost of an entire British general election was far less than the cost of winning election to a single U.S. Senate seat. In Europe it was the political parties, not individual candidates, that raised the money to fund campaign elections.

"By the year 2012, European egg producers will have to provide a perch and a private nesting box of 120 square inches, or two and a half times the space provided for our birds. Veal crates have been outlawed in Britain for many years, and will be illegal in all countries in the European Union by the year 2007. Keeping pregnant sows in individual crates for their entire pregnancy was banned in Britain in 1998 and is now being phased out in all of Europe.

"We can begin in Florida," he said. "A citizens' committee is collecting 690,000 signatures for a ballot initiative that will end the use of crates for pregnant sows. Florida is a good target. There are few pig farms in that state, so there will be less resistance. But the vote will reveal that it is not a lack of sympathy for the animals that causes us to be far behind Europe, but a failure of Democracy."

Offering Honor her moment of justice, Grumpol turned to the 1985 legislation and a recently released audit from the Department of Agriculture. "The USDA has not properly monitored the animal care committees," he said. "Pointedly, in the last 12 years, out of 26 animal care committees, 12 failed to observe the legal and regulatory requirements. Moreover, there is no example of even one case in which any committee stepped in and ended a painful experiment, or insisted on drugs when they were withheld. Nor were any multiple procedures stopped in order to protect our nonhuman friends from multiple surgeries before mercifully being put to rest. The USDA concluded that the animal care committees offer no assurance that the animals will receive better care and be protected against unnecessary pain or operations."

The room was quiet. Eleanor didn't dare gaze at Honor, but she could see that her eyes were on Grumpol as if she worshiped him. But Grumpol didn't dwell on the disunity of the past. Instead, he insisted that they put the past behind them and work to unite the movement on basic issues. He pointed to state initiatives as one way to bypass Congress. He advised the CEOs to redistribute their funds to worthy local campaigns nationwide as a means to an end. The engine of the animal rights movement was to be found on the local level, not in the corporate offices of national organizations.

"The biomedical community used our own government to defeat us back in the 1980s. Today we should begin a new era, an era of unity. Let's agree to unite and finally put an end to factory farming cruelties and stop the slaughter of eight billion animals a year by working through local campaigns. And also, in a united front, let's initiate federal legislation to do the same. Let us endeavor to outlaw the searing of beaks, the veal crates and the iron maidens. Let us start here to end the torture of our nonhuman friends." He received a round of applause.

Grumpol had returned to his opening theme, Eleanor noted. There was a favorable and interested buzz whirling around the room as people wrote down his words on their pads and gazed back up at him with interest. He received another a round of applause. But in the eyes of many veterans Eleanor observed fatigue and skepticism. Eleanor, however, was inspired anew by Grumpol and all the others. Certainly the movement was beginning its march to free farm animals. She was sure of it!

Before he rushed to another appointment, skipping the poolside reception, Grumpol whispered something in Honor's ear. It was apparent to Eleanor that they were devoted to each other. No doubt they were arranging for a night under the desert stars. Hopefully a new era in animal rights would be born, and a more mellow and stable Honor would be in the forefront of the movement with Grumpol at her side.

Eleanor rushed to meet Lenore Davis as the meeting broke up. To her amazement, Lenore told her that she was in the process of rescuing two elephants. "They're owned by this horrible organization that rents elephants to circuses. But I can't reveal any names. I don't dare risk the deal. At this point, anything can happen."

Lenore's large brown eyes sparkled with expectation as she spoke. But Eleanor didn't dare hope. Besides, according to the trainer, the Anderson Bros. Circus owned Eve.

CHAPTER 15

▼

"PEACE, LOVE, VEGETARIAN"

By no miracle, and only with the utmost tenacity, Lindsay Brenner, now an attorney at a Hartford environmental law firm, won a year of life for the surviving deer at Denmark Cliff, including the new migrants: sixty-five deer in all.

It was only a few days after the conference when Lindsay filed an injunction to bar the state-sponsored deer hunt most likely to occur in December. She charged damage to Connecticut's citizens when fawns had been killed in the 1998 hunt. Wildlife was considered a "state resource" and therefore belonged to every resident of Connecticut. Also, in allowing the fawns to be killed, the state had failed to uphold its own legislation which demanded that the deer be at least yearlings before being "taken."

Blott, true to form, attempted to squirm his way out of it at the preliminary hearing. He told the judge that the state didn't actually shoot the fawns. Lindsay contended that it was a state-sponsored hunt that was controlled by state regulations, and so the state was responsible. The judge agreed.

When Blott announced the cancellation of the December hunt, the judge asked how the deer population would be controlled.

"Through natural selection," Blott answered. "Genetic inheritance, the weak versus the strong, diseases, accidents, available resources, and weather-related deaths."

It was Tuesday, February 1, and CFAR had proved Grumpol's point that the most significant changes achieved by the movement were done at the local level. Eleanor returned from Hartford enthralled by Lindsay's courage and expertise. She ran into Honor's office at 3 PM and related the astounding news. Honor, with an icy stare, insisted that it was PAAC's protest and CD that deserved the credit for the canceled hunt.

Eleanor's admiration for Lindsay's efforts earned her another stint as PAAC's omega. But on the morning of Monday, February 16, thirteen months since Honor had hired her, Honor summoned her to her office. She was all smiles and looked ecstatic. "Alison's in the process of liberating two elephants. They were rented out to circuses by this Rydon Corporation. One of the elephants is your Eve."

Eleanor bolted to her feet, her pad and pen falling to the floor. Honor rose to walk around the desk to stand before her, picking up her pen and pad and setting it on her desk. Than she stroked her arms as she explained. Alison's organization contacted the three-year-old Elephant Refuge in Perry, Tennessee. They were thrilled to take Eve and Rosie. PAAC would participate in a campaign to raise funds for the sanctuary.

Honor assured her that bulldogging the circus and the canceled Derbe contract had done the job. The Anderson Bros. Circus dropped their elephant act, and, Eve and Rosie were no longer viable commodities. Both had developed arthritic feet and legs, and circulatory problems: the usual infirmities created when mammoth bodies are chained in place for most of their lives. When the company failed to rent the elephants to other circuses, it considered euthanizing them. Until Lenore Davis brokered the present deal. Lenore warned Rydon that killing the elephants would create a backlash, while retiring them to a sanctuary was cost free and was good PR.

"We're paying for the transportation of both elephants to the sanctuary," Honor said.

Honor returned to her desk, and Eleanor sat down. It was at this point that Eleanor sensed that Honor was about to reveal the real reason she called her in.

"A new legislator, Rep. Tom Buford, a Norfolk Democrat, intends to introduce a spay/neuter bill," Honor told her. "Alison asked us to handle it. They've narrowed their efforts down to their national spay/neuter program and their African and Thai programs. I'm on board. We need people in Hartford."

Eleanor listened through a foggy haze, her mind euphoric and filled with new respect for the movement that was about to free Eve. It had worked perfectly, though it had taken three organizations working independently to do it. She recalled how fearless she was in the face of danger on behalf of Eve. You wear an invincible shield when you respond to universal law, she had told herself. Bodily harm seemed not to matter; yet she never thought she'd come to any harm. Now she realized that her intuition was also telling her that she was not acting alone; she was just one member in the vigilant army.

Honor was describing Buford's bill. No killing of dogs or cats would occur in state shelters for two years. And no puppy mill dogs and cats could enter the state for that period of time. "You stop the killing and you stop the guilt," Honor was saying. "People avoid going to shelters because they feel sad for those they don't adopt."

They would convince the Connecticut Humane Society to rent mall stores to display the shelter animals. No more shelters near the town dump. The state would charge ten dollars each, enough to cover shots, while spay/neuter services would be offered by state veterinarians in exchange for a tax write-off. "Massachusetts euthanasia rates are dropping because they instituted early, eight-week spay/neutering. We'll do the same."

Honor hesitated. "We have all of two months."

"Has she lost her mind?" Eleanor thought. Hartford was hostile, and Buford had no clout. A similar bill had caused a sensation in progressive California. "I can see breeders and pet storeowners spending thousands of dollars on lobbyists as we speak," Eleanor thought. "But Honor's promise to try again next year was the closest she's come to a long-range plan since I arrived."

"Honor, with this bill we're demanding no killing, no selling, no breeding for two years, and also spaying or neutering and shots, for ten bucks! And we want the state to compensate the pet stores and breeders. We'll have to enlist everyone from grassroots to national groups from humane to animal rights, or this will never fly! We'll have to unite! Like Grumpol urged us to!"

"Absolutely!" Honor said. "But let's remember who's in control! I want an appointment with the two chairs of the Environment Committee ASAP. For just you and I."

Thoughts of Eve flooded Eleanor's mind as she entered her own office. Her hands trembled from the prospects of her freedom. No more chains! No more freaky trainers! No more bull hooks! No more stupid tire on the trunk! It was too much! She never expected this! She didn't dare to dream!

She dashed to the phone, dialed information and got the refuge's number wanting to hear a voice connected to what would be Eve's new home. Her desire to witness Eve's liberation was becoming unbearable. But she knew that Honor would turn down such a request, besides didn't she just assign her Mission Impossible? Kate, the friendly receptionist, informed her that the refuge was in a subtropical climate. To Eve, the land and its vegetation would seem like home, Eleanor thought. There were three elephants and 220 acres and they were negotiating for another 500 acres with a 2,000 plus acre refuge being the ultimate goal.

As she hung up, she heaved a sigh and released the anxiety she carried since she first set eyes on Eve on the high school grounds. She remembered Eve begging her to unchain her by lifting her chained front leg and staring into her eyes. The memory brought tears of humility and gratitude. She faced the door, expecting Honor to barge in at any moment with the first of a million addendums. But she had to close her eyes and thank God. Then she smiled when visions of Eve and Rosie exploring and foraging for miles of trails in the thick Tennessee vegetation came to mind. She could see their trunks reaching for fruits and nuts. She saw them immerse themselves in the ponds, streams, and mud swallows, their mud baths protecting their sensitive skin from sun and insects. Properly dusted, they'd spend the hot afternoons in the shade of a tree.

She reminded herself that the refuge's competent staff would have to first address the maladies of mind and body. Eve and Rosie most likely suffered from osteomyelitis, an infection of the bones in the feet and legs that affects many captive elephants, but never those who are in the wild. And, of course, they had so many fears to overcome, the greatest one being not knowing what was in store for them.

She thanked God for caring people, and for a movement that provided an answer. And for Honor for hiring her. When she opened her eyes, they rested on her notes on the messy spay-neuter bill.

One hectic week and hundreds of calls later, she and Honor sat in a private meeting room in Hartford in the Legislative Office Building. Eleanor was relieved to see the friend of the deer, Sen. Hannah Franklin, the Democratic chair of the Environment Committee. She was petite and attractive, with dark hair and blue eyes. "It's not going to happen," Hannah said.

Hannah explained that it was a budgetary year and only members of the Environment Committee could raise a bill, and since Buford was not on the committee, the bill would not be raised. The Republican chair, a woman with icy eyes and a demeaning smirk, promised that the state would not support a bill that threatened jobs.

Eleanor knew that she and Honor seemed uninformed or foolish. And then she remembered Eve's pending rescue. She reminded herself that she was the rookie. Honor obviously thought there was hope. "Why would she put us in these hot seats?" So Eleanor launched into her pitch.

"We're not talking about wheat or corn here, we're talking about lives," she said. "Taxpayers don't want the state to throw out their dogs and cats with the garbage. We have support from teachers, lawyers, secretaries, you name it, from all over the state! The Connecticut chapter of the Women's Club is on board, and a Redding shelter group is collecting 100,000 signatures."

"For every signature you dig up, the opposition will find one for their point of view," Hannah said.

The meeting ended as abruptly as it had begun.

Honor hadn't spoken one word except for salutations and good-byes. As they headed toward the door, Honor's heels tapped loudly across the lobby's marble floor as if they couldn't get her there fast enough. She seemed to have clattering skeletons of failed campaigns trailing after her. Back in the car, Honor slunk into the passenger seat, shivering from the cold. Eleanor started the engine and turned on the heater.

Honor glanced at her. "Call me a crazy optimist, but I think we have a damned good chance!"

"Has she lost her mind altogether?" Eleanor thought. "Given Hannah's grim response, I assumed that the bill was dead! Wasn't the purpose of the meeting with the two chairs to feel them out?"

"Honor, you've been sniffing this legislative trail much longer than I, so you must know something, but I don't. I must admit, the hundreds of calls I placed were received beyond my expectations, but Hannah sobered me. And Steve and Lydia thought it was impossible given the shortness of time. But you're the veteran. Whatever you say, I do."

Eleanor stopped the car and rolled down the window to pay the uniformed man in the booth. Then they entered the flow of capital traffic to Interstate 91 South.

"They aren't a damned island!" Honor said. "Buford's set to submit the bill to several of the committee members, asking them to introduce it. He's certain it'll get that far. Besides, under the pressure of the sheer volume of calls, faxes, and e-mails from us, they'll have to consider it or answer to their constituents. I say we move ahead!"

It was on Monday, February 23, that Eleanor embarked on "Moratorium Impossible." With enthusiasm she began to mobilize the state behind the campaign. Sandy Freedman, a divorce lawyer and the head of BARK, ranked at the top of the list of shelter volunteers. Her first piece of lawyerly advice was to wait until next year.

"But it's such a sad situation at the shelter. The publicity will at least educate the public, if nothing else. We have a sick mother Lab, and her litter of puppies might die of infection if they don't find homes soon."

Other heads of organizations echoed the same sentiments but climbed on board, seduced because PAAC was a national organization.

Eleanor ate at her desk to save time, started early, stayed late, and worked from home on the weekends. Awake or asleep, her mind never rested from planning strategies and themes, drafting new letters to reach the legislators, and hunting for the perfect heart-wrenching words for their literature and letters. Honor pounded down to her office countless times a day for updates, again a happy trooper. Meanwhile, the realization that thousands of family pets were being killed had hit a nerve. Hundreds volunteered to join PAAC's crusade.

Eleanor's editorial on the bill was published in the *Hartford Journal*. Tina and Helen called to congratulate her, radio stations begged for interviews, and Honor held several TV interviews. With the campaign at least igniting the imagination of the general public, if not the legislators on the Environment Committee, Honor and Eleanor laughed and boosted each other's morale.

Their rekindled relationship caused the office to whisper about Eleanor's "new friend."

But after several weeks into the campaign, they had heard nothing from the Environment Committee. Eleanor forged on optimistically, however, thinking of next year. And Hannah's warning words faded in the rush of concern for shelter dogs and cats. Eleanor wondered how she had lived so many years unacquainted with the hundreds of concerned people. Again she thanked God for her job, and couldn't believe she had entertained the thought of quitting.

Meanwhile Hartford remained a depressing place. She'd stake out the legislators in the hallways and doorways, or skulk next to the elevator, waiting for an opportunity to walk alongside them. She confronted them as they returned to their offices after General Assembly meetings, or when they arrived in the morning with their coffee mugs in hand. She also fed them facts of the proposed bill as they waited in line in the cafeteria. She smiled broadly, blinked her thick eyelashes, and cooed to them about the yearly deaths of 30,000 dogs and cats. The answer was always the same. "Come back next year."

But the committee hadn't rejected the bill, so she continued working nonstop. On the days when Hank had stayed overnight, she awoke to the roar of the juicer. He cooked for her and her two cats and brushed her thick hair while she was on the phone, where she spent most of her time mobilizing the state. After watching a stimulating Knicks playoff game, he'd wake her and guide her across the wooden floor to tuck her into bed. Basically she worked twenty-four hours a day, seven days a week. At Sunday church services she prayed for the unlikely bill.

She told Hank, in one of their brief conversations: "This could be the end of the routine killing of dogs and cats. Does it get any better?"

"Yeah," he said. "And they might find the cure for cancer any day now."

Anything was possible, she told herself. But six weeks into the moratorium campaign, on Monday, March 23, after another depressing day at the capital, she rushed into Honor's office to tell her that the campaign seemed a hopeless cause.

"Is the damned humane society calling them? Is NAHS participating? Is everyone else we've taken into this campaign doing anything? Our 'partners'?" she sneered. "What good are they? We have about 40,000 people listed as animal advocates in the state between all of us! Where are they?"

Eleanor slid the tips of her fingers along the smooth wood surface of Honor's desk, seeking a tactile anchor to reality as she assured Honor that a statewide network of people in and out of the movement was hammering Hartford nonstop.

Honor looked at her wild-eyed. "I can't see how they can bloody refuse! Continue pushing. Tom thinks it'll work out with enough persuasion."

That afternoon Buford called telling her to stop hounding the Environment Committee because they were busy with hundreds of bills to consider in a short budgetary session. "There are too many calls coming in! They're complaining to me. We don't want to irritate them! We need them on our side for next year."

With that directive, Eleanor rushed into Honor's office and repeated Buford's instructions. "Honor, at least we know everyone's calling."

Honor remained silent and offered Eleanor a vacant stare. Then she returned to the letters she was signing.

On Tuesday, March 31, eight days later and the day before the deadline to raise the bill, there was still no news from the Environment Committee. Buford and his assistant refused to answer her calls. And Honor still refused to speak to her. As far as Eleanor was concerned it was over for the year.

But it didn't matter. There was next year. And that morning, Eleanor learned that Liddy and Paul Phillips were opening a string of vegan fast-food stands called "Strawberry Fields." She was to meet a TV reporter for the opening of the Strawberry Fields in Bridgeport at 5 PM. Even though she was exhausted beyond belief, she agreed. The cruelty-free fast-food chain signaled an advance in the movement.

As Eleanor sprang to her feet to charge out the door, briefcase in hand, she was stunned to discover Honor standing in her doorway. Honor's left hand clung to the door molding for support. Her skin was a sickly yellow. She looked deathly ill. Eleanor would have run to her, but Honor's scornful expression kept her frozen in place.

"Do we have a bloody fuckin' bill or don't we?"

"It doesn't look good. Nobody's answering my calls" I'll go up there tomorrow first thing and find out for sure."

"Why the hell go up there? It's the deadline, and all you have to do is call the House clerk. If it's not entered it's not entered. Fuck, it's as easy as that. A no-brainer!"

"Well, they sometimes don't record those decisions until the following day. But I guess I can call them."

"I want answers! I want to know why! Why they didn't raise the bill with the thousands of calls they got! What about the 100,000-name petition?" she shouted. "Get me a meeting with the chairs! What the fuck's going on?"

She approached Honor. "Honor, think of next year. The chairs already told us 'why' in person. And petitions don't impress them. Hannah warned us about that. If you charge up there angry, you'll only agitate them further. We have to win over legislators, not alienate them."

Honor instructed her to write a letter of complaint to the governor about the stubborn Environment Committee. "I have two high rollers who are supporting his reelection. I'll get them to sign it."

Eleanor stared at the empty doorway after Honor left. "She still thinks this bill has a chance? After all this time with no word?" She telephoned the Channel 35 reporter, who agreed to delay their meeting for a half hour, allowing her to bang out the two letters and deliver them to Honor's office. Honor appeared calmer.

Eleanor was so anxious to be on her way, she grabbed her parka off the back of the door, leaving the wooden hanger rocking back and forth from the tug. She grabbed her briefcase and scudded across the empty office and out of PAAC's office door, grateful to inhale the sea's fresh mild air. She gazed at the promising blue horizon, and at the couples strolling Compo Beach Road and those jogging, taking advantage of the glorious spring day. It was a wonderful day for Strawberry Fields to open! How inspiring Liddy and Paul were! She charged into her car to travel several miles in the opposite direction from Derbe on Interstate 95, in heavy commuter traffic.

The next morning at eight o'clock, she prepared herself to hear the final word and to tell Honor as she dialed Buford's assistant, who apologetically revealed that the bill hadn't been raised.

"Why didn't they reject this thing seven weeks ago and save us all this work?" Eleanor asked.

"It was all the calls. They didn't want to upset people."

"Why didn't I know that?" With the news came the exhaustion she had held in abeyance. That night she'd sleep the sleep of the dead, and every night that followed for a week or so. She anticipated a few weeks of a calm nine-to-five routine. She needed to refuel. No stress, no deadlines, no Honor, no recrimination, no abuse: just the normal number of calls from pleasant people who were grateful to her for helping them help the animals. Then she looked up.

Honor was again at her door. She held a manila pad in her right hand, and a letter-size manila envelope in the other. Early that morning, Tom had contacted her by phone at her home with the news, she told Eleanor.

"There's next year. We gave it a good try," she said. She moved around the desk to stand right next to Eleanor, who remained seated. The hem of her dress touched Eleanor's left knee in a show of closeness. Eleanor gazed up at Honor's face, which was glowing with honest affection.

"This is so like a bad marriage," Eleanor thought. She wore a fixed half-smile.

"I've come to a decision about the farm animal campaign," Honor said. "I want it to be hard-hitting. The theme is: 'Take Responsibility.'"

Eleanor listened through a veil of exhaustion. Her mind was still focused on the moratorium bill, the waiting letters and calls, all the information to file. Honor wanted a hard-hitting campaign?

Honor continued, telling Eleanor that she wanted people to take responsibility for the animals killed each year for human consumption. There would be demonstrations held in front of supermarkets across the state. And Vegan for Life rosters would be available so people could sign up. They'd get a pin and a free copy of *Howl*.

"Even our own activists eat chicken sometimes. We need to nail them down. We'll tell them: 'Kill your chicken-eating habit, not a chicken! Approximately twenty million chickens killed each day, eight billion a year! Stop the carnage. If you bite into a chicken, you are the slaughterhouse! Take Responsibility! Go vegan!' At least that's the idea, you can fool around with it," she said. "I want a T-shirt with a mother hen on it, saying 'Vegans for Life!'"

Was Honor asking her to head up another campaign? Already?

Honor opened the manila envelope and withdrew several 8" × 10" black-and-white photographs. Then she walked to the corner and pulled the corner chair to the desk. She sat just inches from Eleanor. She showed her several photographs of battery cage hens. She pointed to several of the filthy cages with the panicky, worn chickens peering out of the cages, feathers stuck to the sides, dead chickens at the bottom of the cages.

"Some are pecked to death," Honor began. "There's no bloody room! They sear the baby chicks' beaks so they won't kill each other in the cages! It's a painful process, you can well imagine! Some don't have enough of a beak left to eat or drink water, so they die of thirst or starve to death!"

She had photographs of male chicks being buried alive, pigs being hacked to death but refusing to die, and a Jersey cow being skinned alive. For every cow killed there were about 100 chickens slaughtered, she said. Of the eight billion animals killed each year, seven billion were birds. She wanted literature, posters, stickers, and rosters designed.

"And we should recommend books, such as *Diet for a New America*, *Slaughterhouse*, and whatever else you think of. Our target date is 10 AM, National Meat-Out Day, May 30. Eight weeks from now."

Eleanor's entire body and mind rejected the order. But eating eight billion animals a year was the original sin. Eight billion projected to rise to ten billion by 2004. Didn't Grumpol agree that it was the issue? Wasn't it the original sin from which all others stemmed? Like eating the apple! Wasn't it the basic issue that could unite the whole movement?

She was staring into the eyes of the enthusiastic Honor sitting inches away. But what a hideous thought it was to repeat the journey she had just finished, with the addition of demonstrations. "Honor, before I can start on this, I'll have to write and call people to let them know that the moratorium bill won't fly."

"Oh, they'll read about it in the papers," Honor said.

"I owe them a letter or a call. They're waiting to be told when to go to the public hearing." Eleanor showed her the list of hundreds of people she had personally drafted.

"When they don't hear from you, they'll forget about it."

"Well, I can also tell them about the supermarket demos, too."

"Oh, OK. We'll need to visit each of the sites. Map out the demonstration areas. Tell people where to stand and so forth."

Honor sat waiting for a response from her.

But Eleanor continued to ponder. "I have a little less than eight weeks. It'll take about thirty demonstration sites. I'll have to inspect each one, once I get them, negotiate with hundreds of volunteers, study their demographics, take their calls, and keep them abreast of updates," she thought. Again she was overwhelmed as she perused the paperwork waiting on her desk. She struggled to hold back tears.

"Honor, I can honestly say, I know we'll get all sections of the state with about thirty demonstration sites. I've no doubt that we'll have enough Connecticut activists. I know because there are hundreds of willing grassroots activists. I've been talking to them for the last seven weeks."

"Great!" Honor strummed her pearly-tipped fingers against the top of Eleanor's desk. She stood up satisfied with her employee, and walked to the door. "You can check out the supermarkets on Tuesdays and Thursdays."

Eleanor closed her eyes for a second. She flushed from the humiliation of being treated as an inferior. "There may be as few as two or three or even just one activist at a particular location to pull this off in so short a time. People may have other demands," she said. "All of them will need my knowledge and my moral support from now until the demos. I need to start ASAP."

"But you have other duties here. Freda, Lisa, and I will also visit some of the supermarkets. At least once a week we'll venture out. We can do at least four in one day. That's plenty of time. I'll be leaving for the Bahamas at the end of April for a week."

"Sounds great." Eleanor's eyes seemed to sink into her head as she gazed at Honor. Her thick hair was limp. And her slumping body slumped even more with the image of Honor in a bikini, an indolent beachcomber basking in the Caribbean sun. Eleanor's workouts at the Y were a thing of the past. The lilac knitted dress with the delicate pearl-lilac buttons that hugged Honor's trim figure suddenly affronted her, and she resented her freshly shampooed hair that fell so obediently into place.

Honor left and charged back to her office. Eleanor stared at the empty doorway, thinking. The good news was that Honor would be gone. "Peace, Love, Vegetarian!" The Zen Buddhist mantra was perfect. She'd run a positive campaign but use the hard-hitting photographs. The "Peace, Love, Vegetarian Campaign."

Eleanor took a deep breath and in doing so felt her body's exhaustion. "Peace, Love, Vegetarian," she wrote on her pad. "If we change our society's eating habits, isn't that the beginning of other changes? If one denies the cruel truth of one's food three times a day, doesn't that affect one? Of course it does! Didn't I become a vegan because I wanted perfection somewhere in my life? Isn't that a piece of Eden now?"

It was the eight billion farm animals slaughtered a year that had drawn her to the movement in the first place, wasn't it? She remembered the calf tethered to a crate on her newsroom wall. "I'll get it done," she told herself. "Hunker down!"

But tears of exhaustion filled her eyes. She felt physically ill. The campaign seemed beyond her energy. "Burnout," she thought. "I don't have the heart for the first time in my career. I can't do it. I can't pick up the phone and start all over again!"

She was shocked by her own admission. She continued to sit at her desk gazing at the phone. It seemed an unattainable goal to reach for it and dial the first of thousands of calls to the very people she had just spoken to with fervor over the last seven weeks! Her zealous heart had every right to die for a few weeks, to rise again from the ashes for the next push, she thought.

She grabbed her pad and a pen to make a list. She wasn't a list person. She usually just played out her vision. But a list for some strange reason seemed a good idea. Then it occurred to her that she was actually writing a memo. If she listed every single thing, surely Honor would understand that the undertaking was too much at this point! Surely she'd offer her more help! Or more time! Maybe she'd wait for a united movement effort against factory farming, as Grumpol had suggested!

With a broad smile of satisfaction Eleanor listed the number of tasks, from locating the thirty supermarkets, visiting the sites, finding the volunteers, writing all the necessary literature, and organizing the demonstrations to all the public relations required, including advertisements. With the greatest optimism, she dropped the memo in Honor's in-box while she was out to lunch.

One hour later, Honor returned and entered Eleanor's office holding the memo in her hand. "This about covers it. Add editorials to your list. And, of course, you will demonstrate at one of the markets. Freda and I will demonstrate at one and Delores at another. If you get tight, you can use Lisa."

When Honor left, Eleanor called Hank sounding desperate. "Eleanor, two can live as cheaply as one over a Korean deli."

"Hank, is this a proposal?" In her exhaustion, maybe she had misunderstood.

Hank wanted to give her the option to quit before she began the campaign, he told her, knowing how exhausted she was. She hadn't slept well for weeks. He believed Honor would only punish her for her efforts. And she'd continue to grind her into the ground until she quit. "Eleanor, will you marry me? I promise to repeat these words in person, tonight."

Her heart filled with joy. "I love you," she said. "Can I save my answer for later?"

"OK," he chuckled at her.

The option to quit worked like magic. She even managed to call Sandy at BARK without crying. Sandy promised to cover seven sites and more if need be. That night, on bended knees, as Eleanor sat in the middle of the couch, with Friday and Rusty acting as witnesses, Hank officially proposed and she accepted. Their engagement would remain a secret from Honor.

During the next four weeks she and Honor again worked together, with Honor charging down to her office constantly for updates and clowning around, obviously contented with the campaign. Freda had chauffeured Honor to three supermarkets before Honor departed for her vacation on Friday, April 30. Eleanor assessed the remaining twenty-seven sites, and with the help of her activists the "Peace, Love, Vegetarian Campaign" progressed in perfect order.

When Honor returned from the Bahamas, Eleanor rushed to her office wanting to brief her. But Eleanor felt the sting of humiliation when Honor refused to acknowledge her as she stood at her desk. When Eleanor spoke to her, Honor refused to answer. And the following day, Honor was repelled at the mere sight of her. So Eleanor resorted to memos to gain permission to go forward, knowing they'd come back to haunt her. But the "Peace, Love, Vegetarian Campaign" continued to progress in a timely fashion.

Then came Monday, May 10.

CHAPTER 16

▼

THE DREAM

It was Monday, May 10, with three weeks to go to the supermarket demonstrations. Eleanor pulled out of her driveway and on to Route 7 that bright spring morning, and turned on the radio as usual to catch the news. But in seconds, the road blurred behind her tears.

"Liddy Phillips died of cancer," said the newscaster. "Strawberry Fields was her parting gift to the world, revealed her superstar husband Paul Phillips. The animal rights community is mourning her death as a great loss."

By the time Eleanor arrived at PAAC, she was desperate for company and tore into the lobby. But Ellen wasn't at her desk, and only the trappings of the office staff greeted her. The aroma of brewing coffee, however, wafted from the lounge. Jackets hung haphazardly in the closet, and pocketbooks and keys sat on the tops of desks. As Eleanor ripped through the office, she heard Honor saying, "It's a shame." Her voice traveled from the coffee lounge.

"She must be talking about Liddy Phillips," Eleanor surmised. Near tears again, she prayed. "God, bless this lovely soul and welcome her with open arms!"

She slapped her parka and her briefcase on her desk chair, frantic to reach the coffee lounge. "That's the beauty of working for an animal protection organization," she thought, "we can share our victories and our disasters. We understand! Honor must feel horrible! She's even mingling with the common folk!" At least the tragic event would break the sixteen-day silence between them, she thought as she raced to the lounge.

But Honor's icy glare stopped her at the door. Eleanor was quick to look down to protect herself from it. She was again the omega; she could hardly believe it. But it was unmistakable. It was written in the steady glare, the tight mean line of Honor's lips. "It was the memos!" She knew it when she wrote them. She found herself slinking away, standing back in the recesses of the doorway.

Honor was opposite the doorway leaning against the wall, six feet away. She held a mug of green tea and had been pleasantly engaged in conversation. "One look at me and her mood changed," Eleanor thought. "She looks like she's challenging me to a duel. Like I'm her enemy. Again I've been working my butt off to please her!" Her chest heaved as the air escaped her lungs. This time, she was too exhausted for it. She had the urge to run and hide! But where?

Coretta, Betty, Mary, Lisa, Carla, Pat, and Claudia chatted while doubling up on the four chairs around the crowded circular table, obviously enjoying the rare audience with their boss. Ellen and Delores stood next to the serving table that held the coffeepot and hot water, stirring their morning brews. They recalled RUFFFF's summer fur protest and Liddy in her country yellow floral dress playing her tambourine on the streets of New York, so down to earth and natural. They spoke of the true love she and her husband shared.

Eleanor remained in the doorway. Honor seemed ready to spring if she moved. Her sleek dark-brown turtleneck sweater and slacks clung to her slim body, making her look serpentine. It was Honor's famous paranoia. Eleanor stared at the floor for a break. "She thinks I've taken over." She took a deep breath, straightened her posture, and decided to act normally and join the conversation. "Maybe she took estrogen," she said. "How else would a vegan get breast cancer?"

Honor's head whipped around to face the wall for a second, as if she were recoiling from the insulting idea.

Eleanor at once recognized her mistake. "My days are numbered! This is it! I've personally insulted her! No one survives that! I forgot she's taking hormones! She knows I know and she thinks I'm criticizing her for it! All this talk about cancer must be frightening her!"

Most employees were fired after such infractions, she thought, crushed by her own thoughtless words. She slumped in the doorway. Her heels seemed to sink into the floor. She pulled herself up and leaned against the doorway for support, waiting for the fatal blow. Her heart was hammering as if she were under attack, adrenaline pumping into her veins.

"Nobody has to die from breast cancer these days with mammograms!" Honor hurled the words in a single breath, and sounded as if she wanted to slap Eleanor. Silence fell as her anger roiled the room. The employees' fear of losing their jobs was set into motion, yet they didn't dare run for cover. "Maybe it was in her family!" Honor shouted.

With disbelief, Eleanor studied Honor's hateful eye, her fears disappearing in the rush of her reporter's objectivity. "Can Honor be this ignorant about breast cancer? Does she live in another world? Hasn't she seen the statistics lately? Every naturopath my mother's seen has told her that hormones are a ticking bomb. Besides, she doesn't know if Liddy Phillips was on hormone replacement therapy? She could have been treated with acupuncture and herbs! For all Honor knows, she may have had a hundred mammograms!"

Again, Eleanor decided to act as if all were normal. "With her diet, one would think Liddy Phillips would have been immune to cancer," she said.

With that Honor charged across the room. She stopped just inches from her. She stretched her neck and screamed at her nose to nose. "Nobody has to die from breast cancer these days with mammograms!"

"Is she saying that it was Liddy Phillips's fault? Is that what she's saying? Of course, she always has to lay blame! Yes, she's blaming Liddy Phillips for dying of breast cancer in the 'days of mammograms'! But this is too much!"

She heard a small voice speak. "I heard many people in New Jersey get breast cancer."

It was Coretta. She sat closest to the door. Eleanor looked down at her and was astounded at her courage and her friendship.

"They get it from chemicals in the water. That's what they say."

"Yes!" Eleanor said. "New Jersey is known for its high cancer rate."

With her outraged eyes still on her, Honor took a step backwards. Again she shouted, "Nobody has to die from breast cancer these days with mammograms!"

Honor stomped by her, her eyes boring into Eleanor's. She continued to stomp to her office, her furious footsteps hammering away while the staff scurried from the coffee lounge like ants to burrow into their work and disappear from sight, and at all costs avoid Eleanor. She was the first to leave. Once back in the relative safety of her office, she sat behind her desk shaken. As she reached for her phone to call Helen, she fixed her eyes on Coretta, who like a loyal sentry responded with a knowing nod.

It was Liddy Phillips's death that caused Honor's black mood, Helen assured her. She explained that Honor resented every obituary sure to be published around the world because it would mention Leona Nesbitt and RUFFFF, since she and the famous couple were closely associated.

"Let me get this straight. Liddy Phillips dies of breast cancer…in her early forties…and Honor is the victim?"

"You know, Honor is always the victim." Helen explained that Honor's hatred was egalitarian: she hated Leona, so she also hated anybody associated with her. Indeed, Honor's egalitarian hatred included the entire population of the national animal advocacy movement, she reminded Eleanor. "Except for the rare few," she added, "and she finds fault with them periodically."

Coretta rolled her large dark eyes, signaling the approaching Delores heading toward the mailroom. Eleanor lowered her voice even more whispering to Helen. "I knew being efficient and decisive would be held against me!"

"It's not you."

"Helen, I'm still new to this, but tell me, isn't she supposed to inspire us? She's doing the opposite! That's why Liddy's death is so depressing. She was inspiring. I'm struggling! I'm tired, worn totally out, and after this I have no desire to work for this woman! Why should I work day and night only to be accused of taking over? People follow me because they believe in me! And therefore they believe in PAAC!"

Some even mistakenly called her Honor, she revealed. People had no idea that the head of PAAC was a tyrant, she concluded to the sighing Helen, who again assured her that it was the death of Liddy Phillips that was the root cause of Honor's bad mood, and not her.

"It was so unexpected!" Helen said, near tears. "There'll be a huge candlelight ceremony tonight. All my activist friends are going to it."

Eleanor thought that luxury would be denied her. She'd be too busy dodging bullets. She hung up still shaken from the experience. She stared at the phone with her hand resting on the receiver, finding it hard to conceive that she had been the object of hatred so severe that it could deliver a staggering wallop from across a crowded room. Tears of hurt and exhaustion stung her eyes. She recalled that fateful December telephone call from Honor during deadline at the *Norfolk Daily News*, which seemed a lifetime ago, and how she had believed that some angel of mercy had manipulated her destiny to find her dream job. But Honor would have her believe that she had failed her! Failed the movement too! Failed their waiting friends! That's what Honor wanted her to believe. The very thought enraged her anew. "If anybody betrayed anyone, it was Honor who betrayed me!

At least I'm not standing around asking myself, 'What did I do?' Instead, I'm standing around asking myself, 'What does she *think* I did?' I've made some progress in the last sixteen and a half months!"

An hour later, at 10 AM, Lisa came charging up to her desk in a fit of despair to announce that Honor had initiated a conference call and had purposely excluded her. "Honor said to tell you that when it comes to the supermarket demonstrations she'll call you in. That's insulting! Why is Freda there? She doesn't work on issues!"

Lisa stormed back out. It was the third ambush of the day. Eleanor heaved a deep sigh. Honor was on the warpath. Who's kidding who, she thought, rolling her eyes at Helen's naiveté. She tossed her pen onto her crowded desk and pushed her chair back with the tips of her toes until it hit the wall behind her with a thud. She was ready to punch the walls. Liddy Phillips's death—and the sixteen-plus months of accumulating abuse—were driving her to madness. She could barely stand the place and wanted to scream. "This is hell!" she said aloud.

She stared at Coretta, who dashed around her desk and dared to stick her head in the outcast's office. "She's playing you!" she said. "She's playing you! Don't let her get to you! You're too good for this place anyway! What are you doing here? Huh?" Her large brown eyes stared at Eleanor for a second before she returned to her desk. Most everyone was searching for new jobs. Honor's dismissive treatment coupled with that of the ungracious Freda had proven to be a serious overload.

Eleanor spun her chair around to stare up at the clear blue sky. "God, stay with me here! We have three weeks of madness to get through before touchdown."

A few minutes later, she received Lisa's call requesting her presence in Honor's office. The meeting offered some relief. At least she could update Honor in person on the campaign. Maybe Honor would come to her senses.

The blinds were drawn to temper the brilliant morning light. Freda sat in the closest chair, in front of Honor's desk, so Eleanor crept past her as if going through a minefield to reach the other chair. Honor's scowling gaze directly across the desk was a mere few, unprotected inches away. Eleanor avoided gazing directly into her stalking alpha eyes. Freda wore a conspiratorial grin, and her eyes darted knowingly to Honor's and back again. Freda was chewing bubblegum with the confidence of a student who was the teacher's pet. She even blew small pink bubbles periodically. Her thick legs were stretched out straight ahead of her with her feet, encased in flat black shoes, planted squarely against Honor's desk in a show of confidence. Eleanor sighed warily.

From the peripheral view of her downcast eyes, she observed Honor's signal for her to proceed. Again, Eleanor proceeded as if all were normal. "First, hi everybody!" she began.

"Hi," they squeaked.

Honor gazed across at her with hatred that caused her stomach to convulse. Her adrenaline began to pump again, readying her for additional bombardments. She stretched her neck to move a little closer to the speakerphone and its friendly voices.

"We received about fifty calls from activists offering to participate in or lead a demonstration," she began. "I'm so thrilled with the reaction! With that and our contacts with about eleven grassroots organizations, we have thirty demos nailed down! I expect more! It's been a great response! Our regional newspaper ads will reach each demo site. I've targeted them precisely to do just that. I'll be sending press releases to all the local papers, the weeklies...."

Honor interrupted. "Helen, you've been working on the press release, haven't you? And Tina, you and Helen will decide the particular cities and newspapers that it's best to place our advertisements in, won't you? I want the ads in at least ten dailies. They must reach most of our targeted supermarkets. Our ads read, 'Vegans for Life.' In the small print we list the dangers of eating meat and the benefits of soy products and vegetables. A lovely mother hen with her darling chicks under her protective wings is the graphic. It's still in the works. We'll have it tomorrow. Helen, you and Larry will hammer out some plucky placard slogans for me, won't you?"

Eleanor's face stung from the demoralizing brush-off. But she sat back in her chair determined to hide any signs of dejection. Was this woman actually stripping her of all her major responsibilities before her colleagues, like Dreyfus stripped of his medals before the rank and file? "Why didn't she offer me this help when I wrote my damned list? She waits until now to do it as a punishment!"

Eleanor took a long deep breath and shifted in the unfriendly wooden chair that seemed smaller and harder by the second. She must calm herself. She had to size up the situation. The campaign was threatened. Tina and Helen knew nothing at this point about the campaign. The meeting was fast turning into a war of attrition, with Honor coming to key decisions based on revenge, not wisdom. Eleanor had to protect the campaign at all costs for their "partners" across the state, and the multitude of forsaken farm animals.

"I want the demonstrations kept to thirty, no more!"

It was an order from a general given to a buck private. The heat of humiliation burned in its travels through Eleanor's body.

"Helly, did you begin the press release yet?" Honor asked.

"The press release should note that this is a cooperative effort," Eleanor said.

"It's our 'Peace, Love, Vegetarian Campaign!'" Honor said, bolting up in her chair and mimicking Eleanor's voice and cadence.

Was Honor impugning her for not using her negative "Take Responsibility" name for the campaign? Was that it?

For a few seconds there was an uncomfortable silence. "I could list all the town names," Helen said, "and the groups. That's no problem."

"That'll be OK," Honor said. "This is our bloody campaign! We are the 'spokespeople!'" Again, she imitated Eleanor.

Keep your mind on the text, Eleanor told herself. "We'll have to decide how many posters, handouts, and bumper stickers we'll send for each demonstration," she said.

"That's a no-brainer! You have twenty people—you send twenty signs! Do the math!"

"Terrific!" Eleanor thought. "That was a win. If I had requested that from Freda, I would have been called extravagant and my request would have been denied. Mission accomplished!"

"OK," she said to Honor. "So each activist going to a demo will get a sign! We have to decide how many fliers we'll send to make sure we have enough."

Honor directed the question to Freda, who possessed no knowledge of the supermarkets and their volume, and had never spoken to one activist who lived in the vicinity of the supermarkets.

"Fifteen thousand," Freda said. She wiggled her right foot still braced against Honor's desk, then followed by blowing a small, pink bubble.

The number seemed light, but reasonable. At any rate it would be close to 500 fliers for each site. With the demos lasting for three hours, they could easily hand out thousands of fliers at some supermarket, given the weekend volume. Eleanor let it go and moved on to a more important aspect of the campaign. She suggested that they broaden the campaign by offering additional Vegans for Life bumper stickers for activists to place on their vehicles and to be handed out to their members, along with extra Vegans for Life registration forms. "We want our vegan registration to grow after the twenty-ninth, right?"

"I'm not going to hand out fifty bumper stickers to each activist," Honor said.

"Of course not!" Eleanor's chest was tight. It was clear that she'd be whipped in public until the damned meeting was over. She withdrew the "Peace, Love, Vegetarian" flier from her pad. Helen had labeled it brilliant. She placed it on the desk before Honor.

The flier covered the latest information, Eleanor explained, such as land and air pollution caused by the meat and dairy industries; the toxic chemicals outlawed for human consumption but digested by animals and stored in their fatty tissues, the toxins then digested by the human body upon consumption; the antibiotics used on animals, which were passed on to humans through their milk and flesh—along with the stored hormones fed them to increase their size so farmers could reap greater profits, and which contributed to the early maturation of children. The flier linked accepted farming practices and the consumption of animal products to deadly diseases such as cancers of the breast, uterus, lungs, mouth, pharynx, larynx, esophagus, stomach, colon, liver, pancreas, and prostate. It noted that some 30 to 40 percent of deaths in the male population were diet-related, and 60 percent of deaths among women were diet-related. Coronary illnesses, it noted, were also linked to meat-based diets. The flier mentioned the statistics from the Center for Disease Control of those suffering from *E. coli*, salmonella, and poisoning from rotted meat who mistakenly believed that they suffered from stomach viruses. Then it listed books bearing the documents of proof for all the above, such as *Diet for a New America, Becoming a Vegetarian,* and *Slaughterhouse.* Honor's brutal farm animal photographs were dispersed throughout the flier.

"Humph," Honor said. She opened the flier and spread it on her desk, surveying it with bored heavy eyelids. She folded it back up and thrust it across the desk at Freda and ordered her to make 30,000 copies, not 15,000 as Freda had suggested. "Do that today! We don't want anything left until the last minute, do we?" Her eyes were boring into Eleanor.

"Helly and Tina too," Honor said, "you decide which demonstrations should be highlighted in the press release."

Eleanor interrupted. "Helen, you could check with Larry. Hi, Larry...I asked you to do a demographic study to be sure. But I nailed down the highly populated areas. I also listed the demos with the highest number of activists. You could refer to that before coming to decisions."

"We don't need a bloody fucking demographic study!" Honor said. "We're having this conference call to nail down this 'Peace, Love, Vegetarian Campaign!' Besides, Larry has already provided us with that information!"

The four-letter word stung, but Eleanor kept her mind on the text. Was Honor saying that she was overdoing the job? Was Honor saying that she and Helen had called this meeting because of Eleanor's ineptness? And why did she feel left out of the loop on a campaign that she had built from the ground up? "I didn't see Larry's response," Eleanor said.

"Well, it's right in the file!" Honors said. She pointed to the manila file set in front of her.

The skin on the back of Eleanor's hand crawled as she got closer to Honor and the folder sitting in front of her. She lifted the thin flap of the file, withdrew the memo sitting on top, and set it before her. Her name and Honor's were clearly written at the top of Larry's memo. Her eyes popped up to stare into Honor's, realizing that she had withheld her mail. Eleanor settled back in her seat and drew a deep breath. This was an impossible situation! She turned numb. She waited for the next blow.

"Well, Helly, you talk to Tina and come to those decisions and let me know," Honor said. The meeting was over.

Eleanor remained anchored to her seat for a few moments. Since Honor had pocketed her pound of flesh, maybe she'd ease up now. Freda left the room just short of skipping while she blew bubbles. Honor rose, pushed back her chair, and raced past her to the blinds of the scenic window. Eleanor turned in her chair to observe Honor as she opened the narrow slats to brighten the office. With that done, she spun around and with her eyes on Eleanor issued a triumphal "Humph!"

Eleanor rose to her feet, her eyes riveted on Honor's. She turned her body to fully face her. Only when Honor's eyes dropped to the floor several seconds later did Eleanor feel free to turn to exit. As she traversed the wide room she demanded her exhausted body to stretch to its fullest. She felt the eyes of her fellow workers on her. When she reached her office, she walked directly to her desk and spread the copy of the "Peace, Love, Vegetarian" flier. She gazed at the photographs of the peaceful cow and her calf, three chickens, and a couple of pigs romping in a green meadow on the first flap. The brutal farming facts were written in a cheerful green text on a glossy white background. It covered everything from the searing of baby chicks' beaks to cows that never saw the outdoors until the trip to the slaughterhouse, where they died in terror and often by pieces.

She proudly tacked the flier up in the middle of the empty wall just above her computer in the space that had once been occupied by her dog's photographs. She stepped back and sighed with satisfaction.

"Keep your eyes on the text," she instructed herself aloud, staring at the flier as she reached for her ringing phone. It was the same advice she had given herself on her first day of employment, she thought. "Some things never change," she muttered.

"I have no idea what I'm doing," Helen said. "I have plenty of numbers, but they make no sense to me! And I'm so sorry. I don't know why she's doing this to you! She's not singling you out! You're doing a great job! Please, please, don't quit!"

"Helen, don't forget to mention the activists in the press release! I can't let them down! They'll never do anything for us again! Better yet, I won't do anything for us again!"

"Eleanor, you just tell me what to do. I'll do whatever you say. And I'll send you the press release. Make any changes you think appropriate. I'll work them in."

Eleanor had no sooner hung up when Larry called. "She had no right to hold your mail," he said. He proceeded to reveal yet another threat to the success of the campaign. "Do you know that Honor is going to demonstrate at the Apple Supermarket in Milford? She hates the manager and wants to give him a hard time."

"She's sabotaging her own campaign!" Eleanor sprang to her feet. "She's supposed to be at Super Stop and Shop in Norfolk. I have the reporter from the *New York Times* for the Connecticut section scheduled to interview her. And another from the *Advocate*! There'll be at least thirty activists there; it's our largest demonstration!"

When she called Hank, he became incensed. "Walk, Eleanor. Didn't she just strip you of all your duties? Walk!"

"It'll all be over soon," she said.

Seconds later, Tina called to tell her that she was doing great. "Don't quit! I hate her!"

A Monroe activist informing her of a date change followed Tina's call. Monroe High School's graduation ceremony was on Saturday; she'd do her protest on Sunday. It would have to be noted on the press release. Several others called requesting similar changes. Eleanor worked until 6 PM answering nonstop telephone calls. That evening Hank stayed in Queens to cover a public meeting on tightening up recycling rules. Eleanor spent another restless night and dreaded the dawn of another day at PAAC.

The following morning, Tuesday, May 11, at a few minutes after nine, Lisa again rushed into her office and up to her desk in a state of panic. "Honor told me to send out the press releases! I don't know what to do! That's your job!"

Eleanor grabbed a manila file sitting on top of a stack on her desk. It contained a complete list of media contact names and numbers with instructions and dates for mailing and faxing. Waving the file, she said, "We'll do it together. Just keep coming in here with your questions. Don't worry, Honor's counting on your doing just that."

Hank had another night meeting to attend. That Wednesday morning Eleanor resumed her workouts at the YMCA. She cut into the cold blue water, dominating it, and working out her anger by slashing the water for forty-five minutes of nonstop freestyle lap swimming. She arrived at PAAC at 9 AM instead of 8 AM. With reduced responsibilities came the luxury of more time. Ten minutes later, in came Lisa.

"Eleanor, Honor told me to tell you that you shouldn't send anything out to the press without her approval."

"But this is too much!" Eleanor shouted. She tossed her pad on the desk. This pushed the saucer of her potted plant into the side of the metal file cabinet, and a chip of the saucer broke off with a resounding crack that carried through the office and she was sure into Honor's.

"Eleanor, I've never even heard of anybody being sent to an employee to deliver insults! She's a bitch!"

Eleanor got up and walked around her desk and hugged Lisa. "It'll soon be over."

After Lisa left, she called her mother, Lydia, Hank, and her friend at the newspaper. They fueled her with the required energy for the day. That night Hank, the Dells, and her cats offered comfort. The following morning, Thursday, Eleanor dressed with such care that she noticed Hank looking at her. "I know it's hard for you to go to work," he said. "Remember, you can walk any time." He caressed her. They hadn't set a date for their wedding yet. "Remember, two can live as cheaply as one over a Korean deli."

She chuckled. "I love you too."

At 9:30 AM Lisa entered her office, right on time. "What is it now?" Eleanor asked.

"I overheard Honor talking to Helen on the phone this morning. 'I'm bored. I feel like being nasty. I'm going to harass Eleanor some more.' That's what she said. Then she came out and told me, with a smile on her face, to take your name off the press release as a contact person! Now Honor and I are the only names on it! Who does she think is going to answer all these calls? Me? Me do radio interviews? TV interviews? I don't know anything about the subject! I'm not a PR director!"

"You are now the director of public relations. I haven't received any notice of a demotion yet; that's probably tomorrow's insult."

With that Eleanor rose to her feet and moved around the desk to face Lisa. "Look, you're a quick learner! You just need to read my new flier and Helen's press release—that will prepare you." She pointed to her "Peace, Love, Vegetarian" flier tacked on the wall. "Have you seen that yet?"

"No!"

Eleanor removed the tacks and handed Lisa the flier, easing her mind by assuring her that if she read the flier she'd know more than any reporter. Eleanor advised her to do the telephone interviews in her office, where she could prompt her. "Don't worry about Honor seeing you. She knows damned well where you'll get your information; she's counting on it!"

"Why are you taking this?"

"This is my work. I won't let her warped personality rob me of my job." She had repeated this response so many times it was becoming a cliché.

"But you could do other things," Lisa said.

After Lisa left, Coretta stuck her head in her office. "It's like they're trying to take your dignity away from you!"

"They can't take that from you; you have to give it to them," Eleanor said, but she considered Coretta's observation. Minutes later, Tina called and offered her moral support.

"Tina, all I'm responsible for is the demonstration at the Norfolk Stop and Shop, which Lisa could do if need be. And as sure as the Westport sun shines, each day brings a brand-new insult. I don't know how long I can last!"

As Eleanor continued with the conversation, she realized that her chest seemed tight, as if bands were strapped around it. "Tina, I remember your saying your chest was tight and hurting when you were being abused. Come to think of it, I haven't been breathing well for a while. Yes, my chest has hurt. It's no wonder. I don't sleep well, and when I'm awake I'm waiting for another attack. Hank said he had the same thing! Stress-induced chest pains, I remember!"

"This place makes you sick!" Tina said.

Lisa's visit proved to be the last insult of the day. As Eleanor escaped the office and joined the five o'clock stampede to the door, she comforted herself with the absurd notion that there was little left of her pride for Honor to plunder.

On Friday, when Eleanor entered the lobby, Betty interrupted her morning conversation with Ellen to speak to her. "Nobody should be treated this way," she said. "We t'ink you have a lot of courage and a lot of love for the animals to come in here to be insulted every day!"

"Yes, we do!" Ellen whispered.

At least her office family didn't consider her a total fool, she thought. But her stomach sank when she reached her small office. On schedule, at 9:30 AM, in came Lisa. "Now she wants me to work on sending the materials out!"

"That's impossible," Eleanor said. "She doesn't know who gets what, or how much!"

To save money, time, and effort, Eleanor had arranged to mail the material to the heads of organizations, who would then distribute it to their people. "She doesn't know who gets what!" she reiterated. "Not all the names on the list get packages!"

At 2 PM Honor called her into her office. Lisa was seated in a chair facing Honor's desk with pencil and pad in hand. Eleanor remained a safe distance away at the doorway. Honor gazed across the room at her and said, "We intend to do this right now. Lisa's not working all day on this!"

"Lisa or you don't have to do a thing, I'll do it now!"

"Oh, ho, ho, no!" Honor said. "I saw your list without street addresses and telephone numbers, and you're sending too few pamphlets to some. It's a disorganized mess."

"I asked the activists about the stores' volume and did an assessment after visiting."

"I'll make that judgment." Lisa spent all morning completing addresses and adding telephone numbers! Bollocks! You're not organized!"

"Yes I am!"

"You failed to have full addresses listed! Didn't you?"

"I didn't need them! They aren't getting packages! I'm only sending the packages to the heads of the organizations. I have all the activists' names written down and which group they belong to and the heads of the groups. They're the ones that get the packages. They will disperse the material to their members."

"You didn't warn me that you were doing this today!" Eleanor continued. "We have two weeks before the demos. I was planning to mail them out Monday."

"They need to be in the mail today!" Honor charged. "We're not bloody waiting for the last minute!"

The heat of humiliation filled Eleanor. She raced out, needing to get away. But once she reached her office, she thought of the activists. She rushed back and approached Honor's desk.

"Honor, the thirty demonstrations are numbered and the activists have a number next to their names to show who will distribute their materials to them."

"Well, you are welcome to sit down and join us," Honor offered.

Eleanor took the seat next to Lisa.

"Number 1," Honor began, picking up the most recent list sitting in front of her on the desk, "gets the material for numbers 2, 3, 4, and 5." She slowly said the numbers to allow Lisa to write the numbers down on her list. "Number 6 gets the material for 7…8…and…12."

It took a minute for Eleanor to figure out the process. "Oh no, Honor, you can't do it that way," she interrupted. "Your lists don't match. You and Lisa have two different lists. Lisa's got an earlier one and I readjusted all the numbers, so they don't coordinate with yours. Why don't you just read off the names? And then Lisa can just write them down. Such as 'Ann Best will send materials for the following,' and list their names. Lisa can find the names on her list easy enough. That'll work."

"Oh, no, we'll stick to the numbers," she said.

"Honor," Eleanor began to attempt to explain again, but Lisa signaled her to stop.

"OK," Lisa said to Honor.

Eleanor sat back in her seat and watched the farce.

"Number 10 gets 13…15, and let see, 19!" Honor said. She smiled contentedly, looking up from the list and glancing at Lisa in total satisfaction.

For a half hour Honor read out numbers that made no sense and Lisa dutifully wrote them down on her pad, which made very good sense.

After the charade, Eleanor was back at her desk for only a few minutes before Lisa barged in at full stride.

"Bitch! The way she talked down to you! I'm surprised you didn't walk out!"

"I did." Eleanor said.

"I mean out the door! Forever! Eleanor, I have no idea what she was saying! I'll do whatever you tell me!"

"We'll go back to poor Pat," she said. "Between the three of us we'll probably get one package mailed today. It's now 3:15 on a Friday afternoon! That gives us one hour and fifteen minutes. Do you realize we were all in there wasting our time, three of us, as she went through this list, this charade? I could have been peacefully doing that work in my office! And doing it right!"

"You know what the problem is?" Lisa asked. "This kind of secretarial work is actually what she enjoys doing best."

This nugget of truth cut through the dysfunctional air.

The two women proceeded to the mailroom to mail at least one package, so they could honestly lie to Honor in case she asked. There wasn't time for any more, at any rate.

"She'll stop harassing you now that she thinks the packages are out," Lisa said.

Eleanor heaved a sigh of relief with that thought, thinking the wise Lisa knew Honor best. She was ready to enjoy the weekend, thinking her season of harassment was over.

On Monday, however, a few minutes after nine, a reporter visited the office to interview Honor about the Peace, Love, Vegetarian Campaign. Helen had also arrived early that morning. She was meeting with Honor and then would leave for her two-week vacation in Germany. Honor not only failed to invite Eleanor to the meetings, but her mocking laughter targeted her as it traveled through the office straight to her. Eleanor moaned aloud as she sat at her desk, realizing Honor's abuse hadn't ended with Friday's supposed mailing.

Two more weeks of this? Her knees grew weak at the prospect. She gazed at her open door while she dialed Hank. "Hank, she'll meet with this reporter and then Helen and she won't invite me. She'll follow a path I've seen before. Hank, I'm in such pain, and my body is saying 'no more.' We worked shoulder-to-shoulder up to three weeks ago. Soul sisters in the movement, my boss and leader. I'm having chest pains."

"Eleanor, I want you to quit. I'll come now if you want."

"They're coming...I'll call you back."

She could hear the approaching trio. The long, thin, superior Honor in her light gray business suit dashed past Eleanor's office laughing raucously. At her side were Helen and the amused, lanky male reporter, obviously charmed by PAAC's charismatic president. As the three passed her door, Honor's mocking eyes glanced into hers, checking the damage.

The mocking glance delivered Eleanor's second epiphany. She had seen it all before: it was the Colorado campaign all over again. Honor's abusive behavior began with her working shoulder to shoulder and went through all the same stages of abuse right down to the distribution of materials. It was an identical twin.

"Why didn't I see this?" Eleanor asked herself. "She's trying to ruin me. She's not a fading hero reacting under pressure and fearful of being wrong. No, on that ugly and mocking, superior face, I see the intent to hurt me with her power, reduce me, and show me who's boss. These painful attacks on her managers are not the result of her fear, her alienation from the movement, as Tina and Helen claim! From the beginning of the campaign to the end, she's got a hidden agenda! 'Use them then lose them.'

"She allowed me to work day and night for her. She was my pal while it served her! Why didn't I see this? Then she stripped me of all my duties and her friendship, deceived me! Betrayed my trust! Demoralized and played me before my colleagues! She allows just enough reign to fill her needs. Then she demoralizes and destroys you, turning your moral effort into a mockery, all to put you in your place.

Another burst of laughter put an end to her thoughts for a second. She watched the door. The overt ridicule in Honor's pointed laughter triggered the waiting rage. "Her abuse is routine. Every step calculated. I'm only the most recent target! Hank, Tina, me, and God only knows how many before us in the last forty years, and no doubt all those who will come after us—all damaged by her! And so many fine people were lost to the movement! Yes, I was blind! I forgave and felt compassion for her! Oh no! Not anymore! She's a spoiled and vengeful woman working beyond her capabilities! A fake!"

The trio passed her office chatting, and all she saw was the back of Honor's perfectly coiffed head.

"What a joke," she thought. "She's no Malcolm X! No Gandhi! She's not even a proper CEO. She's an empty suit with a wig, a skinny broomstick of a woman posing to lead. She's no CEO and no leader either. What comes first is not the animals, or the movement, it's control."

With this revelation she wanted to run, to run as fast as she could because she had demeaned herself. In the demoralizing process of holding on to her job, she had become Honor's girl. Just like the animals they tried desperately to free in zoos whose natural lives had been stolen from them, she'd been caged, and she had lost a sense of herself, her own nature. She had fought to keep her confidence under the ear-shattering downpour of Honor's criticism, her moods, her dislike, her shunning, her rampages, her arrogance, her intolerance, her showing favor to another purposely to hurt. All those acts were links in Honor's rusty chain to keep her employees in their place, in their cages in her own private animal-rights zoo.

Eleanor's heart was pumping away. Everything was up in the air now, disjointed and crazy. Leaving her desk, she stood in the center of her office. She felt the cage around her closing in. Her eyes were on her open door, waiting for her predator. She leaned on the back of her desk, ready to leap at her and crush her! She reached for her phone. She called Helen, who was in the conference room alone. She requested that they meet like spies in the privacy of the lavatory located outside the lobby door, in the hallway. Minutes later she faced Helen.

"Helen, what is she doing to me?"

"She said there's a power struggle going on," Helen said.

"A power struggle? She has all the power. What's she talking about?"

"She thinks you're trying to take over the project. She said that you were acting like a CEO."

"She has control of her board of directors, she's the CEO and the president, and she can fire me at will. Why all the drama? Why not just fire me if I'm trying to steal her job? Why? Why?"

"She needs you. I know it's unreasonable, illogical."

"Helen, it's not because she's nervous about the campaigns! It's not out of fear of failure that she tortures us! It's all calculated to put us in our places! She's diabolically torturing me, demeaning me, demoralizing me to put me in my place. I see it all as clear as day now! She follows a pattern of abuse; it's as routine and calculated as brushing her teeth in the morning. I'm defenseless except for one out: to quit! But don't worry, don't worry. I won't do that! I won't do that," she lied.

If she quit, Helen's vacation would be canceled. This troubling thought came to mind as she spoke to her. Honor would lay the responsibility of the entire campaign on Helen. No! That wouldn't do! The better plan was to wait until Helen was safely on her way to Kennedy Airport. Helen would have her vacation, and the full weight of the campaign would fall on Honor's shoulders. She would be the beast of burden for the first time in a couple of decades. She was out of shape and out of steam. Let her struggle with the dregs of her energy! Let her handle the mind-boggling demands of a statewide campaign, juggling hundreds of calls, and all the infinitesimal details! Let success or failure rest with her!

As Eleanor plotted, Helen begged her once again not to quit. She promised Helen that she wouldn't quit at that moment, as she examined Helen's trembling hands. She grabbed hold of her hands in an endeavor to make her understand. "Helen, Honor is no leader. She's merely a withered, frightened woman. The leader she once was got lost along the pioneer trail someplace a long time ago. That leader is gone forever."

"She's in over her head."

"Helen, I thought she was saving the animals, but at this point in time, they're saving her. Without this cause, she'd have nothing. But Helen, she's costing the movement. It's time!"

Helen left first, and Eleanor followed a few minutes later. In her office, standing in the center of the room, she gazed at her desk, her printer, her file cabinet, and the window as if they were part of her cage. She thought of the newsroom, her old battered desk that was like a friend, Rob and Fran and the editors and reporters, and their standing ovation on her last day there. Then she overheard Helen departing for the airport. Her mind raced. She closed her door and paced in the small area in the center of her office, mumbling to herself. Her chest began to tighten and became painful, as if the straps around it were tightening. Her breathing was shallow. She sat down at her desk taking deep breaths. Trembling, she again called Hank, complaining of chest pains.

"Eleanor, write your resignation." There was an appeal in his voice that reached her. "Leave it on your desk and get out. Don't expose yourself to a scene. You haven't slept well in months. I'm not surprised. Leave."

As she listened, she remembered that Honor's pattern of abuse had continued for months after the Colorado campaign. With this untenable forecast all reservations about walking out evaporated. As Hank continued to urge her to leave, she eyed the philodendron sitting on her desk with the broken chip, her books sitting on top of the file cabinet, and the file drawers holding her personal files, all of which had to be carted down to her car.

"Won't she be blown away when she learns that the whole burden of this campaign will now rest on her scrawny shoulders," Eleanor asked, interrupting Hank. "Helen will be in Germany and Tina is leading a demonstration in Boston. Larry's doing one in DC, and Freda will be walking down the isle as maid of honor for her best friend. Lisa will, of course, have to do my demonstration. Neither Lisa nor Delores has ever run a campaign. Honor will virtually fly solo for the first time in a couple of decades."

After hanging up, she turned to her computer to write her letter of resignation. At once she was traumatized at the notion of quitting her dream job. With her resignation, she was relinquishing her leadership role in the animal rights movement, the movement that defined her life and enabled her to fulfill her mission. She plummeted into a daze as she began her brief statement. It was as if someone else were writing; she was outside her body watching. In her dissociation, she observed her fingers on the computer keyboard as if the tapping fingers belonged to someone else. She saw herself take the letter out of the printer tray, and she read it as if in slow motion. She then slowly opened her top desk drawer and hid the letter in a computer instructional booklet in her desk, and in slow motion she closed the desk drawer.

Quietly, and still a spectator of her own actions, she began to remove her personal belongings. She picked up her plant and carried it through the office, through the lobby, into the hallway, down the stairs, and out into the wide parking lot and the blazing sun. The coastal air was light and warm against her skin. The ring-billed seagulls swirled and glided, their bellies turning brilliant white as they caught the noonday sun. Eleanor took a deep breath of freedom.

She opened her car door on the passenger side and placed her lovely philodendron on the roomy floor. She stood up and closed the door, her eyes on the endless blue wide sky that faded into the horizon. "It feels so normal out here," she said aloud, gazing up at the sea's horizon. It was then that she realized that when she left at 5 PM, she would never have to return.

"I will never have to work for Honor one more day in my life! No more trying to please her! No more trying to read her mind! No more trying to read her mood! No more trying to win her affection! No more trying to win her respect! No more! No more, period! Yes! God! It's like a very bad marriage and it's finally over! And I never took one lousy swim in the Sound!"

She reentered the building, glancing at the inspiring beach one last time. She could hardly wait for five o'clock. Her reaction in the parking lot proved to her that quitting was indeed the positive thing to do. The employees paid little attention to her. They were accustomed to her toting things in and out. Finally, having deposited the last of her items in her car, she glanced at the inspiring sea and turned back to the office to enter the building for the last time.

It was 4:30 PM, and she had just one half hour to go for a clean getaway. As she headed toward her office, she regretted that she was unable to say good-bye to the office staff. But she wouldn't dare implicate them in her escape. As she slipped into her seat behind her desk, she envisioned the trauma to be inflicted on them. The questioning. The warnings. The not so subtle threat of losing their jobs if they dare speak to her again!

The thought drove her into a righteous fury. She ripped open her top drawer and whipped out her resignation, which seemed as lethal as a sword. With all the independence of her namesake, Eleanor of Aquitaine, she charged out of her office. As she walked through the large office, she appeared casual and avoided eye contact with her fellow employees. But entering Honor's office, she strode up to her desk and slapped her resignation on it, and uttered a resounding "Humph!"

Honor read the letter, then gazed up at her, and down again, her eyes inquisitive and hard.

"'The servant doesn't know what the master is doing!'" Eleanor quoted. "I'm not your servant, and I have only one master, and believe me, lady, it ain't you! So I quit! You've stripped me naked before my colleagues and friends, ripping responsibility away from me, leaving my roots bloody and raw! Well confiscate this, lady! Have Lisa do the Norfolk protest and talk to the press! You're finished abusing and battering this sucker!"

She leaned across the desk to deliver her tirade. Honor seemed frightened of her and pushed her chair back in fear. Eleanor seized the advantage and leaned forward across the desk, heightening Honor's fears. "I believed in you! So you used me! You abused and battered me as much as any abusive husband, as much as any zookeeper, factory farmer, furrier, or circus owner! You became what you beheld!"

Honor pushed her chair against the wall and slid out of it to put further distance between herself and her raging employee. She stepped behind her chair, as if to use it as a shield, and drew herself up in a haughty rigid pose. "I never battered you! And nobody caged you! You were free to leave at any time!"

"My allegiance to you and the animals caged me, Honor, and you, damn you, you counted on that! I'm just one of many! And I'm sure others will follow me!"

"Eleanor, I'm not going to beg you to stay, but you're mistaken." Honor began to tremble. "If the activists get wind of this! Tina, Larry, Freda, Helen, all of them, bloody gone. Chaos, that's what this is, bloody chaos! It could all fall apart, the whole campaign!"

Honor fell silent and just stared at her. Eleanor turned to leave.

Honor called to her. "Your activists are counting on you!"

Eleanor turned with a smirk on her face, but to her horror Honor was standing in the center of the room clutching her throat, her mouth gaping open. She stared at Eleanor silently, pleading for her assistance.

Eleanor lunged for her, but Honor folded onto the floor in a heap before she could reach her. Then Honor fell backward, her mouth gaping open as she slipped into unconsciousness, her long legs bent underneath her.

Calling for Lisa and Freda, Eleanor darted to the desk to dial 911 and confiscate the resignation, shoving it into her pants pocket. It was nothing less than a crime scene to Eleanor. Honor was the murder victim, and she had as much as killed her. As she gave the operator the basic information, Freda and Lisa bolted in, with Freda rushing to Honor's assistance. She checked her wrist for a pulse. Then she put her head to her chest and announced that she was still breathing.

"Thank God," Eleanor whispered. She squatted to pull Honor's legs out from under her and pull down her skirt and jacket.

The rest of the staff gathered and gasped standing in the doorway. The ambulance arrived in five interminable minutes. Two young male medics guided a gurney covered in a clean white sheet through the office to Honor's side. With great efficiency, they set to work affixing an oxygen mask to her face. As the tall, slim young man checked her vital signs, Eleanor stared into his pale blue eyes searching for hope. "It looks like she had a massive heart attack," he said. "She's in critical condition." His facial expression implied the worst.

The staff parted as the medics, with all speed, rolled the gurney out of the doorway. They followed in dreaded silence like a funeral procession. Betty said, "Death has no favorites. Everybody dies. Even the president!" Then she whispered into Eleanor's ear. "She was hurting you. But she paid. I t'ink she gave herself a heart attack with her meanness!"

Did she know? Eleanor examined Betty's large black eyes. She decided she didn't.

They nimbly wheeled the gurney across the carpeted floor of the crowded large office, through the lobby door past Ellen's petrified eyes, exiting PAAC's entrance door and entering the hallway. They lifted the gurney and descended the stairs, and left the building. For a second, Honor's inert body was bathed in the light of the May sun. A crowd from Hancock Insurance, on the bottom floor, gathered outside and at their windows, and sunbathers peered from the beach at the commotion around the ambulance with its doors gaping open. They hoisted the gurney up to the ambulance floor, and Freda followed, managing to hoist her heavy body up to accompany Honor to Norfolk Hospital. Eleanor would follow after she had reached Helen.

The employees returned to PAAC's office and went to their respective desks to collect their things to go home. It was close to five. Eleanor stood in the center of the large room, while Delores rushed to Honor's files for Helen's cell phone number. The staff began to swap opinions about Honor's declining health, saying they had noticed some changes. After a few minutes, Eleanor interrupted them. "When you go home, please pray. And then pray some more that she makes it! But your jobs are secure no matter what the outcome."

She closed her office door, took a deep breath, and began to dial Hank. Her fingers trembled to such a degree that she was unable to push the buttons down. She placed the receiver on the desk to free her left hand so she could guide her trembling right index finger to the numbers.

She informed Hank that Honor was in an ambulance being transported to Norfolk Hospital after suffering a massive heart attack. "I killed her. I handed in my resignation and I was hateful, full of anger. She was afraid of me! I wanted her to suffer! And the thought of handling the campaign was too much for her! She had a heart attack! I as much as killed her!"

After Hank prodded her to be more precise, Eleanor had begun a blow-by-blow description of what had taken place when Coretta charged in to announce that Helen was on the phone, ending the conversation. Eleanor related the same story to Helen, who was calling from a taxicab. Helen interrupted her to direct the cabdriver to take her to the hospital.

"Oh, I was afraid of this!" Helen said. She wasn't shocked. And she seemed to dismiss Eleanor's confession of guilt. "Eleanor, listen to me carefully. This is not your fault! Honor suffered from severe coronary artery disease. Her doctor recommended a second triple bypass after she returned from Tucson. She had symptoms at the conference. Her arms were going numb at times, and her throat was tightening up on her. And she had severe indigestion. These were the classic signs of her having insufficient oxygen. The doctor told her that she had silent ischemia, a condition that masks the damage and progress of heart disease." Helen's voice began to tremble. "But she refused to go through the surgery again. She was taking nitroglycerin. It's an accepted treatment, but not what the doctor recommended.

"I expected you to quit a long time ago," Helen said softly. "I want you to help me. Honor could pull out of this! Just pray for her!"

Honor could survive? The thought was a reprieve.

"I've got to call Grumpol," Helen said. "'I'll book two rooms for us at the Norfolk Hotel. He can catch a flight from DC to New York in no time. The sooner the better. If she pulls through this, he'll need to talk some sense into her. She won't be able to continue as CEO. Her doctors warned her that if she had a heart attack, it would result in massive damage. And from the sound of it, she's lucky to be alive."

Helen was to wait at the hospital for Grumpol's arrival. When the time was appropriate, she would request that he sit on PAAC's board of directors. Helen's resolute and controlled voice ushered calm into the chaos. At the same time, as the acting CEO, she at once put an end to PAAC's insanity. An hour later, at the emergency room, and behind a white partition, Eleanor, Helen, and Freda stood at Honor's side. Honor was stretched out on a bed covered by a white sheet. For a few minutes she had regained consciousness before falling to sleep. The doctors had been able to stabilize her condition and predicted that she had a "fair chance" to pull through. But massive damage to her heart was evident.

Eleanor could feel nothing but guilt and shame as she stared at Honor under the bright lights of the hospital emergency room. Helen convinced her to go home to rest. She would continue to wait for Grumpol. That evening Eleanor paced her living room awaiting news from Helen. Hank had returned and gone out to pick up some Chinese food, insisting that she eat. Still haunted by guilt, Eleanor phoned her mother to give her a detailed description of what she had done.

"I was hateful! Vengeful! I don't want her to die! Even if I hate her! But I hate and love her! I would have done anything for her! Anything! I believed God sent me here to help her!"

"Eleanor, you believed in her," Lillian said.

"Mom, with Helen as CEO, PAAC will transform into Grumpol's vision of a company that works side by side with grassroots organizations. It'll change the movement. The eight billion animals killed for food every year, they will be our priority! Grumpol will be on the board of directors. He'll focus on factory farms! He'll draw in other national organizations to unite around this major issue. It is the issue of the twenty-first century! Grumpol knows this. It'll be a new era in animal advocacy. The first thing we'll do, I'm sure, is set aside a major chunk of the budget for worthwhile legislative campaigns across the country to outlaw some factory farming practices. That's why I feel so guilty! I wanted this! Right from the start! If only I hadn't given her that letter!"

Eleanor collapsed on the couch shivering and trembling, her teeth chattering. "If I could only turn back the clock! Let it be as it was! I was so furious! So hateful! I failed God!"

"Darling, listen! I've got something very important to tell you. Darling, remember when I was carrying you, and I had the dream?"

"Of course!"

"Well, I didn't tell you about the whole dream. I was afraid."

"I know. What is it?"

"In my dream there was a woman who looked just like you sitting on a gray stallion wearing the red cross of the crusades over a full coat of armor, as I told you. When I woke up, I knew that I was carrying a baby girl, but I also knew that she'd be a crusader. I decided to name you after Eleanor of Aquitaine because she led a band of women to the crusades, not because she was a liberated woman. Of course, I didn't want to saddle you with living up to such expectations. You had every right to seek your own destiny, whatever that was. And, I might add, I wasn't crazy about your being a modern-day crusader."

"But your keeping it a secret didn't change fate."

"Right. So do you still believe that you caused Honor's heart attack? Or if she dies, that you would be the cause of her death? When your destiny was written before you were born?"

Her mother's words caused her to take a long, deep, quieting breath. In that moment she was carried back to the beginning. It was the eyes on the newsroom wall that had brought her to PAAC in the first place: the calf, the three-legged doe, the black Lab; the face of her mission. If Honor lived or died it wasn't her doing. She wasn't God, she concluded. She remembered what she had learned years ago: her father's alcoholism and her former husband's lack of character had nothing to do with her. She began to weep with relief.

The knock on the front door almost escaped her. She rushed to it while wiping the tears from her eyes. There stood a couple dressed in business suits, the Route 7 traffic in the background. For a moment, she barely recognized the famous Grumpol and Helen at his side.

"I didn't want to spend the night in the hotel," Helen said. "I hope you don't mind."

"Mom, Helen and Grumpol are here," she said. She waved them in. "Don't worry about me. I'm OK. Mom, I understand what you're telling me, and thank you," she said. "I love you."

She ushered them into the living room as Helen announced that Honor's crisis was over. Eleanor showed them to the cranberry couch while she perched on her rocking chair across from them. Then she suddenly remembered the burgundy and rushed into the kitchen to emerge minutes later with the wine and three wineglasses.

The damage to Honor's heart would force her retirement, as they had suspected, Grumpol revealed. Honor hid her illness from him, but he had feared the progression of the disease. In recent telephone calls her voice at times had seemed breathless and exhausted. Luckily, he was in New York for a meeting when Helen's call reached him, which allowed him to be at Honor's side in a couple of hours.

"I thought it important that the three of us meet," Helen said. "I wanted to tell you in person that you must stay. Your work with the activists convinced me of this a while ago. I knew this was coming. It was just a matter of time. But we won't discuss any changes until I've been officially voted in as the new CEO and president by the board. Honor will need months of recuperation before she can even consider consulting work. But factory farming and those slaughtered each year will be our priority." Helen gazed at Grumpol.

Grumpol looked far older for the trauma, Eleanor thought. His hair seemed to be flat and thin, his facial muscles sagged under the weight of worry, and his pallor was a sickening gray. "Honor's retirement marks the end of an era," he said. His voice began to shake.

"You should have seen her with her long brown hair flowing down her back, so haughty, so like a princess. She was flushed from the damned heat in the DC hearing room, it was always so hot in there, and, of course, there was a whole room of people who hated her righteousness. But to me she was like the courageous women I read about in history books, like the suffragettes. I was just a teenager. Believe me, she was my superwoman and my role model. She wasn't living life for material gain and status. She was attempting to make the world a better place for those less fortunate. That's the gift Honor gave to me." His voice broke.

Eleanor rose to fetch the tissue box in the bathroom and dashed back with it, handing them both a tissue and using one to wipe away her own tears. She set the box on the coffee table and returned to her seat.

"In later years, I came to understand her problem with trust, believe me," he said. "But I knew we'd have time to devote to each other at the tail end of our careers. I planned for it. She won't refuse me now. She'll be forced by her limited health to accept the role of consultant, and finally she'll be my life partner. That ought to keep her in enough trouble." He chuckled mischievously.

Grumpol stood up and appeared anxious to leave. He refused Eleanor's invitation to stay for dinner, explaining that he needed to get back to Honor. This was the first of many meetings, he assured them. He intended to stay in Westport for the transitional period. He'd help Honor in her adjustment, and would draw up documents to legally seal the changes at PAAC. "Then I want her to come home with me. I'll try to sweeten the pot for her. Long-stem roses and digitalis." He laughed.

Eleanor stood at the door next to Helen and watched Grumpol drive off. She couldn't help but be in awe of him and the enormity of the changes that had taken place in just hours. She invited Helen into the kitchen for a second glass of wine. They sat at the table staring at each other for several seconds in silence. Eleanor noticed that Helen's hands were not trembling.

"After the supermarket demonstrations," Helen said, "don't you think we have to check out this Elephant Refuge? Can you think of anyone we can send? Somebody who could write a story about Eve returning to Eden thanks to the movement?"

With that Eleanor threw back her head and laughed. "I'll pay for my own transportation!"

Their conversation was interrupted by the sound of Hank entering the house. Seconds later he stood in the kitchen doorway with two bags of Chinese takeout. He broke into a devilish grin at the sight of Helen. "Moo shu vegetables?" he asked.

The End

Recommended Reading

Eisnitz, G. A. *Slaughterhouse: The Shocking Story of Greed, Neglect, and Inhumane Treatment Inside the U.S. Meat Industry.* Prometheus Books, 1997.

Francione, G. L. *Rain without Thunder.* Temple University Press, 1996.

Garner, R. *Animals, Politics and Morality.* Manchester University Press, 2005.

Guillermo, K. S. *Monkey Business: The Disturbing Case That Launched the Animal Rights Movement.* National Press Books, 1993.

Jasper, J., and D. Nelkin. *The Animal Rights Crusade: The Growth of a Moral Protest.* Simon and Schuster, 1991.

978-0-595-36489-3
0-595-36489-6

Printed in the United States
53222LVS00003B/424-447